BY MICHAEL J. SULLIVAN

THE LEGENDS OF THE FIRST EMPIRE

Age of Myth • *Age of Swords*

Forthcoming: *Age of War* • *Age of Legends* • *Age of Wonder* • *Age of Empire*

THE RIYRIA REVELATIONS

Theft of Swords (contains *The Crown Conspiracy* and *Avempartha*)

Rise of Empire (contains *Nyphron Rising* and *The Emerald Storm*)

Heir of Novron (contains *Wintertide* and *Percepliquis*)

THE RIYRIA CHRONICLES

The Crown Tower

The Rose and the Thorn

The Death of Dulgath

The Disappearance of Winter's Daughter

STANDALONE NOVEL

Hollow World

ANTHOLOGIES

Unfettered: The Jester (Fantasy: The Riyria Chronicles)

Blackguards: Professional Integrity (Fantasy: The Riyria Chronicles)

Unbound: The Game (Fantasy: Contemporary)

Unfettered II: Little Wren and the Big Forest (Fantasy: The First Empire)

The End: Visions of the Apocalypse: Burning Alexandria
(Dystopian Science Fiction)

Triumph Over Tragedy: Traditions (Fantasy: Tales from Elan)

The Fantasy-Faction Anthology: Autumn Mists (Fantasy: Contemporary)

Help Fund My Robot Army: Be Careful What You Wish For (Fantasy)

Age
OF
Swords

Age
OF
Swords

BOOK TWO OF
The Legends of the First Empire

MICHAEL J. SULLIVAN

DEL REY
NEW YORK

Copyright © 2017 by Michael J. Sullivan
Map copyright © 2016 by David Lindroth Inc.

Published in the United States by Del Rey, an imprint of Random House, a division of Penguin Random House LLC, New York.

DEL REY and the HOUSE colophon are registered trademarks of Penguin Random House LLC.

LIBRARY OF CONGRESS CATALOGING-IN-PUBLICATION DATA
Names: Sullivan, Michael J., author.
Title: Age of swords / Michael J. Sullivan.
Description: New York : Del Rey, 2017. | Series: Legends of the First Empire ; 2
Identifiers: LCCN 2017013600| ISBN 9781101965368 (hardcover) |
ISBN 9781101965375 (ebook)
Subjects: LCSH: Imaginary wars and battles—Fiction. | Elves—Fiction. | Dwarfs—Fiction. |
Magic—Fiction. | BISAC: FICTION / Fantasy / Epic. |
FICTION / Action & Adventure. | FICTION / Fantasy / Historical. | GSAFD: Fantasy
fiction. | Adventure fiction
Classification: LCC PS3619.U4437 A745 2017 | DDC 813/.6—dc23
LC record available at https://lccn.loc.gov/2017013600

Printed in the United States of America on acid-free paper

randomhousebooks.com

2 4 6 8 9 7 5 3 1

First Edition

Book design by Christopher M. Zucker

This book is dedicated to Tim Gerard Reynolds, the narrator of my Elan novels, whose vocal interpretations breathe life into mere letters, give voice to my imagination, and make me sound better than I am. Thanks, Tim, I owe you another dinner, and sorry for disrupting the recording sessions by making you laugh.

Contents

Author's Note

Welcome back to The Legends of the First Empire! I want to start by thanking you for the warm reception extended to the new series. It's a risky business setting aside a well-established franchise and creating something new, and I'll admit I was a bit anxious with the release of *Age of Myth*. I love the new characters and hoped you would, too, but until a book gets into the hands of the readers, I'm never sure how it'll be received. Well, the book has been out for seven months and the results are in. *Age of Myth* has garnered more than ten thousand reviews and ratings from Goodreads, Audible, and Amazon. Even better, 90 percent have rated it a 4 or 5 and only 2 percent a 1 or 2. I don't think I could ask for more than that! So thank you for assuaging my fears about not being able to write anything that didn't have Royce and Hadrian in it.

Speaking of characters, one of the things I love most about *Age of Swords* is shining a light on more of the key players for the series. From its onset, I wanted The Legends of the First Empire to consist of an ensemble cast, but had I fully introduced all the players in the first book, it would have significantly dragged down the pacing. *Age of Myth* already had a lot to do: introduce two major races (Rhunes and Fhrey), set up the cultural differences between them (primitive and technologically advanced), and tell a self-contained story while starting threads that will weave across the entire narrative—such as what's up with Malcolm and Nyphron, and who is Trilos and what part does he play.

In *Age of Myth,* you've briefly met Gifford, Roan, Brin, and Moya, but with *Age of Swords,* you'll start to see why I love them so much and what unique aspects they'll be bringing to the rest of the story. Of course your old favorites will be back, including Persephone, Raithe, Malcolm, Arion, and I couldn't leave out Suri and Minna. You'll also have a chance to meet the Dherg, a race that we don't get to see much of in The Riyria Revelations. Traveling to their homeland will be a major aspect of this story, and I'm pleased to introduce the last of the triumvirate that makes up the major races in the world of Elan.

There is something else I would like to mention before sending you off to the tale. In the author's note of *Age of Myth,* I mentioned that the whole series was written before I submitted the first book, and this was, and is, true. But I fear I may have unintentionally given the wrong impression, and I want to clear things up. What I'm referring to is the difference between *written* and *done,* which is a pretty wide chasm. Having all the books *written* means: I completed the first draft to my satisfaction. But *done* is something much more. It requires polishing the books after receiving feedback from others I trust, including my alpha reader, my beta readers (generally fifteen to twenty people), my agent and a few others at his agency, my editor, and my publisher. And then the line editors, copy editors, and proofreaders need a chance to further groom the manuscript and turn it into something I couldn't do on my own. All those finishing touches take time, and that's a major factor in the release schedule.

I will say that we are going to try to shorten the time between books for the rest of the series. Yes, there was a one-year gap between the first book and this one, but that was largely because some major rework was required. You see, when Robin (my wife and alpha reader) finished the series, she proclaimed the first three books to be in really good shape, but believed that the end of the series had a number of issues. There were a few plot points she felt were confusing, and some logic that she didn't agree with; most important, she felt that the ending was rushed. As is usually the case, she was right.

To address these concerns, I spent over a year working on the ending, and in the process, the series grew from five books to six. You see, I was trying to smoosh (a highly technical literary term) two books together when the story really wanted a natural break at a particular point. While I was off doing that, *Age of Swords* sat untouched. Until I had the series ending reworked, I didn't know what changes would be needed in *Age of Swords*, and as it turned out, some tweaks were necessary. I would have hated to release it and then been unable to make the required adjustments.

Anyway, I turned the revised book over to Robin in May 2016, and for the rest of the year we gathered additional input, incorporated changes, and line and copyedited the manuscript, which was finally locked down in early February 2017. It's a fascinating process seeing a manuscript morph into a finished book. If it's something you are interested in, Robin is creating *The Making of Age of Swords*—a free ebook that provides an interesting peek behind the scenes. We did something similar with the third Riyria Chronicle (*The Death of Dulgath*), and you can receive either of these just by sending an email to: michael@michaelsullivan-author.com. Please make sure the subject of the email includes "Making of . . ." and the title (or titles) you are interested in, and we'll send them out to you.

Okay, last thing, I promise. If you read the acknowledgments of *Age of Myth*, you might have noticed that I mentioned wanting to hear from people. I've had hundreds of letters, most of which apologize for intruding on my time. I always get a chuckle out of that, as if knowing people like my books could ever be an imposition. I've enjoyed these letter so much that I thought I would once again extend the invitation. So if you like this book (and even if you don't), feel free to drop me a line at michael@michaelsullivan-author.com. I'm always interested in hearing what you have to say.

And that's the end of my preamble. Now sit back, adjust the volume if you're listening to an audiobook, or adjust the font and background of the ebook, or run your fingers down the paper and take a deep breath of the ink of your printed copy. It's time to dive in. *Age of Swords* is my favorite book of this series, and I hope you'll enjoy reading it as much as I did writing the tale.

HENTLYN

ERIVAN

Ervanon

Estramnadon

Harwood

Avempartha

Seon Hall

Swamp of Ith

North Branch

Under
the
Dragon

Mount Mador

AVRLYN

The Forks

Alon Rhist

High Spear
Valley

River

Bern

Nadak

Dureya

Gula

Rhen

Merredydd

Urum

River

RHULYN

Melen

Menahan

Tirre

Warric

Green Sea

BROKEN LANDS

Neith

BELGREIG

Blue Sea

100 Miles

🏰 Fhrey towns
🏰 Rhune towns
🏰 Dherg towns

Age

OF

Swords

CHAPTER ONE

The Storm

Most people believe the first battle of the Great War occurred at Grandford in the early spring, but the first attack actually took place on a summer's day in Dahl Rhen.

—THE BOOK OF BRIN

"Are we safe?" Persephone shouted up at the oak.

Magda was the oldest tree in the forest, massive and majestic. Standing before her was like staring at an ocean or mountain; each made Persephone feel small. Realizing her three-word question might be too simple, too vague, she added, "Is there more that needs to be done to protect my people from the Fhrey?"

Persephone waited for an answer.

Wind blew; the tree shook, and a massive branch fell.

She jumped when it hit the ground. Falling from such a height, the limb would have killed her if it had landed a few inches closer. Broken branches suspended in the forest canopy were called widow-makers. Since Persephone had already lost her husband, the dead wood lying beside her must have been an overachiever.

"What's that about?" Persephone asked Suri.

The young mystic with the white wolf glanced at the fallen branch and shrugged. "Just the wind, I think. Feels like a storm is coming."

Once before, when Persephone had sought the great tree's counsel, Magda's advice had saved her people. Now she was back, seeking answers again. Months had passed since her last visit, and life at Dahl Rhen had returned to a comfortable routine. The destruction created by the battle between two Miralyith had been cleaned up, but Persephone knew that hadn't ended the conflict. Questions remained—questions no human or Fhrey could answer. And yet . . .

Persephone looked at the fallen tree limb. *It's not a good sign when Magda starts a conversation by trying to crush me.*

"Something wrong?" Arion asked. The Fhrey was still learning their language and stood beside Suri and Minna watching the proceedings with great interest. She wore the green hat Padera had crocheted for her; its whimsical quality made the Miralyith appear more approachable, less divine, more—human. Arion had come along to witness the oracle in action, although Persephone had expected more talk and less action.

Suri looked up at the tree. "Don't know."

"What's Magda saying?" Persephone shouted to Suri over the rising howl of wind.

That was how it was supposed to work. Persephone posed questions to the tree and the mystic revealed the answer after listening to the rustling of leaves and branches. But Arion was right about something being wrong. Suri had a perplexed look on her face—more than merely puzzled; she looked concerned.

"Not sure," the girl replied.

Persephone clawed a lock of hair away from her mouth. "Why not? Is she talking in riddles or just ignoring you?"

Suri's face twisted in frustration. "Oh, she's talking, all right, but so fast I can't tell what she's saying. Just babbling, really. Never seen her like this. She keeps repeating 'Run . . . run fast . . . run far. They're after you.' "

"*They?* Who? Is she talking to us? Is that the answer to my questions?"

Suri shook her head, short hair whipping across the tattoos on her forehead. "Nope. She was yelling *before* you said anything. I don't think she heard you. I'm not even sure how Magda knows the word *run*. I mean, seriously, how does a tree know what that is?"

"Are you saying the tree is hysterical?"

Suri nodded. "Scared to death. I know mice who have made more sense. She's not even using words now, just making noises." Suri's brows jumped up, her face tensing, eyes squinting, mouth pulling tight.

"What?" Persephone asked.

"It's never good when a tree screams."

Tall grass slapped Persephone's legs, her dress whipping and snapping. Ripped from their branches, the oak's leaves flew thick as snow in a blizzard. Under the dense canopy, Persephone couldn't see the sky, but the wind was stronger than ever. Stepping out, she discovered that what had been clear blue just moments before had turned a tumultuous gray. Dark clouds bubbled one upon another, turning midday into twilight. A strange green light cast everything in an eerie, unnatural hue.

"What's happening?" Arion asked.

"Tree is panicking," Suri answered.

"Maybe we should return to the dahl," Arion said, her head tilted up. "Yes?"

Minna whined and drew closer to Suri, nearly knocking the girl down. The mystic knelt to comfort her wolf. "Not right, is it, Minna?"

Looking more serious, Arion gave up speaking Rhunic and returned to her native tongue. *"We need to——"* She was cut off by a blinding flash and horrific crack.

Minna yelped and bolted down the slope.

Persephone staggered. Blinded by the afterimage that left a bright, splotchy band across her vision, she vainly tried to blink it away. Her nostrils filled with wood smoke, and she felt the heat of a blaze.

Magda is on fire!

Arion lay on the ground at the base of the tree, both hands raised, shielding herself. The Miralyith shouted a single word—nothing Persephone recognized—but it sounded like a command. The fire engulfing the old oak vanished with a *pop*. In its place was a terrible hiss and smoke swirling in a malevolent wind. Magda was split down the center, cleaved in two. A horrible blackened gash with bright-red edges flared with each gust of wind. The ancient and wondrous mother of trees had taken a mortal blow from the gods.

Persephone helped Arion to her feet.

"We need to run," the Fhrey told them.

"What? Why?"

Arion grabbed her by the wrist and pulled. *"Now!"*

Persephone's scalp tingled as Arion dragged her down the hill and out of the glade toward the thick shadow of the Crescent Forest. Suri and Minna were already ahead of them, sprinting.

Crack!

Lightning struck the ground somewhere behind them.

Crack! Crack!

Two more bolts rent the air close enough for her to feel their heat. Running together, Persephone and Arion followed Suri and Minna as they plunged headlong into the forest through thickets, brambles, and thorns. Gasping for air, Persephone glanced back. A series of scorch marks smoldered in a direct line between the oak and where they stood.

Crack!

They all jumped as the sound exploded directly overhead. Like the old oak, the trees above caught fire. One huge branch fell like a giant torch—another widow-maker wannabe.

"Need shelter," Arion said, and pulled again.

"Rol nearby," Suri shouted. "This way." The girl dashed deeper into the wood, Minna bounding at her side.

Persephone might not understand the language of trees, but she understood anguish. The wood shrieked. Branches snapped, trunks groaned, and the forest cried out as the wind stripped away summer gowns of green. Then a new sound rose, a loud, all-encompassing roar from everywhere at once. At first, Persephone thought it might be sheets of rain, but the noise was much too loud, far too violent. Balls of ice tore through leaves and branches. Fist-sized missiles assailed the canopy, ricocheting off limbs and trunks. With arms raised over her head, Persephone screamed as two huge chunks of ice struck her back, glancing blows, but they carried the sting of a switch and the force of a punch.

Ahead, Suri stopped at the foot of a sheer, rocky cliff and slapped the face of it with her palm. To Persephone's immense relief, a section of the stone's face opened, revealing a little room neatly carved out of rock. The mystic leapt inside, followed closely by the wolf. From the doorway, Suri swung her arms in huge circles, waving the other women to safety. The chieftain of Dahl Rhen and the Miralyith crossed the threshold together, crouching to avoid hitting their heads. Once in, Persephone turned to witness the destruction.

Crack!

Another bolt of lightning split the air, and for an instant, a dazzling array of translucent shades of green illuminated the leaves, a light brighter than the sun.

Crack!

A nearby cottonwood caught fire. Sheared in half, the tree fell in a rain of sparks and flame. The wind fanned the fires started by the strikes, spreading an inferno—ice and fire, wind and debris. Persephone stared, lost somewhere between horror and awe.

Suri slapped the keystone, and the door closed.

Outside, the lightning cracks and hammering hail continued, but from a safe, muffled distance. Panting from the run and realizing they'd escaped without significant injury, the three exchanged the stunned looks of survivors. Relief washed over Persephone . . . until she noticed they weren't alone.

Gifford would never win a footrace. Although he came to this realization late in life, everyone else knew it the day he was born. His left leg lacked feeling, couldn't support his weight, and dragged. His back wasn't much better. Severely twisted, it forced his hips in one direction and his shoulders in another. Most people pitied Gifford and a few even despised him. He never understood either.

Roan was the exception. What everyone else saw as hopeless, she took as a challenge.

The two were out in front of Gifford's roundhouse, and Roan was lashing the wood-and-tin contraption to his left leg, tightening its leather straps. She knelt in the grass before him, wearing her work apron, a smudge of charcoal on the side of her nose. Her dark-brown hair was pulled back in a short ponytail so high on her head that it looked like a rooster's crest.

Dozens of cuts from working with sharp metal marred her clever little hands. Gifford wanted to hold them, kiss the wounds, and take the pain away. He'd tried taking her hand once, and it hadn't gone well. She'd pulled away, her eyes widened with fear, and a look of horror crossed her face. Roan had an aversion to being touched—Gifford had known that—he'd simply forgotten himself. Her reaction wasn't limited to him. She couldn't suffer anyone's touch.

Yanking hard on the ankle strap, Roan nodded with a firm, determined expression. "That should do it." She rose and dusted her clean hands symbolically. Her voice was eager but serious. "Ready?"

Gifford answered by pulling himself up with the aid of his crafting table. The device on his leg, constructed from wooden sticks and metal hinges, squeaked as he rose, a sound like the opening of a tiny door.

"Do you have your weight on it? Try. See if it holds."

For Gifford, any attempt to support himself with his left leg was akin to leaning on water. But he'd gladly fall on his face for her. Perhaps he could manage a roll and make her grin. If he'd been born with two stout legs, strong and agile, he'd dance and twirl like a fool to amuse her. He might even make her laugh, something she rarely did. In her mind, she was still a slave, something less than nothing. Gifford longed for Roan to see herself the way he did, but damaged as he was, he made a poor mirror casting back a broken image.

Gifford tilted his hips, shifting some weight to his lame leg. He didn't fall. A strain tugged on the straps wrapped around his thigh and calf, but

his leg held. His mouth dropped open, his eyes widened, and Roan actually *did* smile.

By Mari, what an amazing sight.

He couldn't help grinning back. He was standing straight—or as
straight as his gnarled back allowed. Using magic armor fashioned by
Roan, Gifford was winning an impossible battle.

"Take a step," she coaxed, hands clenched in fists of excitement.

Gifford shifted weight back to his right side and lifted his left leg, swinging it forward. The hinges squeaked once more. He took a step the way
normal people did a million times, and that's when the brace collapsed.

"Oh, no!" Roan gasped as Gifford fell, barely missing the newly glazed
cups drying in the morning sun.

His cheek and ear slammed into the hardened dirt, jarring his head. But
his elbow, hand, and hip took the bulk of the punishment. To Roan, it must
have looked painful, but Gifford knew how to fall. He'd been doing it his
entire life.

"I'm so, so, so sorry." Roan was back on her knees, bent over him as he
rolled to his side. Her grin was gone, the world less bright.

"I'm okay, no pwoblem. I missed the cups."

"The metal failed." She struggled to hold back tears as her injured
hands ran over the brace.

"The tin just isn't strong enough. I'm so sorry."

"It held fo' a while," he said to cheer her up. "Keep at it. You'll make it
wuk. I know you will."

"There's an added force when walking. I should have accounted for the
additional weight when your other leg is raised." She slapped the side of
her head several times, flinching with each strike. "I should have realized
that. I should have. How could I not—"

He instinctively grabbed her wrist to prevent additional blows. "Don't
do—"

Roan screamed and jerked away, drawing back in terror. When she re-
covered, they exchanged embarrassed looks, mirroring each other. The
moment dragged unpleasantly until Gifford forced a smile. Not one of his
best, but it was all he could manage.

To ease past the uncomfortable pause, he picked up the conversation where they'd left off, pretending nothing had happened. "Woan, you can't know ev-we-thing when doing something new. It'll be betta next time."

She blinked at him twice, then shifted her focus. She wasn't looking at anything in particular; she was thinking. Sometimes Roan thought so intently that he could almost hear it. She blinked again and emerged from the stupor. Walking over to Gifford's crafting table, she picked up one of his cups. The awkward moment vanished as if it had never happened.

"This design is new, isn't it?" she asked. "Do you think it could hold its shape at a much larger size? If we could find a way to—"

Gifford's smile turned genuine. "Yew a genius, Woan. Has anyone told you that?"

She nodded, her little rooster crest whipping. "You have."

"Because it's twue," he said.

She looked embarrassed again, the way she always did when he complimented her, the way she looked when anyone said something nice, a familiar unease. Her eyes shifted back to the brace, and she sighed. "I need something stronger. Can't make it out of stone; can't make it out of wood."

"I wouldn't suggest clay," he said, pushing his luck at trying to be funny. "Though I would have made you a beautiful hinge."

"I know you would," she said in complete seriousness.

Roan wasn't one for jokes. Much of humor arose from the unexpected or preposterous—like making a hinge out of clay. But her mind didn't work that way. To Roan, nothing was too absurd and no idea too crazy.

"I'll just have to think of something," she said while unbuckling the brace. "Some way to strengthen the metal. There's always a better way. That's what Padera says, and she's always right."

Roan had good cause to think so highly of Padera's opinion. The oldest resident of Dahl Rhen, she'd seen it all. She also had no trouble expressing her thoughts, regardless of whether people wanted to hear her opinion or not. For reasons beyond understanding, Padera had always been particularly harsh with Gifford.

As Roan struggled with the buckle, the wind gusted and blew his cloths from the crafting table. Two cups fell over, making a delicate *clink*. Thick, voluminous clouds rolled in, blotting out the blue and blanketing the sun. Around the dahl, people urgently trotted toward their homes.

"Get the wash in! Get the wash in!" Viv Baker yelled to her daughter.

The Killian boys raced after chickens, and Bergin rushed to shut down his new batch of beer. "A perfectly blessed day just a minute ago," he grumbled, peering up at the sky as if it could hear him.

Another gust made Gifford's entire set of cups collide and ring. Two more toppled, rolling on their sides and making half circles on the tabletop. He had been having a productive day before Roan had stopped by, but she was always a welcome distraction.

"We need to get your pottery inside." Roan redoubled her effort to remove the brace but was having trouble with one of the buckles. "Made it too tight."

The wind grew stronger. The banners on the lodge cracked with a sharp report. The fire braziers near the well struggled to stay lit but lost their battle, both snuffed out.

"That's not good," Gifford said. "Only time they've blown out was when the lodge's woof came off."

The thatch of his little house rustled, and dirt and grass pelted his face and arms.

Frustrated with the buckle, Roan reached into one of her pockets and pulled out another of her inventions: two knives bound in leather so they could both cut at once. She used them to release the brace's straps, freeing him. "There, now we can—"

Lightning struck the lodge. Splinters, sparks, and a plume of white smoke preceded a clap so loud that Gifford felt it pass through him. Giant logs exploded and thatch ignited.

"Did you see—" Gifford started to say when another bolt of lightning struck on the other side of the lodge. "Whoa!"

He and Roan stared in shock as a third and then a fourth bolt hit the log building. Cobb, the pig wrangler and part-time gate guard, was the first to react. He and Bergin ran toward the well, picking up water gourds on their way. Then another bolt of lightning exploded the well's windlass into a cloud of splinters, and both of them dived for the ground.

More lightning bolts rained, both inside and outside the dahl. With each shaft came screams, fire, and smoke. All around Roan and Gifford, people ran to their homes. The Galantians, Fhrey warriors who had been welcomed to the dahl when exiled, rushed out of their tents and stared up at the sky. They looked just as frightened as everyone else, which was as disturbing as the cataclysmic storm. Until recently, the Fhrey had been thought to be gods.

Gelston the shepherd ran past. Lightning hit while he made his way between the woodpile and a patch of near-ripe beans in the Killians' garden. Gifford didn't see much, just a snaking, blinding brilliance. When his sight returned, Gelston was on the ground, his hair on fire. Bergin rushed to the man's side and doused his head.

Gifford shouted to Roan, "We need to get to the sto'age pit. Wight now!"

He grabbed his crutch and pushed himself up.

"Roan! Gifford!" Raithe yelled as he and Malcolm hurried toward them. Raithe still carried two swords: the broken copper one slung on his back and the intricately decorated Fhrey blade hanging naked from his belt. Malcolm held a spear with both hands. "Do you know where Persephone is?"

Gifford shook his head. "No, but we need to get to the pit!"

Raithe nodded. "I'll spread the word. Malcolm, help them."

The ex-slave moved to Gifford's side, put his shoulder under the potter's arm, and practically carried him to the big storage pit while Roan followed close behind. With the first harvest still more than a month away, the pit was nearly empty. Lined with mud bricks, the hole retained the smell of musty vegetables, grain, and straw. Other members of the dahl were already there. The Bakers huddled with their daughter and two boys against the back wall, their eyes wide. Engleton and Farmer Wedon peered out the open door at the violence of the storm.

Brin, the dahl's newly appointed Keeper of Ways, was there as well. "Have you seen my parents? They're not here," she said in an unsteady voice.

"No," Roan replied.

Outside, thunder cracked and rolled continuously. Gifford could only imagine the lightning strikes that accompanied them. Being down in the pit, he couldn't see the yard, just a small square of sky.

"I need to find them." Brin bolted toward the exit, springing like a fawn. Unlike the crippled potter, Brin *could* win a footrace, and she was easily the fastest person in the dahl. The fifteen-year-old regularly won every sprint during the Summerule festivals, but Gifford had anticipated her dash and caught her wrist.

"Let me go!" She pulled and jerked.

"It's too dangewous."

"I don't care!" Brin yanked hard, so hard she fell, but Gifford still hung on. "Let me go!"

Gifford's legs, even his good one, were mostly useless, and his lips slid down the side of his face because he didn't have the muscles to support them. But reliance on his arms and hands turned them into vises. Gavin and Krier, who always picked on him, had once made the mistake of challenging Gifford to a hand-squeezing contest. He humiliated Krier, making him weep—his name magnifying the boy's embarrassment. Gavin was determined not to suffer a similar fate and cheated by using both hands. Gifford had held back with the first boy but didn't see the need to do likewise with a cheater. He broke Gavin's little finger and the tiny bone that ran from the second knuckle to his wrist.

Brin had no possibility of breaking free.

Autumn, Fig, the Killians, and Tressa stumbled through the door, all of them exhausted and out of breath. Heath Coswall and Bergin came along just after. They dragged Gelston, who remained unconscious. His hair was mostly gone, the scalp red and black. Bergin was covered in dirt and grass and reported that the lodge was burning like a harvest-moon bonfire.

"Has anyone seen my parents?" Brin asked the newcomers.

No one had.

As if the wind and lightning weren't enough, hail began to fall. Apple-sized chunks of ice clattered, leaving craters in the turf on impact.

More people raced into the shelter of the pit, running with arms and baskets over their heads. They filed to the back, crying and hugging one another. Brin watched each come in, always looking for but not finding the faces she sought. Finally, Nyphron and his Galantians charged in with shields protecting their heads. Moya, Cobb, and Habet were with them.

"Let me go!" Brin pleaded, struggling against Gifford's unrelenting grip.

"You can't leave," Moya said, her hair a wild mess. "Your house is burning. There's nothing—"

Outside, a roar grew like the angry growl of a colossal beast. Everyone stared out the doorway as the sky turned darker still, and the wind blew with even more force. Without warning, the Bakers' roundhouse ripped apart. First the thatch blew away; then the wood beams tore free; finally, the log walls succumbed and disappeared, sucked into the air. Even the foundation of mud bricks was sheared and scattered. After that, a whirl-wind cloud of dirt and debris consumed everything outside the storage pit.

"Close the door," Nyphron ordered. Grygor, the giant, started to haul it shut just as Raithe arrived.

"Has anyone seen Persephone?" Raithe asked while scanning the crowd.

"She's not here. Went to the forest," Moya replied.

Raithe drew close to her. "Are you sure?"

She nodded. "Suri, Arion, and Seph went to talk to Magda."

"That old oak is on top of a hill in an open glade," he said to no one in particular. Raithe looked like he might throw up. There had been rumors that the Dureyan was in love with Dahl Rhen's chieftain, but a lot of recent gossip had turned out to be untrue. Seeing Raithe's face removed any un-certainty. If Roan were still outside, Gifford would have looked the same way.

Everyone sat or knelt in tearful silence as the roaring grew louder. With the door closed and guarded by the giant, Gifford let go of Brin, who col-lapsed and sobbed. All around, people quivered, whimpered, and stared at the ceiling, no doubt wondering if it, too, would be ripped away or cave in.

Gifford stood beside Roan, the crowd pressing them together. He'd never been this close to her for so long. He felt her warmth and smelled charcoal, oil, and smoke—the scents he'd come to associate with Roan and all things good. If the roof collapsed and killed him, Gifford would have thanked Mari for her final kindness.

The shelter was little more than a hole in the ground, but because it protected the dahl's food supply, the pit was solidly built. The best materials went into its construction. The walls were dirt and stone, the ceiling braced by logs driven into the ground. Most of Gifford's work ended up in that pit. Huge clay urns held harvests of barley, wheat, and rye. Their tops were sealed with wax to keep out the mice and moisture. The enclosure also safeguarded wine, honey, oil, vegetables, and a cache of smoked meats. At this time of year, most of the urns were empty, and the pit was little more than a hole, albeit a sturdy one. Still, the ceiling shook, and the door rattled.

The only bit of light entered through the narrow cracks where the door didn't precisely meet its frame. This sliver of white flickered violently.

"It'll be okay," Gifford told Roan. He said it in a whisper, as if a secret chosen to share with her alone.

Around them, people wailed, and not just women and children. Gifford heard Cobb, Heath Coswall, Habet, and Filson the lamp maker weeping openly as well. But Roan didn't make a sound. She wasn't like them; she wasn't like anyone. The light from the door highlighted the contour of her face, and she didn't look scared. Instead, intensity shone in her eyes. If not for the dozens of people between Roan and the exit, he had no doubt she would have opened the door. She wanted to see. Roan wanted to see everything.

After what felt like hours, the clatter of hail stopped, but the rain continued to fall, hard at times then lighter, only to pound once more. The howl of the wind faded. Even the cracks of lightning fell silent. Finally, the light from around the door became bright and unwavering.

Nyphron shoved the door open and crept out. A moment later he waved for the others to follow.

Everyone squinted against the brightness of the sun, struggling to see. One of the lodge's banners lay on the ground, its ends frayed. Thatch and logs were scattered everywhere. Not a single roundhouse had survived. Branches, leaves, and broken bodies littered the yard, none of them moving. Overhead, clouds were breaking up, and patches of blue emerged.

"Is it over?" Heath Coswall asked from the back of the crowd.

As if in answer, a loud boom sounded, and the dahl's front gate trembled.

"What is that?" Moya asked, speaking for everyone.

Another bang hit, and the gate began to buckle.

The rol where they sheltered was like the one under the waterfall that Suri had shown Persephone months ago, which had provided refuge from a pack of wolves and a deadly bear named Grin. Carved from natural stone, the room was about the size of a roundhouse and had strange markings near the ceiling. While the waterfall rol was slightly larger and square, this one was perfectly round and contained six stout pillars surrounding a gemstone the size of a storage urn. Embedded in the floor, the standing crystal gave off a green, unnatural light. Six heavy benches encircled the stone, as if it were a campfire and the room used for telling ghost stories. In front of the bench farthest from the door stood what Persephone first thought were three small men. Each was less than four feet in height, their faces illuminated by the eerie emerald light. She might have screamed, and certainly would have recoiled, if their expressions hadn't been so clearly marked by shock and fear.

"He . . . hello," Persephone stammered, a bit embarrassed and out of breath. "Sorry for barging in. A bit scary outside."

None of the three replied.

Stocky to the point of appearing square, with large hands, broad noses, deep-set eyes, and bushy brows, they stood as motionless as statues. They wore shirts of metal rings, and a row of metal hats lay on the nearby bench. The reflection of the green light from their armor made them appear to glow in the dark.

Dherg.

Persephone had met their kind before. She'd traveled with several caravans to Dahl Tirre and the nearby port town of Vernes where the Dherg had shops. She and her husband, Reglan, had traded with the Dherg on behalf of Dahl Rhen, swapping antlers, hides, and pottery for bits of tin. The Dherg were far less intimidating than the Fhrey but even less trusting.

The Dherg on the left had a long white beard and a sword. The one on the right also had a sword, but his beard was gray. The fellow in the middle had no sword at all and almost no beard. A massive pickax was strapped to his back, and around his neck he wore a golden torc.

"Is this your rol?" Persephone asked.

The Dherg didn't answer. They didn't even look at her. Instead, the three focused on Arion with a mixture of hatred and terror.

"Do you mind if we share it until the storm passes?" she continued, undaunted.

Still no answer.

Persephone wondered if they even understood Rhunic. Not all Dherg did. There were orthodox factions that shunned outsiders and foreign ways, including language.

"I need to sit," Arion said, and staggered toward the benches.

At her approach, two of the Dherg—the ones with the beards—bolted for the door. One slapped the keystone, and it started to slide open. The moment it did, the noise outside grew deafening.

Neither the voice of hail nor the roar of fire, this rumble was louder, deeper. The growl of whirling wind. Persephone had seen it before. As a girl, her father had held her high on the dahl's wall to witness a god's wandering finger scratch the back of Elan. Across the distance of more than a mile, the whirling black funnel ripped up trees. Persephone had wondered what it would be like to be a rabbit or mole caught in that cataclysm. Now she knew. Outside, leaves, grass, dirt, stones, hail, branches, and whole tree trunks flew sideways, smashing into one another. A loud shattering *crack* issued from somewhere in the storm—another tree snapping in half. Persephone felt a pull like the current of a powerful river dragging on her as air was sucked out through the opening.

The white-bearded Dherg felt it, too, and braced himself at the threshold. He looked at the raging storm then glanced back to Arion, trying to decide. With his beard whipping, he shouted, "Close it! Close it!"

The gray-bearded one clapped hand to stone. The door reversed direction, the stone rolling back into place until the roar was shut out once more.

"You're doing that!" the white-bearded Dherg accused in Fhrey, pointing at the door while glaring at Arion.

She shook her head wearily while sitting on the stone bench. *"Not of my making. Believe me."*

"I don't believe you!"

Arion flexed her fingers. Shock and worry creased her brow. She reached up and put a hand to the back of her head.

"It's okay. It'll come back." Suri pointed at the series of runes chiseled along the top of the walls. *"The markings."* They were the same as the ones on the bandages that had prevented Arion from using magic.

Arion nodded slowly. She was frowning but looked relieved. Seeing that the Dherg were still glaring at her, she pointed to the runes and said, *"Those are yours, so you know I'm not responsible for what is happening out there."*

Persephone had never seen Dherg quite like them. None of the others she'd met were dressed in metal. The traders in Vernes wore floppy wool hats of bright orange or red, and long tunics usually dyed yellow or blue. Metal in the southern regions wasn't common, and the Dherg coveted it like sacred relics—*their* form of magic. They haggled stubbornly for even small bits of tin. But it was their other metals that were truly remarkable: wondrous bronze, which could be forged into invincible weapons, and gold and silver, which shone with divine light. She wondered if these three were rulers or otherwise-powerful members of Dherg society. Whoever they were, it'd be a mistake not to make a good impression. Or at least the best that could be made after barging in on them.

"I'm Persephone, chieftain of Dahl Rhen," she said, thinking it was time someone did the polite thing. "This is Arion of the Fhrey. And this"—she gestured toward the mystic—"is Suri. Oh, and her wolf, Minna, who is very nice, and will do you no harm."

Perhaps because they realized Arion wasn't capable of performing magic, or because Persephone had been the first to address them, the three finally appeared to notice her existence. They looked at her with no less suspicion but far less fear.

"Now then," she said, offering the friendliest smile she could conjure. "Who might you be?"

They all offered one more glare at Arion before the white-bearded one spoke. "I'm Frost of Nye. This is Flood," he said, clapping a hand on the shoulder of the one beside him, making the gray-bearded Dherg wince. "And he"—Frost pointed at the one with the pickax who hadn't run for the exit—"is called Rain. My companions obviously weren't properly watching the door."

"Us? And what were *you* doing?" Flood asked Frost. "Why was guarding the door our responsibility?"

"I was busy trying to remove a pebble from my boot."

"Careful, it might be your brain. If you toss it away, then . . . well . . . now that I think of it, we likely wouldn't notice any difference, so go ahead."

Frost scowled.

"Honored to make your acquaintance." Persephone bowed formally, which appeared to surprise them.

"Now, how did you know about our rol?" Frost asked no one in particular. "These are secret places, safe areas known only to our kind."

"Suri is a mystic and has lived in the Crescent Forest all her life." Persephone glanced at the girl. "She led us here."

The Dherg smirked. "All her life? How long could that possibly be?"

"Suri is . . . well . . . special. She's located many rols. Haven't you?"

Suri was petting Minna's neck, oblivious to the conversation.

"Suri?" Persephone nudged the mystic with an elbow.

"What?"

"I was telling them that you have a knack for finding rols. Could you explain how you do it?"

Suri shrugged. "Empty places feel different from the ones filled with dirt and stone. It's fun to find the spot that opens the door. Although Minna sometimes gets bored if I take too long. Don't you, Minna?"

"We just came here to get away from the storm," Persephone said. "No idea it was occupied. I hope you don't mind, but as you can see the storm is . . . the storm is . . ." A thought wriggled into her head—and then more than one. A whole set of puzzle pieces fell together: the suddenness of the storm, Arion telling them to run, and the trail of scorched divots left in their wake.

She turned her attention to the Miralyith and spoke in the Fhrey language, *"Arion, how did you know?"*

The bald woman sat on the bench, head resting in her hands. *"Know what?"*

"You told us to run. And that lightning, it . . . it wasn't random. I don't know how, but it was trying to hit us. Right?"

"Yes," the Fhrey said, looking up. The relief that Suri's explanation had provided earlier was gone, replaced by a painful expression as Arion rubbed the knit hat on her head.

"This was how it was in the war." Frost seemed to be talking to his companions, but spoke in Fhrey. *"When the Fhrey attacked, we'd shelter in rols."*

"You couldn't know anything about the war," Arion said. *"I was young, but I remember. You don't. You only know stories. Dherg don't live that long."*

"Don't call me a Dherg . . . you . . . you . . . elf!" Frost's hand went to his sword.

Arion's brows rose at the term *elf*.

"Hold on, hold on," Persephone said. "Maybe we should all calm down a little. I'm sure Arion meant no disrespect. The storm is too dangerous for any of us to leave, so let's make the best of it. We don't know how long we'll all be stuck in here."

Overhead, thunder boomed, and the wind's howl continued.

Persephone moved to take a seat on the bench beside Arion and was unpleasantly reminded about the hail that had struck her back. She also had time to notice the many cuts along her hands and legs from the thornbushes. Her left ear hurt as well, though she didn't know why.

"Might as well sit down," Persephone told the three.

Frost and Flood looked at each other and then returned to the benches on the far side of the glowing green gem. Rain, who hadn't stopped looking at the runes since they'd been pointed out, had wandered into the shadows. He stood near the back wall, head tilted up, studying the carvings.

"Pardon me for asking, but if Dher . . . er . . . what Arion said isn't the correct way to refer to your kind, then what is? It's the only term I've ever heard."

"*Dherg* is a Fhrey word meaning 'vile mole.' How would you like it if we called you *Rhunes?*" Frost asked. "That's also a Fhrey word. You know what that means, right? 'Barbarian,' 'primitive,' 'crude'? Do you like being called that?"

Persephone hadn't thought about it before. To her, to most everyone in the Ten Clans—few of whom spoke Fhrey—Rhune was just a common term, a name. Now that he mentioned it, she realized it had been an insult. "So what do you call yourselves, then?"

"Belgriclungreians," Frost said.

Persephone took a breath. "Really? That's . . . that is a mouthful, isn't it? And what brings you to the Crescent Forest? I don't remember your kind ever coming this far north."

The three exchanged looks—uncomfortable expressions—and Frost growled, "That's really none of your business, now, is it?"

Persephone was becoming exasperated by the effort of the conversation. Even idle chitchat seemed to provoke their ire.

Outside, the noise grew softer, only rain now; the storm was lessening. The patter became a pleasant, comforting, non-threatening sound. *Does that mean it's over?* Persephone wondered, realizing she wasn't at all certain what *it* was. Not exactly.

That morning had begun so agreeably. A clear sky and a leisurely walk through the forest made a refreshing change from the growing tension about a potential war. Prior to a few months ago, the Fhrey were thought to be gods—seemingly immortal. Then, Raithe of Dureya had killed one, throwing everything in doubt. A few weeks later, he slew Gryndal, the seemingly all-powerful Fhrey Miralyith, and all skepticism had vanished. The Fhrey were not gods, but they were powerful. Retaliation was only a matter of time. Still, Persephone had expected an army, not lightning bolts.

"*Headache?*" Suri asked after seeing the Fhrey rub her temples.

Arion replied with a shallow nod and got up. Her movement sent a jolt of fear through the two bearded Dherg, who briefly jumped to their feet. When Arion lay down on the floor and rested an arm over her eyes, they relaxed.

"What's wrong with the elf?" Flood asked.

"Don't talk to them," Frost snapped.

"Why do you call her *elf*?" Persephone asked.

"That is what they are to us," Frost said. *"Nightmares."*

Persephone said, puzzled, "But *elf* is a Fhrey word."

"Not much sense calling them names in our language. What good is insulting someone if they don't know you're doing it?"

"You aren't pronouncing it right," Arion said. *"It's* ylfe, *not* elf."

Persephone moved to where Arion lay and knelt beside her. The Fhrey used both hands to rub her eyes.

"The pain is bad?" Persephone asked.

"Yes."

"Is there—" Persephone stopped when the ground shook.

Everyone exchanged glances with similar worried expressions.

The earth quaked again, accompanied by a muffled thud.

"What is that?" Persephone asked.

No one answered.

The Dherg were on their feet again, all three looking up.

Another thud, louder this time, sent a tremor through the rol, and dust, bits of rock, and pebbles rained down from the ceiling, glinting off the gemstone. Persephone got to her feet and approached Frost, who, along with Flood, was backing away, moving toward the door again.

"During the war, did the Fhrey ever manage to get into these rols?"

The two Dherg looked at each other with so much concern that Persephone didn't need an answer.

"How?" she asked, as another shudder shook the room. The stone ceiling cracked, and a large piece of rock fell, followed by a shower of dirt. Through the gap, a massive eye peered in.

CHAPTER TWO

Giant Problems

The first giant I ever saw was friendly and liked to cook. The second one might have as well. I do not know; I never asked. It is hard to pose questions while screaming.

—THE BOOK OF BRIN

The huge eye drew back, and a fist punched through part of the rol's remaining ceiling. The tawny-skinned hand was ten times the size of a normal man's, its knuckles coarse and caked in dirt. Persephone and the others scattered as rock and dirt fell, bursting on the floor. Another blow and the great fist smashed through again, this time opening a hole large enough for an aurochs to pass through.

Frost and Flood were the first to the door.

"Arion!" Persephone cried.

The Fhrey was still on the floor. She'd sat up, but that was as far as she'd gotten.

Two massive hands slipped through the opening. They gripped the sides of the hole and tore back the roof. Brilliant sunlight entered as the unmistakable silhouette of a giant loomed. The mountainous man crouched on his knees, digging with bare hands, his tongue poking out of his mouth in concentration. Tossing aside a fistful of heavily rooted forest floor, the giant thrust his craggy face into the opening, blotting out the light once more. He peered in, as if examining the contents of a sack. The green glow of the gemstone worsened an already terrifying visage. Narrow eyes set beneath a precipice-brow bulged with a maniacal leer. Shadowy canyons lay to either side of a promontory nose, beneath which gaped a cavernous mouth of uneven, intermittent, tombstone-shaped teeth.

"Hag-la!" the behemoth bellowed with hot breath smelling of rotted meat and strawberries.

The head drew back and a hand thrust in.

"Run!" Persephone yelled.

Frost and Flood had already escaped with Suri and Minna close behind, but Arion never had a chance. The giant grabbed at her as she struggled to her feet. As the massive hand closed, Rain swung and planted the spiked end of his pickax in the giant's fist. The colossus let go and jerked his hand back. He clutched his blood-gushing wound while looking down with snarling fury. Persephone and Rain took that moment to help Arion, and together they dived out the open door just before the giant rose and slammed his foot down on the rol. The ground shuddered as dirt and dust blew through the door.

Outside, the trees were gone. Some had been uprooted, others snapped, leaving only splintered trunks. Mangled limbs, logs, branches, and leaves littered what was now a bald spot within the wood.

Frost and Flood leapt fallen trees on their way toward thicker cover. Suri and Minna paused atop a toppled hickory to look back as Persephone labored to get to her feet in the tangle of branches. Unlike the others, Arion wasn't fleeing. She sat still, arms out, anger in her eyes.

The giant howled as he struggled to free his foot, which had become lodged in the hole where the rol had been. He became frustrated as it slipped deeper despite his attempts—sinking first to the ankle, then to the shin. Finally, the ground swallowed him up to the knee. The giant's other leg was finding similar difficulty, as if the mutilated forest floor had turned into a swamp of tar.

"Arg rog!" he shouted in what sounded like a mix of anger and fear. Two huge hands came down in an effort to push himself up, but there was no solid ground, and they, too, were sucked into the mire.

Slowly, steadily, and with an occasional snap of a branch or rustle of leaves, the floor of the forest pulled the giant down. He sank past his waist, then his shoulders, and as the rich, leafy soil inched up around his neck, Arion lowered her hands and the descent stopped.

Flood clapped Frost on the shoulder and pointed at the Fhrey, and for the first time Persephone saw them both smile.

"Did you see *that?*" Frost asked.

Flood nodded. "Maybe there *is* a way back, after all."

The giant began screaming then. A number of words Persephone didn't recognize were shouted before he cried out, *"Help!"* in Fhrey.

"You speak my language?" Arion asked from where she had taken a seat on the fallen trunk of a maple.

"Yes! Yes!" the giant cried.

"Lucky you." Arion got up and carefully stepped through the carnage. Finding the hat Padera had made, she reached down and withdrew it, sighing at the dirt and leaves covering the garment.

"Let me live, " the giant begged. *"I yield. You win. I'll quit."*

"Quit what exactly?" Arion asked.

The giant hesitated.

Arion looked up from her hat with an irritated frown, and the giant began to slip deeper, the soil now up to his chin.

"Trying to kill you! Trying to kill you. We were sent to kill you!"

Arion nodded as she brushed the dirt and leaves from the hat. Then she stopped, looked up puzzled, and glared at the giant again. *"What do you mean—we?"*

The thick-beamed brace snapped in half, and the front gate of Dahl Rhen burst open. Over the last few months, Gifford had seen many strange things enter through them—the dead body of a chieftain and before that his son; three groups of Fhrey, two of which had held a magical battle before the lodge's steps; and Raithe, the famed God Killer. Gifford imagined he'd seen it all, but standing outside the storage pit in the wreckage left by the storm, he realized he was wrong. What entered that afternoon was a sight beyond his imagination; or more accurately, it was a sight that should only exist there.

Giants. A lot of them.

Everyone knew they existed, just as everyone knew gods, witches, goblins, and crimbals did. Dahl Rhen had even played host to one, but Grygor, who had accompanied the first set of Fhrey, turned out to be a pleasant sort. He enjoyed cooking and kept mostly to himself. These were different: angry and ferocious. They were also bigger, much bigger, wearing kilts and vests poorly stitched from the hides of numerous beasts of different species.

Taller than the gate, they had to duck to pass under the parapet. Their feet were the size of Gifford's bed, and they carried wooden mallets that looked to have been fashioned by shoving a thick branch through a hole in a tree trunk. In total, there were twelve, and they broke through the gate with bared teeth and wild eyes. Rushing in, the giants swung their mallets, smashing the already ruined piles of thatch and fractured logs. They hammered the wind-strewn rubble and crushed a goat that had survived the storm but had made the mistake of not running. A few took the time to lift the thatch and peer underneath, then one looked Gifford's way.

Much of the surviving citizenry of Dahl Rhen was still in the pit. Those outside, like Gifford and Roan, watched as one of the giants howled with excitement, pointing directly at them. The other eleven turned, and the ground shook as the group hurried forward. Having seen what had happened to the goat, nearly everyone cried out and retreated in terror.

Roan didn't. She stood her ground, watching in awe.

From behind, the Fhrey warriors charged out of the pit, weapons drawn, too impatient to wait the few seconds for the giants to close the distance. The first to land a blow was the one called Eres, who threw two javelins. One pierced the throat of the nearest giant, which Gifford believed to be a female Grenmorian, as she had breasts and a shorter beard.

The other javelin caught one of the larger attackers in the eye, driving itself so deep that only the rear portion poked out of the socket. The giant staggered, then collapsed face-first into the remains of the lodge, flipping a log into the air and shaking the ground so violently that Gifford had to take a step to keep his balance.

Sebek, the Fhrey with short blond hair and a pair of swords, ran directly into the pack of invaders. He sprinted past the first two, and Gifford couldn't understand why until he realized that the Galantian had picked out the biggest for his target. Sebek reached his prey, ran between the giant's legs, and drove a sword into the middle of each foot. The giant howled a long deep note of rage and pain, which grew louder as he tilted forward and struggled to free his feet from the ground. The blades dislodged but not before the giant lost his balance. Once more Gifford staggered and nearly fell when the giant crashed to the dirt. Fast as a rabbit, Sebek retrieved his weapons and sprinted up the giant's stomach. He leapt across the invader's chest and stabbed both blades into his neck.

Anwir was the next Galantian to land a strike. Pulling forth a loaded sling, he swung it in circles over his head and unleashed the stone. The rock staggered a medium-sized giant just as Tekchin reached him with his long, narrow blade. After severing three fingers of the giant's mallet-like hand, Tekchin stabbed the giant's chest, cutting a semicircle before withdrawing the sword.

Roan took a step forward. She had that familiar single-minded curiosity in her eyes, a sort of blind fascination that was impossible for Gifford to understand. Once, she'd broken an ankle after falling into Crescent Creek while preoccupied by a butterfly. Gifford didn't know what had caught her eye this time, but in a battle between Fhrey and giants, it hardly mattered. If she wandered too far, if she tried to get ahead of Nyphron, who'd taken up a position between the giants and the people of Dhal Rhen to act as a final bulwark, Gifford would take hold of her wrist as he'd done with Brin. Yes, she would panic and lash out, but he'd gladly endure the pain inflicted by her reaction if it was the only way to keep her safe.

He reached out but stopped when, to his relief, she didn't move any farther. Roan wasn't interested in the giants; she was shifting her gaze between Anwir and Eres, staring with intensity as Anwir wound up another stone and Eres launched another javelin. She muttered softly, "There's always a better way."

To Gifford's surprise, Grygor joined the other Galantians in the fight against his brethren. Grygor didn't appear to care about their kinship as he raised his huge sword and hewed down a slightly larger giant with a single stroke.

Vorath, the only Fhrey who had a beard—which he'd grown in the style of the Rhunes—advanced with a three-spiked ball on a chain in one hand and a star-shaped mace in the other. He waded into the fray, a whirling cyclone of whipping metal. The giants appeared confused by his weapons until Vorath solved the riddle by crushing knees and then skulls.

With a shout, which may have been a command that Gifford didn't understand, the giants retreated, dragging their fallen with them. The Fhrey didn't pursue or interfere, even when one giant strode toward the well to reclaim the body of his comrade, which was just a few yards from where Sebek stood.

As the giants fled, Gifford noticed other dahl residents who hadn't reached the storage pit but had survived the storm. Old man Mathias Hagger stood near the waste holes behind what used to be the lodge, sodden with muck. Arlina and Gilroy, their three boys, and daughter, Maureen, were clustered around the grindstone where the millhouse once stood. Arlina's face was covered in blood, but otherwise she looked fine. Many more weren't as lucky. Bodies were strewn everywhere. Feet and arms protruded from under wreckage. The battle was over, but the toll had yet to be tallied.

CHAPTER THREE

The Circle of Fire

I will never forget the day my parents died. I was a child of fifteen, and my world had been destroyed. Then Persephone led us away from what had been our home, and I was not a child anymore.

—THE BOOK OF BRIN

Arion lay on her back, eyes closed, in a small area cleared of debris inside the walls of Dahl Rhen. When a shadow covered her face, she was reluctant to open her lids. Her head was still throbbing, the pain unbearable.

"Try this," Suri said.

If it had been anyone else, Arion would've pretended to be asleep, but Suri could always tell.

Arion opened one eye. The Rhune mystic stood over her with a steaming cup. Just behind the girl was the old woman Padera. The two had become something of a team lately, joining forces to concoct primitive recipes to ease Arion's pain. None worked. Knowing the two would continue to pester her until she drank, rubbed, or gargled whatever they brought her, Arion sat up and took the cup. Miraculously, the delicate vessel, called a Gifford Cup by the dahl's residents, had survived the attack. The exquisite chalice was as out of place as Arion in that world of mud and logs.

Suri made a gesture indicating that the brew should be drunk. Arion sniffed the cup's contents, then recoiled at the stench.

"You sure?" Arion inquired.

"Pretty sure," Suri answered with an encouraging smile.

The hot tea was bitter but not nearly as repugnant as its smell. The liquid had a woody aftertaste. *"What's this one?"*

"White willow bark."

"Good for headaches?"

Suri nodded. *"The best."*

Arion knew the young mystic was stretching the truth. If the concoction was *the best,* it would have been the first the pair tried, and they had gone through nearly half a dozen attempts. She took a second sip, which also made no improvement, but at least the steam was pleasant. The old woman didn't speak Fhrey, so Arion forced a smile and nodded in her direction. Padera said something unintelligible and her sour face turned even more acidic. Suri had been teaching Arion Rhunic, just as Arion worked at improving Suri's mastery of Fhrey. But Arion's vocabulary was still limited to a few hundred words, and Padera hadn't used many of those.

"What did she say?"

"She doesn't understand why you aren't getting better."

"That makes two of us."

Looking around, Arion saw that not much had changed since she'd lain down, except that now neat rows of wrapped bodies were carefully laid out in a mass grave. Each building was still destroyed. Logs, thatch, and rock foundations were scattered everywhere. She considered repairing the damage—not that she knew exactly how it all went back together—but she didn't dare take the risk.

Earlier that morning before she'd gone to the forest, Arion had thought she'd finally mended. Her head hadn't hurt for days, but now the throbbing announced most emphatically that her hopes of being healed were, at best, premature.

Months ago, after arriving at the dahl to bring Nyphron to justice, Arion had been hit in the head with a rock by one of the villagers. She'd yet to discover the culprit's identity, but it didn't matter. What had mattered was being completely cut off from the Art. After the injury, she couldn't manage even a simple weave. It wasn't until after the bandages wrapping her head were removed that the Art returned. Apparently, Suri had been afraid Arion would retaliate against the dahl because of the attack, so the young mystic had painted Dherg runes on the bandages, and they had inhibited Arion's use of magic.

With the restoration of the Art, Arion had fought Gryndal, but by the end of the battle the pain had blinded her. She couldn't walk and had to be carried back to bed. She hadn't fallen asleep after the fight; she'd passed out. When she awoke a full day later, Arion was physically sick and emotionally devastated, but at least she had the Art once more, or so she'd thought.

Using the Art to extinguish Magda's flames, then later to trap the giant, had brought the pain back. So while she was no longer blocked from accessing the power of the Art, using it was another matter.

"You're awake. Good." Nyphron waded toward her through a pile of thatch that had been someone's roof. The Galantian leader was wearing his armor for the first time in weeks, the bronze shining brilliantly in the late-afternoon sun. He towered over her. *"Do you still think a diplomatic solution can be found?"* he asked, his tone forceful, aggressive. He wanted to fight—verbally at least. No surprise there, the Instarya tribe were the warriors of their people.

Suri and Padera rushed off, but Arion couldn't avoid Nyphron so easily.

The pain was coming in hammering waves that blurred her vision as if from the pummeling of blows. She rubbed her forehead while making a pained expression, hoping he would get the hint and leave her alone.

He didn't.

Nyphron gestured at the destruction around them. *"Do you think this was a random accident? A rogue band of Grenmorians wandering some three hundred miles away from home? A weirdly large group who managed to avoid Instarya patrols, who walked right by Alon Rhist to smash this dahl for the sheer joy of it? And the storm? Was that just a freak occurrence?"*

"No, I don't think any of that." Her words were slow, tired, and dribbled out of her mouth. He must grasp that she was miserable. Common decency should cause him to—

"So what are you thinking?"

She wasn't. That was the point. Thinking hurt. Of course the attack was deliberate, but who exactly was being targeted? The Rhune village for Gryndal's death? Nyphron for his defiance? And it was impossible to discount the accuracy of the lightning strikes. Had Prince Mawyndulë convinced his father that she was a threat for the part she had played?

"I think this isn't the time to have this conversation. I'm tired, my head hurts, and I just want to rest."

"Your hesitation has already cost us valuable time. Months have passed while we've lingered and done nothing." He gestured at the devastation around them. *"This is the result. We need to take this war to Fane Lothian himself."*

"War?" Now it was her turn to use an incredulous tone. *"What war? Yes, Dahl Rhen has been attacked, but I really can't blame Lothian for that. This dahl has harbored you and your Galantians, and one of its residents killed First Minister Gryndal. This was retaliation, plain and simple. But a war? What I need to do is defuse the situation, not fan the flames."*

"Are you really so naïve? This isn't about a single dahl. Did they even tell you why you were sent to retrieve me? What my transgression had been?"

"Yes. You attacked Petragar, the new leader of Alon Rhist."

"I chose to avoid arrest for disobeying an order, a directive to destroy the Rhune villages—all of them. Lothian wants the Rhunes gone. The fane has declared war."

Arion did remember passing through a burnt set of ruins, but it wasn't until then that she realized how it had been destroyed and why.

"But you can't fight a war against Estramnadon. Will you kill your own kind? Break Ferrol's Law? You can't possibly be willing to be barred from Phyre. Living the rest of your life as an outlaw is one thing, but being banned from the afterlife is unthinkable."

"I don't have to do any killing myself. I'll teach the Rhunes to fight. They can do the slaying. Raithe has proved that. They just need training."

"And you think with a few lessons they can stand against the full might of the fane?"

Nyphron smirked, shifting his eyes as if she'd said something both amusing and distasteful. *"The fane? What does Lothian know about war? What do any of those across the Nidwalden know of battle? We Instarya have protected them for centuries. If my host of Rhunes can present a credible threat, then the rest of the Instarya will join our cause."*

"As simple as that, is it?"

"At the very least my brothers-in-arms will stay out of the conflict. And without them, the fane will have no strategists, no skilled commanders, no warriors, no army, and no clue how to fight."

"And the Miralyith? Fenelyus single-handedly defeated the entire Dherg army at the Battle of Mador. Your mighty Instarya were merely spectators."

"We'll use the Dherg runes. Put them on every shield, every helm."

Arion was surprised. He'd thought this through more than she'd expected. *Clever, but filled with holes overlooked out of ignorance or stupidity.* She remembered the words of Fenelyus: *It's easier to believe the most outlandish lie that confirms what you suspect than the most obvious truth that denies it.* Apparently, lying to oneself wasn't restricted to Artists.

"The Dherg's runes won't win a war for you," she said, blinking against the pain that was making her eyes water. *"Your thinking is limited, skewed toward what you want, what you need to believe. The runes will only prevent the Art from affecting the wearer. If I wanted to kill you right now, my first thought might be to incinerate you. Fire is easy and doesn't take much effort. It is one of the first things aspiring Miralyith learn, but I'm guessing that wouldn't work, would it? The flames would be conjured and you've already lined the interior of that armor with protective markings."*

Nyphron's brows lifted, confirming that Arion was right, and that he was surprised she had guessed.

"But what if I opened the ground beneath your feet? Or caused a tree to fall on you. What if I rerouted a river through your army's camp . . . a big, powerful river? The Miralyith are a creative lot. We call it the Art for a reason. So how will you and your Rhune army stand against a team of Miralyith who are able to turn Elan herself against you?"

The pounding in Arion's head was lessening. Maybe the tea was helping. She was finding it easier to think.

"I'll overwhelm them with numbers. Do you know how many Rhunes there are?" he asked.

"Thousands."

Nyphron smiled with equal parts pleasure and mischief. *"One of the tasks of the Instarya is to keep a census of the Rhunes, the same way we track animal populations and the status of the Grenmorians and goblins. Every ten years we take a count. When the numbers get too large, we promote warfare between the Gula-Rhunes and the Rhulyn-Rhunes to cull the herds."*

"That's terrible."

Nyphron shook his head. *"What would be terrible is to let them breed uncontrolled. In a few generations, the Rhunes would be a flood upon the world, and the Fhrey and Dherg could be pushed aside and eventually erased. And it's not like they don't enjoy killing one another. They would fight more if we didn't stand between them. But we should have been more vigilant. Once they settled in villages, even primitive ones like this, their population exploded. When they were nomadic, their numbers were kept small by predators like the goblins and Grenmorians, and by a lack of food. But then they learned farming."*

"Did we teach them?"

"No, they started using copper and tin around that same time, so we think it was the Dherg." He shot a glare in the direction of the three, who huddled near the outer wall. They weren't close enough to hear the conversation, but there was no mistaking the disgust in Nyphron's venomous expression. All three got up and moved farther away.

"The Dherg taught the barbarians all sorts of things, and soon the Rhunes were erecting granaries and buildings, settling down, and spreading out. Suddenly there were thousands, then tens of thousands, and now . . ." He lowered his voice for dramatic effect. *"Arion, there are more than a million Rhunes."*

"Million?" she asked, certain that she heard incorrectly, or that her sluggish, wounded brain wasn't recognizing a jest.

There were only about fifty thousand Fhrey, and the idea that Rhunes could outnumber them twenty to one *was* disturbing.

"And it's only going to get worse. Next year, Estramnadon will welcome,

what, ten or twenty births? That same year the Rhunes will see twenty-five thousand."

"But . . . but they die so quickly. I've heard they don't even reach a full century."

"True. About fifteen thousand die each year, but that still means ten thousand are added to their population. Two hundred thousand could be born to this coming generation. When they were thought to be as docile as rabbits, they didn't represent a threat. But now . . . well, Raithe killed Gryndal, didn't he? The Rhunes once considered us immortal gods, but now that they know we bleed and die, will they sit idly by when Lothian attacks or will they rise?"

He looked past her at the inhabitants of the dahl, *"War is inevitable, and we can be trampled or we can learn to harness and ride. I've made my choice, and I suggest you do the same."*

The bonfire roared as it consumed a hundred years of civilization in a single night. From the moment Raithe had arrived in Dahl Rhen, he'd considered this place to be the high point of mankind's achievements. He'd never seen a place so rich and luxurious. Every family had a home— a roundhouse constructed from wood. The storage pit was deep enough to last a whole winter and beyond. The fields were lush and fertile, growing multiple varieties of seed grass. The residents of Dahl Rhen had excesses of beer, mead, bread, meat and fish, herbs and spices. And all their riches had been protected by a high wall and a massive gate, but the gate hadn't been strong enough.

The bodies had been buried by nightfall. Otherwise, the scent would've lured animals out of the wood. Without a secured perimeter, everyone felt it best to put their loved ones safely underground. Raithe had worked hard all day. Covered in sweat and dirt, he was pleased to see that the well was working again. The Dherg, three small-statured people who had returned with Persephone's group, had created a vessel made from beaten metal. They called it a bucket, and it worked better than the gourds the villagers had used in the past. Raithe poured water over his head and let it drain down his hair and soak his chest and thick black beard.

Those who'd survived were gathering around the bonfire built on the ruined foundation of the lodge. They fed it splintered logs, thatch, and the other broken pieces of their lives. Not including the Galantians, fewer than three hundred had survived, and when he'd first arrived there had been almost a thousand people in Dahl Rhen. Given the destruction, Raithe would have expected the toll to be higher.

Somehow the oldest resident, Padera, had weathered the attack. She claimed her dead husband had something to do with her survival, but Raithe hadn't listened to the reasons why. He'd been busy burying Brin's parents while the girl sobbed into Persephone's chest. There had been a lot of crying that day. Gelston, whom Raithe had only just discovered was Delwin's brother and Brin's uncle, was still alive, having survived the lightning strike. Still, he was in no shape to care for his niece. The man had barely spoken and hardly moved all day.

Some villagers hadn't been in the dahl during the attack. A number of folks benefited that afternoon from tending their fields or being in the forest cutting wood or hunting. If the giants had attacked at night, the death toll would have been higher. And without the Galantians, there might have been no survivors at all. The Fhrey had saved them, but after seeing what was left of the dahl, maybe *saved* wasn't the right word.

With the destruction of the gate, Dahl Rhen was just a hill, an exposed mound surrounded by wilderness. Neither the lodge nor any of the roundhouses had survived the storm. In one cursed day, generations of labor had been lost. They were back to how it must have been when the clan first paused in that spot and built a similar fire from the wood of the forest.

And yet despite the losses, there was cause for appreciation. Gone was the idea of Fhrey gods, but there was plenty of room for heroes in the Rhen pantheon. Any reservations or suspicions the dahl's inhabitants had held about the Fhrey warriors were erased by the feet of giants. Around the fire, the men of Dahl Rhen sat shoulder to shoulder with the Galantians, sharing beer and mead and toasting the dead.

"There you are," Malcolm said as he headed toward Raithe with a wooden cup in each hand. "Here. Bergin opened his best jugs of beer to honor the dead. Thought you could use a drink."

"Thanks, but do you know where—"

Malcolm tilted his head, and Raithe turned to see Persephone, Nyphron, and Arion approaching them from behind. He offered her a smile as she passed but didn't receive one in return. She looked tired, her eyes sore and red. He'd seen the same expression on many faces throughout the day. Not for the first time, Raithe questioned his own callousness. The deaths meant little to him. He rationalized that he didn't know the people of Rhen well, or maybe the impact of the devastation was somehow delayed. But Raithe was still waiting for the arrival of grief over his father's passing, and he suspected it might never come. He was Dureyan, and the simple truth was that his people had little use for mourning or sympathy. Sudden, inexplicable death wasn't a surprise to them. The only constant was suffering. Those of Clan Dureya learned this lesson well, and they learned it young. They also knew anything could be endured—even life.

Raithe and Malcolm found seats around the fire not far from where the three Dherg clustered just inside the ring of light. Raithe looked at Malcolm and indicated the visitors, to which Malcolm merely shrugged. The conversation around the fire quieted when Nyphron and Arion sat. Persephone remained standing. She clasped her hands and took a deep breath.

"This has been a dark and grievous day," she said. "A sad and bewildering one that saw the loss of many beloved friends and family." Her eyes strayed toward Brin, who sat between Moya and Roan, her cheeks still streaked. "Tonight we say goodbye, tonight we grieve, tonight we remember the past." She paused and looked up at the stars overhead. "But tomorrow will bring a new day, and the question before us is: What shall we do with it?"

"Why did this happen?" Hanson Killian asked. The woodworker sat cross-legged next to his wife, who clutched their remaining three children. Earlier that day, Raithe had been in the burial pit when Farmer Wedon handed down the other four Killians.

Raithe didn't think Hanson expected an answer. The question was at the forefront of everyone's minds, but the same question arrived with every tragedy. *Why my son? Why today of all days? Why us again?* The clans suffered loss with such regularity that the questions often felt as pointless as prayers. At least that was the case in Dureya, and there was never an answer, at least not one mortals could understand.

"Because the Fhrey seek to kill us," Persephone said.

Some of the gathered were drinking, some shifting their seats because smoke was blowing toward them, most were just staring out into the dark or into the flames with the same vacant expressions they'd worn all evening. But at that moment, everyone focused on their new chieftain. For a full minute, the only sound was the crackle of the fire.

No one had explained the full details of what had happened when Arion and Gryndal waged a battle of magic outside the lodge, the day Raithe killed his second Fhrey. All the residents of the dahl had witnessed the fight, but the verbal exchanges had been in the Fhrey language. Only Persephone, Suri, and Malcolm understood it well, and none of them, nor any of the Fhrey, had volunteered explanations. Raithe knew more than most. He wasn't fluent, but his father had taught him enough to understand part of what had been said, and it was clear that Gryndal's death wouldn't be the end of the conflict.

"The rumors we heard during Chieftain Konniger's first clan meeting are true," Persephone said. "The Fhrey have destroyed the dahls of Dureya and Nadak and have added Dahl Rhen to the tally. But we now know the Fhrey aren't gods, and their actions weren't revenge for the death of Shegon, the first Fhrey killed by Raithe. The fane, leader of the Fhrey, has had plans to rid the world of us for years. They fear us because of our growing numbers and because we are a people capable of challenging them, able to defeat them."

Again, Persephone paused to look around at their faces, to give those gathered the chance to comment. No one did. The fire crackled, a burst of sparks floated skyward, and Persephone went on. "Some of you already know, or have guessed, that Nyphron and his Galantians are hiding here because they refused orders to slaughter us. Likewise, Arion risked her life defending this dahl against Fane Lothian's sorcerer. You saw what happened for yourselves. Now the Fhrey ruler has sent giants and storms. But we're still alive. We endure. I'm sure this most recent attack will not be the end of his aggression. Yes, they will be back, and next time they'll likely send an army."

Raithe watched fear creep back into the faces of those who thought they had faced the worst life could muster, and the combination was a current dragging everyone toward hopelessness.

"But," Persephone began again, this time with a louder voice, "we aren't helpless. We who were never a threat before will become what they fear the most. When news of the other dahls' destructions first reached us, I stood in the lodge and told everyone of a plan to save ourselves. No one listened to me then, but you must listen to me now." She took a step forward so that the fire's light shimmered on her face. "I've already sent runners to Menahan, Melen, Tirre, Warric, and the Gula clans, asking their chieftains to convene a summit at Tirre. We will unite all our leaders, form a war council, and appoint a single keenig to lead us."

"But how can we fight against giants and storms?" Cobb asked.

Nyphron stood up. "I will teach you. Many of you saw our battle with the giants. Twelve against seven, but we won without a single wound."

"But that's because you're Fhrey," Filson the Lamp said.

"And was it a Fhrey who killed Gryndal?" Nyphron pointed at Raithe. "He's already killed two of my kind, and he isn't particularly special. He has, however, been trained. My father taught his father how to fight, and he passed those skills on to his son. I can do the same with you. The only differences between Fhrey and Rhunes are training, tools, and experience. I can give you all of these. My Galantians are the best warriors in the world, and they will teach you all they know."

"But even you were powerless when Gryndal came," Engleton said. "What chance have we against magic?"

Nyphron pointed to Raithe. "Have you seen the markings on the shield Raithe carries? Did you see what happened when the fane's sorcerer turned his magic against the Dureyan? The answer is *nothing*. Nothing at all. Raithe was unharmed, protected by markings discovered ages ago by the Dherg people. We will use these markings to negate the power of those who would wield the Art against us. You have superior numbers. You have the protection of the Dherg runes. And you will be trained by the most capable warriors Elan has ever known. If I thought you wouldn't be victorious, I wouldn't be here. I and my Galantians would have left long ago."

Nyphron pointed to Persephone. "Your chieftain is wise. The fane will not stop until your kind is exterminated. This war is winnable, if you're willing to fight." He took his seat once more, and all eyes went back to Persephone.

"In the morning we will begin preparations to leave our home and travel to Tirre. There's nothing left for us here, and the farther we can get from Alon Rhist the safer we will be," Persephone told them all. "Within the week Clan Rhen marches south."

CHAPTER FOUR

Rapnagar

As far as I know, Suri was the first of our kind to use the Art. It must have been wonderful to do magic, except when it was not.

—THE BOOK OF BRIN

Bodies were broken in half, collapsed on one another or lying side by side. Hundreds were dead, maybe thousands. Many were strangers; some mere acquaintances; others friends, but a few Suri considered family. The horror was almost too much to bear as she moved through the forest of fallen trees ravaged by the storm. She'd seen storms before, windstorms, ice storms, floods, and fires, but those had always been the will of Wogan— this wasn't.

And then there was Magda.

Suri and Minna led the way through the decimated forest; they traveled quickly, but Arion managed to keep up, so her headache must have improved. She moved with a nimble, youthful grace that contradicted Arion's past comments about being old. She seemed anything but elderly. Even without hair, and perhaps because of its absence, Suri thought Arion was the most beautiful person she'd ever seen—on par with the big swans from the high lake or the snowy owl that used to winter near the mountain's western face. Arion had that same smooth elegance and otherworldly serenity. And her skin was perfect: no pimples, blotches, wrinkles, or marks. Most of the time, she didn't seem real at all.

Also with them was Nyphron, the leader of the Galantians. He wasn't nearly so beautiful, but he was silent. Not that he didn't talk—though none of them said much as they hiked the ridge—it was more that he made no noise at all. Dressed in layers of metal and adorned with sword and shield, he trotted up the forest slope with a ghostly quiet. Suri prided herself on moving noiselessly through the wood, and Minna was no slouch herself, but Suri had to stop occasionally to make sure Nyphron was still there. He always was, and closer than she expected.

Nearing the top of the rise, Suri found herself looking upon that holy glade where all other trees refrained from growing out of deference to the Grand Lady of the Wood. She stopped at the sight of Magda. The ancient tree, sheared in half, was naked, her leaves gone. One side of her trunk was blackened; on the other, bark-stripped wood splintered from the trunk. On the ground lay a severed limb. Suri stood staring, unable to move. Minna brushed her side and nuzzled her hand, but Suri couldn't take her eyes off the horror that had been the oldest tree of the forest.

The wind blew, then blew again.

Silence.

A tear slipped down Suri's cheek, and then another. Minna once more prodded her, whimpering slightly as she nudged. The wisest of all wolves knew it was best not to dwell on such horror. The two moved on, following Arion and Nyphron, who hadn't bothered to stop and pay their respects.

"Who's there?" The voice came from down the slope and through the thicket, where an enormous head poked out of the ground. Shifting into the Fhrey language, he added, *"Come to finish me, have you?"* The giant, still sealed in dirt, must have smelled them; he was facing away from their approach and unable to turn his head fully. Suri wasn't an expert on giants and their ability to detect scents, but the four of them had made no more noise moving through the woods than a gentle summer breeze.

Nyphron took the lead then and marched down the length of the devastated hillside and right up to the colossal nose.

"Rapnagar, what a surprise . . . and by surprise I mean it's not, and by Rapnagar I mean you son of the Tetlin whore."

Arion followed the Fhrey warrior. *"You know this Grenmorian?"*

Nyphron nodded and put a booted foot on the bridge of the giant's nose, leaning in toward his left eye. *"Shouldn't have left Hentlyn."*

"No food in our mountains."

Nyphron frowned and put more weight on the giant's nose. *"Yeah, right. So, who sent you?"*

"Go fill a pig," Rapnagar growled back.

Nyphron drew his sword and pierced the giant's left nostril, pinning it to the ground. The Grenmorian cried out.

Arion took a surprised step backward. *"What are you doing?"*

"I came here for answers." Nyphron spoke just as much to the giant as to Arion.

"You won't get any from me," Rapnagar said through gritted teeth. *"But why don't you enlighten me? I'm sorry I wasn't there to see my brothers' destruction. How many did we kill? Was Grygor among them? How is it that you survived? Were you hiding like a coward?"*

"Your brothers died before they even reached the dahl's gate. They trampled some flowers and frightened a goat, but that's all."

"Liar!"

Nyphron twisted his sword and the giant cried out again.

"Stop doing that!" Arion shouted, stepping forward. *"Listen,"* she said, addressing the giant, *"your attack did fail. That should be obvious by the fact that we are standing before you. When I told Nyphron of your predicament, he insisted on an audience. The only thing you have to bargain with is knowledge. I think it's in your best interest to cooperate."*

Rapnagar didn't answer right away. His big eyes blinked twice and his lips shifted once to the left and then to the right. At last he asked, *"What's in it for me?"*

"How about an easy death and proper burial?" Nyphron asked. *"I'll slit*

your throat from ear to ear. Be real quick about it, and then the Miralyith will bury you so the animals won't feed on your body . . . only the worms."

"Not good enough. I'll talk, but in return you have to let me go."

Nyphron was shaking his head even before Rapnagar finished. *"We don't need to know that badly. I can already guess most of it. The storm was a pretty big clue."*

"I can tell you their next move."

"No, you can't. They thought this attack would succeed. Any plans already in existence have changed."

"I can tell you who we were after. Who specifically."

Nyphron paused and took a moment to think. *"Was I singled out?"*

"I'd nod but I have a sword in my nose."

With a quick jerk Nyphron pulled his weapon free, causing the giant to grunt, his eyes to wince. *"Who else? Did they mention any other names?"*

The giant shook his head. *"No, no. I won't say anything else until you promise to let me go."*

"Okay, you tell us what you know and you can go free," Nyphron said.

Rapnagar shifted his eyes and focused on Arion. *"She agree?"*

"Yes," Arion replied.

"Okay. Okay. Arion of the Miralyith, Nyphron of the Instarya, and all the Rhunes in the wooden fort, especially the one called Raithe, the one known as the God Killer."

Arion furrowed her brow, thinking. *"And no one else?"*

Nyphron looked at her curiously. *"Who were you expecting?"*

"Her." Arion pointed toward the mystic, who lingered partway up the slope. *"Mawyndulë didn't tell his father about Suri. I wonder why. If Lothian has decided to slaughter the Rhunes, it's only because he considers them nothing more than animals. Knowing they can wield the Art could change that perception. Discovering our similarities would make it impossible to annihilate a whole race. It would end the conflict, save lives on both sides. Suri proves Rhunes and Fhrey are more similar than anyone previously knew."*

Nyphron shook his head. *"No, you have it wrong. Rhunes with the Art would be seen as an even greater threat. The last thing people in power want is to share. Lothian won't welcome them as equals. It'd harden his resolve against them."*

"I don't agree, and I know Lothian better than you."

"Well, you have your opinion and I have mine. Guess we'll never know for sure, especially now that the fane knows about your part in Gryndal's death."

"He doesn't know the circumstances. He's only heard one side of the story."

"Oh, so you think he'll believe you over his own son? And exactly how are you going to get an audience with him? You have as much chance getting into the Talwara as I do. Welcome to—"

"Hey," Rapnagar interrupted. *"Haven't you forgotten something? Let me out."*

"Seriously?" Nyphron smirked. *"You think your life is worth three names? You'll have to do better than that."*

"What else do you want to know?"

"Well, you can start with who hired you."

"His name was Vertumus, but he spoke on behalf of a fella named Petragar."

"Vertumus went to Hentlyn?"

"Came right to the Yarhold. Actually knocked on the door. He was very cute."

"He didn't go alone."

"No. Sikar was babysitting."

"Did Sikar look pleased with his orders?"

"Sikar looked as if he hoped we would step on Vertumus. Only reason we didn't was because Furgenrok thought it was a trap."

"Strange," Nyphron said.

"Yeah, that's why we let them leave. Figured it was a trick."

"No." Nyphron leaned over to clean his blade on Rapnagar's hair. *"I meant it's strange that Furgenrok is capable of thinking."*

Arion took another step forward, coming so close that she could touch the giant's ear if she wanted. *"What did this Vertumus say? What did he ask of you exactly?"*

"Said there were herds of Rhunes in the south for us to eat if we killed Arion, Nyphron, and Raithe. He also said Petragar was the new lord of the Rhist now

that Zephyron was dead and his son Nyphron had turned traitor. We were also told that the Instarya wouldn't enforce the ban anymore, and we'd be allowed to feast on any Rhunes we came across."

"Were any Miralyith with you?" Arion asked.

"Nope. Not even Vertumus showed up for the fight. But they said we'd have help. They were sending a storm to soften things up and show us where to go. The lightning would indicate where you were. Most hit the Rhune fort, but I noticed the bolts up here and came to check."

"From how far away can a Miralyith create a storm?" Nyphron asked Arion.

"Depends. If they used the Valentryne Layartren . . ."

"The what now?"

"It's a room in Avempartha, the tower that sits on top of a waterfall just west of—"

"I've seen it."

"Ah, well, the tower gathers the power of rushing water and channels it to a chamber. It significantly improves the ability of anyone utilizing it. The tower is excellent for finding things. Working together, teaming up, I suspect a group of Miralyith could attack us all the way up here. Lothian would just need to issue waivers from the Law of Ferrol."

"Oh, I'm sure he's done that." Nyphron frowned as he rubbed his chin, a hard look in his eyes. *"My guess is he's granted universal immunity to everyone. Probably placed a bounty on our heads as well."*

Arion looked concerned. She stared at the ground near her feet, wet her lips, and then said in an ominous tone, *"They can kill us, but we can't kill them."*

Nyphron smiled at that. *"Well, not exactly. We just can't use our own hands. So long as it isn't our arms that swing the sword, Ferrol will look the other way."*

"When did you become an Umalyn priest?"

"It's true, isn't it? If I convince you to kill another Fhrey, the Law of Ferrol descends on you, not me. The act, not the instigator, is punished."

"Strikes me as manipulative and self-serving, even cowardly."

He shrugged. *"I didn't make the rules. Ferrol did. Personally, I prefer to see it as allies coming together in a common cause against a common enemy. Sounds so much better that way, don't you think?"*

Arion sighed.

"Now, if you don't have any other questions, I'll be putting Mr. Rapnagar out of the misery he's called his life."

"What?" Arion gasped. *"No!"*

"No, what?" Nyphron asked. *"No, you don't have anything else to ask?"*

"No, she doesn't want you to kill me," Rapnagar shouted.

"Stay out of this," Nyphron snapped. *"This has nothing to do with you."*

"This has everything *to do with me. You said if I talked, you'd let me live. And I did. You need to hold up your side of the bargain."*

"The giant is right," Arion said. *"You aren't going to kill him. You made the deal. Now honor your word."*

"See, that's the difference between you and me. While I tend to be pragmatic, you let idealism cloud your judgment. I can't kill you . . . well, I could, but not without severe repercussions for breaking Ferrol's Law . . . but I most certainly can kill Rapnagar. And believe me, he deserves it."

"I don't, and you made a vow!" the giant shouted.

"He's right, you did," Arion said.

Nyphron rolled his eyes. *"No, I didn't. I only promised. A vow is different. I promised my father I'd accept Lothian as my fane if he failed in the challenge; I also promised Tekchin he could have the last chunk of bread last night, and I promised myself I wouldn't drink to excess anymore. I'm lousy at keeping promises."*

"Well . . . well . . . then I vowed on your behalf," Arion said.

Nyphron shook his head. *"No, you didn't."*

"Someone did!" Rapnagar yelled.

"There wasn't any vow," Nyphron said. *"Neither one of us swore to anything. We just engaged in a weak agreement, which I am willing to break."*

"I'm not," Arion declared.

"Fine." Nyphron pointed. *"You stand over there. Look away if you like."*

"Absolutely not! I assured this Grenmorian he would be set free, and he will. Now put your sword away before I melt that little toy."

Nyphron hesitated. Arion's hands came up.

"Okay." He dropped the sword back into its scabbard. *"But you're making a mistake. Rapnagar, well all of the Grenmorians really, is monstrous. Grygor being the one exception. If the situation were reversed, Rapnagar would be burping you up right now."*

"Suri." Arion waved the mystic over. *"Remember how I discussed teaching you? Well, today you're going to begin your first practical lesson in the Art. You're going to free this giant."*

Suri had never done anything more than start fires and cast bones, and freeing the giant was as unlikely as restoring the trees or bringing Magda back to life. If such things were possible, she certainly wouldn't put any energy into helping Rapnagar.

As a rule, Suri didn't dislike anyone, but she would make an exception for him. He had destroyed the rol—one of her favorites—and was, by his own admission, in league with those who'd murdered Magda and Suri's other friends, like the beautiful young maple. Suri had only recently become acquainted with the sapling who was now lying in a pile of debris, snapped in half three feet up from her roots. Suri had been surprised Wogan hadn't killed the giant during the night. She imagined rodents gnawing out the giant's eyes and burrowing into his head. While Suri wasn't overly fond of Nyphron, she sided with him about how to deal with the giant.

"This might take a little while," Arion told the Instarya. *"I don't want to rush her. So you can go back if you like."*

"I wouldn't dream of leaving," he said, moving to sit on the body of a freshly fallen birch. Suri didn't know the birch, but he looked like he'd been nice. *"I'd love to see how one teaches magic, this Art of yours."*

Arion shrugged. *"Suri, we in the Miralyith call the ability to use the power of the world the Art, because it's such a creative process. While there are basic foundations, principles, and techniques, just as you would find in any artistic endeavor, these are only guides. They are mostly designed to assist students to grasp ideas, to get them started. But I think you'll find there are no genuine rules except those you set for yourself. Some of these will be choices you make; others will be made for you, simply because of who you are."*

Suri assumed Arion was speaking to her, and she heard all the words clearly but still struggled with their meaning. Over the last month, the bald Fhrey Miralyith had improved Suri's understanding of the Fhrey language, but she still had to guess at a few of the words, and Arion was talking fast.

"*Thing is,*" Arion went on, "*everyone is capable of using the Art, in the same way that everyone can draw, but not all drawing is considered art. In this same way, people use the power of nature all the time. Speech, for example, is a form of mundane magic. A base branch of summoning, in fact. The natural powers of sound, pitch, and tone can 'magically' transfer ideas from one person to another. Smiling and causing another to smile back is another form of the same idea. Do you understand?*"

Suri shook her head.

"*Creating fire—the way you already know how to do—is yet another form of basic magic. Nyphron can also create a fire. To do so he'll harness the power of friction to summon heat. A more advanced wielder of nature's powers might use metal and stone to generate sparks, an easier and faster method. And to the person who uses friction, it can be seen as magical, but* magic *is merely another word for 'I don't know how you did that.' You, of course, know an even better way to start a fire.*"

Suri smiled, having understood this last part. She had seen Tura start fires using both methods, but the old mystic never started one the way Suri did.

"*Your method, Suri, is even more elegant, easier, and faster. And to you that's all it is, another way of making a fire. But to Nyphron, with his lack of understanding, it's magic.*" She turned to the Galantian. "*I apologize for using you as an example, but you chose to stay.*"

"*Not a problem,*" he replied. "*I enjoy seeing how you instill a sense of superiority in your student along with the lesson. I can see how it happens.*"

"*How what happens?*"

"*How you've come to see yourselves as gods.*"

Arion paused, and a shadow of self-doubt crossed her face.

"*I'll do the same thing when I teach the Rhunes to fight. Confidence is important, particularly in a war.*"

Arion hesitated a moment longer, then turned back to Suri. "*So where *was I? Oh, yes, there's a divide between those who trace or copy a picture that someone else drew and people who can create a drawing out of their own imagination. The people who have a natural talent, something they are born with or develop at a young age, are Artists. But there are others who can only use magic by relying on physical constructs such as wood, water, minerals, and metal. Those who must rely on the crutches of physical items are known as faquins or stylists. You, Suri, are a true Artist."*

Suri smiled again, certain that was a compliment. She liked Arion. The Miralyith wasn't just beautiful; she was fascinating, too. The Fhrey was like an elegant version of Tura, kindly, understanding, and wise. They both dripped with knowledge like an overloaded sponge. No one could be around either and not learn something.

"You improve as an Artist by understanding the basics of how elements interact and how to affect them," Arion explained. *"This is similar to learning to communicate. You learn to speak by discovering which sounds mean what. A lot of magic is based on sound. Sound and motion can create weavings and bindings like knots, similar to the string game you play. They fasten aspects of natural power into patterns that can be used by the Artist. Knowing the language of the world and how to speak in usable patterns allows an Artist to effect change.*

"Everything in the world is connected to everything else. Understanding the paths allows you to make new connections. To do this, an Artist needs to be in contact with a source of power. In terms of the string game, this would be your fingers. In the real world, power comes from life, heat, and movement. So you can use sunlight, fire, the flow of water, or life itself. Seeds are a good source; the potential they hold is extremely powerful and you can carry many with you, which makes them convenient as well. Of course, here in this forest, you have an abundance of power to tap. Now, there are several categories of source power. Elemental, which is most common and is the manipulation of elements: Rubbing wood makes fire, adding heat to water makes steam. There are subcategories of this such as weather art, water, fire, and such. There's also Life and Vision art, but there's no sense going into those yet. Today we're going to begin with dirt."

"Dirt?" Suri asked.

"Yes, dirt. It may seem inert, but like seeds, it holds the power of life. The soil has provided strength and nourishment to these massive trees, and it will provide the power to free Rapnagar. Now, you should already know how to tap. You do it every time you start a fire. It's that sensation, the drawing in of elemental strength that is akin to taking a deep breath, the summoning you do just before you clap. I want you to do that now. Close your eyes. That'll make it easier to concentrate. Listen to the wind; feel the ground beneath your feet. Reach out with your senses and explore. Try to feel the dirt around Rapnagar. Imagine the ground being an extension of yourself. It is. Everything in the world is part of everything else. We are all related in that we affect one another. You just need to pull on the right thread and manipulate the string pattern so that the dirt moves away from Rapnagar."

Suri tried to do what Arion asked, but she didn't have much to go on. Her eyes were closed, and she was imagining the dirt—seeing worms wiggling around. That was pretty easy. She also felt her feet on the soil but wasn't sure how that helped.

As if understanding her difficulty, Arion said, *"Try humming."*

"Humming?"

"Yes."

"What should I hum?"

"Nothing. Don't hum a tune, just a single, even tone. Just make a steady sound."

Suri did.

"Feel the vibration? Now change tone and feel the difference. This will help you center yourself. It's a good base point. It'll help focus your mind on what you're looking for. Now reach out and search for a similar tone outside of you, the same way you do when summoning fire."

Suri did feel the vibration in her throat, chest, and head as she hummed. It almost tickled when she changed notes. She thought of how she found fire. Suri always thought she called to the fire spirit, but maybe she summoned it, sucked it in like a breath. As she hummed, Suri sensed another vibration outside herself. The vibration was familiar—fire.

Suri grinned broadly with this discovery. How exciting it was to learn more about something she'd done for years, like the time she found out it was impossible to swallow without touching the roof of her mouth with her tongue.

At the same moment, she became aware of other tones, other vibrations.

Sound and motion can create weavings and bindings like knots, similar to the string game you play.

Suri realized it then: The vibrations were like strings she could pull and twist. Without thinking, she raised her hands, moving her fingers just as she would when playing the string game. The movement was familiar and helped her balance, helped her focus.

"That's it," she heard Arion say. *"Work it out just like the game. Form a pattern to draw the ground apart."*

Suri struggled. She didn't know which strings did what, and the more she concentrated the more strings she found. She became overwhelmed. This was a game with an infinite number of strands.

"There's too many. I don't know which—"

"You're standing on it," Arion replied.

Suri grinned again. This time a bit more stupidly because the answer was so obvious.

She found the chord, big and deep, heavier than most of the others. This was less a string and more a rope. Without thinking, she dropped her humming to a lower tone and let her fingers play out before her. She heard a sound through her ears, a faint rustling as she bent the chord slightly.

"That's it," Arion said. *"You've got it. Just hook and draw apart."*

Suri slipped her fingers underneath, as she would have if she were playing the game, and pulled her hands apart. As she did, just as in the game, the chord slid around her fingers and tightened.

"Suri, no!" Arion shouted. *"Stop! Stop!"*

Stopping wasn't easy. Just as with the game, after looping a finger she had a natural desire to pull the strings out to their full extent. Suri craved to feel the pattern complete, to feel the loops tug near her knuckles, and it was all happening so fast.

The rustling became cracking as if trees were being broken.

"Suri!"

Arion grabbed her hands, and Suri opened her eyes.

The expression on Arion's face was one of horror, and Suri turned her head to search for signs of what had caused it. Suri was terrified that she may have inadvertently harmed more trees, but they looked exactly as they had before. This left her puzzled as she had heard the cracking of trunks.

"What's wrong?" Suri asked.

Arion said nothing and just closed her eyes while putting a quivering hand to her mouth.

Suri looked over at Nyphron who remained sitting on the fallen birch, a smile on his lips. *"Nothing at all,"* he told her. *"You did wonderfully."*

Only then did Suri notice Rapnagar.

The giant's head had slipped farther, only the crown exposed above the surface, and it was crushed like an egg. Suri hadn't opened the ground. She had closed it.

CHAPTER FIVE

Small Solutions

Roan was, without overstatement, the most intelligent person I have ever met. To our great misfortune, we did not realize this fact for far too long; to our great luck, we discovered it in the nick of time.

— THE BOOK OF BRIN

Persephone had grossly underestimated the time it would take to get her people moving. Even if Dahl Rhen hadn't been destroyed, it would have taken weeks to evacuate. The people just didn't know how to move a village of that size. Hundreds of years had passed since Clan Rhen was migratory, and the techniques of their nomadic ancestors were lost. She considered asking Brin to provide some insight. As the Keeper of Ways, Brin was the repository of their people's history, but the girl was in no condition to think. Even if Persephone had been able to quiz her, the forebears had lived in a world much different from the current one. Their existence had been lean. They wouldn't have been able to imagine the wealth amassed by future generations, and therefore they couldn't help make decisions about what to bring and the things to leave behind.

Adding to the task was the overwhelming grief. Most days Persephone spent time prodding people who'd become stagnant while sifting through debris. Just this morning, she had come across Eli the Miller as he struggled to pull a shoulder basket out of the remains of his home. When he spotted his daughter's hair-tie in the wreckage, he stooped, picked it up, and then crumpled to the ground. Persephone gave him the next hour to cry, but then had to assign him a task or he would have been there all day.

"How's it going?" Moya asked, trotting over and catching Persephone near the well.

"Slow . . . real slow." She stopped and fixed the young woman with a harsh look. "Are *you* packed?"

Moya's face assumed one of her indignant expressions, consisting mostly of sour lips. "Let's see . . ." She glanced down at herself. "I'm wearing my dress and have both my arms and legs, so yes, I'm packed."

"Good, then you can help carry food. Do you think you and someone else could carry one of the pots of wheat?"

"Oh, sure. No problem. While we're at it, would you like me to carry the miller's stone too? Seph, that pot must weigh three hundred pounds."

She was right, of course, and Persephone nodded, adding another task to her already long list. "We'll need bags, and lots of them. We'll divide each urn among ten or fifteen people." She sighed. "Even if every man, woman, and child carried a thirty-pound bag of wheat or barley, we still wouldn't be able to take half of what's in the storage pit, and it's nearly empty. And what about the elderly? I can't ask someone like Padera to haul a heavy load."

"I wouldn't worry about her. She's tougher than all of us. That old woman will likely carry a goat under each arm."

"We need to find a way to bring it all. What if Tirre refuses us? If they keep their doors barred, we'll have to camp outside for who knows how long, surviving on only what we bring. They don't have a forest to hunt in. And what happens in autumn when there's no harvest for the coming winter?" Persephone turned, caught sight of the well, and sighed again. "And then there's water. I know where there are a few small streams on the way, but in the middle of summer, they might be dry. We'll need *a lot* of water."

Moya nodded and pointed in the direction of Dahl Rhen's patron god. "And what about Mari? She's none too light."

"Oh, for the love of Elan, I almost forgot." Persephone looked over at the stone statue. "I don't think abandoning our god is a wise idea right now."

"Exactly." Moya nodded toward the Galantians, who were clustered around more than a dozen jugs of Bergin's beer. More than half of the containers were empty, lying on their sides. They hadn't stopped celebrating their victory since the battle with the giants. "Maybe Grygor could carry her."

The two walked over to the group.

"And then Sebek, he runs right for the biggest one," Vorath was saying. The stocky Fhrey with the fledgling beard stood before the others, gesturing broadly with a cup that sloshed over the brim.

"Just trying to get ahead of my javelins," Eres said.

"We could use some help packing up," Persephone told them, and folded her arms in what she hoped was a commanding manner. She looked around their circle for Nyphron but failed to spot him, which did nothing for her confidence.

They all looked at Persephone for a moment. Then Sebek, with as charming a smile as she'd ever seen, said, "We are helping. We're working hard to lighten the weight of beer that needs transporting."

They all laughed.

Persephone waited for it to calm, then asked, "Where is Nyphron?"

"Went off with the Miralyith and that mystic this morning."

"Great," she muttered.

"Why don't you join us?"

"Sorry, I have a village to save."

"Moya," Tekchin said, "you can stay, can't you? I saved you a place on my lap."

"There's always plenty of room there, because there's precious little else to get in the way," the young woman replied.

Tekchin's eyebrows shot up, and Sebek laughed so hard he fell off the broken log he'd been sitting on.

Moya opened her mouth once more, but Persephone latched on to her wrist and dragged her away.

"Why do you always do that?" she asked. "Why do you antagonize them?"

"They're warriors, Seph." Moya pulled her arm back. "You think kissing their ass is the way to impress them?"

Persephone was still pondering the question when she spotted Raithe and Malcolm trudging up the recently cleared eastern walkway.

"There you are," Raithe said. "Hard to find anyone anymore." Both men were slick with sweat. Raithe had bundled his shirt into a bag made from his leigh mor and hung it from his belt.

"We saved twenty-three sheep," Malcolm said. "Found most of them nicely clustered in a little valley a few miles to the northeast. They were a pleasant lot, but a handful led us on a merry chase. Habet and Cobb are watching them."

"That's wonderful," Persephone said, and she meant it, though her tone was less than happy. The efforts to round up the scattered flock served to remind her that Gelston, the shepherd, was barely alive, and Delwin was dead. Then she couldn't resist thinking about Sarah, Brin's mother and Persephone's best friend. She bit her lip, sucked in a quick breath, and walked on, struggling to beat down the emotion.

We still have so much to do.

Persephone's feet led her to the area cleared for packing. Bundles of the spring's wool harvest were piled, waiting to be carded, spun, and woven into cloth. If Sarah were there . . . Persephone squeezed her quivering mouth closed. As she fought back tears, she saw the three Dherg sitting on the far side of the wool piles, lounging in the bundles as if they were giant pillows. Emotion boiled up. Tears or rage were her choices, and Persephone didn't have the luxury of appearing weak.

"What are you still doing here?" she shouted at them.

They jumped, but for a moment none of them said a word.

"We . . . ah . . . would like to talk to the one you call Arion, the bald Fhrey. You see we have a problem that—"

"Arion isn't here right now, and if she were, she wouldn't have time to be bothered. Neither do I. Can't you see how busy we are?"

Frost started to say something but Persephone became distracted by what she saw over his shoulder.

"Roan?" she yelled. "What in Mari's name are *you* doing?"

Roan's old roundhouse—the one originally built by Iver the woodcarver—had been reduced to little more than a lean-to by the foot of a giant. One pole remained upright and held a single crossbeam in place, but that was enough to grant her cave-like access to most of the tools and supplies. She and Gifford worked out front. He was hammering on what appeared to be a giant wooden box.

Both Roan and Gifford paused in their fevered labor to look at her, each with a guilty expression.

"Roan," Persephone said, walking past the wool and the Dherg to confront the two. "I thought I made myself clear. You of all people need to get your things together." She looked at the chisels, mallets, and ax spread out on the ground. "We need to hurry. You know that! Why are you still—"

"Woan got an idea when she was helping me pack my spinning table," Gifford said.

"Roan always gets ideas!" Persephone nearly screamed in frustration. "We have no time for her *ideas*. We need to pack up and get out of here. I have no clue when the next attack is coming, but if we're still here when it arrives, we're all going to die. Do you understand *that* idea? We have no gate anymore, Roan. No protection, and the Fhrey are getting drunk!"

Clutching Gifford's large, round pottery table to her chest, Roan retreated toward the devastation of her home.

Gifford shoved himself as upright as possible and hobbled toward Persephone. "This idea is impowtant," he said as firmly as his lisp allowed. Leaning heavily on his crutch, his twisted back and dead leg made him a tragically comic figure, but Persephone saw fire in his eyes, a familiar sight.

We'll do it together, Aria had said on a day long ago when Persephone's shortcoming had ended their friendship. She saw the intensity of her childhood friend's stare again, this time through the eyes of Aria's son. That stopped Persephone, and she looked past Gifford to Roan, whose lower lip was trembling.

I didn't mean to upset her. I didn't mean to yell. I was just so . . . Persephone felt tears bubbling up again. "Okay, I'm sorry. Tell me. What is this
great idea?"

Roan stared at her a moment, then said, "No, I'm the one who should
apologize. I didn't . . . I didn't think it would take so long. We'll stop, and
I'll get packed." Roan set down the pottery table and began picking up her
tools, tears streaming down her cheeks.

"Tell me the idea, Roan," Persephone said, softer still.

Roan straightened up and wiped her face. She looked at Gifford, who
nodded his support. Walking over to where he'd been hammering, she
retrieved a long pole.

She wiped her cheeks again. "Gifford was sad because his pottery table
is too heavy to move. Well, it's round, so I thought maybe we could roll it.
You know how we move rocks, right?" Roan asked.

Persephone shrugged.

"Well, we put them on a sled with logs underneath and then push.
When a log comes out from underneath, we pick it up and put it in front of
the others and keep pushing. It's a lot of work moving those heavy logs,
and it's hard pushing the sled over them, but look . . ."

Placing the pole into the hole at the center of the table, she tilted the
large round stone up on its side. She swung the pole, and the pottery table
moved easily along an arc. "Now imagine another pottery table, just like
this one, on the other end of the pole. Then, if that big box"—she pointed
at the wood Gifford had been hammering when Persephone first came
over—"was sitting on top of the pole, we could put stuff in it."

"So what are you saying? Could we put pots of wheat and barley in the
box and move heavy things?"

Roan nodded. "It reduces rubbing. Instead of the entire surface of a sled
grinding against a set of logs, all the weight is on just two small points."
Roan indicated where the pole passed through the disk. "I'll put pins on
the ends to keep them on." Then her face saddened. "But it'll take time to
make the other side. It took nearly a week to chisel Gifford's first table. But
if I work real hard . . . I don't sleep much, you know . . . and I could work
on it night and day, then—"

"She's made a wheel," Frost said as the three Dherg strode over.

"She's put a pottery table on the end of a pole," Moya said.

Frost's bushy eyebrows knit together and he looked amused, as if she'd made a joke. "Don't you people know what a wheel is?"

Silence.

The three Dherg laughed.

"Wow. So she didn't make *a* wheel," Frost said and looked at Roan with newfound respect. "You made *the* wheel. The first one invented by your kind, I'm guessing. Very impressive in a sad and stunningly pathetic sort of way."

"Don't call Woan pathetic!" Gifford said, the fire once more in his eyes. "She's bwilliant."

Frost scowled. "Belgriclungreians have used the wheel for hundreds of years, mostly in mines. We put carts on them. That's like what the cripple is making. Our wheels are made of metal, as are the axles. That's what the pole part is called. We move thousands of pounds of rock with them."

"Thousands? How many Belgric . . . Belgriclung . . . oh, blessed Grand Mother! There must be an easier way of referring to your kind that isn't as insulting as Dher . . . well, that Fhrey word. How about Bels?"

Scowls all around. "We don't jingle."

Persephone had no idea what that meant.

"How about little men?" Roan asked.

Flood's brow rose. "We are not *men!* And our size is perfect. It's your kind that is freakishly tall."

"But you are little. How about *dwarfs?*" Persephone said. "You know, like dwarf rabbits or dwarf wheat. They are smaller but just as good. In the case of dwarf wheat, it's even better because we get higher yields with less acreage. Would that be okay?"

The two frowned but shrugged.

"Fine. So, how many *dwarfs* would it take to move a thousand pounds with your carts?"

"On level ground? One."

"One?"

"Well, it takes a bit of effort to get it rolling, but then not much at all. Of course we affix our wheels to the axles and grease the bearings."

"Grease the bearings?" Roan asked, looking at the little man with stern intensity.

"Yeah, at the places where the axles rub on the wheels."

Roan nodded, a smile forming.

"Without using metal," Persephone said, "doing what she's trying to do here, could this thing carry a lot of clay urns of wheat and barley? And what about jugs of water and beer?"

"Easily," Frost said. "But why not use barrels? They'd be much lighter."

"What's a barrel?" Persephone and Roan asked together.

Frost raised his hands in exasperation. "I'm starting to understand why the Fhrey refer to your kind as Rhunes. A barrel uses planks of wood bound with hoops of metal. Smaller than your pithos, but they weigh a fraction of all that clay."

"And that, what did you call it, *wheel*? Could you help Roan carve more of them so we could make several of these carts?"

"Well, we could . . . but it'd be faster to down one of those huge trees from the forest and just saw disks from its trunk."

"Saw?" Roan asked.

Frost rolled his eyes. "Dear Drome, are you really so backward? Yes, a saw is used to cut through wood. We could use one to make wooden wheels and staves for the barrel."

"And how long would that take?" Persephone asked.

"Well, not long if we could get our hands on some metal. Rain, do you think you could dig some up?"

He nodded. "The surface around these parts has been picked clean, but there is plenty below."

"I'll make you a deal," Persephone said. "You help Roan, and I'll ask Arion to talk with you. Agreed?"

"Agreed." Frost nodded.

"What do you say, Roan? Wanna work with the dwarfs and learn to make some new things?"

Tears were back in Roan's eyes. She nodded enthusiastically while Gifford beamed a smile in her direction.

In less than three days, the Dherg had helped Roan create six carts and more than a dozen barrels, which were truly remarkable. When first filled with liquid, they leaked, but then the wood swelled and the metal bands held the staves in place until not a single drop escaped. Not only was Persephone able to pack up every last grain in the storage pit, but she had six full barrels of water to ensure that the people of Dahl Rhen wouldn't go thirsty on the trip even if the streams along the way were bone-dry from the summer's heat.

The saw was an even greater miracle. With it, a dozen wheels had been created in just a few hours, simply by slicing through the trunk of a large tree they felled at the eaves of the forest. Watching two of the Dherg push and pull it back and forth was a comical sight. Especially since they argued constantly.

With the tasks completed, it was time for Persephone to honor her promise, and she offered to act as an intermediary. She'd already obtained Arion's consent to the meeting, and given how helpful the Dherg had been, she wanted it to go well. Besides, the Dherg were better at speaking Rhunic than Fhrey and she didn't want any mistakes in communication to cause a rift before their request was fully aired. She led the three over to a small lean-to that was acting as Arion's living quarters.

"Is now a good time?" Persephone asked in Fhrey.

"Good as any."

Persephone was impressed with the change in the Dherg's demeanor. Gone was the hostility and distrust, and they reverently bowed in greeting. *"As I mentioned, the dwarfs have been very helpful. Our travel to Tirre will be much easier. They have a problem and would like to speak to you."*

"Dwarfs?"

"Yes, that's what we're calling them now. Can I impose on you for their audience?"

"Yes, of course."

Persephone smiled, stepped back, and Frost came forward. "Flood and I are from Nye, that's a small town in the south of Belgreig. We met Rain in Neith."

Persephone translated for Arion, *"These three live in a city across the sea."* Then to Frost she said, "I've heard of Neith. That's directly across the Blue Sea from Dahl Tirre. It's near Caric, right?"

"Yes. Caric is a small port city, but Neith was the first home of the Belgriclungreians. It's largely abandoned now. Few people go into the mountain anymore. Mined out, they say. But Flood and I thought we could still find treasure there. So we put together a team and set off. That's how we met Rain." He gestured in the direction of the younger Dherg, and Rain bowed once more. "Rain is a digger—the finest there is. Flood and I are builders."

"Hah!" Flood erupted. "One of us is."

Frost ground his teeth and glared up through the bristles of his brows. "When are you going to get over that? It wasn't my fault that the scaffolding broke. And besides, you weren't even hurt."

"Then why do I have this limp?"

"You don't have a limp!"

Flood folded his arms. "No thanks to you, I can tell you that."

"You're an idiot." Frost shook his head and smiled apologetically in Arion's direction.

Before Frost could continue, Flood retorted, "Yeah, well, your mother slept with the entire village."

"We're brothers!" Frost replied.

Flood turned then. With a smirk on his lips and hands moving to his hips, he said, "That's your answer for everything, isn't it? *We're brothers. You don't have a limp. My name isn't Shirley. Fish don't fly.* You're always the one with the answers, aren't you?"

Frost lowered his voice and addressed Flood, "Now isn't really the time. Can you just keep your big mouth shut?"

Frost tugged his brother's beard and glared. Flood scowled back just as intently. For the first time, Persephone noticed that the two had similar eyes, the same nose, and most certainly the same exact scowl. She had no idea how she'd missed the family connection before.

Immersed in their altercation, the Dherg were oblivious to Arion's irritation, and Persephone cleared her throat to get their attention.

Frost looked sheepish, and he bowed respectfully toward Arion once more, then repeated the gesture to Persephone. "I apologize for the interruption, Your Majesty."

Persephone addressed Arion, *"They went into a mountain to find treasure."*

"Seriously? All that boiled down to they are treasure hunters?"

"Well . . ."

"Doesn't matter. What is it they want?"

"I think it would be best if you got to the point," Persephone said to Frost.

"Of course, of course," he said apologetically. "As I was saying, we were part of a team, exploring the depths of Neith . . . the unmapped areas . . . the old places. Eight of us including Rain. We were in a corridor when we heard it coming. That happens in the deep places. You hear things, feel them, too, and there's no place that goes deeper than Neith."

Fear crept into Frost's face. "It came from behind us. We were at the end of a corridor with no place to go. I'm not exaggerating when I say we feared for our lives. We would've died. Should've really. But Rain, well . . . he started digging. No one digs like he does. He gets going and it's like he's a mole. The giant ignored us and chased him; it follows sounds, you see. The rest of the party scattered. Easy to get lost down there. Of the remaining seven, only Flood and I got out. We never expected to see Rain again. And we didn't, not for a long time. Then one day he popped up. He'd spent months in the deep, in the dark, with hardly any supplies. No one knows how he survived. He don't talk about it, and we don't ask."

Persephone asked, "Is he also related to you two?"

"No, but we've sort of adopted him. Flood and I are alive because of Rain, so we owe him. First thing we did was get him out of Neith, out of Belgreig entirely. Away from all of it, because, well . . . it wasn't exactly

legal what we done . . . digging in the old mines. So we crossed the Blue
Sea and headed north. No idea about where to go, just traveling, running
really. But now we're here and after seeing what she did, well . . ." Again
he looked at Flood, then at Arion. "I think we might have discovered a
way to fix things so that we can go home, if you understand me."

Persephone shook her head. "Sorry, not a clue."

"Not surprising," Flood said. "Your people only recently discovered
the wheel. How bright can you be?"

Frost slapped Flood across the back of his head, making the gray-
bearded Dherg flinch. "Show some respect to the lady. She's the queen
of her people." Frost turned back to her. "Please forgive Flood, Your
Majesty. Our mother never cared for him, and this is what neglect
yields."

"So what is it you need?" Persephone asked. "To go home, that is?"

"Oh, see, it was huge, a giant about the size of the one Arion subdued a
few days ago. It's still down there, barring our people from their homeland. If Arion could come to Neith and get rid of it, then we wouldn't be
in so much trouble for digging around in places we shouldn't have been.
Gronbach would surely grant us pardons." Frost smiled hopefully.

Persephone said to Arion, *"They went to forbidden area and found a giant.
Now can't go home. If you could get rid of it, they might be forgiven."*

Arion shook her head, and Frost's face fell. *"I'm sorry. I appreciate their
situation, but I need to focus on stopping the war. Perhaps if I manage to do
that, then maybe I can do something for them, but right now I have more important problems."*

Persephone spoke to Frost, "I am sorry. You've been a great help to us
these last few days, but Arion is needed here. She's trying to stop a war
between the Rhune and Fhrey peoples. You are welcome to join us during
our trip to Tirre. There are many of your kind down south, and perhaps
you can find a group to take up with."

The three bowed formally once more. "We thank you both for your
time and for the invitation." Then they turned and walked away.

———

"You really messed that up," Flood told Frost when they were once more back among the piles of wool. "A giant? Seriously?"

"What? It's big, isn't it?" Frost replied.

"What are we going to do now?"

"I don't know. That elf is our best chance. Maybe if we convince her that Balgargarath is a greater threat than the war, she would help."

Flood shook his head. "In order to do that, you'd have to tell her the truth."

CHAPTER SIX

The Prince

The land of the Fhrey is called Erivan, a vast nation of great cities and numerous woodland villages set within the ancient forests of the east. The capital is Estramnadon, the seat of the fane and his son Mawyndulë.

— THE BOOK OF BRIN

Mawyndulë was certain he hated Vidar. The senior councilor was old and he smelled, a bit like sour milk. Thinking about it, Mawyndulë realized he hated most people, but made a distinction for those he truly despised. People like Vidar, Arion the Traitor, the God Killer, and Mawyndulë's own father fell into this especially loathed group. The rest of the world was filled with individuals he merely disliked. As Mawyndulë followed Vidar up the marble steps to the columned building where the Aquila met, he realized Gryndal had been the only person he honestly liked. Gryndal had been the greatest of the Fhrey and he had been killed by Mawyndulë's ex-tutor-turned-traitor, Arion. Although the God Killer had removed Gryndal's head from his body, it had been Arion's fault for helping the Rhune get so close.

As the new junior councilor, Mawyndulë was to assist Senior Councilor Vidar in representing the voice of the Miralyith tribe in the Aquila.

Mawyndulë's task was quite simple. He did nothing. Only the senior councilors could vote or speak in the Aquila, which relegated Mawyndulë's role to that of an observer. He was there to learn, which meant Vidar was another tutor—his third in less than two months.

"The Aquila was formed in the year 8901 as a formalization and public recognition of the group of Fhrey who had been assisting Gylindora Fane for more than a century." Vidar had stopped, turning back to lecture.

As he did, Mawyndulë noticed the gleam of sweat on Vidar's ample forehead. *He's pretending to teach me, but the dusty old relic is really out of breath from the climb.*

"Gylindora had always asked the leaders of each tribe their opinions on matters of governance. They worked as her general council, and their role, as she explained it, was to present problems, make suggestions, and assist in the overall administration of our people. At the time, the Fhrey nation was small, but she knew it would grow. One person couldn't hope to effectively run the whole thing."

He thinks he's being so clever, but if he's stopping to catch his breath, why does he talk so much?

Mawyndulë stood with one foot on the next step, wondering what would happen if he just went on ahead; the two wore identical purple-and-white asicas, which Mawyndulë believed was the only requirement to gain entrance to the main floor. Instead, he tapped his foot to show impatience. Vidar, being the oblivious lout that he was, didn't notice.

"The Aquila is still composed of six councilors and the fane, but he doesn't attend often. The councilors usually have assistants, like yourself."

Assistants? As Mawyndulë's father had explained it, the prince was to be the *junior councilor*. Since he was paired with Vidar, Mawyndulë saw his responsibilities more along the lines of making sure the older Fhrey didn't embarrass himself by drooling or forgetting his own name.

Forget you are the prince while you are with Vidar, his father had said. *Learn from him, from all of them. See firsthand how the Aquila works. This will be invaluable to you in the future when you are fane.*

Mawyndulë didn't know why he should listen, especially given that the fane was under no obligation to take advice from the Aquila. Gryndal wouldn't have cared what they thought. Mawyndulë wished he could have been made junior councilor when Gryndal represented the Miralyith in the Aquila, one of only a few First Ministers to share the dual roles. Serving with Gryndal, Mawyndulë would have certainly learned things, lots of things.

Vidar prattled on, "Imaly is the Curator of the Aquila and presides when the fane isn't present. She's very clever for a Nilyndd, and not to be trusted. In the event the Curator is unable to conduct the responsibilities of their office, the Conservator of the Horn appoints a new one."

Mawyndulë had lost interest, if he ever had any to begin with. Not his fault, he reasoned. The old Fhrey had a droning manner that could put a rushing river to sleep. The prince's gaze strayed, as did his thoughts. Since he'd never had any interest in the meetings of the Aquila, Mawyndulë had never bothered to climb the stairs to the Airenthenon, where the council met. Although the stairs were not above the forest canopy, they neverthe-less granted an impressive view of the capital. The city was nestled in the valley amid three hills: the one where the Airenthenon sat, the one where the palace stood, and the one with the Garden. At the foot of the hills, the Shinara River snaked its way among great trees, homes, and shops. In sev-eral places, it was crossed by bridges, the largest near Florella Plaza where artisans set up stands to hawk their wares.

From this vantage point, Mawyndulë saw the Garden as a small ring of rich green surrounding a great edifice of stone. *The most sacred place in the world* was how the Garden had always been described. Mawyndulë had never thought much of the Garden, or of the wall at its center that sup-ported a great dome. The wall had only one entrance, a permanently sealed door. From above, it didn't look so sacred. It looked small.

He soon grew bored with even the bird's-eye view and his attention was drawn to the nearby fountain built as a decoration on the marble steps. The excessively noble-looking statue of a stag stood within a gurgling pool of water, its head bent down as if to drink. With a flick of his wrist and a swirl of his fingers, Mawyndulë summoned up three balls of water the size of fists. He made them whirl in the air, chasing one another in a circle. *So much easier to do with the Art. The Traitor was a fool to force me to juggle by hand like a common Fhrey.*

"Stop that!" Vidar snapped.

Mawyndulë let the balls drop, splashing on the steps. A few drops sprayed the bottom of Vidar's asica, causing him to glare. "This isn't playtime, my prince. And it is forbidden to use the Art in the chambers, so restrain yourself."

Should have dropped the balls on his head.

"Now, back to what I was saying. The Aquila holds no direct power, since the fane's authority is absolute, ordained by Ferrol. However, this esteemed body has an important role in determining who shall be given the right to blow the Horn of Gylindora. They don't decide who will be fane. Ferrol does that. But they determine who gets the opportunity to challenge, and this makes them very powerful."

For the first time, Vidar had caught Mawyndulë's attention.

"How is that done?" Mawyndulë asked, and he noted a superior smile on the senior councilor's lips as if the old Fhrey had won something. Then Mawyndulë realized Vidar *had* done just that. How could the prince maintain an air of indifference, proclaim he already knows everything worth knowing, if he asks questions? This defeat—his thoughtless misstep— irritated Mawyndulë, and Vidar's little smile was a gloating insult.

"The Horn of Gylindora is kept by the Conservator who is charged with keeping it safe and producing it when, under the leadership of the Curator, a decision is made as to who shall blow it. In theory, anyone of Fhrey ancestry has a right to challenge, but since only one Fhrey can do that every three thousand years, it is an important responsibility to determine who that will be. Challengers must apply to the Aquila for the right. Then from those applicants, the council decides. Applicants appear before the council to argue their case. All this is done confidentially. No identity is revealed until the horn is blown. Those who aren't chosen remain anonymous, and the deliberations and the proceedings are never disclosed. This hill, on which the Airenthenon sits, gives our council its name. Aquila literally means 'place of choosing.' "

So endeth the lesson, Mawyndulë thought when Vidar finally resumed his climb.

Mawyndulë didn't follow immediately. He remained on the step staring up at the marble columns of the Airenthenon, wondering about the list of applicants. His father had been challenged by Zephyron, the leader of the Instarya. Until that moment, Mawyndulë had assumed he had been the only challenger.

Were there others? How many? Who were they? Since Gryndal had been a senior member of the Aquila, had he known who they were?

Mawyndulë turned to look back at the city. Below him, the Fhrey went about their lives on that beautiful summer morning, and the prince wondered how many of them were his enemies.

Mawyndulë had been told about his first and, until that day, only visit to the Airenthenon. He had no memory of the occasion, seeing as how he was an infant at the time. The council chamber, while open to the public, wasn't for children. And as far as the world of the Fhrey was concerned, he'd only recently crossed the line into adulthood by reaching the age of twenty-five. Before entering the Aquila, Mawyndulë had expected something truly wonderful, but after arriving, he couldn't say he was impressed.

The hall wasn't overly large, nor unusually grand, nor particularly breathtaking. He imagined some might think so—those who hadn't grown up in the palace—but for Mawyndulë, the meeting chamber was a disappointment. The place was little more than a simple stone room with meager adornment except for the ghastly frescoes of Gylindora Fane and Caratacus painted on the underside of the dome. The two wore almost-smiles as they looked down on everyone from thrones of intertwined birchwood. Gylindora wasn't pretty. Mawyndulë didn't understand why anyone would create a painting and make her unattractive. He wondered if she had been alive when they painted it, and if so what became of the artists after she saw the fresco. Her famed adviser, Caratacus, wasn't terribly handsome, either, which made Mawyndulë wonder if all the Fhrey from those days were homely.

The rest of the chamber was a semicircle with three rows of tiered benches capable of seating twenty or thirty people. Mawyndulë was surprised at how small the space was but also curious at the number of seats. If there were only six councilors and their junior counterparts, why were there more than twelve seats? This led Mawyndulë to wonder who else was present. Not everyone wore purple and white, which identified the senior and junior members. Maybe some councilors had others on their staff. He considered asking Vidar about it, but remembered the smirk the old Fhrey had given him after his last question, and he refused to provide any further entertainment.

In the center of the room sat a large chair. Like everything else inside the Airenthenon, it was carved of stone, but it was also endowed with lush gold cushions. That must be where his father would sit, if he were there. He wasn't. Fane Lothian was still at the tower of Avempartha. Mawyndulë didn't know the details of his father's visit. Maybe Vidar did, but, again, the prince refused to ask.

An old woman approached the gold-cushioned chair and took a seat. Like Gylindora Fane, she, too, was homely. She had a wide, flat face, thin lips, brittle hair, and eyes just a tad too big—like a bulbous-eyed fish. The woman was tall and stocky, with wide shoulders and masculine hands. He didn't like her, could tell that even from such a distance. She was odd, different. Ladies shouldn't be so strapping. She sat with too much confidence, too much authority. She wasn't fane, not even related, and yet she looked back at the gathering crowd of purple and white like a teacher waiting for a class to assemble. Mawyndulë was tired of teachers and tutors. This looked like another one, and he didn't care for her in the least.

Vidar directed him to a bench, where they seated themselves. The stone was cold and hard, and the back support too straight, forcing him to sit more upright than he was used to.

"Is that the Curator?" Mawyndulë asked grudgingly, figuring if he guessed correctly it would deny Vidar the upper hand and prevent the insidious grin.

Vidar didn't even look at him, but whispered, "Yes, that's Imaly Fane, mind yourself around her."

"Fane?" Mawyndulë ventured, without even realizing he had added yet another question.

"Imaly is a direct descendant of Gylindora Fane." Vidar paused, then looked at him. "You do know Gylindora was the first fane, yes?"

Mawyndulë rolled his eyes as dramatically as he could. "I *know* that," he said, stretching out each word to properly demonstrate his annoyance.

Vidar did grin derisively at him then.

"This fifth meeting of the Aquila in the Age of Lothian is hereby called to order," someone said in a deep voice, and Mawyndulë leaned forward to peer down. The speaker was a tall, thin fellow holding a huge staff. "May our lord Ferrol grant us wisdom."

"His Greatness, Fane Lothian, will not be with us today, as he is still dealing with issues at Avempartha," Imaly said. She remained sitting, addressing the audience with legs crossed at the knee. The top foot bounced slightly under the long folds of her asica. "His son, however, is here, and I'd like everyone to please welcome our newest member, Prince Mawyndulë—junior councilor for the Miralyith."

Everyone, including Imaly, began applauding.

"Stand up," Vidar said sternly.

Mawyndulë pushed hurriedly to his feet, so quickly he nearly fell head-long over the rail. This brought a scowl and shake of Vidar's head.

One more reason to hate you, Mawyndulë thought. He did, however, like the applause. Something about the dome made the clapping of just twenty-some people sound rich, full, and satisfying. He was smiling before he knew it, a broad, tooth-filled grin. He'd never been applauded before. People always clapped when Mawyndulë was with his father, but never just for him. The sound, and all the smiling eyes, made him feel buoyant in a way he'd never experienced before.

The moment was over all too soon. The clapping stopped, and Vidar tugged on Mawyndulë's sleeve as if he didn't trust the prince to know enough to resume his seat.

All the faces turned back to the Curator then—all but one.

She sat in the third tier—the row where those not dressed in purple and white were relegated. Young, and displaying the immaculately bald head of a Miralyith, she continued to smile at him long after the others had turned their attention back to Imaly. Mawyndulë looked away, feeling uncomfortable. He wasn't accustomed to being stared at; he wasn't accustomed to being seen. He'd spent most of his life in the Talwara alone with servants, who were far too busy to pay attention to him.

At first, he thought the girl was about his age, but then he decided she was probably older; almost everyone was. Births were so rare that they were greeted with citywide celebrations.

". . . resulting in a surplus of acorns and mint tea," Imaly was saying, but Mawyndulë hadn't been listening. He was still thinking about the girl in the third tier.

Is she still looking? It felt like it. Funny how he could almost feel the stare, like an itch on the side of his face, making his cheek hot. He had to look. He performed the most modest of glances.

She *was* still focused on him. Her big, wide eyes were as cute as a kitten's. And at that moment, she was biting her lower lip in a manner that made his stomach feel odd, sort of light and fluttery.

Mawyndulë heard a *humph*. Vidar was scowling at him and took that moment to fold his arms in a severe manner.

Mawyndulë looked back toward the center of the room, to the chair, which was now empty. Imaly was walking in slow thoughtful steps before the spectators.

". . . no, I'm afraid not," she said as if answering someone's question, and she may have been. Mawyndulë, who'd entered the Airenthenon with noble intentions of listening closely to the concerns of the day, found himself lost in deafening thoughts about the girl in the third tier. At least he was until he heard Imaly say, ". . . former First Minister Gryndal."

His head snapped around, and he fixed his attention on the Curator.

"By all accounts the assault was less than successful. Seers report that neither Arion nor Nyphron was so much as scratched. As for the God Killer, they saw a Rhune with a copper sword on his back and a Fhrey sword in his belt, so I'm guessing he wasn't harmed, either. Mawyndulë, does that description fit with your recollection of the Rhune known as Raithe?" she asked him directly. "The one who killed Gryndal?"

"Yes," he replied, not certain if he was expected to stand before speaking.

Imaly hesitated a moment, as if anticipating he'd say more. Then she went on, still walking with her hands clasped behind her. "The Grenmorians were slaughtered, and only a few escaped. Despite the surprise of the attack and the disarray caused by the storm, the Galantians weren't shaken. I had predicted as much when I voted against the action."

"What is being done now?" Volhoric asked. Mawyndulë knew him from many holiday celebrations. Being the leader of the Umalyn tribe, he was the Conservator of the Horn, and he officiated at all religious events. Although not a Miralyith, the priest was completely bald. Mawyndulë decided he didn't hate him. Volhoric had a quirky sense of humor that Mawyndulë appreciated, and the priest could usually be counted on to smile at most things. At that moment, however, he wasn't smiling. No one was. "Is that why the fane is still at Avempartha? Will there be another attempt?"

"I don't know," Imaly said in her brash voice. "His Greatness has not included me in his thoughts on this matter. Perhaps his son can tell us more?"

Again, Mawyndulë felt many sets of eyes, and his cheeks burned.

Vidar shot to his feet. "His son is here to observe . . . for the present. But I'm sure that the fane will not rest until these rebels are brought to Ferrol's justice."

"Such good news." Imaly smiled gently at Mawyndulë, then turned to the senior councilor. "Vidar, as senior representative of your tribe, could you enlighten this esteemed body on how a primitive village and a handful of Instarya managed to defeat the might of the Miralyith?"

"I can't say I care for your tone or insinuation," Vidar shot back.

Imaly lifted her eyebrows in surprise. The response was just a tad overdone to be sincere.

"Might I ask what tone you would like me to use? One of greater disappointment and surprise, perhaps? Oh, wait. No, that doesn't work, does it? I distinctly recall being the one to say the attack was a bad idea. So surprise wouldn't be appropriate, would it? How about dismay? How about despair at how easily those who defy this assembly's advice stand here and pretend to be insulted when an explanation is requested?"

"The fane isn't accountable to this assembly," Vidar shouted with indignation.

Imaly stretched her thin smile. "And you are not the fane." She turned to face the rest of the members, throwing out an arm in a sweeping gesture. "Or are you claiming the title in his absence, and Lothian is simply tardy in sending us the good news?"

This brought a muffled bit of laughter, most of it coming from the third tier.

Despite her ugliness and her large brutish body with its ungraceful movements, Mawyndulë enjoyed seeing Imaly belittle Vidar. He also hoped the girl in the third tier was one of those who laughed.

Vidar said nothing. He stood rigid, making fists with his bony hands.

"I hope the fane isn't intending to repeat such a performance," Imaly went on in his silence. "One humiliation should be more than enough for anyone to learn from. Don't you think, Vidar?"

The rest of the meeting was too boring for Mawyndulë to process. He heard what was said, even understood some of it, but instantly forgot it all once the doors to the Airenthenon finally opened. When the light of the day spilled into the stone cave, Mawyndulë felt he could breathe again. His excitement at being a member of the grand council had been replaced with the dread that he'd have to do this again in less than a week. The idea depressed him.

He had imagined the Aquila as an exciting place of grand debates on the nature of the world. He saw himself arguing eloquently about how the Miralyith should be recognized as a distinct and superior race, separate from the general Fhrey population, much as Gryndal had believed. He would, by virtue of his logic and poetry, convince everyone of this sensible course. Instead, the grand total of his first day's impressive elocution was a single word, *yes*.

He lingered near the door as the attendees, including Vidar, streamed out and down the steps. His Aquila tutor was no longer in the mood for lessons, and Mawyndulë caught just a flash of the senior councilor's robes as out the door he went.

Mawyndulë looked up toward the third tier, already emptied. She wasn't there.

He sighed and plodded toward the exit, nearly walking into Imaly. She was even bigger face-to-face, a good two inches taller than he was.

Was Gylindora Fane that tall? No wonder she took charge of the seven tribes. No, six tribes—he mentally corrected himself. *The Miralyith hadn't existed back then. They came later.*

"I hope you enjoyed your first day with us," Imaly said in a pleasant, friendly voice—so different from the booming one she'd used when addressing the assembly. "It's not always as boring as this. Sometimes it's fun. Extremely *fun*." She spoke the last word as if referring to something in particular, and that it wasn't actually fun but something more sinister. She didn't bother to explain, but proceeded as if he already knew. He didn't, but Mawyndulë appreciated that Imaly wasn't talking down to him the way Vidar did, as if he was an idiot or a burden. She spoke as if they shared secrets, even if he had no idea what those might be.

"Don't let Vidar ruin you," she said. "Stand up for yourself. You might be young, but you're still Lothian's son, and quite possibly the next fane. Remember that and the fact that Vidar will never forget it, either." She grinned at him.

He felt she was saying more than her words suggested. He could see Imaly was the sort of person who did that—who spoke in innuendo, a complex language he wouldn't always understand and maybe wasn't supposed to.

Mawyndulë smiled back. The moment he did, he squashed his lips into a forced frown. He didn't want to like the big, ugly lady with fish eyes. She wasn't Miralyith. She wasn't his equal. In all likelihood, she was his enemy and the enemy to his aspirations. He didn't need her to remind him he would be the next fane—and what did she mean by *quite possibly*? There wasn't any *possibly* about it. He *was* the prince. And when his father died—and his father was already old—Mawyndulë *would* sit on the Forest Throne. He didn't need her to tell him this.

"You'll be just fine," she assured him. "See you next week." She offered him a wink, and once again, he wondered if there was a hidden meaning in that last bit, as if perhaps next week would never come, or he wouldn't live to see it, or maybe she would end up blind and unable to see him. He found speaking with Imaly exhausting.

He nodded and ducked out the door, following behind the oldest and slowest councilors. The elderly wave of purple and white spilled down the steps of the Airenthenon. Some were caught up into conversation by small waiting groups. Mawyndulë recognized most of them, but he didn't know a single name. They all knew him, of course. Everyone in Estramnadon had filed past his crib, or visited the Talwara over the last few years to see the new heir to the Forest Throne. And they all knew one another because they were centuries old. Mawyndulë was a sapling in an ancient forest. Still, he was the prince, and one day he would rule. But at that moment, he felt like a foreigner, an outsider looking at a world he didn't know.

Alone, he descended the steps to the ancient interlocking stones of Florella Plaza. Artists displayed examples of their work: statues of animals, glass sculptures as delicate as moths' wings, and breathtaking paintings of the sweeping frontier. A group of landscapes near the Fountain of Lon caught Mawyndulë's attention, and he went over to examine a particularly large image.

The painting depicted a dramatic view of Mount Mador, caught in the light of a setting sun. The image was bold, passionate, emotionally stirring—and also a lie. Mawyndulë had stood at the same vantage point as the artist. He'd seen the view, and the pinnacle didn't look anything like the picture. There were no bright oranges and deep purples, no gold ridges on the slopes. And while the mountain was large and impressive, it wasn't *that* big. Not to mention, the clouds didn't swirl so dramatically. Everything was embellished for effect. Looking at it, Mawyndulë thought the artist managed the opposite of their intention. The lurid colors and exaggerated size cheapened the truth, replacing grandeur with garishness.

"Hello." He heard a soft voice and turned.

His muscles froze and rooted him in place. He was face-to-face with the girl from the third tier. She stood within arm's length, smiling at him, and just as pretty up close. Prettier even.

"That's mine." She pointed at the painting. "Do you like it?"

He nodded, his mind searching for his voice. "Yes . . . much . . . ah very much. It's . . . it's wonderful. Amazing really."

Her smile grew bigger and brighter.

Mawyndulë's heart began to gallop. He could feel it throbbing and worried it might be noticed under the layers of his asica.

"I wasn't actually there," she admitted. "I borrowed from other paintings."

"I was," he said.

"I know. Did it look like this? Do you think I captured it?"

"Absolutely. Better than absolutely. Better than perfect. You improved on perfection. Really." Mawyndulë tried not to listen to himself. He knew he was babbling. His fingers trembled, and he was starting to sweat.

Again she smiled, and his stomach became buoyant, feeling the way it did when he went swimming. Actually, no—more than that—he felt a tad nauseous, but in an impossibly pleasant way.

"I'm Makareta."

"I'm Mawyndulë."

She laughed a short, light sound. "Of course you are. Everyone knows you." Her smile disappeared, and a worry wrinkle appeared over her eyes. "Is it okay for me to talk to you? I mean, is that allowed?"

He didn't know what she meant.

"I wouldn't have, except you were looking at my painting. I thought . . ." She turned away with troubled eyes. "Maybe I should just stop talking now."

"Why wouldn't it be all right?"

Her brows went up. "You're the fane's son, and a council member of the Aquila, an important person. I'm . . . well . . . I'm nobody."

Mawyndulë was stunned that such an amazing girl as Makareta— a Miralyith—could see herself as a *nobody,* but he did like that she considered him too important to speak to.

"You're Miralyith, aren't you?"

She nodded.

"Then how could you be *nobody*?"

"I'm not important, not like you. I'm just—"

"*All* Miralyith are important."

She smiled again. He liked making her smile, and he managed it so easily. Up close, she was dazzling. He would've likened her blue eyes to pools of water, or fiery gems, or the endless skies, if any of those things had been remotely as beautiful.

"You sound like friends of mine," she said. "They go on and on about how the Miralyith are the chosen ones of Ferrol. The Blessed Ones, they call us. Why else would Ferrol give us such gifts? They chide me when I struggle to accept my own position, my birthright."

"These friends sound very wise."

"A lot of Miralyith our age feel that way. Would you like to meet them? We're having a gathering next week on the first night of the new moon, under the Rose Bridge in the north end of the city."

"Under the bridge? Why there?"

She paused and looked around them. Lowering her voice, she said, "Not everyone would appreciate the things we talk about."

"Really? Like what?"

"Come and find out." She looked down at her feet a moment, then back up at him. "If nothing else, it would be nice seeing you again."

Mawyndulë couldn't argue with that. He gave her a nonchalant shrug, but in his mind, he was already making plans to find the bridge.

CHAPTER SEVEN

The Road to Tirre

So I had this idea. A crazy one—or so I thought at the time. I did not have a clue what I was doing. No one else did, either. That is how it was at the beginning, and maybe it always is like that at the start of great things.

—THE BOOK OF BRIN

Roan checked the carts as she had every morning, afternoon, and night since they set out from Dahl Rhen. She crawled underneath each broad wooden bed and looked at where the axle passed through the wheels to make certain it wasn't shearing. The long wooden poles had developed deep, splintered grooves, and the weight was taking a toll, but they were still holding up. Persephone had packed the carts solid. All the grain, slabs of smoked meat, barrels of water and beer, tools, weapons, wool, and even the stone figure of Mari bounced along, riding in style. Roan prayed the carts would last the trip. It'd be her fault if they didn't. The stress made eating impossible, and walking all day without food made her dizzy.

The procession had stopped, and the midday meal was being prepared. All around, people were gathered in small groups. Roan wasn't a social person. She'd spent most of her life trapped in a little roundhouse with Iver, who didn't let her go out and punished her for speaking with others.

She'd learned early, and painfully, that it wasn't wise to defy him. So, while Roan found most everything in the world intriguing, she shunned people. Now that Iver was dead, this was more out of habit than need, but old ways were familiar ways—safe ways—and Roan had become an expert at hiding from the world.

Still, the dwarfs fascinated her. Their metal shirts, fashioned from hundreds of tiny rings, were amazing. *And the things they know!* They'd called what she'd built *wheels* and *carts*—giving names to her ideas as if they had known what was in her head before she did. One of them had helped her build the *axles,* another new word. He called himself Rain. He was the one who brought her copper and tin that he'd dug down to—something she'd never thought of doing. And with it, he suggested making something he called *bushings,* reinforcements on the axles to protect the area of rubbing to prevent the wooden poles from being sawed in half.

Sawed was another new word, derived from the remarkable metal tool that could smoothly cut through wood. Roan couldn't count the number of ideas that little device was birthing inside her head. If Roan were a god with a divine anvil she'd make dozens of saws, but she didn't even have a workbench anymore. She didn't have anything. Iver's home had been mostly destroyed, and what had remained had been left behind.

Her master had been dead for over a year, but he had continued to surround her. His house, his things, had always been a reminder. Now the house was gone, the last physical connection broken. Leaving her past behind, Roan had expected she'd feel something: relief, peace, hope. But she found none of those things. The world was the same as it had been, except now she didn't have a workbench.

"Well?" she heard Gifford say.

Looking out from under the grain cart, Roan could see Gifford and Rain down on their knees, peering under the wagon at her.

"Still weakening, but it should survive another day." She turned on her side and rolled back out into the sun. "I thought a few of those bumps today might have cracked the axle, but it's fine." Roan loved saying the world *axle.* She liked how the word formed in the back of her mouth like she was coughing up phlegm. "How much farther to Tirre?"

Gifford looked to Rain.

The little man shrugged, staring out across fields dotted in daffodils. "Hard to gauge distances here." He talked with the same rolling accent as the other two dwarfs, a melodious trundling of thick tongues that stretched words into growls. But his voice was higher, his words clipped, halting, and precise, as if he didn't have the same amount of time that the others did.

Roan understood his point. In the vast rolling uplands of few landmarks, it would be difficult to tell how far they'd come. Endless fields of tall grass swayed everywhere, interrupted only by an occasional clump of trees or small creek. She was about to nod her agreement when Rain added, "Directions aboveground are impossible to gauge with any accuracy."

Roan looked at him for a moment, perplexed. She used a hand to shade her eyes and glanced upward. "The sun rises in the east and sets in the west. And if the rising sun is to your right then you're facing north, and south is behind you."

Rain squinted his eyes at her. "North, south, east, west? What good are those?" He pointed up at an angle. "What direction is that?" He pointed in the exact opposite direction toward the ground. "Or that? It's not east or north, is it? And it's not exactly up or down, either. And how far is *far*? How near is *near*? What's the length of a finger? And what is the distance to the sun? Underground it all makes sense. There are rules down there. Logic in the rocks. Up here . . ." He scowled at the sky. "Up here it's all just a wishy-washy mess. All air and open space that can't be measured or gauged."

Roan thought about this and realized measurements were indeed a problem. When she'd asked the question, she hoped to hear they were close, but how far was that? Without specifics, she couldn't hope to determine whether the carts would finish the journey. That the carts had managed the trip so far was—as Persephone put it—a miracle.

The miracle applied to people as well as the carts. Just two days after setting out, the crowd had grown to almost six hundred. The injured from Dahl Rhen had been left at the first outer Rhen village, and at each settlement, Persephone urged people to stay in their homes and wait for further instructions. Even so, the parade south gathered a few more citizens from each town before moving on. *Parade* described the procession well. Padera had saved the one remaining flag, which had flown from the top of the lodge, and Habet carried the tattered cloth, flying it on a long stick right out in front.

Each day the column stopped just twice, once for the midday meal, and then well past sundown to make camp for the night. As always, Padera and Grygor orchestrated the cooking.

That day, Raithe had borrowed Roan's ax to cut a nearby tree. But Grygor became too impatient to wait for the God Killer, and snapped logs over his knee for firewood. Wide-shouldered Engleton and two other men were busy digging a pit to put it in. Habet, after planting the Rhen banner nearby, worked at igniting the kindling using a strip of rawhide held taut by a bowed stick. The strap was looped around another vertical piece of wood that spun quickly as he moved the bow back and forth. Where the vertical stick was pressed against a log, wool placed in a knothole started to smoke. Those who had nothing else to do gathered to watch Habet— the master of the clan's fire. Or maybe they just knew that the sooner he got the wool to light, the sooner there would be food.

Satisfied that her carts would reach the next camp, Roan walked with Gifford and Rain toward the sound of laughter. On the far side of those watching Habet, another group formed a circle, clapping and cheering as if being entertained by a minstrel show. At the center were the Galantians, who themselves were ringed around Moya.

At first, Roan feared her friend was being punished, beaten the way Iver had done to her. *No,* she thought, *Moya would never let anyone beat her.* She should have known better. As she and Gifford got closer, Roan realized Moya was fine. She didn't appear the least bit frightened and laughed along with the rest. In her hands, she held a thin sword.

"Maybe it would be best if you just stand back and throw something," the Fhrey named Tekchin was telling her. He stood in front of Moya brandishing a stout stick and making everyone laugh as he pushed aside Moya's swings.

"The Fhwey twaining the women too?" Gifford asked.

It stunned Roan how Moya could stand in front of so many people—in front of the gods—without fear.

They aren't gods. Roan had to constantly remind herself of that fact, just as she had to convince herself that Iver was dead. She'd seen him laid in the ground and even dropped in a handful of dirt. During the burial, she'd thought his pale, bluish cheeks had twitched when the dirt hit. She'd nearly screamed; not because she thought he had come back to life, but because she was terrified of the punishment for throwing dirt in his face.

"Eres," Tekchin said, "let her throw one of your javelins."

The Fhrey with the little spears glared back in alarm.

Tekchin rolled his eyes and shook his head. "They're weapons, not sacred artifacts, for Ferrol's sake. Let her try one."

Eres scowled for a moment then reluctantly waved Moya over. He held out one of the spears.

"You throw it from the shoulder and follow through," Eres explained. "Try and hit that deadwood over there."

"The stump or Tekchin?" Moya asked with a mischievous grin, and everyone laughed again, but louder this time.

Moya was a marvel. Roan watched astounded, as if the woman stood in the center of a roaring fire. Roan couldn't imagine being stared at by so many, much less a ring of Galantians. They were all grinning, and Moya grinned right back. She was closer to being one of them than Roan was to being like Moya.

Moya took the javelin and threw, but the little spear made it only halfway to the deadfall.

Eres took what looked like a stick with a cup on its end. "This is an atlatl, a thrower. See?" He took another javelin and inserted the butt end in its cup. Then he flicked the javelin, making it move faster and travel farther. The weapon hit the stump with a loud *thwack*.

Moya looked at him as if he were insane.

"She'd do better with this," Anwir said. He demonstrated his technique for whipping a stone with a sling. Swinging the long straps in a circle over his head, he let one fly. When Moya tried, she managed to shoot the pebble much farther than the javelin, but in completely the wrong direction. A distant *crack* was followed by someone cursing, and Moya cringed.

"Maybe you should just stick to the sword," Tekchin said.

Roan looked at the javelins and the sling and thought about Habet starting the fire. *There's always a better way.*

"*I* could heave a stone betta than that," Gifford told Roan.

"So can she," Roan replied. This caught the attention of both Gifford and Rain.

"What do you mean?" Gifford asked.

"Moya can knock a squirrel off the branch of an elm tree when pitching a rock, and with either hand. I don't know why she's faking, pretending that she can't throw well."

He focused on Roan. "Have *you* done that? Faked being bad at something."

Roan looked up. "I don't need to pretend. I *am* bad . . . at everything."

Gifford laughed. "Woan, you made a joke. That's wondiful."

She looked at him, puzzled.

Gifford stopped laughing. His expression changed; he grew sad. Roan hated when that happened. Too often she made Gifford look that way. She made a lot of people sad, but none more often, or as deeply, as him. He looked like he might cry, and she didn't know why. She hated not knowing things and began thinking, looking for answers. *Has to be a reason. Everything has a reason.* Then she realized what it was. "I'm sorry."

"It's okay."

"No, really, it's my fault. And it was so beautiful, too."

"What you talking about, Woan?"

"The amphora you made . . . the one with the woman on it who you said was me . . . it got smashed in the giant attack. I should've taken it to the storage pit when we ran. I'm sorry it's gone. That's why you're sad, isn't it? I knew you shouldn't have given it to me. So beautiful, and it's my fault it's gone."

Gifford put a hand to his mouth as he sucked in both his lips. He leaned forward and she saw his arms come up as if he might try to hug her again.

She cringed.

He stopped.

Then he did cry. Tears spilled down his cheeks. "No, Woan," he whispered. "I wasn't thinking about the amphora. And I don't mind that it was smashed. And I would . . . I would give you a million mo', each one betta than the last if I thought they could help."

He moved away from her, away from everyone, sniffling as he went. She let him go. He wanted to be alone. He didn't like people seeing him cry. She understood that; she understood that very well.

Suri lay deep in the field, the tall grass swaying overhead. Bees buzzed from one flower to the next. She was close enough to hear that everyone had started eating, but far enough away so that no one would stumble on her. She felt Minna's head pop up and realized someone had. It wasn't hard to guess who.

"I've been *looking* for you," Arion said in Rhunic.

"I've been *avoiding* you," Suri said truthfully, and not just because Arion had been traveling near the goats, which were frightened by Minna. *Very stupid animals. Who couldn't love Minna?*

"Not your fault," Arion assured in tender tones.

"You're right," Suri replied. "It was yours."

When she had moved close enough, the Fhrey's shadow blocked out the afternoon sun, but Suri still didn't look at her. She closed her eyes instead.

"You are right. It was," the Fhrey said.

"Did you *want* me to kill him?" Suri asked.

"No!" Arion was so shocked she switched into Fhrey. *"But . . . I suppose I should have realized you might not be entirely committed to releasing him. The Art is powered by the forces of nature, and they aren't tools like a hammer or ax . . . more like fire or wind. In that way, it can have a will of its own. It can sometimes assist in unintended ways, like a too-helpful friend. What you want and what you think you want need to be aligned, or the results can be . . . well, you know."*

"I didn't *want* to kill him," Suri said. She felt she needed to say it out loud, and not just so Arion could hear.

"I believe you. I was foolish to expect such a complex weave so early in your training."

"I don't want to be trained. I like being who I am."

"But you could be so much more. You are like a caterpillar becoming a butterfly."

Suri frowned. *Why did she have to pick butterflies as her example?* "Maybe I like being a caterpillar. What's wrong with inching along and eating leaves?"

Arion sighed and switched once more to Fhrey. *"You don't really believe that. Now that you know . . . now that you've seen what it's like, you've had a taste and are hungry for more. Now that you've touched the chords, you can't help wanting to fly. None of us can. I remember my first time. Nearly a thousand years ago, but I remember it so clearly. I never felt so alive as when I first touched the chords, when I saw what was possible . . . like being born a second time. Do you honestly think there are any caterpillars who, upon learning that they can become one of those beautiful winged creatures, say, 'No, thanks. It's not for me. I don't really want to fly. I don't want to be beautiful and soar to the sun on painted wings.' "*

"Maybe not, but I would."

Arion sat down. "Why?"

Suri wished she would just go away.

"Why not be a butterfly, Suri?"

"It's a long story."

"We have much time."

Suri sighed to show she didn't want to talk about it, but Arion just waited. So did Minna, who looked at her friend with expectant eyes; Minna loved stories. Suri sighed again, took a new breath, and spoke in Fhrey because she didn't want to have to repeat the whole thing. *"I once found a grove of perfect strawberries. I love them, and these were big, and ripe, and wonderful. Usually, other animals get to them before I do, but that time I was first. Completely alone, I considered myself so very lucky, didn't have to share. I ate all of them, one after another, whole handfuls at a time. So wonderful! I should have taken some for Tura, but I didn't. I devoured them all. I became very sick. My stomach twisted and cramped. I went home to ask Tura for help, but she wasn't there. I lay in bed for hours, feeling terrible."*

"Are you saying that pain can come from too much—"

"Quit trying to get ahead of me," Suri snapped. *"This has nothing to do with the strawberries; they were just what brought me home."* She waited, and Arion didn't say any more. *"So all night I was sick. I called out for Tura, but she never came, even though she had always done so in the past. The next day I went looking, and I found her facedown in the garden."*

"Are you saying—"

Arion stopped when Suri pushed up and glared at her.

"Boy, you are impatient." Suri huffed. *"Do you want me to explain or not?"*

Arion made a show of closing her mouth.

Suri frowned at her then went on. *"Tura was dead, and I was alone. All my life Tura had taken care of me. Told me what to do and what to avoid. She was the mystic, and I was her apprentice. That's what she always said. And she also said that when she finally died, I would be the mystic—just me, no one else. The forest would be all mine, and I wouldn't have any more rules to obey, no more restrictions, no one to report to. I used to long for the day when I would finally be in charge of myself. But that morning, I knelt beside Tura and begged Wogan to wake her. All of a sudden, I didn't want to be the mystic anymore. But"*—she paused and this time looked right into Arion's eyes— *"once you're a butterfly it's impossible to go back to being a caterpillar, even if you want to. You're stuck with those wings, and you have to fly away, and life stops being a simple thing of inching happily along leaves and eating in the sun. Life becomes something else entirely. You don't get to stay in the Hawthorn Glen beside the gurgling brook. You're forced to go away, away from the forest that had been your home, away from everything you've known and loved. You have to be something different and give up everything. There's always a cost. And I can't imagine those pretty wings come cheap. Nothing has so far."*

They sat for a while, not speaking.

The sun was warm enough to be called hot. The bees didn't care. They labored as they always did, going from one flower to the next, landing and straining the stalks with their weight. When they left, the stalks sprang back and waved goodbye. Suri didn't know these bees—at least she didn't think so. She was already too far from home. The breeze was nice, and she was certain it was the same one she knew from the forest. Nothing like a good breeze on sweating skin to make a person feel loved.

"*I know why you did it,*" Suri finally said.

"*Did what?*"

Suri wasn't looking at Arion. She stared out at the hazy summer horizon where hills rose above hills until they became mountains of faint blue. "*Why you had me free the giant instead of doing it yourself. It's because of your head. It hurts when you do magic. You haven't done any for a long time, but you put out Magda when she was on fire. That's why you needed to lie down. And after you had trapped the giant, you could barely walk. You slept even though it was the middle of the day. You wanted me to free him so you could avoid the pain.*"

Suri didn't know what she wanted Arion to say, or even if she wanted her to say anything. She told her because the knowledge had been trapped inside and needed to get out. Otherwise she would feel as if she was holding a secret, and having secrets was like keeping a weasel inside a house. They don't like it one bit and dig and claw to escape. A weasel will make a terrible mess of a home, and a secret does the same to a friendship. Suri had come to think of Arion as a friend, a good friend. They had known each other for only a short time, but already Suri knew that, next to Minna, Arion was her best friend.

When Arion didn't say anything for several minutes, Suri turned to look. The Fhrey was sitting hunched forward in the grass surrounded by wildflowers that gently patted her. The sun was on Arion's face, and Suri saw glistening silver lines running down both cheeks. Her eyes were closed and her body trembled, but she didn't make a sound.

Suri was puzzled, but just for a moment. Then she understood, and she slid over to the Fhrey. She put her arms around Arion and felt her lean in. "*It wasn't your fault, either,*" Suri told her. "*Wogan wanted the giant to die. After what he and his brothers had done to the forest, I imagine all of creation wanted revenge.*"

"I don't believe in revenge," Arion said in a wet whisper as she clutched at Suri's waist.

"Then I suspect you're the only one."

Suri held her, feeling Arion quiver, then pause, sniffle, and quiver again. She had never held anyone before, except Minna, and it felt strange. Not bad, really, just odd because she didn't know exactly what to do. Maybe it didn't matter. She only had to be there.

"Suri," Arion said, *"I'm scared."*

"Of what?"

Arion didn't answer, and the two went on hugging each other among the swaying flowers under the afternoon's summer sun.

After the meal was over, Roan found Brin. The girl sat on her knees, a wad of rumpled cloth on her lap. Before her parents' death, Brin had been cheerful, an eternal spring of happiness. She had been a warm fire on a cold night; cool water to parched lips; her beaming smile just as important as the lodge's eternal flame. But neither had been seen since the giant's attack. Roan wanted to say something, do something, but she didn't know what. If an axle broke, Roan could fix it, but she hadn't been able to help Gifford's leg, and she knew she couldn't fix Brin. There always seemed to be a better way, except when it came to people. Once broken, people couldn't be repaired.

"Have you eaten?" Roan asked.

"Not hungry."

Roan sat down beside her.

The camp was breaking up. People hoisted the belongings they carried in baskets and moved up the slope. The dirt that had been dug for the fire pit was now used to smother the flames. Men armed with staffs set off with dogs to gather the sheep and pigs. Parents found children and started walking down the road to give tiny feet a head start. Gifford had left before anyone since he was slower than most of the children, slower even than Padera. Only Brin, Roan, and Malcolm remained. The ex-slave sat across from the women, searching the inside of his shoe for something.

"What's this?" Roan asked Brin, pointing at the strips of cloth.

"It's . . . it's . . ." Brin took a deep breath and pushed the strips away. "I don't know. I don't know. I'm too stupid." She began to cry.

Roan watched her. Malcolm looked up as well. Unlike Gifford, Brin didn't seem to mind them watching her cry. She didn't seem to notice. Roan didn't know what to do, so she did what she could and began picking up the mess. The strips of cloth had deliberate markings on them, little pictures placed one after another all along their lengths.

Brin was calming down but still crying. She waved dismissively and shook her head. "Bandages . . . those are the ones that were around Arion's head. I thought . . ." Brin sucked on her lips as she wiped her tortured eyes. "I don't know. I was thinking that those markings are like the pictures I used to paint on my walls."

Roan nodded. One did look a bit like a mountain and another sort of like a person with missing arms.

"Well, I thought . . . I sorta thought that a picture showed a moment or an idea, but a series of pictures could tell a story. Look." Brin raked her heels over the ground, scrubbing clear a patch of dirt. Then she drew a circle with a line under it with her finger. "Let's say that's Persephone. I know it doesn't look like her, but just listen a second." Brin drew a vertical line. "That divides the *that* time from *this* time." She added a bigger circle and put a head on it with eyes. "That's the big brown bear." Lastly, Brin drew the same circle and line as before.

"Persephone again," Roan said excitedly.

Brin looked up. "Yes! Exactly!" Then the girl drew another dividing line, and in the last space available before the grass started again, she drew another Persephone and another bear, but the bear's eyes were little lines instead of circles, and another line came out of its center.

Roan stared at this image for a long time. While she did, Brin didn't speak or move.

"Persephone again . . ." Roan muttered, trying to work it out. "The bear again . . . but different, and this line . . ." She pointed.

"Yes?" Brin asked, her voice tense.

"It almost looks . . ."

"Yes?" Brin inched closer.

"I mean, it's sort of like . . ."

"Like what? Like what?" Brin was bouncing on folded knees.

"Almost like a spear is in its side and the bear . . . the eyes look closed, so the bear looks dead."

"Yes!" Brin exploded.

Roan studied the pictures. She pointed to them in order and said, "Persephone. Then the bear. Then Persephone meets the bear, and the bear dies."

She looked up and saw Brin smiling. "You understood it!"

"But Persephone didn't kill the bear with a spear."

"It doesn't matter. It represents an idea, not a real thing. Do you understand?"

Roan didn't, not entirely, but sort of. What she did understand was that Brin was smiling.

"It would be too hard to draw a picture of everything, but"—Brin picked up the bandages with the runes—"if I could turn the ideas into markings like this, then I would put down stories on cloth the way Suri painted these symbols. So much was lost when Maeve died. She never had the chance to tell me everything. I've tried to pick up the pieces from others, but I hear different accounts from various people. And this . . . I mean look at it." Brin took the bandages, crushed them in her hands, pulled at them, as if she hated the strips, and threw them down. "See? You can't hurt it. The markings are still there. If I get this right, I could put down all the stories that Maeve taught me, and whenever anyone wanted to know something, they could just look at it, even after I'm gone."

Roan stared back at the dirt and the drawings there. The idea fascinated her. When Roan looked back at Brin, she was holding the rags once more.

"No one would ever forget them," Brin said, and wiped her eyes. "My mom and dad, our home, our lives together, everything. If I could do that, they'd never be forgotten. And maybe in some small way, they'll never truly die. I suppose that sounds stupid, doesn't it?"

"No, not at all. I think it's wonderful," Roan said. "Better than the saws made by the little men. Better than my cart or barrels. It might just be the most amazing idea I've ever heard."

Roan continued to look at the rags in wonder as Brin gathered them up and set off down the road.

"I think . . ." Malcolm said, punching his foot back into his shoe, then standing up. "I think we've just witnessed the world shift, and I doubt it'll ever be the same again."

CHAPTER EIGHT

Ride of the Stone God

No one can tell me Mari is not the greatest of the gods. I saw her charge forth and single-handedly fight for us, and then she sat down and generously shared food and drink with the conquered.

—THE BOOK OF BRIN

The first thing Persephone noticed were the seagulls. The white birds circled in flocks, squawking in a chorus of lonesome cries. The dahl's survivors were a full five days from Rhen. *Five days!* She could hardly believe it, and had begun to wonder if Tirre, along with the Blue Sea, had been moved farther away. The trip had never taken so long. On the few occasions when she and Reglan had traveled there, it had only taken two days. Of course, they hadn't traveled with a host of hundreds that included scores and scores of children and the elderly. Persephone didn't have the heart to drive the column harder. This wasn't a vacation to visit and trade with neighbors. They were broken families grieving for loved ones, children without parents and parents without children. They walked into an unknown world, and on their backs they carried their whole lives. Letting them sleep, giving them time to prepare hot meals, and providing rest were the least she could do, even if it prolonged her own torment.

Today we'll discover how strong the bonds are among the clans.

Tirre knew she was coming. Persephone had sent runners to all the dahls the day after the giants' attack, explaining what had happened. She'd had the messengers draw sticks to see who would go to the Gula clans in the north, the people who had been their enemies for centuries. Aberdeen, Montlake, and Morgan were the unlucky ones, all three farmers. Two of the men had families who'd survived the attack, but both had nodded grimly and set out without complaint on the perilous road north. All of them knew it might be suicide, but they went anyway. They left Persephone to care for their families—and cultivate a tremendous feeling of guilt.

I should have gone instead of one of them. I gave the order, and I should live, or die, with the consequences. But I didn't even draw a stick.

Dahl Tirre was larger than Dahl Rhen had been, more elaborate, too. While Rhen had the forest with its wood, berries, and animals, Tirre had the sea. The water was more than just a source of fish and salt. Across its aqua waves lay Belgreig, the land of the Dherg, and from there came riches. The Dherg influence was impossible to miss. Dahl Tirre was built of stone. Although some buildings were fashioned from clay bricks, the wall that surrounded the dahl was constructed of neatly stacked slabs, as was the lodge. Unlike Dahl Rhen, some of the village had grown up outside the fortification.

The most abundant wealth of Dahl Tirre existed in the settlement around the docks. Hundreds of brick buildings were stacked upon one another as they climbed the steep slope from the water's edge. The people of Tirre called this dock-village Vernes, which she'd been told was the Dherg word for "pier."

As Persephone's parade rounded the bend that sloped down to the rocky coast, they could see the whole of the dahl, the village, and the sea stretching into the horizon. The dahl could see them, too. Hard to miss a column of several hundred people marching toward their gate, which at the moment was still wide open.

"You all right?" Raithe asked.

He walked beside her as he had every day of the trip. She hadn't asked him to. She almost never asked anything of Raithe. She didn't feel she could. Persephone was the chieftain of Clan Rhen, but Raithe was Dureyan, and he certainly wasn't anyone's servant. Raithe was the God Killer, a valuable asset to a clan chieftain about to go to war with the Fhrey. Still, he was more than that—she felt comfortable with him. Except for the Fhrey, who still frightened her, it felt as though everyone else depended on her for something. Raithe didn't need anyone. At times, when things grew bleak, she shamefully indulged in his fantasy of running away together. She imagined slipping off the shackles of responsibility and living with Raithe in his carefree world, but it was only an illusion. The real world didn't work that way.

"No, I'm not all right," Persephone replied, and she could tell it wasn't the response he had expected. "I'm waiting to see who has more power: Mari or Eraphus."

"Eraphus?"

"Clan Tirre's god."

The gate remained open as they began their descent. Just as Persephone started believing everything would work out, at least for the next few days, she heard the horn.

This is the moment, the hinge our future swings on. What has Tirre decided?

As the first horn's wail faded, Persephone held her breath. Her heart sank as a second blew and then a third—no mistaking what that signal meant. One horn indicated a greeting, two horns indicated potential danger, but three horns . . . three horns warned of a threat, calling all the residents to arms.

Remarkably, the gates didn't close—not at first. The initial movement came from people just outside the wall. Wherever they had been going, and whatever they had been doing, became unimportant as they rushed inside, shoving one another in their haste to reach the protective walls before the gates closed.

What she had feared the most had come to pass: Tirre wouldn't welcome them.

Lipit, the dahl's chieftain, had never impressed her as a courageous man. Pompous and arrogant, made so by his dahl's wealth, he'd faced few real threats. Rich men—especially those who came to their wealth through no effort of their own—didn't like risk, and challenging the Fhrey was as risky as it got. As far as Tirre was concerned, Clan Rhen carried a plague, and they didn't want it spreading to their shores.

Just when she imagined things couldn't possibly get worse, Persephone heard a scream.

Behind her, the lead cart crested the hill and began to descend. Most of the men driving it had been behind, pushing. Only Malcolm and Cobb pulled. The trip to Tirre had, until that point, been across reasonably level ground. So it came as a surprise to everyone when the cart began to roll downhill under its own power. Malcolm leapt aside, but Cobb had been too slow. The cart lurched as its front left wheel rolled over him. The following wheel ended Cobb's screaming. Yet the cries weren't over. Everyone ahead of the cart panicked, because Cobb's death hadn't stopped or even slowed the rampaging cart. If anything, it rolled faster.

Roan's creation rumbled down the hill on that horribly smooth road, picking up speed until it ran faster than a rabbit. Mari bounced in the back, trapped amid barrels of water, wheat, and beer. The god looked furious as she rattled by. The wobbly wheels shimmied badly, but Roan's invention held together, and the cart gained astounding speed.

Everyone who could, scrambled out of its way, diving to one side or the other. Some were too slow. Raithe pulled Persephone aside, but a man and his wife were struck. The cart finally raced clear of the column of people, rolling hard and fast down the remainder of the road, wobbling and whistling as it headed straight toward the gates of Dahl Tirre.

The great gates were still admitting latecomers. Seeing the cart, they cried out and scattered. Even the guards ran for their lives when seeing a god rattling straight toward them. The cart appeared as a living thing, a wobbly beast, angry and charging in rage. Striking sacks and uneven paving stones, the cart leapt and crashed, rocked and shook, but it never faltered, never slowed.

Then it struck the gate.

The crash was loud, a crack like thunder. One wheel was sheared off in a burst of splinters as the gate's two wooden doors were slapped aside.

With the impact, the rear of the cart came up, and the whole thing flipped, throwing barrels of grain and beer, along with rakes, hoes, winnowing forks, mattocks, and the god Mari. What remained of the cart, and its chaos, passed within the wall and beyond Persephone's view. Shrieks were followed by another crash. Then everything went quiet.

The stillness that followed was worse than the screams. Overhead, seagulls cried, and they weren't alone. Clan Rhen wept, some for the loss of those who had been killed by the runaway cart, and others because they couldn't do anything else. The silence came from inside the dahl, where Persephone couldn't see. She was blind and deaf to whatever terrible conclusion had occurred, and as she walked the remaining steps down the road, she couldn't even begin to imagine what she might find inside.

Persephone ordered all the other carts stopped. They, and the rest of Clan Rhen, were to wait while she, Raithe, and Malcolm went to the dahl. Looking back, she spotted Roan, who stood clutching herself, glaring wide-eyed at the body of Cobb. Persephone wanted to talk to her, needed to explain that it hadn't been her fault, but Persephone had a bigger crisis to deal with. She had to talk with Lipit, Clan Tirre's chieftain, and salvage what she could.

One of the big doors of Dahl Tirre's gate had been nearly torn off. It hung at a twisted angle. Passing inside, Persephone searched for blood but found none. No one lay on the ground. No one looked hurt. The cart had mostly destroyed itself when it hit the gate. What was left had crashed and rolled. The empty cart lay on its side. Mounds of wheat and barley lay among shards of broken barrels. Tools were scattered. Miraculously, the four barrels of beer rested on their sides, undamaged. Several bushels of peas and berries had spilled out of baskets. In the center of it all, in the middle of the courtyard of Dahl Tirre, stood the stone figure of Mari, upright and unharmed.

The people of Clan Tirre gathered in a circle around the god. Many were on their knees, heads bowed until Persephone and her escorts entered. They looked up then, fearful. On the stone steps of the lodge, Chieftain Lipit knelt along with his wife, Iffen, and his three sons. All of them wore soft white linen, typical of the Tirre people. Around Lipit's neck was a stunning gold torc, while a silver one circled Iffen's throat.

Persephone said nothing as she waded through the grain until she stood beside Mari. She considered how best to apologize for the disaster, but couldn't find the words. How could she begin to explain, and how could she ask for safe haven after such a catastrophe?

"Forgive us." Lipit spoke first, lifting his face to look at her.

Persephone glanced at Raithe and then Malcolm, uncertain whether she had heard correctly. Both raised an eyebrow in response.

"We were misinformed," Lipit said, and took a moment to glare viciously at a man who knelt in the dirt at the bottom of the steps. "Calab said Eraphus was greater than Mari, that Clan Rhen was weak, and that you came as beggars to spoil our lands." He spat on the prostrate man, who quivered and moaned, his face still pressed to the ground.

Lipit looked back at Mari, rising out of the sea of grain. "Your god is great and generous." He looked up at the broken gate. "She is fierce and powerful. I can see why you believe Rhunes can fight the Fhrey. Your god is a warrior god. Forgive us. We didn't know."

Persephone nodded thoughtfully. "And what about my messenger?"

"He's here and safe. He said you called for a Council of Clans to choose a keenig to lead us in a war against the gods of the north."

"And what are your thoughts on this matter?"

Lipit once again stared harshly at the prostrate man.

"We thought it was ill advised." The chieftain cringed slightly while shifting his gaze to Mari, who did nothing.

"And what do you think now?" Persephone asked.

"We think we were rash."

Persephone nodded with a sympathetic face and hoped that only she knew it wasn't genuine. "Chieftain Lipit, Lady Iffen, allow me to introduce Malcolm, who lived nearly his whole life in the famed outpost of Alon Rhist, and Raithe of Dureya, also known as the God Killer."

Lipit nodded to Raithe. "We've heard of you."

"He is my Shield."

"A worthy choice indeed. You do yourself a great honor by selecting so mighty a warrior. Allow us to express our extreme sympathies for the passing of Reglan and your son Mahn. They were both great and honorable men."

"Thank you," she said. "Now I must ask. Is Clan Rhen welcome in Tirre?"

Lipit looked over at the stone god that faced him. "Of course, of course. The people of Clan Rhen are our brothers from the wood."

"In that case," Persephone smiled and said, "may the blessings of Mari be upon this dahl and this land."

Lipit's shoulders relaxed. He closed his eyes and took a breath. All around the courtyard, his people did the same as they got to their feet.

"Persephone, my good friend, please come in," Lipit said in the more familiar tone she was used to. "I'll have wine and cheese brought."

"And my people?"

"The streets are crowded. Would it meet with your approval for them to camp outside, along the north wall?"

Persephone waited a moment, and Lipit licked his lips and wiped a bead of sweat from his brow.

"Yes, yes, of course." Persephone nodded then whispered to Raithe and Malcolm. "Would you please let everyone know they can come down, and see to . . . well, take care of things until I return."

They both nodded and headed back.

By the time the two returned, Cobb's body had been covered in cloth and his large family were still weeping over it. As for the husband and wife who had also been run down, only a young boy was draping their bodies. The three must have joined the procession from one of the outer villages, as no one appeared to know them. About fourteen years old, the lad was thin as a stick and had a lock of hair standing straight up. He didn't cry. His eyes weren't red. His lips didn't tremble.

Tough one, that kid. Like a Dureyan. He has that weathered, forsaken look.

Roan also stood among the dead. She didn't cry, either, but she looked sick.

Raithe wasn't good at public speaking. He didn't care for talking in general, but it had to be done. He took a deep breath and straightened. "Persephone has asked me to tell everyone that Clan Tirre has welcomed us," he said loudly, and everyone nearby turned to face him. Those farther away moved closer to hear. "We can make a camp outside the north wall." He looked down at the bodies. "But we'll have to do something about the carts so we can bring them down safely."

Roan's jaw tightened, and her eyes squeezed shut as if he'd hit her. When she opened them again, she mouthed, *I'm sorry.* Not even a whisper gave the words sound. She did this over and over, her hands clenching and unclenching, her arms frozen at her sides.

Raithe didn't know what to say, and stood with his eyes downturned.

Malcolm stepped forward. "We mourn those who left us this day, but their sacrifice gave us, and possibly all of the clans, a chance at survival. Dahl Tirre had been planning to close its doors, but Mari's ride showed them the wisdom of unification. These people didn't die in vain. Their deaths, and Roan's carts, saved Clan Rhen. Let us honor them all." He bowed his head reverently, whispering a quiet, unheard prayer.

"How can we fix the carts?" Raithe asked Roan softly. "Make them so they don't"—he hesitated—"harm anyone else."

"She didn't kill those people," Gifford said. The crippled potter stood beside her then took a step forward, putting himself between Raithe and Roan.

Raithe had often seen the two sitting together during mealtime and speculated they were sharing more than each other's company. But in five days, he hadn't seen them so much as hold hands.

"I know that," Raithe said. "And Persephone knows that, too. But it's important that—"

"No one can know what will happen with something so new," Gifford went on, not hearing him. "When you toss a pebble in a lake, you can't know all the places that will be affected by the wipples. If it wasn't fo' Woan, all the food and supplies would be left behind."

Raithe didn't try to interrupt. Gifford wasn't talking to him; he was looking at Roan.

"It's widiculous to think it was Woan's fault. If I make a cup and someone swallows so fast that they choke to death, am I to blame? It's the same thing. It's the *same exact thing*. So don't blame Woan."

Gifford stopped and Raithe looked back at her. "Can you fix the carts so they don't roll so fast?"

She nodded.

"Good."

Raithe gave another glance at the boy who'd lost his parents. Something about him was familiar. Nothing obvious stood out, and Raithe wasn't going to intrude on the kid's grief, but he felt he ought to know. Raithe had spent a lifetime feeling that way, as if some important truth was just out of reach.

He stared hard at the kid.

Nothing.

With a shrug, he turned away.

CHAPTER NINE

Under the Rose Bridge

I have always found it fascinating that the Fhrey are divided into seven tribes, just as the Rhulyn are divided into seven clans. But Rhulyn clans are based on bloodlines and regions, and the Fhrey tribes are distinguished by class, occupation, and power. At the bottom is the Gwydry, the working class, at the top, the Miralyith.

—THE BOOK OF BRIN

Mawyndulë was certain that if he'd been at Avempartha—or better yet, if his father had let him lead the attack—Nyphron of the Instarya, Arion the Traitor, and all the Rhunes of that despicable village would be dead. Instead, his father foolishly counted on Jerydd.

Jerydd the Stupid, as Mawyndulë had recently dubbed him, was the kel of Avempartha. Mawyndulë had met him once, the oldest Fhrey the prince had ever seen, so old that he no longer needed to shave his head; all his hair had fallen out years ago. In its place were brown spots, making him as speckled as the owl he kept as a pet. Like an old couple, the two had been together for so long they had begun to look alike—a pair of ancient, mottling incompetents. Neither one knew how to fly.

Upon their first meeting, Mawyndulë had mistakenly liked Jerydd. He met the kel when Mawyndulë and Gryndal had spent the night at the tower on their ill-fated trip to Rhulyn. The old Fhrey and his bird had seemed friendly, even wise. Mawyndulë knew better now. The imbecile had sent giants to do the work of Miralyith, trusting the power of the ancient tower to do what was best dealt with in person. Plus, he and his cronies had used too weak a hand. *Lightning and hail?* Mawyndulë shook his head at the absurdity. Better to have sent fire and wind. They should have burned the entire forest: every building, blade of grass, and tree. All of Rhulyn should have been reduced to smoldering ash. Mawyndulë wouldn't have stopped there. He would have rent the ground with quakes, breaking their roads and leveling hills. What did Miralyith need giants for? Conviction was what was required, but that virtue had died with Gryndal.

Mawyndulë realized all this as he sat in the council room of the Talwara. He wasn't allowed at the big table where the new First Minister, the Master of Secrets, the fane, and the commanders of the Shahdi—the Erivan home guard—had gathered. Instead, he was relegated to a little desk beside the pitcher of water and glasses. He wasn't there to contribute, only to listen. Attending was part of his ongoing education, his chance to learn how a fane ruled. But observing from his exiled corner, Mawyndulë saw only what *not* to do.

"Petragar reports resistance in obtaining the cooperation of the Instarya stationed in Alon Rhist," Kabbayn said.

The new First Minister was a pathetic excuse for Gryndal's successor. *He's not even Miralyith!* Although apparently he didn't mind impersonating one, dressed as he was in an elaborate asica. Why his father had picked such a feckless fraud was beyond Mawyndulë's comprehension.

"Cooperation?" Lothian appeared both surprised and amused. "How is that an issue? They will do as I command. I have decreed that Petragar is their leader, and they are to abide his authority."

"Of course, of course," Kabbayn said, retreating, "but they won't have their heart in serving him."

"What need have I for their hearts?" Lothian asked.

Kabbayn opened his mouth to speak, but nothing came out, and he closed it again.

"What else?" Lothian asked.

"I've obtained news that the Rhunes are gathering, my fane." Vasek folded back the sleeves of his gray robe but left the hood up. Where the sleeves were pulled back, Mawyndulë spotted the burn marks on his wrists. The skin was puckered and shriveled, redder then the rest. Seeing even that small glimpse made Mawyndulë grimace. "It seems they're going to appoint a keenig."

"Keenig?"

"Their version of a fane, I believe. A single leader who'll unite all the clans under one banner. It's possible they're making plans for war."

"War?" The fane chuckled. "With whom? With us, you mean?"

"I believe so."

Several at the table laughed, none more heartily than the commander of the Lion Corps, who, when he was able, added, "Of all the nerve."

Vasek didn't laugh or smile. "There are a great many of them, my fane. And they sent messengers to the High Spear Valley as well. It could prove serious if the Gula-Rhunes join forces with the Rhulyn clans of the south."

"Unlikely," Lothian said. "We've taught them to hate, trained them to slaughter one another." He waved his hand in dismissal. "We'll have the Instarya instigate another conflict. That should douse any would-be flame. Things will settle back down then."

Mawyndulë couldn't hold his tongue any longer. He'd been excluded from the plans for the giant attack—*The Punishment,* as his father had called it—which hadn't punished anyone. He couldn't continue to sit idly by while fools blathered so. The prince pushed to his feet, slapped the little desk with the untouched water pitcher, and said, "Settle back down? Are you hearing yourselves? We need to slaughter them all!"

"Mawyndulë!" his father snapped. "You don't have a voice at these proceedings."

"I'm a councilor of the Aquila."

"A *junior* councilor, and as you might have noticed, there aren't any senior councilors in attendance."

"But I *should* have a voice. I'm the only one making sense, and it's the same thing Gryndal would say—"

"First Minister Gryndal isn't here," Vasek interrupted. "And no one knows what he may or may not have—"

"He's not *here* because they murdered him! And that's why they *must* die. All of them!"

"You are excused," his father told Mawyndulë with a sharp voice.

"But I—"

"Out. Now!"

Mawyndulë left, but before he did, he overturned the desk, shattering the pitcher and the glasses. Childish, but then they were acting like children, too, and it felt good to break something.

Mawyndulë wasn't planning on going to the Rose Bridge. He told himself that even as he ducked into the Garden, avoiding the evening crowds in Florella Plaza. He would come out on the north side of the city, which *would* put him in easy reach of the bridge—just in case he changed his mind. All he really wanted was to get out of the Talwara and away from his father. He thought the fane might go looking for him after the meeting, and Mawyndulë decided he'd rather not be found.

I might go after all. Wouldn't mind seeing Makareta again. I'm already in the area.

Mawyndulë had liked talking to her. She didn't seem like a genius or anything, but in some ways that made her even more appealing. Nearly everyone knew more than him, or acted as if they did just because they were centuries older. Mawyndulë liked that Makareta didn't put on airs. In a way, that made her smarter—or at least more genuine.

While walking through the Garden, Mawyndulë considered the design and decided the rocks were a little too perfectly placed and the shrubs too neat. He supposed the intent was to fool visitors about a pristine origin. History held that it had been designed by Gylindora Fane and Caratacus, and then built by the founders of the Eilywin tribe. He would have preferred to see the Garden more natural, which meant messy and haphazard.

The longer he studied his surroundings, the more certain he became that Gylindora had everything wrong. What did she know anyway? Yes, she had been the first fane, but she wasn't there when life sprouted on Elan. Mawyndulë was convinced the cradle of life had been in utter disarray.

People always expected order, they liked believing in symmetry and equity, but no such things existed without applying force. His father likely felt he was being *evenhanded* by dismissing his son in the council chambers rather than hearing his extremely valuable advice. If life were fair, his father would see the righteousness of his son's wisdom. With his father's realization would come remorse, and justice would be served. *That* would be fair, but the world didn't work that way, nor was it pretty or perfect.

As he approached the Door, Mawyndulë slowed. Not that he wanted to savor the moment, or to show reverence or respect. He did so because the Door scared him.

Mawyndulë had heard about children daring one another to knock on it, a rite of passage. But he hadn't known any kids when growing up. There were never too many to begin with, which made him think the rumor wasn't true. He'd only approached the Door once, on his twenty-fifth birthday. The Umalyn High Priest had pressed Mawyndulë's palm against its surface and declared him a true Son of Ferrol. The rough wood had felt like a dead tree. No—not a tree—a dead *person*. Remembering it now, Mawyndulë imagined his hand on the face of a corpse, and a chill raced up his back.

Supposedly, paradise lay on the far side of the Door, the place where everyone went upon death. *So what would happen if it opened when I was standing too near? Would it suck me in like a whirlpool? Would I die when crossing the threshold? Maybe it isn't paradise. Maybe it's something else. Something so not-paradise that it had to be locked away.*

Mawyndulë worked his way to the circle that surrounded the Door. The Garden was designed to bring everyone to the center, so he couldn't avoid it entirely, but he kept to the outside ring, skirting the area around the benches. The sun was down, and only a faint gray light remained. The dimness made the Door appear that much more ominous. When he was young, Mawyndulë had had nightmares about being there alone at night. In his dream, someone was always knocking. As he drew closer, he realized the sound came from the Door's other side. He'd struggle to keep himself from reaching out, a battle perpetually lost. Even as he extended his hand, Mawyndulë tried to convince himself it wouldn't matter, because the Door couldn't be opened. But of course he was wrong. He always woke before seeing what horror was on the other side, and maybe that was worse—the not knowing.

As Mawyndulë went around, he spotted a person sitting on one of the benches. During the day, that wasn't unusual, but after dark it was downright creepy. The guy wore a dirty brown robe, stained and tattered. He had dark hair and the ghost of a beard.

Not a Miralyith.

The figure sat leaning forward, staring at the Door. Mawyndulë didn't pause; he kept moving and slipped by. The fellow on the bench never looked up; he didn't move a muscle.

Maybe Mawyndulë would go to the Rose Bridge after all. He was curious about the meeting and who attended. Perhaps they were a bunch of nuts who turned their backs on Ferrol and worshipped the moon or something crazy like that. He wondered how many would be there—he'd prefer just Makareta. As much as he hoped that might be, he knew it wouldn't happen. She didn't seem like the type to stand alone under a bridge at night, but hadn't he already determined she wasn't too intelligent? Odd for a Miralyith, but he supposed not all the gifted could be smart. The creative ones could be pretty dumb, actually—Arion, for example.

He started picturing Makareta, standing in the dark, rubbing her chilled arms, searching intently. Maybe she had concocted the whole story to lure him to a place where they could be alone. He imagined her shyly admitting her attraction. She'd have to confess the truth when he arrived and no one else was around.

Is it okay for a nobody like me to be out, unescorted, with the prince? she would ask.

He found himself grinning as he slipped out of the Garden, and he was walking quickly by the time he turned onto the narrow lane that went downhill toward the river. With any luck, he wouldn't even go home that night, and his father could search the palace all he wanted.

If Mawyndulë needed any further proof that the world wasn't fair, he didn't have to look any farther than the Rose Bridge.

Makareta wasn't alone.

Fifteen, possibly twenty, people clustered under the span that crossed the Shinara River. At midsummer the water level was low, and there was plenty of room among the flat rocks. The gathering looked like an odd late-night picnic. Several had brought cloths, laying them over the stone. They had baskets of fruit and cheese and bottles of wine by the crate. Several people stood around, sipping from wooden cups. Each attendee had a dark, hooded cloak, though few actually wore them. They carried the garments across an arm or tossed over a shoulder. Perhaps they expected colder temperatures as the night wore on. Mawyndulë wondered if he should have brought something warmer as well, but the night was muggy and he didn't expect needing more than his asica. If anything, he wished he had worn his short linen one, but he had dressed for the council meeting and hadn't taken the time to change.

Without a moon, the space below the bridge was dim but not dark. Illumination came from buoyant lights. Sparkling balls of various colors bobbed and floated like bubbles. He'd seen them before, usually at Miralyith-hosted festivals. The lights reflected off the surface of the Shinara and lit the underside of the bridge. Everything under the span was splashed with the strange upside-down illumination that rippled across the stone pylons and people's faces, giving it all a carnival glow.

"You made it!" Makareta shouted as she appeared out of a clump of people and rushed to his side. She was wearing her cloak, though it was cast back over both shoulders like a cape. In her hand she held a wooden cup.

Makareta hugged him.

Mawyndulë froze. He hadn't expected an embrace, and he didn't know what to do. He'd never been hugged before. Rumors said mothers hugged their children; Mawyndulë knew for a fact fathers didn't.

When she drew back, he saw the cup that had been in her hand was floating beside her. She offered an embarrassed half smile and said, "Didn't want to spill wine on you. What a nice asica. Little warm for tonight, though."

"You're the one in the cloak," he blurted out, and hated the confrontational tone. Thankfully, she didn't seem insulted and let out a little laugh.

"We all have these. They were Aiden's idea. He thought we should have a symbol of unity, you know? A little silly, I suppose. I mean they're too hot in summer and not nearly warm enough in winter, but we're expected to wear them at every meeting. No one does, but at least we bring them. Better than tattoos. That's what Rinald wanted. He thought they would show a real commitment. But we couldn't agree on a design or where they should go. The whole thing became too much of a hassle, so we settled for the cloaks. Inga and Flynn make them."

"By hand?"

Makareta laughed. "Of course not."

Mawyndulë was still thinking about the hug. In retrospect he decided he liked it. She had smelled like lilacs, and he recalled the warmth of her cheek against his neck and her bald head against his jaw. The squeezing was nice, too, the way her arms felt around his back. If he had known, if he hadn't been so blindsided, he would have returned the hug. He would have liked to let his palms solve the riddle of what was clothes and what was Makareta. Maybe, before the night was over, he'd have another chance.

"Here. Have some wine," she said, and the cup drifted toward him. "It's really good. Inga brought it. So much better than the ghastly swill Rinald said was supposed to be a rare vintage from a famed vintner. Everyone hated that. But this is excellent; try it."

Mawyndulë grabbed the floating cup, which was wet on one side where it had spilled a little. He didn't want it. He didn't care for wine. He mostly drank water, and loved apple cider when it was in season. He disliked the sensation of wine and mead. He hadn't touched either of them since his first taste at the age of thirteen. He also had never shared the same cup with anyone. He was the prince. He didn't share anything, but Mawyndulë took it from her. He looked inside, but saw only a dark liquid. Over the brim, Makareta's big kitten eyes peered at him expectantly. Placing the cup to his lips, he took the tiniest of sips. He got mostly air, but a little of the wine as well. *Fruity,* he thought, sweeter than he remembered. He took a second taste, a bigger one. The wine surprised him—light, not biting or bitter.

After another sip, he noticed a crowd of bald heads around him. "Is everyone Miralyith?"

"Oh, yes," she said with sudden gravity. "Non-Mira aren't allowed."

"Why?"

"We talk about stuff; things others wouldn't understand."

"Like what?"

"Like how Miralyith shouldn't have to hide under a bridge to speak the truth. Am I right?" The speaker was a tall Fhrey—taller than Mawyndulë—who approached them carrying two fresh drinks, one of which he handed to Makareta.

"This is Aiden," she said.

"And this is the famous Mawyndulë." Aiden grinned. "Makareta said there was a chance you might visit our humble gathering, but I didn't believe her. Who would? Let me just say, it is an honor to have you here."

Aiden looked older than Makareta, but he was still young—under five hundred maybe, in his first millennium certainly. Older people had a dusty way about them. *Dusty* was a word Mawyndulë had recently begun applying to people with dated mannerisms and tastes, as well as an archaic mentality that mirrored something left on a shelf too long to be useful. Those in their second millennium—while they didn't appear too old—moved, talked, and possessed attitudes that betrayed their age. They screamed *old*, as if from another world, an ancient one covered in sediment. Aiden was young. So was Makareta, as was everyone under the bridge that he'd seen so far.

"And what exactly do you do? I mean what is everyone here for?" Mawyndulë asked, looking around.

Closer to the river, three fellows in gray cloaks held a water war. They coaxed balls of liquid from the stream, much as he had at the fountain with Vidar, and launched them at one another. Mawyndulë had seen Miralyith play the same game at holiday festivals, and it had always looked like fun.

"To enjoy the company of the *right people* without having to suffer fools, inferiors, or those who are too stupid to tell the difference. Am I right?" Aiden replied, and Makareta nodded.

Aiden had a little smile that stayed on his lips as he spoke. Probably fake. Mawyndulë believed most smiles were. But maybe Aiden's was real; most young people didn't fake-smile. That was a *dusty* trait. Aiden could genuinely be awestruck by his princely presence.

"We believe our culture is on the cusp of a new era. It's been nearly twelve thousand years since Estramnadon was founded, since Gylindora Fane and Caratacus led us here and established our society. Did you know Gylindora was a Nilyndd . . . a crafter?"

Does he think I'm an idiot?

"Of course he knows that," Makareta said with enough disdain to put a genuine smile on Mawyndulë's face.

Aiden looked annoyed, or maybe it was embarrassment at being corrected in front of the prince. "Okay, but did you know she used to make *baskets?*"

Mawyndulë was pleased to see just as much surprise on Makareta's face.

"Ah-hah!" Aiden declared victory. "I thought so. Most people don't know that, but it's true. That was her craft, making baskets from river grass. Can you imagine? A fane. A basket weaver! Life was very different then. So much of our society was established in a time before . . . well . . . before the Art for one. I think it goes without saying that if the Miralyith had been one of the original founding tribes, Gylindora wouldn't have been our first fane. Am I right?"

Mawyndulë found himself nodding as he took another sip of wine. At first glance, he hadn't liked Aiden. He didn't care for anyone taller than himself, and Aiden's habit of repeating *Am I right?* was certainly annoying. But most of all he didn't like that Aiden had given Makareta a cup of wine. Maybe it didn't mean anything. Perhaps they were just friends, but it bothered Mawyndulë all the same.

He couldn't argue, however, with Aiden's high opinion of Miralyith. What he had said was as comfortable as old slippers. Mawyndulë had thought the same for years. And while he knew Gylindora had been of the Nilyndd tribe, he'd never heard about the basket-weaving thing. That was pathetic, but also exactly what he would've expected.

"What your father did to that Instarya leader in the Carfreign changed everything. It showed that not even the warrior tribe can hope to challenge us for dominance. And the way he played with him? That was awesome. When Lothian finally obliterated Zephyron like a toy, that really sent a message. All the other tribes now know the truth about the Miralyith. We aren't just a stronger tribe; we're a different people altogether. A higher sort of being."

"Gryndal used to say the Miralyith were the new gods," Mawyndulë said.

Aiden grinned. "Did Gryndal tell you he was part of our group?"

Mawyndulë was stunned.

"The founding member, actually. A genius." Aiden's grin faded to a sickened look. "I can't believe what happened to him. To be killed like that . . . by a *Rhune*."

"Mawyndulë was there, weren't you?" Makareta said.

He nodded and finished the last of his wine—a large mouthful—and he found himself wishing there was more.

"That must have been horrible," she said, shortening the distance between them.

Mawyndulë didn't like people standing too close, but Makareta was an exception. He also liked that she was now nearer to him than to Aiden.

"Everyone heard how you tried to kill the Rhune. You were summoning fire, yes?" she asked.

Mawyndulë nodded.

"A perfect choice," Aiden said. "I would've tried the same."

"No, you wouldn't," Makareta said reproachfully. "Neither one of us would. We would've been struck stupid, paralyzed at the sight of Gryndal's headless body. We wouldn't have been able to *think*, much less *do* anything."

"Maybe *you* wouldn't, but I certainly would have," Aiden said, sounding angry and perhaps a little hurt.

Mawyndulë didn't want to gloat, but he couldn't help smiling.

"I don't think you know what you would or wouldn't have done," Makareta said. "The last time, and I bet the only time, you saw anyone die, much less witnessed anyone being *killed,* was that Instarya leader in the arena. He wasn't Miralyith, not one of our people, but I still cried."

"That's *you,*" Aiden said. "I didn't cry. I laughed."

Mawyndulë hadn't laughed or cried. After seeing what his father had done to Zephyron, Mawyndulë left the stands, went behind the support pillar near the service gate, and vomited. He worked hard to avoid thinking about the challenge, and he'd pushed away the memories of the day Gryndal died. Mawyndulë had tried to erase the dual visions of blood and gore, especially the horror when the First Minister's head came free and fell. There had been so much blood. He thought he could still taste the vomit on his tongue.

"You're such the hero, aren't you?" Makareta told Aiden.

Aiden's expression soured. "I'm just saying that fire was a good choice. That's all."

"Well, I agree with that," Makareta conceded. Taking Mawyndulë's empty cup, she handed him her full one.

"Maybe," Mawyndulë said. "Won't ever know because The Traitor stopped me." He refused to refer to Arion by name anymore. His old tutor would forever be known as *The Traitor.*

All three shook their heads in disgust. "Bitch," they said in unison.

Such a perfect harmony made them all smile, and in that shared moment, Mawyndulë felt at one with the universe. Everything made sense in a way it never had before. It all felt good and right. He liked the wine—the way it tasted and how it made him feel. The floating carnival lights and the people playing with water were wonderful. He liked the silly robes, the hidden secret fellowship, and the atmosphere provided by the dark underside of the bridge. Mawyndulë even decided he liked Aiden. But more than anything else, he liked Makareta. He liked *her* a lot.

"This is fun," Mawyndulë said, and took another sip of wine, surprised that his new cup was already mostly empty.

"Does that mean you'll come back?" Makareta asked.

"If I do, can I have a cloak?"

"Only members get those. Would you like to join?"

Mawyndulë decided with barely a thought. What was there to think about? These were the most sensible people he'd ever met. They were smart, welcoming, and more like a family than anything he'd experienced in the Talwara. And then there was Makareta. Mawyndulë licked the wine from his lips and wondered what it would be like to kiss her.

"I'd love to," he said. "You're my kind of people."

CHAPTER TEN

Something to Believe In

We were the same age, but I do not recall seeing him in Tirre. I have been told that he was little more than an animal then, an abandoned boy surviving the aftermath in the shadows and tall grass. No one could have guessed what he would become. I know I did not.

—THE BOOK OF BRIN

The tent still leaked.

Raithe watched water fall from sagging cloth where overhead pools had formed, three of them, and each one dripped. He wasn't complaining—quite the opposite. He was amazed that pieces of stretched cloth could keep the area mostly dry after four solid days of rain.

Clan Rhen had settled along the northern wall of Dahl Tirre. The stacked-stone barrier ringing the village had provided shelter from the wind, which blew in endlessly from the sea. The open field afforded plenty of room to spread out, and after the villagers unloaded the carts, they dug a series of fire pits and stored the supplies. Water had been pulled from Tirre's well, originally a source of tension with the locals who insisted the newcomers needed to wait each day until all the Tirreans were finished. Despite this, everything had worked out fairly well until the rain.

The downpour made the days difficult and sleeping a misery. Under such deplorable conditions, frustration led to anger and dissent spread. Complaints grew frequent, including regrets about accepting Persephone as chieftain and the decision to leave Dahl Rhen. After hearing them, Raithe stayed close to her and walked with one hand on his sword.

This is how it'll end. How everything will fall apart, he had thought with irony. *Not with war or the might of the Fhrey's magic but with rain.*

Then Roan had started unrolling the wool.

For centuries, hunters had built shelters from animal skins, but there hadn't been many of those in the dahl. What they did have plenty of was wool. Roan adapted the concept, and soon Persephone had assigned a small army to follow Roan's directions. Using spears as poles, a series of taut awnings were fashioned that butted against the wall. When supports ran out, Roan dismantled the carts. The trick was in the angle that caused the water to run off. Soon a narrow porch was erected, providing enough shelter to sleep and cook beneath if everyone took turns. A few hours out of the rain to eat a warm meal or take a nap eased rebellious thoughts—at least for a while. Raithe worried what winter would bring, even though he had no intention of being there when the snows fell.

"Mind if I have a look?" Flood asked, pointing at Raithe's sword.

Raithe had ducked under the wool near Padera's cooking pit for his midday meal. He'd picked a bad time, as the three Dherg were there, too. Why they were still around he couldn't understand. They were always underfoot, and more than a little annoying. "Why?"

Flood shrugged. "Strange seeing someone like you with a bronze sword. I thought your kind still used stone-tipped spears."

Raithe didn't like the tone. "And *your kind* are just plain strange."

Flood harrumphed, folded his little arms, and scowled.

Raithe pulled the sword from his belt.

The Dherg flinched.

"Relax. You said you wanted to see it."

"See it not feel it."

Raithe flipped the weapon around, presenting the pommel. Flood hesitated, then reached out and took the blade. He held it up to the light and studied the edge.

"Took this from that elf you killed?" Flood asked.

"Elf?"

"Elf, Fhrey, same thing. Only they hate *elf* more." He gestured once more toward the weapon. "So is that where you got this blade?"

Raithe nodded. "Elf-made bronze." The Dherg scowled and shook his head as if the sword had insulted him.

"Best weapon I've ever had. What's wrong with it?"

The Dherg handed the weapon back. "Feel how light it is."

"Yeah, that's what makes it good."

Flood rolled his eyes. "This is the product of laziness. Look at the blade. See the color? It's almost white."

"So, why is that a problem?" Raithe asked, certain Flood was trying to find fault where there wasn't any.

"Bronze is made from combining copper and tin. Tin has a lower melting point, so it's easier to liquefy than copper. This sword is tin-heavy. That's why it's so light in color and weight. If it had more copper, it'd have a golden hue and would be stronger. Copper . . . good copper . . . is scarce. Can't really make a good bronze sword without it, and there are better uses for copper if you come across it. For instance, black bronze is used to make our most revered statues. It's made by mixing gold and silver with copper." He pointed at the sword as Raithe put it back in his belt. "That's not a sword. Not a real one. It's cheap cosmetic jewelry."

"Well, it cut right through this." Raithe hauled out the broken end of his father's blade, which was sheathed on his back.

Flood looked it over. "Where'd you get this?"

"Handed down by members of my family. Supposedly a Dherg made it."

Flood frowned. "Belgriclungreian, if you please."

Raithe smirked. "Is that a word or did you belch?"

"Point is we didn't make this. We haven't made copper swords since before the War of Elven Aggression. And no one would make a sword this long out of copper, too weak. But I guess I don't have to tell you that."

It didn't surprise Raithe that his family heirloom, the thing his father loved more than his wife, daughter, and sons put together, was worthless. He expected Flood to toss the half-a-sword back at him, but he kept it, turning the hilt over and over in his little hands. The Dherg licked the metal, and amazement washed over his face.

"What?"

"It's copper."

"You had to lick it to tell that? Of course it's copper."

"I mean it's *pure* copper. I'd say"—he licked again—"ninety-five, ninety-eight percent." Flood looked up at him as if this should mean something. "I told you copper is scarce. Most of it was mined out during the war. Pure copper is more valuable than gold these days. I'm not a swordsmith, but in the hands of a good one, this sword could be melted down and turned into quite a few excellent weapons. Much better than that elven ornament you're carrying."

Flood handed the broken end back, and by then the line for food had moved up. The Dherg went on ahead, leaving Raithe to consider that his father's belief in the value of that blade might not have been so misplaced.

A short time after Raithe finished his meal, the rain was either stopping or taking another of its momentary pauses. Persephone ventured out from under the wool, and he watched her take a few tentative steps, navigating the brown puddles. She paused, looking up with a squint, and then she winced, as the rain hadn't given up entirely. She wiped her face, held out her palms for a few seconds, and then set out into the open, walking down the length of the encampment.

Raithe, who had been scraping a rabbit skin, stuffed the pelt into the folds of his leigh mor and jogged after her. She hadn't gone far, following the wall to the main gate, which wasn't completely repaired—the work having been delayed by the rain.

"And where might you be going?" he asked.

She turned with a quizzical eye. "A Shield isn't supposed to question their chieftain's actions."

"And a chieftain isn't supposed to be running off without their Shield, and yet you do so often. Are you trying to avoid me?"

"No, it's not like that." She shook her head. "I like having you around.

I was just going for a walk, tired of being trapped under wool. It's good you're here, though. We need to talk."

"Oh?" He raised an eyebrow.

"Yeah, but it can wait. Come. Walk with me. I need some time away from all that's going on. Have you been down to the ocean yet?"

"Saw it from the hill on the road when we arrived."

She laughed, and it almost sounded carefree. Almost.

"That's not the same thing. From up there it's not alive." She held out her hand, and he took it in his. "Come, let me introduce you."

She led him to a narrow trail that wove between wet rocks down to a sandy beach strewn with seaweed. From a distance, the plants looked like clumps of a giant's hair, torn and scattered. Beyond the sand, the sea was a flat blue-gray, stretching out to eternity. Near the shore, waves rolled in, first a line of dark rippling blue that slowly moved toward them. Then the ripples reared up like a gaping maw, showing white teeth before crashing with astounding fury. Foam spewed and surged across the sand, chasing the feet of gulls.

"It's massive," he said, staring out at the endless expanse.

She nodded. "Rumors say oceans have no end; they go on forever. This is just a narrow strait." She pointed to the horizon. "Caric and Neith are out that way, but if you were to sail south around the coast of Belgreig, you'd enter the endless water of the Blue Sea."

"What makes the big ripples?" he asked, thinking about the size of a boulder that would create such things.

"The sea god, Eraphus. The people of Dahl Tirre believe he's splashing out there somewhere. They don't have the same relationship with their god as we do with Mari. Rather than expecting blessings, they fear his reprisals. Many a massive storm has ravaged their seaside home. Eraphus's Wrath is what they call such a storm, and only after it arrives do they determine which transgression brought the destruction."

Staring at the water and the hammering waves, Raithe considered that if Eraphus really existed, he'd have to be considerably bigger than the largest giants and more powerful than any Fhrey. Since learning the Fhrey were mortal, he had wondered if there were *any* real gods.

"It's frighteningly beautiful."

She nodded. "Indeed. It's also where we came from. All the Rhunes. Can you imagine what it must have been like? I mean, being Gath of Odeon and telling everyone to get on floating bits of wood and sail out into that expanse of nothingness? I don't know how he convinced them. He must have believed it was the only way to save our people. He couldn't know where he'd end up, how long it would take, or even if there was anywhere else. He risked the lives of everyone, on the hope of finding something he didn't know existed."

They said nothing for a time, each lost in their own thoughts, then she said, "Tegan of Clan Warric and Harkon of Melen arrived last night."

"I heard."

"That's the last of them. All the Rhulyn chieftains are assembled. I really didn't expect the Gula chieftains would show up. But I wish they had. The meeting will begin tomorrow."

"Heard that, too."

"This is the first time in a hundred years . . . probably more . . . that all the chieftains will be together."

"Not *all* the chieftains," Raithe said. "Walon and Eten are dead."

"A man named Alward is the new chieftain of Nadak. You probably saw them. The whole clan is just fifty or sixty people now, mostly men. They're camping near the eastern end of the wall."

"And Dureya?"

Persephone looked down at her feet for a moment. "That's what I wanted to talk to you about. I've asked the other chieftains, and they all say the same thing. There haven't been any other survivors . . . no refugees from even the most remote village. As far as we can tell, you're the only one that's left of the Dureyan clan."

"Lucky me," he said with more bite than he intended. Having his whole clan wiped out by the Fhrey wasn't Persephone's fault.

"In a way, you are fortunate. As far as the other leaders are concerned, you're the Dureyan chieftain."

"Meaning what exactly?"

"It means you'll have a vote, an equal say in who becomes keenig. It also means you can't be my Shield anymore. So I'm officially dismissing you. If you were both, the others might think I was influencing your vote. Besides, the post never really suited you. You don't like taking direction from anyone."

"I can't be a chieftain if there's no clan."

"We don't know for certain that all the Dureyans are dead. A month or a year from now survivors could turn up, and they should be represented."

She sighed and ran a hand through her hair. It was wet with the fog and the sea's spray. The mist left jeweled droplets along the strands. Her cheeks were moist and glistened in the intermittent sunlight. She stood facing the water, hands on her head, the constant wind blowing her dress.

He tried to stop himself from what he was about to say but couldn't. "Persephone . . . I have to ask. I mean, a lot has happened since . . . what I'm trying to say is, have you reconsidered leaving with me?"

"Going with you to Avrlyn?" The sadness in her eyes deepened. "You can't still be thinking about that."

"Just hear me out. Before, you wanted to stay for the people you considered your family: Sarah and Brin, Moya and Padera, Gifford and Roan. You had a home to fight for, and Konniger's incompetence was threatening everyone's future. But your village has been destroyed, just like mine. In Avrlyn, we could build something new. Something good and lasting. You've done what was needed for your people. You've convinced the chieftains to band together and appoint a keenig. Nyphron has agreed to train the troops. You've done your part. Now let others do theirs."

She started to reply, but he interrupted her.

"I'm not saying it has to be just the two of us. I'm not asking you to leave the ones you love behind. Bring whoever you want. We can all go, Malcolm and Suri, too. If we leave now, we'll have time to build a shelter before the snow flies. As for food, there's an abundance of game, and the rivers are filled with fish. I have the perfect place picked out. A bluff overlooking the Urum River that has an exposed cliff with flint shards. It's perfect."

She stared at him again for a long while, and her expression became confused, then upset. "You can't be serious. I can't leave. I'm responsible for more than just a handful of people. All of Rhen is counting on me."

"Not anymore." Raithe pointed back at the dahl. "Once the keenig is appointed, it'll be *his* responsibility to keep everyone safe. Not yours. You did your part. You're done."

"I'm not done . . . and you can't be, either. This doesn't end with the appointing of a keenig. We're chieftains, leaders of our people."

"I—have—no—people! You said so yourself. It's just me, and I have no interest in being the keenig. Look, you've lived your whole life in Dahl Rhen, protected from the Gula–Rhulyn wars. You have no idea what lies ahead. And you know what? Neither do I, but I understand better than you about what's coming. If we fight, we'll die. If we leave, then we have a chance to live. And if we live, *then* we might be able to do some good. Maybe we can build something that will withstand the Fhrey if for no other reason than they don't know we exist."

Persephone threw up her hands. "You're right. I know nothing about war. But let me tell you what I believe. I think running from responsibility breeds self-loathing and despair. I think people can, and do, rise to the occasion, and even a single person can make an incredible difference. What they need are leaders who believe in them, a belief that gives birth to hope. With hope, people can do remarkable things, amazing things. Between hope and despair, I'll take hope every time."

"Hope without cause is insanity."

"I have cause. I believe in us. I believe we can win if we're brave, if we're committed. I believe people can do anything if they try hard enough."

"Then you believe in fantasies."

"I would call them dreams. Maybe that is all they are, but aren't those ideals worth believing in?" She took a deep breath. "If you want to leave, then go. But I'm staying here. You say you don't have any people? Well, open your eyes. We're all in this together. We're all the same people. It's not about Dureya or Nadak or Rhen. We're fighting for the lives of all of us. Maybe you should think less about yourself and more about others."

She grabbed the hem of her skirt and headed back up the beach.

Raithe marched back toward his spot under the wool with a singular purpose: *I'm leaving.*

Coming to Tirre was a huge waste of my time. She'll never leave. She doesn't give a damn about me! She would rather die in a futile war than make a new start and be happy.

He didn't need Persephone. He could go alone if he had to. Other people had always been a problem. His brothers had beaten him. His father had dragged Raithe across the river and gotten himself killed. His clan's reputation had labeled him a villain since the day he was born. The only thing others had ever given him was grief.

I'll be better off without her. Why did I stay so long?

The rain was falling again by the time he rounded the corner and reached the tiny niche where he and Malcolm stored their possessions. Malcolm's spear leaned up against the stone wall next to Bergin's brewing equipment and his daughter's bed. Not being Dureyan, Malcolm didn't feel the need to carry his weapon everywhere he went.

Overhead, the rain drummed on the cloth as Raithe knelt and grabbed the big bag Padera had given him. Roan had shown the old woman how to incorporate a clever drawstring, which kept the mouth closed. He jerked the bag open and started stuffing things in: a half-dozen flints, three knives, the hand ax he'd made in Dureya, a little hammer, a gift from Roan that replaced the smooth stone he used to use. Needle and thread that he got from Moya went in, along with the blanket Sarah had woven. Last, he dropped in the bowl Gifford had made. Standing, he slung the sheep's bladder waterskin over his shoulder, another gift from Roan.

How did I get so much stuff?

Before coming to Dahl Rhen, he'd had only a handful of things. Now he'd accumulated so much that he needed a bag. What he didn't need was excess weight. Reaching up, he pulled the copper sword off his back and tossed it to the ground. It might be worth something to the Dherg, but not to him. Not anymore.

"Going somewhere?" Malcolm asked.

"Leaving," Raithe replied without turning. He held the bag with one hand while searching with his other for whatever else he might have missed.

"Sounds urgent. Something happen?"

"Yeah, I woke up. I remembered I'm Dureyan, and the world hates me." Raithe scooped up a stick with a wad of woolen thread wound around it and stuffed it into the bag.

"Who hates you?"

Raithe turned and saw that Malcolm wasn't alone. He stood beneath the edge of the awning, his arm on the shoulder of a barefoot boy who clutched a stone knife in his right hand and a wood carving in his left. While both of them were wet, the kid was soaked. His hair and tattered shirt lay plastered to his pale slick skin, and his ribs were clearly outlined above his rope belt. The boy's eyes were dark and shadowed as if he hadn't slept in weeks.

"Is it a secret?" Malcolm reached for a blanket to dry himself, and when finished he offered it to his young companion. The lad ignored him and just stood there, waiting and letting water drip down his face. Raithe recognized the kid. He was the same boy whose parents had been killed by the runaway wagon.

Raithe frowned. "Huh? No. I was referring to Persephone."

"I'm guessing she's not going with you, then."

"And you'd be right." Raithe reached into the bag and adjusted the contents so the sharp edges wouldn't jab as he carried it. "Turns out she'd rather stay here and die than be with me. But I guess that's to be expected, right? I mean, I'm still Dureyan." Raithe looked over and pointed at the boy. "Remember that, kid. You might think your life is terrible right now, but it could be worse. You could be Dureyan."

The boy stood a little straighter. "I am Dureyan."

Raithe stopped packing. "But your parents, they didn't look . . . their clothes—"

"Weren't my parents." The boy wiped the rain from his face with the inside of his elbow.

That was what Raithe had seen the day the wagon got loose, the strange sense of familiarity he'd noticed. Clan Dureya had a way of moving, a way of speaking. "Who were they?"

He shrugged. "Just some farmers from one of the Rhen villages. The man was called Lon and the woman Rita. They gave me food and let me sleep in their house."

"So where *are* your parents?"

"Dead." That one word, and the casual way the boy dropped it, brushed aside all doubt.

"You *are* Dureyan."

The boy looked back at him with a hard gaze. *"So?"*

No truer word was ever spoken. The kid was from his clan. At least two of them had survived. "I'm from Clempton village, on the west side."

"East side," the kid said. "No name, was just three families. The Fhrey killed everyone."

"Rumor has it they're not done yet." Raithe looked to Malcolm. "I'm heading out. You coming?"

"Do you really think Persephone refused to go with you because you're Dureyan?"

"I don't know, maybe. Sure, why not? Why should she be any different?"

"Why are you so angry?"

"I'm not angry. What makes you say I'm angry?" Raithe jerked the mouth of the bag closed by pulling on the drawstring so hard that it broke. He looked at the torn bit of leather in his hand and frowned. "I just . . ." He sighed. "I was trying to save her life. There's no winning against the Fhrey, and she won't listen to reason. Everyone here is going to die."

He looked at the boy. "Sorry, kid, but it's true. Persephone believes determination is all that's required. That's the difference between Rhen and Dureyan thinking." Raithe toggled his finger back and forth between himself and the boy. "We know better. Believing in something isn't enough, and luck is never on your side. The only luck is bad luck. And while disasters happen all the time, there's no such thing as miracles. You wanna know why? It's because the gods hate us, and they take every opportunity to prove it."

"So you're just going to leave?" Malcolm asked.

"That's the plan." Raithe hoisted the strap of the bag over his shoulder and adjusted it. "If you're coming, grab your spear. You're gonna need it. I suppose the kid can come too, as long as he doesn't whine or anything."

"You're a coward," the boy said.

He fixed the kid with a cold stare. "What'd you call me?"

If Persephone, or even Malcolm, had made the remark, Raithe would have ignored it, but the boy was Dureyan and knew the consequences of his words. In the parched desolation that was their shared homeland, there was no greater insult. Blood always followed that accusation. The kid knew that, and he held his knife at the ready.

"Your mouth is making promises your body can't keep, boy."

The other Dureyan didn't back down. He rose on the balls of his feet and shifted his right foot back slightly. He knew how to fight—not unusual for a Dureyan. Such an education came right along with walking and talking.

"You're running from the Fhrey who killed our people. What else do you call that? I'm not a chieftain, and I don't even have a sword, but I'm going to kill them," the kid said in cold measure. "All of them. Every last one, just like they did to us. I owe that to my parents, to my clan. You do, too."

"My *people* are dead and so are yours."

"That's right," the kid said. "Don't you hear 'em? How can you ignore their cries from the pits of Phyre? Are you *that* deaf?" The boy had the courage to take a step forward. "I watched them kill my father, and when my mother was weeping over his body, one of them . . . one of them . . ." He squeezed his lips together, and clamped his jaw for a moment, sucking air through his nose so that the nostrils flared with his short puffs. "I'm going to kill every last one."

No tears, and the kid's voice was steady.

Raithe smiled. Dureyans weren't the smartest, or prettiest, and they certainly weren't the richest, but his people were a breed above when it came to grit. They were the granite amid sandstone. Still, the kid was being stupid. "If you try to fight, they'll kill you. You'll be slaughtered like everyone else."

The kid shook his head. "I'll sneak up at night and—"

"Won't help. Their pointed ears hear everything. You won't catch them off guard. And they see much better than you do in the dark. And they're more skilled in combat than any human."

"Not you. You're the God Killer." He pointed at Malcolm. "That's what he said."

"I was lucky."

"Only real luck is bad. You just said so."

If nothing else, the boy paid attention. He was starting to like the kid.

"You could teach me," the boy said. "Train me to kill Fhrey like you have."

Raithe shook his head. "I'm leaving, and you seem to want to stick around for the war."

"You *have* to train me."

"I don't *have* to do anything, not anymore."

"The clan chieftain is responsible for teaching young men to fight. That's Dureyan law."

"I'm not the chieftain." Raithe paused to think. "I never said I was the chieftain, did I?" He looked at Malcolm, who shrugged.

"Who is then?" the boy asked. "In the meeting tomorrow, who will speak for Dureya?"

"There is no Dureya."

The look on the kid's face was a potent mix of shock and disappointment. He pointed at Malcolm. "He told me you were the God Killer and that you could teach me." He shook his head in disgust. "Only things I've learned are you run from a fight, ignore the cries of your clan, and break our laws." The kid frowned. "Who knows. Maybe God Killer is an undeserved title, but I'm certain of one thing. You aren't Dureyan."

Raithe hated his people. They were vicious, crude, and cruel. Elan would be a finer place without Dureyans. Despite this, the kid's words hurt. Raithe didn't know why. It made as much sense as his father sacrificing his life for a copper sword.

Pride. The idea spilled in as he looked at the kid. How many boys his age could have lost their family—their whole village—and still challenge the God Killer. That took guts, stupidity too, but guts nonetheless. Where did that strength come from? Raithe was proud of the kid, and couldn't help but feel pride in the clan who bore and raised someone like him. Dignity was the one gift his father—his people—had bestowed, and this boy was stripping it away. As foolish as it was, Raithe couldn't deny such things still mattered. *What good is surviving, if I have to give up everything I am to live?*

The irony was so complete it stung.

Raithe picked up the broken copper sword. The moment he did, the kid shuffled back and lowered his crouch. Raithe shook his head. "Relax. I already lost this fight, and it wasn't with you." He looked at the copper, sighed, and then returned the blade to its place on his back.

"Where'd you find him?" Raithe asked Malcolm.

"Out in the field. He was watching a Galantian training session. He's so thin that I was afraid he wouldn't last the night. And seeing as how you and I are kinda misfits, I thought he'd feel right at home."

"When was the last time you ate, kid?" Raithe asked.

The boy didn't answer.

Raithe laughed. "You can remember everything I say, but you can't remember the last time you ate. Either you're being stubborn, or it's been quite a while. I'm guessing both."

"I have some leftover seed cake," Malcolm said, and dug through the pile of supplies near the wall.

"Leftover?" Raithe asked.

"Meaning I didn't finish it all."

Raithe stared at the man, confounded. "Since when has that ever happened?"

"I lived a long time in a place without want, but being with you has made me pick up bad habits. I now save food for lean times." Malcolm pulled out a thin cloth which was wrapped around torn chunks of the caraway-flavored cake. He held them out to the boy.

The kid didn't move. He hardly breathed as he stared at Malcolm's outstretched hand.

"Go on, take it," Malcolm said.

"What for?" the boy asked.

Malcolm raised his brows. "To eat. Honestly, you Dureyans aren't terribly smart, are you?"

"That's not what he means," Raithe said. "He's expecting a trade. Listen, kid, we are part of the same clan, which means we're family. So, I'm responsible for you. That's how it works."

"Never worked that way before," the boy said. He was still looking at the seed cake. His tongue licked his lips, but his hands never moved. "No one gives food for nothing. I don't have anything to trade, so what do I have to do?"

Raithe thought a moment. "Well, if I'm going to be taking on the *enormous* obligation that is Clan Dureya chieftain, I'll need a Shield."

The boy's sight slipped from the food to look at him. Those dark, hollow eyes tightened in confusion. "I thought you were leaving? I won't go if that's what you're up to. I'm staying to fight, and if you won't train me, then I—"

"If you'd shut up, I'll stay. Apparently, I have traditions to uphold and a very dirty, very hungry, but surprisingly brave clan to lead." Raithe focused on the kid. "I'm not going to say you're the best man for the position. You aren't. Honestly, you'd be more effective if I used you as an *actual* shield, but it's not like I have any better options."

"What about him?" The boy nodded his head toward Malcolm. "Why isn't he your Shield?"

"He's not Dureyan, but I suppose you already knew that. Just look at him."

"I assume you're referring to my unusually good looks," Malcolm said.

Raithe ignored him and addressed the boy. "You're all I have. And I suppose with some food you might eventually amount to something. The one thing you have going for you is that you were born Dureyan, and Dureyans are like flint. If anyone beats us or tries to break our will, they'll chip away an edge sharp enough to cut. So I'm offering food and shelter in return for being my Shield."

"Does that mean you'll train me? What good is a Shield if he doesn't know how to fight?"

Raithe sighed. "Yes, I'll train you. Don't want to be breaking any laws I'd have to punish myself for."

The boy looked at the seed cake again. Then, after stuffing his knife into his belt, he reached out his hand—not to Malcolm, but to Raithe. They shook. The boy squeezed hard. "Agreed," he said.

The boy took the cake and devoured every bit of it in seconds, allowing no crumb to escape.

"*That's* how you treat food," Raithe told Malcolm. Then, looking back at the boy, he asked. "What's your name?"

The kid was still licking his fingers and getting more dirt than crumbs. "Do I have to use my old one, or can I pick something new?"

"I don't care," Raithe said. "I'd just like to know what to yell when I want you."

"Then call me Fhreyhyndia."

"I'm not calling you that."

"It's a Fhrey word," the boy said.

"I know." Raithe wasn't exactly sure what it meant, but he'd heard Nyphron use it several times, usually while pointing his way, so it probably meant ugly or clumsy. "I thought you hated the Fhrey?"

"Do you know what it means?" Malcolm asked.

"Doesn't matter. It's too hard to pronounce."

"It means 'the killer of Fhrey,'" Malcolm supplied.

The boy nodded. "That's what I want to be called because that's what I am going to be. I'll be the greatest warrior who has ever lived, and I'm going to kill every last one of them."

Raithe smiled. *I really do like this kid.* The boy hadn't sprouted a single hair on his chin, and yet he was eager to take up arms against an entire race. "You can't go around with that as a name."

"Why not?"

"It would insult the Galantians, and I need a Shield, not a target. Pick something else. Something simple that won't tie my tongue in knots."

The boy frowned but relented. "I suppose you could call me Tesh."

"Tesh?" Raithe said. "I like Tesh. That's a good Dureyan name."

"I like Fhreyhyndia," the boy grumbled.

"Too bad. It's settled. I'm calling you Tesh," Raithe declared in his best chieftain voice, which he felt lacked all authority.

"Why did you pick Tesh, anyway?" Raithe asked.

The boy shrugged. "That's what my mother named me."

CHAPTER ELEVEN

Under the Wool

As a person who loves words, I take great joy in knowing that I was there when the saying "under the wool" came into being, even if no one these days has any clue about where that phrase originated.

—THE BOOK OF BRIN

The rain finally stopped, and the people of Rhen made an exodus from the wool awnings to bask in the muddy but sunlit field. In a matter of hours, the world returned to a form of normalcy as folks resumed daily tasks. Moya went back to spinning wool, Bruce to carving, and Riggles to his leatherwork. The sheep and pigs were driven out to graze. The only difference was that they were driven by farmers deprived of their fields, who took care of livestock deprived of their shepherds.

"That's much too big," Gifford told Roan as he hobbled over on his crutch.

She looked up and lifted a hand to shield her eyes from the sun that had finally reemerged after days in hiding. Gifford stood over her, a shadowed silhouette in his draped leigh mor, drawn up in summer-style so his knees showed.

"You'll not make a flame with that," he said.

Roan looked at the stick bowed by the taut string secured to the ends.

"Has to be small." Gifford chuckled. "That's as big as you."

She shook her head. "No, it's supposed to be this size. Might need to be thinner though. I'm still working it out."

She plucked the string with a finger and listened to the twang, a deep throaty sound.

"That's not fo' making flames, is it?" Gifford asked.

"No," Roan replied. Setting the bow down, she glanced at Gifford. He didn't ask where she got the wood, and she wondered if he knew. Gifford was smart and a good guesser.

Limited room in the carts meant she could only bring a few things from Rhen, but this was special. She'd heard about the lightning strike that split open the old oak, and something that unusual needed to be seen. Just as described, Magda had been divided in half. Her trunk had been splintered and Roan found one great sliver standing straight up. Blackened only at the tip, the rest was perfect. She took the staff from the exposed heart of the tree with no more intent than bringing a part of Magda home. Now, it was the only wood she possessed suitable to the task.

"What's it fo' then?"

"Throwing things."

Gifford squinted at her and at the stick but didn't ask anything more.

"What have you been up to? Are you making cups again?" she asked, knowing that almost all of Gifford's work had been destroyed. "Yesterday Moya and Brin went down to the village near the sea. Said a bunch of people were trading stuff in a place called the market. According to them, the pottery here is terrible . . . thick and uneven. Everyone uses the coil method. Don't think they know how to spin clay."

"That's because they don't have a Woan to make them a spinning table." He grinned broadly—the good smile.

"They also don't use glazes. They just fill the insides with pitch. Makes everything taste like tar, I'll bet. They would love your stuff. You could trade your pieces."

"And get what?"

"Food, wine, metal, salt. They have a lot of salt here . . . oh, and cloth.

They have something called linen! It's really light and would be great for the hot weather. They dye it in different colors. Moya's got her eye on a purple dress she found. You could have your own stand, a kind of table where things are sold. Brin said the market is filled with crowds of people who wander through and make deals. You'd be huge."

"Maybe we could both use the same stand." Gifford pointed toward the wall. "Those big wooden pots you make is fantastic."

Roan narrowed her eyes. Usually, she understood what he was trying to say. His inability to make the rrr sound, and the embarrassment from trying, made him avoid certain words. Sometimes he got a bit too creative with his substitutions. She knew how much stress talking caused, so whenever possible, she worked out his "Gifford-speak" on her own, but sometimes she just had to ask.

"Barrels?" she posed.

"You named them that?" Gifford sounded hurt, his eyes lowering, his sight falling off her.

"No. I made that mistake once before." She looked at his crutch and frowned. "Barrels is what Rain called them. The little men have names for all kinds of things."

"What would you have called them? Not wooden pots, I suppose."

"No."

"What then?"

"I would probably call them *casks*."

"Why?"

Roan shrugged. "It's short. And there's no 'r' sound in it."

Gifford smiled. He looked out over the field for a moment then said, "Will we be staying long enough to build an oven? Do you know?"

Roan shrugged. "But it doesn't take long to build one. I'll help."

He nodded. "Also need stuff to make glazes."

"There's a sandy beach and a salt sea here. I saw some cliffs, too. With any luck, I might even find some metal. Let's go explore after lunch." Roan looked at the bow. "I wonder if some tin might help strengthen this."

"How is it supposed to wuk?"

"Oh, let me show you. She picked up the javelin from a pile of sticks.

Gifford's eyes nearly fell out. "That's one of the Galantians' javelins."

She nodded. "I borrowed it."

"Does he know? Did he give it to you?"

Roan paused in thought. She hadn't asked, but the one called Eres was there when she borrowed it. He hadn't objected, so he must not have minded. Thinking back, though, she wondered if he had seen her.

She shrugged. "No. Might not have noticed. Now feel this." She held it out. "See how it's weighted?"

He didn't take it, but he did step closer. With an intense look he whispered, "Woan, you . . . you . . . *took* the Fhwey's weapon?"

Gifford never used the word *Fhrey* unless it was important. She didn't understand why he was using it now, but it concerned her.

"Yes, I needed to study it."

"How long have you had it?"

Another shrug. "Couple of days."

"Days!"

"What?"

Gifford took the javelin from her. "I'll deal with it."

"With what?"

"It's not a pwoblem."

Problem? He's nervous about something.

Gifford let bees land on him without flinching, swam in the deep parts of the lake, and even challenged chieftains at meetings. He was the bravest man she knew, so it worried her that he seemed frightened.

"What are you going to do?" she asked.

"I said it's fine, Woan. I'm just going to give it back." He smiled then, but it wasn't his good one. Gifford had many kinds of smiles, and she'd seen them all. When she scolded herself, he wore the sad one—she never understood why. The cheerful grin was often used like a mask for him to hide behind. Then there was the stiff, toothy-faced expression that usually meant he didn't understand—and it was usually accompanied by a slow nod or two. She rarely saw the good smile. She liked that one.

"Oh. I almost fo'got. Bwin wants to see you."

"Where is she?"

"Still un-da the wool."

Roan nodded. "She's been under the wool since the giants attacked."

Gifford looked at her puzzled for a moment. Then he said, "Yes. Yes, I think so. A lot of us have been *un-da the wool* a long time."

Gifford hobbled toward the Galantians' camp, Eres's stolen javelin in one hand, his crutch under the other arm. The warriors respected strength and beauty; he had neither. For years, Gifford had clung to the hope that things could change. He'd believed that if he tried hard enough for long enough, he could will himself to straighten and stand on two feet. It never happened.

But his leg and back weren't the worst of it.

Gifford was also cursed with half a face. Everything was where it ought to be, but like his bad leg, one side was useless. The left sagged and couldn't move, making it difficult to see and torturous to talk.

But his face wasn't the worst of it.

When he was eight, Gavin Killian dubbed Gifford "the goblin," and Myrtis, the brewmaster's daughter, had called him *broken*. Of the two, Gifford preferred goblin—at the time, he'd had a crush on Myrtis. While growing up, it seemed everyone had called him something. Over the years, the names faded, and although people probably still considered him broken, no one said it to his face.

But the name-calling wasn't the worst of it.

For most of his life, Gifford's "morning baths" *had* been the worst of it. He had trouble controlling his bladder; and thankfully the accidents usually occurred at night. He frequently woke in a soaked bed, humiliated and embarrassed. As with his other adversities, he'd found a way to cope, a way to persevere. He drank little, never at night, and made a point to sleep alone, which was easier than he would have liked. He wasn't *that* broken.

Although Gifford's roads appeared narrower, rockier, and strewn with more thorns, he always found a way to cope. Nothing came easy, but he refused to see himself as a victim. It was only when he looked at Roan that he *knew* the worst of it—the worst part of being him—was that the only thing he truly wanted was forever beyond the reach of his feeble body, and no amount of positive thinking could change that.

Gifford would have preferred to stand tall, admit the mistake, and defend Roan like a hero. Instead, he would do what he could, what he was good at, perhaps what he did better than anything else.

Roan found Brin sitting with her back to the wall, wedged between two bushels of grain. On her lap was a flat gray stone, a shard of slate or perhaps shale.

"Roan"—Brin looked up—"you need to help me."

"Okay." Roan expected Brin would want more paint. That was what she usually asked for. Maybe she was planning to start a mural on the dahl's wall.

"Look at this and tell me what it says." Brin held up the stone with several chalk markings. "Ignore the ones I crossed out. Those are mistakes."

"What *it says?*"

"Yes. What is the message? I think I finally got it right. Took a lot of tries."

Roan knelt down beside her, nudging her way in beside one of the bushels, and studied the markings Brin had drawn. They were lines and circles mostly. Four looked like clouds, with lines below. The next was the same fluffy ball without lines. The third was a circle with lines shooting out from it in all directions. The pictures were simple but pretty, and she marveled at Brin's artistry.

"This is beautiful."

"I don't care about that. I want to know if you understand it. Can you figure out what I'm trying to say?"

Roan nodded.

"Don't nod, tell me. What does it mean?"

"It rained for four days, and then the sun came out."

Brin's jaw dropped, and a huge smile pulled at her lips. "Yes! Exactly! That's perfect. That's wonderful. You understood a dozen words from only three pictures." Brin reached out and hugged her.

Roan sucked in a sharp breath and went rigid. Her shoulders seized to her neck; her hands and teeth clenched. She started to shake.

Brin let go. "Sorry, sorry. I'm so sorry . . . I . . . I'm just so happy. Are you all right?"

Roan focused on breathing. Pulling in air and pushing it out. She tried to stop the tears, but they slipped down her cheeks, first the left then the right. The left was always first, and she could never understand why. Maybe its socket wasn't as deep.

Roan heard a pounding, faint and muffled, as if from far away. She heard low thuds repeating over and over. Then she heard Brin yelling.

Brin? Why is she yelling? Is she all right?

"Stop it!" Brin shouted. "Roan! Roan, stop it! Stop it."

Roan looked down and saw her fists pounding her thigh. She was hitting quite hard and yet could only dimly feel the pain.

"Oh, blessed Mari, Roan." Brin was crying, too. "I'm so, so, so sorry."

Roan stopped hitting herself and went back to breathing. *He's dead. He's dead. He's dead.* Her breath slowed. The tears stopped. She wiped them clear and looked at Brin. "Are you okay?" Roan asked.

Brin looked incredulous. "*I'm* fine. Should I get Gifford?"

She shook her head. "I'm okay, really. And I'm sorry for . . . for being me."

Brin didn't say anything. She had both hands up to her mouth. She looked frightened, as if Roan were some horrible creature.

Roan wanted to crawl into a hole and bury herself. At times like this, she used to go back to Iver's house and curl up on her mat and hide in the blanket. But Iver's house was gone, and she didn't know where her blanket was, lost with everything else to the storm. All she knew was that she couldn't stay there with Brin staring at her in horror.

"I'm sorry," she said, and walked away, escaping from under the wool.

As she did, Roan noticed people were looking down the length of the wall toward the Fhrey camp. The Galantians had made their settlement away from the others near the eastern side. A commotion was causing several people to point that way.

"What happened?" Viv Baker asked Tressa, who was sitting in the sun, sewing.

"The cripple did something he shouldn't, I guess."

Roan started running then. She raced toward the Galantian camp. Most of the Fhrey were standing in a circle. Gifford lay at its center, his face blotchy, cut, and bloody. One eye was already puffed up and closed. Blood dribbled out his nose and mouth. He was curled up, coughing and spitting. After one last kick, the Galantians moved away.

Roan froze, unable to move any closer. Gifford's one good eye stared at her. A tear slipped free and down his cheek.

Iver was dead, but Roan still heard his voice, *"You killed your mother, Roan. You've been a burden to me your whole life, and you'll be a curse to anyone who cares about you. That's what you really are, Roan. That's right, an evil curse, and you deserve what I'm going to give you now . . ."*

"What did you expect?" Padera asked Moya. The old woman was sitting under the awning in a pile of wool, carding away like a spider in her cloud-like web. Padera hadn't looked up. Not that she could see much through the slits she called eyes. Still, Moya found it disturbing that the old lady could always tell whenever Moya entered, as if she could smell her.

"Huh? What? Try making sense, old woman," Moya replied. She ducked under the wool drape and flung herself down on the ground where the grass had been pressed flat. "Or were you talking to yourself again?"

"I don't talk to myself. Although I should start. I'm two hoots and two halves more entertaining than anyone I know."

"That would be three hoots. Whatever in Tetlin's name a *hoot* is."

"You're only proving my point, dear."

Moya poured a cup of water from a jug. She drank half, then poured the rest over her head, letting the water drizzle down her neck and soak the top of her dress. She sighed.

"Not sure why Roan went to all the trouble to put up these roofs if you're just going to douse yourself," Padera told her.

"It's hot out. Hot and muggy. I just wish I knew where Bergin stored his beer." Moya took a seat with her back against the cool stone of the wall, the empty cup still clutched in her hand. The wind blew the drapes, but she didn't feel any relief.

The old lady continued to scrape the wool out. The sound annoyed Moya. "Okay, I'll bite. What should I have expected?"

Padera opened one eye and fixed her with it. "They are men of war. They speak through violence. That's their language."

"They aren't men," Moya said. "They aren't human. They're Fhrey."

"Close enough."

"And what do you know about it? How do you always know *everything!* You weren't even there."

"Bet you're wishing you could say the same."

"Shut up, you old witch." Moya slammed the cup to the ground, and turned away.

Tekchin had been teaching Moya how to use a sword. Every day she trekked to the Galantians' camp for personal lessons. He'd often stand behind her, his chest against her back, his arms guiding her movements. Whenever they stopped, she could feel the fast beat of his heart.

Everyone else was terrified of the Fhrey, but Moya was a regular fixture in their midst. She had become accepted. Moya loved the way the Fhrey welcomed her, the way they smiled as if she were one of them, a Galantian-in-training. They all liked her, but none more than Tekchin. And she liked him, too, so different from any man she'd known before—aggressive, funny, clever, and confident. His looks didn't hurt, either. He wasn't *pretty* like the other Fhrey. Tekchin looked rugged with his scar, leathery skin, and rough hands.

She had been there when Gifford showed up with Eres's javelin.

Gifford was always doing things he shouldn't. Always pushing people and breaking rules. There were times she felt he used his ailments to manipulate others, knowing no one would stand up to him because it would make *them* look like the bully. This time he'd gone too far. This time he'd pushed someone who wasn't afraid of what others thought.

Before the potter could say anything, Eres sprang. He took the weapon in one hand and Gifford in the other. For one terrifying instant, Moya thought he might thrust the javelin through Gifford's twisted little body. Instead, he held him by the throat while he gently laid his javelin aside.

"I'm sow-wee," Gifford had said. "I just wanted to look at it."

When the beating began, Moya was relieved Eres had used his fists. Fleshy sounds filled her ears as he pummeled Gifford, who cried out only once before losing the air to make any sound. Crumbled into a ball, he endured Eres's kicks, hugging himself and gasping for breath as tears rolled down his cheeks.

The other Galantians watched with passing interest. Moya had stared in horror. For the first time, she found she didn't have the courage to speak or even move. She silently watched Gifford take the beating. *I should have helped him. If I had asked Eres to stop, he would've, wouldn't he? Why didn't I?*

Sitting under the wool with Padera watching her, Moya started to cry. "He's a cripple, for Mari's sake! They didn't have to . . ." Moya bit off the rest and crushed her lips together.

"People never *have* to be mean," the old woman said.

"Gifford should have known better. The Fhrey treat their weapons like children. They name them, for Mari's sake! I've seen how protective they can be, and Eres is the worst of the lot. Gifford shouldn't have taken it; he shouldn't have even touched it."

"Gifford didn't take the little spear."

Moya looked over at Padera and shook her head. "Well, I guess you don't know everything, do you, old woman? Gifford came right out and said he did. And it's a *javelin* not a spear."

Padera looked at her once more. Strange how that one eye could make Moya feel so small.

"He lied."

Moya laughed. "So you can tell what's in people's hearts now? Know their innermost secrets from all the way out here?"

Padera didn't reply and went back to her carding. The old woman was so self-assured she didn't even feel the need to argue.

"Gifford took the javelin. He had it. I saw him bring it back. How could he have—" The answer came to her then, and the revelation felt like running into a wall. Moya felt her stomach rise and catch in her throat. "Oh, Grand Mother. It was Roan. She took it."

Padera nodded and Moya felt sick.

Roan likely just wanted to see how it was made. Probably took better care of it than Eres would have. Roan couldn't have asked permission. Roan wouldn't dare speak to a Fhrey, and when she got into her thinking mode, she sometimes blocked out everything else.

Gifford must have seen her with it. He knew what would happen when he brought it back.

I might have stopped it. I should have at least tried.

Gifford was her friend, but she hadn't helped. She stood by and watched him take a beating because *he* refused to let anyone hurt *his* friend. He was willing to stand up against the Galantians for someone he cared about, but she couldn't say the same. *Who's the real cripple?*

Then the worst thought of all entered Moya's head. Gifford wouldn't even be upset with her for standing by and doing nothing—he would have expected it.

Moya's stomach twisted into a knot. She hated herself so much it physically hurt. Her pain must have been painted on her face because Padera added, "You shouldn't feel so bad. It's not like you or I were beaten. Gifford is used to pain."

CHAPTER TWELVE

The Council of Tirre

The famous Council of Tirre that everyone speaks so highly of was not a grand thing. The chieftains were not eloquent, or geniuses, or selfless heroes. And they did not sit at a table of gold. The gathering that changed the course of human history was nothing more than a circle of chairs filled mainly with stupid, vain men.

—THE BOOK OF BRIN

The day was sunny and warm, so the chieftains' meeting was held in the open courtyard of the dahl. Unlike Rhen, Tirre's inhabitants didn't live near the lodge. Long ago, fishermen, craftsmen, and traders saved themselves the daily walk by moving down the hill to the village of Vernes. Only the chieftain, his family, and his staff remained in the roundhouse, which was much larger than the one Persephone had lived in. Uncluttered by other structures, the yard of beaten grass and dirt patches remained open, breezy, and both majestic and dismal. Seven chairs were set in a circle in front of the lodge. Lipit's people brought jugs of mead from his storage pits. Refusing drink would have insulted her host. Still, she wanted to keep her wits, so Persephone intended to have just a sip. She nearly changed her mind after discovering the mead was not only good but cold.

All seven Rhulyn chieftains were there, and Persephone knew each one except Alward, the new leader of Clan Nadak. The sickly thin man with oily hair wore a ragged version of the brown-and-yellow pattern of his people. Lipit had positioned Persephone to his right—as she had been the one to call the meeting—and Raithe on her other side, probably because they had arrived together. She was surprised to see him and hoped his attendance indicated a change of heart. Maybe she had managed to talk some sense into his thick Dureyan head.

Outside the circle, behind each of the chairs, others stood. These were the elders, the Shields, and the Keepers of Ways. Tegan of Warric had eight advisers behind him. Harkon of Melen had six, including a man who looked as old as Padera. Persephone had Brin and Nyphron. The girl had come with a thin slate of gray stone in her arms; Persephone had no idea what for. She was equally confused by Nyphron's presence. She hadn't asked him to attend, but given he was going to aid them in a war against his own people, she thought it fair for him to be there. His presence drew stares from the other chieftains.

Only Malcolm and a young boy she didn't recognize stood behind Raithe.

"Well, let's get to it," Tegan of Warric bellowed. "Who's going to be the keenig? *You*, Lipit? Is that why you brought us here?" he added with bombastic poison.

Their host straightened up and scowled. Lipit had dressed for the affair, wearing earrings of silver and bracelets of gold. "Are you saying I'm unfit?"

"Since you're asking, you must agree."

"And who do you think would be a better choice?" Lipit asked. "You, perhaps?"

"Of course. Why else would I come all this way? I am here to accept the crown of the united clans."

Harkon of Melen laughed, slapping his bare thigh with a loud smack. "And the rest of us came all this way to make certain that *wouldn't* happen."

This ignited a round of laughter. Persephone only smiled.

"I won't support Lipit as keenig," Tegan declared, pounding the arm of his chair with a big fist. He wasn't a tall man, but he had broad shoulders, strong arms, and huge hands. The thump of his fist cut the laughter short.

"Nor I," Krugen said. The chieftain of Menahan emphasized his unsolicited vote by adjusting his robes. Only Krugen wore robes—rich, lavish garments of dyed material embroidered with patterns of fine needlework. The opulence of so much material to clothe just one person seemed absurd.

"I think we are getting ahead of ourselves," Lipit said. His words were sharp, maybe in response to the quick, unnecessary rebukes. "Perhaps we should hear from Persephone. After all, she was the one who called for the gathering."

Persephone saw skepticism on their faces. To them, she had always been Reglan's wife.

"*She* did?" Tegan continued to speak to Lipit while casting cursory glances at Persephone. "I thought the messengers calling for this meeting came from here."

Harkon folded his arms and scowled. "A summit called by a chieftain's widow, war with the Fhrey, is this some kind of joke, Lipit?"

"Not unless you consider the death of thousands of men, women, and children funny," Persephone replied. "Do you? Do any of you feel that the destruction of Dureya, Nadak, and now Rhen is humorous? Maybe you'll feel differently when you find your own dahls in similar straits."

No one answered. The smiles and bravado shrank into uncomfortable shifts and awkward glances. Persephone had their attention and planned to use it. She stood up. "The Fhrey have declared war on us. Those whom we once thought benevolent gods revealed themselves as treacherous enemies. Without warning, without cause, they attacked and erased two of our clans, and very nearly a third."

"The way I heard it, one of ours killed one of theirs." Tegan let his eyes shift toward Raithe.

"A man killed a Fhrey," Raithe said, "because the Fhrey killed his father."

"And I heard the men trespassed where they weren't allowed," Tegan said. "They crossed the river. Something all the chieftains agreed would never happen."

"This is your fault then?" Alward glared at Raithe.

"The trespass and the death are not what has turned the Fhrey against us. Do you *really* think they would unleash so much destruction because of the loss of just one of their own? Does that make *any* sense?" Persephone said.

"Perhaps I could lend clarity," said Nyphron. "May I say something?" He stepped out from behind Persephone's chair and into the center of the ring. No one moved or replied. The Galantian's long golden hair flowed off his shoulders. His face, unblemished and unscarred, was the perfect canvas for his dazzling blue eyes. The morning light enhanced the yellow metal of his armor.

Nyphron didn't wait for the permission he'd requested. "I am Nyphron, leader of the Instarya tribe, commander of the famed Galantians, and the legitimate lord of Alon Rhist. I'll bear witness to what Lady Persephone asserts. A single death didn't launch this curse upon your people. Shegon's death was an excuse. The Fhrey have long planned to remove the Rhunes from Elan, and now their campaign has begun."

As he spoke, he rotated slowly and made eye contact with each chieftain. "Our fane has decreed that your kind has grown too numerous. Your very numbers are seen as a threat. Your success upon this land, your mere existence, is the cause of your doom. The fane fears a growing horde of Rhunes as numerous as the stars, and he wants you gone. *All* of you."

He paused, but remained in the center of the circle.

"If that is true," Tegan was the first to find his voice, although not the same as he used before. It lacked the loud, brassy bellow it once had. "Then why is the lord of Alon Rhist here? Do you come to parley our surrender?"

"You are Tegan, chieftain of Clan Warric? Your people are great traders of jade from the eastern hills of Galesh along the western banks of the Galeannon River. I've heard your people are great drinkers and speakers, but I wasn't aware that Clan Warric also possessed such wisdom, for that is a very good question." Nyphron paused, making them wait, making them wonder if he would answer at all. "While I am the true lord of the Rhist, sadly the rest of my people, including the fane, don't see it that way. I was cast out for refusing to butcher Rhune women and children. I wasn't able to stop the slaughter of Dureya and Nadak by my brothers-in-arms, but my band and I reached Rhen in time to prevent its total destruction. We defended that dahl first against my own people, and then against a band of Grenmorian giants."

The word *giant* was passed around in hushed whispers.

"I stand before you this day to confirm that war with my kin is upon you. I am forbidden by my god, Ferrol, to slay another Fhrey, so I cannot fight this war for you. This is a battle you must win for yourselves, but you do not have to do so alone."

"Men can't fight gods," Lipit said, looking horrified at the very suggestion.

"Why not?" Nyphron asked.

"They'll strike us dead."

"If you don't fight, they'll kill you anyway."

"But . . ." Lipit couldn't hold Nyphron's stare, and he faltered. "Men can't kill gods."

"This man here "—Nyphron pointed at Raithe—"is the God Killer. He has killed two of my people, one of whom was so powerful he called lightning from the sky and rent the earth with powerful magic. That Fhrey, Gryndal, was one of the most powerful Miralyith of our kind. To you he would truly seem godlike . . . and yet a Rhune . . . this one . . . ended him."

Once again, Nyphron rotated, rocking from foot to foot, and this time he lifted his gaze to include those who were gathered behind the chairs, and his voice rose to address the whole courtyard. "You will fight. There is no choice in that regard. Your only other option is death . . . the death of Rhunes everywhere. You can fight separately and die alone, or join together and use your vast numbers. You can become the very thing the fane fears. I will teach you how to win against my people—I will show you how to prevail.

"You need to appoint a single leader," he went on. "I know your custom is to choose the largest and strongest, the warrior most capable to command your people in battle. But don't limit your thinking so foolishly. This war will not be won by virtue of one man's ax, spear, or courage on the field. What if he falls in battle? The clans could break, the alliance falter . . . and you can't afford to lose this war. There will be no second chance, no truce possible, no peace. You must select a person capable of leadership, a person who isn't mired in the petty bickering that might divide you through past grievances. This person does not need to take the field with you, nor do they need to be capable of fighting your enemy with blows. The person you should appoint should be a symbol of unity who can lead with intelligence, wisdom, and strategy. Look for someone above the squabbles. Someone you can put your faith in. Someone you won't doubt. Someone who can win this war for you."

Nyphron stopped rotating and stood before them, waiting.

No one spoke.

He glanced at each of them. When he looked at Persephone, she saw impatience in his eyes.

Overhead, gulls cried. Near the lodge a door creaked on a weak hinge.

The Fhrey sighed, and disappointment replaced impatience. Nyphron clapped his hands against his sides. "May all the gods that be, lend you wisdom in your decision."

With that, Nyphron walked away.

The first clan meeting in several hundred years had adjourned for the day after Nyphron's speech, in order for the chieftains to confer with their advisers and reflect on what had been said.

The next morning, they met again, each sitting in the same chair. Tegan started things off with his own speech. His tone was less pompous, less arrogant. This time he spoke about the necessity of fighting the *enemy*. Reglan had always thought Tegan was the smartest of the chieftains, and Persephone saw evidence of this in how he avoided the words *Fhrey* and *god*.

After him, Harkon spoke, saying much the same, but adding that uniting the clans was essential. Krugen repeated the others' words and included the suggestion of creating a list of candidates for the position of keenig. This was agreed upon, and the second clan meeting ended to allow the chieftains to confer with their advisers as to the names that would be offered.

Persephone considered going to Raithe. He and Malcolm had made their camp with Bergin, his daughter, Myrtis, and Filson the Lamp. Except for the meetings, she hadn't seen him since that evening on the beach, probably a good thing. It was easy for her to forget just how young he was. She'd been unfair. Persephone had spent decades immersed in leadership. She was used to looking out for her clan. But Raithe didn't yet know what it was like to feel responsibility for others. He hadn't even been a father.

She liked Raithe, respected him, but he wanted more from her than she could give. In her heart, she was still married to Reglan. The memory of her husband had been tarnished by his betrayal and cowardice, but he was still a part of her. She continued to meet him in her dreams, and she was reminded of his devotion each time she fastened her bracken mor with the copper brooch he'd given her. Persephone could still recall the sound of his voice, the smell of his hair. In some small way he was still alive—just away somewhere—and she couldn't imagine being with another man. The very idea was ridiculous, but Raithe didn't see it that way. Men viewed the world differently, especially young men. Perhaps it was better that she kept her distance, for his sake as well as hers. What she had to say could be said in the next council meeting.

The third meeting began in the same chairs, and Persephone wondered if the servants put them in the same places each day, or just left them in the courtyard all night.

The gathering began with Tegan again. "I would like to open this meeting by nominating the obvious person for the task: myself." He said this while arching his back and placing his palms on his chest in a noble, yet humble, gesture.

Persephone expected reactions of disapproval, but no one so much as coughed. The other chieftains sat patiently, listening.

"I am Tegan, chieftain of Clan Warric, son of Egan the Stone, son of Hagen, son of Gan. My bloodline traces back to Bran of Pines, Shield of Gath of Odeon, who slew Orr the one-eyed dragon on the Banks of Wailing. I have the blood of heroes in my veins. My lineage is undisputed. Warric is a great and fierce clan with hundreds of experienced spearmen." He held out his own spear, a fine seasoned shaft with a beautiful jade point. "We mine the stone for these tips in our mountains, and my people are never wanting for meat."

Tegan went on discussing the virtues of Clan Warric, and his own personal prowess in battle, bringing up a fight he'd won seven years earlier against a challenger in which he'd outsmarted the younger man, who was also bigger and faster. He talked for a long time before finally sitting down. He did so with a grin on his face, as if they would all cheer and agree that he should be the keenig.

They didn't.

Instead, Harkon stood up and said, "Well said, Tegan. Your lineage and abilities are formidable indeed, and I think you might make a fine Shield when I am appointed keenig." Harkon then went on to explain why he should be made leader of the clans and pointed out that he was descended from Melen himself, the founder of his clan, who was said to have been a giant who slew an army of goblins with the trunk of an oak tree.

Persephone wasn't at all surprised when Krugen stood up next and also nominated himself. This was why no one had complained about Tegan. They each planned on doing the same, and they did. Next came Alward, who, oddly enough, given his recent appointment to chieftain, managed to trace his lineage back to a demigod hero who helped Rasra, the patron god of Clan Nadak, defeat the West Wind.

They took their turns while going around the circle, and when it was Lipit's time, he took advantage of his role as council host to impress the others with a demonstration. With a snap of his fingers, he summoned a cohort of several hundred men who entered the courtyard and surrounded the chairs. Each was tall and naked to the waist, lean muscles on display. They carried large wooden shields and fine spears. Their faces were painted with fierce streaks of white and red that made them look ferocious.

Lipit raised his hand and the crowd of men clamored spears against shields and shouted, roaring at the sky. They stopped when he lowered his hand.

Then it was Persephone's turn, but the eyes of the chieftains skipped over her and turned instead to Raithe.

Persephone stood up.

This incited strange looks. For an instant, she considered nominating herself just to watch their faces, and to see if they would extend her the same courtesy they had provided one another. But unlike the rest, Persephone wasn't there for political gain. She didn't want to be keenig. She wanted to win the war.

"I nominate for keenig . . . Raithe of Dureya." She said it simply, without drama, and didn't bother to explain who his father or grandfather was, or what great ancestor he might have had. She merely pointed at him. "He knows how to kill them. He's the only one who has proven he can. No one else can claim that. And that's what we really need. His clan is gone, and he doesn't have any existing treaties or alliances that would incite jealousy. As such, he can be fair and impartial. But most important, while each of you might be *descendants* of heroes and legends, he *is* one."

She sat back down, folding her hands on her lap and waited.

They all looked at Raithe again. Unlike with the other nominations, she saw surprise and even a degree of affirmation in their eyes. Krugen and Alward—whether they knew it or not—were nodding.

"While I appreciate Persephone's vote of confidence, there's only one problem," Raithe told them. "I refuse to be keenig."

The chieftains looked puzzled.

"What do you mean?" Lipit asked.

Harkon said, "Being keenig is the greatest honor a man could have. It comes with absolute power. Your word will be law in *all* the clans."

"Don't want that," Raithe said.

"I thought you desired to build something," Persephone said. "Here's your chance to build a nation."

"Wars don't build anything."

"You know you're the only one for this task," she said. "You *are* the God Killer, and that doesn't just mean that you killed a Fhrey. You killed the very idea that they are gods. You've already won that first great battle all by yourself. Just by existing, you give the rest of us hope. Hope that we can survive, that we really can win this war. Who else can claim that?"

"That's why I won't do it." Raithe ran a hand over his face. His sight focused on the dirty patch at the center of the ring. "I refuse to give false hope. I won't be the one everyone blames when we fail."

"Fail?" Tegan stared. "Are you saying you don't think we can win?"

"That's exactly what I'm saying." He looked squarely at him. "At Dahl Rhen, if it hadn't been giants, if it had been Fhrey, Nyphron and his Galantians wouldn't have stopped them. They don't fight their own kind."

"But Nyphron can teach us to—" Persephone began.

"Teach us what?" Raithe pulled the broken copper and held it up. "This was my father's sword. A metal weapon, envied by every Dureyan warrior. Yet when I fought Shegon, he cut through it as if I held a dead twig. Yes, I killed Shegon. I killed a Fhrey, but I did so while he lay unconscious, knocked out by Malcolm, who'd hit him from behind with a rock." He paused to let this sink in. "You're right. I'm the only one to kill a god, and I only managed it while he was lying unconscious on the ground."

"And Gryndal?" she challenged. "He was a Miralyith, master of the Art. And you killed him as well. He wasn't unconscious."

"And do you think I could have defeated him if I didn't have Shegon's sword? Or Arion's help? When the Fhrey didn't consider us a threat, we could get close, but that advantage is gone. They will be on their guard and won't underestimate us now."

Persephone's eyes shifted while she thought. "You also battled Nyphron at Dahl Rhen's gate. You fought him sword-to-sword and won. So I think you are understating your abilities."

He nodded his agreement. "Yes, we did fight, *sword-to-sword*. I used Shegon's and would have died without it. What weapons will the men in our army wield? Will stone spears prevail against the Fhrey's bronze swords?" Raithe got up. He drew Shegon's blade and advanced toward Lipit. Two of the soldiers stepped forward to intercept. Raithe sliced the heads off both spears.

The men fell back. Others rushed forward, but Raithe turned and strode to the middle of the courtyard, to the thick wooden post that held up the courtyard's central brazier. He swung down, cleaving into the grain so that the blade wedged deep. He left the sword and turned back to the circle of chairs.

"You'll face better swords than this when they come," he said. "Maybe Nyphron *can* teach men to fight, but what good is training when we have sticks and stones and they have this? So, yes, we've seen Fhrey die, but only two. That proves they aren't gods, but they might as well be. We've already lost this war. Don't you see that? This war isn't winnable. That's why I can't be your keenig. You would need someone crazier than yourselves, and I am not that much of a fool."

Raithe walked out of the courtyard, leaving all of them to stare at the sword he'd left behind.

Persephone looked for Raithe after the meeting, but he wasn't under the wool, and she couldn't find him around the wall. She went down to the village, thinking he might have gone there, but no such luck. She needed to speak to him, had to change his mind, though she didn't know how. Everything he said was true. They might have overwhelming numbers, but for how long? If their weapons snapped as easily as the spears held by Lipit's men, they would need a miracle to prevail.

She stopped looking as night fell, realizing she was glad she hadn't found him. *What would I say? What could I say?*

The next day brought rain again, so the fourth chieftain meeting was postponed. When the council reconvened the following morning, they moved inside the lodge due to continued showers. Raithe wasn't there. At first Persephone was fearful he might have left, but Malcolm explained that he was still in Tirre and training a young boy to fight.

Because of the lodge's tight quarters, few others besides the chieftains were present. Alward was alone, and so was Harkon. Tegan only had his Shield, whose name Persephone thought was Oz. No one joined Persephone except Brin.

"Awful way to treat such a fine sword," Alward said as he stood at the door looking out at the rain. A wet breeze fluttered his linen shirt, revealing him to be thinner than Persephone had originally thought. Chieftains always ate well, but Alward had only recently become one. "Why has no one pulled it out?"

"Go ahead," Tegan told him. "No one is stopping you."

Alward returned to his chair and faced the others. "So what do we do?"

"Nyphron makes a good case," Tegan said. "We have to fight."

"Raithe also makes sense," Krugen responded. "We've already lost."

"Perhaps we could go back," Alward said.

"Back?"

"Across the sea. Can't we just get in boats and head off across the water and escape all this? Isn't that where we came from? Can't we just go home?" Alward looked at Brin. "You're Rhen's Keeper, right? What do the ways say about that?"

Everyone looked at the girl, who appeared shocked that she was expected to speak.

"Well?"

Brin looked at Persephone.

"Tell him," she said. "Tell him what you know. This is why we have Keepers."

"We did come across *a* sea," Brin said. "No one really knows which. It might have been this one or another. But it wouldn't matter. There's no place to go back to. The old world sank. That's why we had to leave. That's why we sailed here. If you sail out there, you could fall off the world."

"What about Caric?" Alward asked. "The Dherg city isn't too far away, is it?"

Lipit shook his head. "We trade with the Dherg in Tirre, but they wouldn't welcome us. They are not a trusting lot, and would assume we were invading. One war is more than enough."

Alward's face drooped. He folded his arms and slumped in his seat.

"It all just seems so hopeless," Krugen said. He was leaning forward, his elbows on his knees and his chin on his hands. "Maybe instead of deciding which man to make keenig, we should first decide which god to pray to. And I will be the first to say, it shouldn't be Mehan. He's not been kind to us as of late. He's turned a deaf ear to his people, and this"—he swept his arm toward the doorway—"only confirms he's abandoned us."

"I can't suggest Krun," Harkon said. "He's fine with wheat and helping the sick, but he's no god of war."

"I would have proclaimed the might of Eraphus," Lipit told them, "but . . ." He looked at Persephone. "Her god is greater. We closed our gates to them, and Mari blew them off their hinges. Then she flew in, bearing gifts of food, drink, tools, and furs. Rhen's goddess is a powerful and generous god."

The chieftains looked to Persephone.

"Is that true?" Alward asked.

Persephone looked out through the open door at the stone figure still there, slick and dark with rain. "I've always felt she listened when we prayed to her."

"Then perhaps we should do that," Lipit said. "Pray to Mari for a way out of this. Pray for an answer."

"I brought a prized pig with me," Krugen said. "Tomorrow I'll offer it in sacrifice."

"We'll all offer sacrifices," Tegan said. "Offer her our best and pledge our loyalty in return for saving us. Maybe she can send someone who will draw that sword from the pillar. And then she'll rain down thousands of swords. Tens of thousands. Enough to equip every able-bodied man. Then . . . with Nyphron's training and Mari's swords . . . we'll have a chance." To no one in particular he asked, "Do you think that would work?"

Lipit looked out the open door with a surprised, almost frightened, expression.

"What?" Tegan asked.

"She's looking at it." Lipit pointed at the statue of Mari. "She's facing the sword in the post. It's a sign. If we reject all other gods in favor of Mari, she will send us a worthy keenig and swords for our warriors."

The sword belonged to Raithe. Everyone knew that. They also knew his reputation. He killed gods. That blade would remain in the post until Raithe himself retrieved it. Persephone suspected Lipit thought the same thing, but neither of them said anything.

"What do you think?" Brin asked as she and Persephone left the meeting. Brin was still carrying the slate clutched to her chest.

"About what, exactly?"

"If we . . . I mean . . . do you think Mari will help us?"

Persephone paused in the center of the courtyard beside Raithe's sword; its pommel was wet and dripping with the rain that had dwindled to a half-hearted sprinkle. "There's always hope."

The other chieftains were spending the night in the lodge. Persephone didn't feel comfortable sleeping with the men. Her place was with her people. And yet she had no doubt the other chieftains spent their nights drinking and talking. Alliances were being formed and trade agreements brokered in that dark and stuffy tomb. Rumor held that Harkon and Krugen had already agreed to trade wool for amber, and during the most recent meeting, they'd sat side by side. Persephone and Rhen were becoming isolated, growing even weaker than they already were. She was a poor leader and Rhen was suffering because of it. But what would trade agreements matter if they didn't find a way to fight the Fhrey?

Persephone's feet felt heavy as she and Brin walked out the gates. Her neck and back hurt from sitting in those stiff chairs, and she was hungry. Lipit had served food at midday, but she couldn't eat much. Stress killed her appetite. Hungry, stiff, and sore, the two made their way up the path that wound around the wall.

"Your Majesty."

Brin and Persephone turned to see Frost and Flood jogging up the trail behind them.

"They're still here?" Brin whispered.

Persephone shrugged.

"A word, Your Majesty," Frost begged in a breathless voice.

The two Dherg were still in their metal suits, with broad belts and knee-high boots. The interlocked links of their armor jangled as they jogged to catch up.

"Your Majesty?" Brin asked.

Persephone shrugged again.

"Now that you've had your clan meetings, I wonder if we could enlist some help in approaching Arion once again? Neith is just a short boat trip away. She'll only be gone a few days. I can't begin to express how important her help would be."

"I'm sorry," Persephone told them. "We have our own problems to deal with. We're on the verge of . . ."

The sun poked out of the rain clouds and the last rays of the setting sun glinted off the Dherg's metal shirts.

Persephone's eyes narrowed as she focused on the shimmering rings, then shifted her sight to their sheathed swords. She nudged Brin and pointed.

The girl appeared confused for a moment. Then her eyes widened, and she began to nod. "Of course! There's many stories about them making weapons. They make fine ones."

Frost raised his voice. "Belgriclungreians make the best weapons in Elan. We alone possess the secret of metal alloys and we wrought them into works of art for generations before your kind even came to Rhulyn."

"As good as Fhrey weapons?" Persephone asked.

Both Dherg spat on the ground in unison.

"Everything the elves know, our people taught them," Frost said.

"They stole, you mean," Flood corrected.

"Have you seen the sword Raithe carried?"

"Which one?" Flood asked.

"The Fhrey blade. Can you make better swords than that?"

"Well, ah . . ." Frost looked at his companion. "Not me personally. Flood and I aren't weaponsmiths. I told you, we're builders. Walls, pillars, and bridges are our specialty. You want a fortification? We can do that. Rain is a digger. If you need a tunnel, he's your Belgriclungreian. None of us knows much about metallurgy or swordcraft. Those are closely guarded secrets."

"But your people can make a decent sword, right?"

Both of the Dherg looked at her, aghast.

"Of course!" Flood declared.

"And how many could be made?"

"What do you mean?"

"If your people were so inclined. How many swords could they make?"

"If you were so inclined, how many loaves of bread can *your* people produce?"

Persephone smiled. "We can make thousands of loaves in a very short time. Are you saying yours could do the same with swords?"

"If we wanted to, certainly. Once, we were very good at such things. Back in the days of King Mideon, the furnaces of Drumindor provided thousands of swords each day for the war against the elves. And all were better than the one Raithe carries."

Persephone grinned at Brin, who smiled back.

"The giant you spoke of," Persephone said. "How badly do you want him dealt with? If I could convince my friend Arion to help you, could you convince your weaponsmith friends to help us?"

Frost and Flood exchanged looks of surprise. Then Frost said, "I can honestly say Gronbach would be most grateful to be rid of the, ah . . . the . . . giant we spoke of. While I can't make any guarantees on his behalf, I think I can arrange a meeting for you to make your case. Would that suffice?"

Suffice: The word sounded so weak and tenuous, especially when the fate of an entire race of people might rest upon it. "Yes," she said. "I would be in your debt."

CHAPTER THIRTEEN

Crossing the Bridge

Every life is a journey filled with crossroads. And then there are the bridges, those truly frightening choices that span what always was, from what will forever be. Finding the courage, or stupidity, to cross such bridges changes everything. For me, the life-altering choice was a literal bridge, the one I followed Persephone across on the dock in Vernes.

—THE BOOK OF BRIN

"You're thinking about it, aren't you?" Arion asked. *"What it felt like to touch the chords of creation."*

The mystic and her wolf were sitting in the open field, out from under the wool. Suri had a string pattern in her hands. She'd been holding it for some time, just staring. She'd made the same design on countless occasions and knew hundreds of ways to manipulate the weave to construct any number of patterns, but she didn't move her fingers.

Suri ignored the question, and Arion sat down beside her, wet and smelling of the ocean.

"Did you fall into the sea?" Suri asked.

"I bathed. You should try it. But I'm not as clean as I would like. I still feel dirty."

"Of course you do. You're odd that way."

"*No, I think it's the salt. The water was full of it. Dries the skin something terrible. Fun, though; you would like the waves. They pick you up and heave you along. Like flying.*"

Suri gave her a smirk. Arion had spewed nonstop butterfly metaphors for days. "*Was raining, you know? Works even better than the ocean. No salt.*"

"*And yet you look no cleaner for it. Don't smell better, either.*"

Suri glanced down at herself, puzzled. After days of constant showers, during which she and Minna had explored the tide pools of the rocky coast and the windswept fields surrounding Tirre, she didn't have a spot of dirt on her—except for her legs and feet, where there was no avoiding the mud. Finding no sense in the comment, Suri focused once more on the string between her fingers. She still hadn't decided what to do next.

Arion watched her, making Suri feel self-conscious.

"What?" Suri snapped in Rhunic.

"*That's the problem with that game,*" Arion replied. "*And why only beginners play it. Once you've touched a real chord, a string is just a string. You realize there are only so many patterns to make. Worse, you see that it's only a toy in comparison with the chords of nature. With the Art there are an infinite number of possibilities. Everything in the world is woven into the same fabric, all linked, and each moment lived creates a new connection, alterations to this unimaginably complex web of life. Some strands can't be moved; others can. Some that don't appear movable at first can be altered if the right conditions are met. Once the strands are aligned, you can strum the chords and play their music. The various tones are a language, the language of creation and the building blocks of all things. At times, it feels as if anything is possible if only you can work out the complexities.*"

Arion reached out and stroked Minna's coat. The wolf opened her eyes but didn't bother to lift her head. "*You have the gift of being able to see behind the veil, to view the mechanics of how the world was made and how it works, and the talent to adjust all that to your purpose. Of course, you yourself are part of that weave. You exist in the web. You create the web.*"

"*I am a spider?*"

Arion shook her head. "*No, you don't spin the string. Just as you're doing now, you always start with a loop. Artists can't create anything new; they merely make connections from what exists. But we are also part of what exists, so we are the web itself, individual strands in our own string pattern. As you alter the patterns in that string, you are also altering the world around you, and because you are part of this world, you are altering yourself. If you can see this, then you can see the truth. The string you weave is really yourself, and the pattern you make is your own life."*

"*Every time I hear you talk about the Art it seems less appealing.*"

Arion smiled. "*Tell me the truth. Just before I sat down, you were thinking that your beloved string game isn't anywhere near as much fun as it used to be, weren't you?*"

"We don't like her anymore, do we, Minna?"

The wolf lay on her side, a long tongue lying on the dirt as she panted.

Suri scowled. "*You ruined my game, and now look what you've done to Minna. Must be someone else you can—*"

Persephone came out of the dark, trailed by Brin and the little people, who jingled wherever they went. "Sorry," Persephone said to them both. "I didn't mean to interrupt."

"Please interrupt," Suri said.

Persephone looked puzzled for a moment. Then she said, "I need to speak with Arion."

"About what?" Arion asked.

Persephone looked at the Miralyith, surprised. "You're learning our language so quickly."

"No, she's not," Suri said. "If you're going to talk about anything important, speak in Fhrey. She has a terrible habit of nodding as if she understands. You'll jabber on for an hour, and she'll nod and nod, smiling all along, but she won't understand a thing. Look, she's doing it right now. Do you have any idea what I just said?"

Arion bit her lip. "You are speaking about me," she said each word precisely, deliberately. "Something bad. Something . . ." Frustrated, she finished in Fhrey, "*. . . insulting.*"

"Maybe you *are* getting better," Suri retorted.

"I'll stick to Fhrey," Persephone said. *"Are you aware of the meetings in the lodge?"*

Arion nodded. *"You and the other Rhune chieftains are selecting a leader. Planning for war."*

Persephone nodded. *"Not going well."*

"Can't decide on a leader?"

"No, but that's only one problem. We need supplies. Weapons. Without them, our people will be . . . how do you say . . . ?" She made a cutting motion across her neck.

"Killed," Suri provided.

"Slaughtered," Arion said.

Persephone nodded, pointing at Arion.

"And they will supply you with weapons?" Arion asked, nodding toward the little people who'd followed silently behind Persephone. All three were there. The two long-bearded ones watched the conversation intently, while Rain, the one with the big pickax, knelt to pet Minna.

"That's the plan—in exchange for a favor."

"Nyphron's idea?"

"No. In a way, it was Raithe's. He refuses to be keenig because without better weapons we don't have a chance."

"He's right. This war isn't feasible. I have a better idea. A more reasonable way to mend the break between our peoples."

"Feasible? Reasonable? A break?" Persephone's brows rose as her hands reached for her hips. *"Thousands have been massacred. I think that counts as a bit more than a mere* 'break between our peoples.' *I don't think it's unreasonable to—"*

"To what? Kill thousands more? What good will that do? Why in Ferrol's name would I . . . would anyone . . . want that? We need to find a way to coexist. Waging war won't bring that about."

"And exactly what will?" Persephone asked, throwing up her hands in frustration.

"Her," Arion said in Rhunic, and pointed at Suri.

Suri had only been peripherally listening to the conversation. She was more interested in introducing the one named Rain to Minna. He bent down to join Brin and together they discovered what Suri had known for years, that Minna loved being scratched behind her ears. But there was no mistaking that last part. "Me?" she asked.

Arion nodded. *"My people think Rhunes are animals, mindless beasts. They feel no guilt about killing your kind. Just like you don't consider it wrong to kill a deer. I know. I thought the same way before I met you. We need to prove to my fane . . . to all the Fhrey . . . that you are worthy of life and deserve respect, dignity, and sovereignty. If they can see we are more similar than they think, they'll see their mistake."*

She turned to Persephone. *"You want to save your people, and so do I, but not at the expense of my own. Both our people can live together peacefully, and Suri is the key. She's not Fhrey, but she can use the Art even without training. I'm not sure you can appreciate what an amazing discovery that is. Artists, true Artists, aren't common even among the Fhrey. If my fane could see that the Rhunes can use the Art, it will prove that the things that divide us are fewer than the many things we have in common."*

"So that's why you have been pushing so hard," Suri said.

Arion frowned. *"You're special, Suri. I can feel it the same way I sense the seasons. It's not merely that you can use the Art. It's you, yourself. I'm certain you're the key to everything. You need to prove to the fane that Rhunes are just as wonderful, as important, and as deserving of life as the Fhrey. If you can do that, they will see their mistake and change their minds. But this can only happen if you accept who you are. Only then can you change the world."*

Persephone didn't say anything for a long while. Her brow furrowed in thought. Finally, she said, *"I wish it could be that easy, but the reality is that my people are vulnerable. As long as we can't defend ourselves, we're helpless. Obtaining weapons is crucial to our survival. Suri, what do you think?"*

"I think summers should last longer than winters. I think dandelion wine isn't nearly as good as Tura said it was. I think Minna is the wisest of all wolves, and she sees several problems with Arion's plan. Don't you, Minna?"

"Such as?" Arion asked.

"First, I'm not an Artist. Yes, I can light a fire, but I don't think that is very impressive, and your fane wouldn't think so, either. The only other time I used *magic it ended in disaster, remember? That giant paid for my mistake with his life."*

"*You* killed the giant? The one from the rol?" Frost asked, his astonishment unmistakable.

Suri was equally surprised—she didn't know the Dherg knew the Fhrey language well enough to follow the conversation.

"Yes, but I was trying to free him." She turned her attention back to Arion and continued. *"And second, I'm not likely to meet the fane. Am I? He sent giants and lightning to kill you, so you probably won't be able to return home at all, let alone with me tagging along."*

"It's definitely more difficult than it once was. If Gryndal hadn't been killed, it would've been easy, but now things are more complicated."

"Can I say something?" Frost asked Suri politely.

She looked at him curiously. The tattoos around her eyes shifted with her furrowed brow. "You just did."

"Can I say something else?"

Suri sighed and looked to her wolf. "If he's going to keep this up, we could be here for a very long time, isn't that right, Minna?"

"I was just thinking that if *you* can kill a giant, then maybe we don't need *her*." He nodded his head toward Arion.

"Why would you want that?" Suri said.

"We have one in the city of Neith, which keeps us from our homeland; your chieftain wants to trade Belgriclungreian weapons in exchange for getting rid of it."

"I just told you. The first time was an accident," Suri said.

"Another accident would be fine." Frost smiled.

"Nobody has to kill anyone," Arion said, and then switched back to Fhrey. *"Why must everyone turn to such drastic actions as death and war! There are dozens of ways to deal with a giant, and none of them would require its death."*

"I'm sure you wouldn't feel that way if you met him," Frost said.

"That's because you're not an Artist. We're trained to think creatively."

"Suri," Persephone said. "We really need help with this. It's very important."

"I'll do what I can, but caterpillars really aren't much help."

"Huh?" Persephone was as confused as the others.

Arion waved a hand dismissively. *"It's her way of saying she's not quali-fied, but she could be. How about this. Suri and I will go to Neith and deal with the giant . . . deal with, not kill. Rapnagar's demise was a mistake. One which we both need to atone for. I shouldn't have asked her to attempt such a compli-cated weave with her current abilities. If properly trained, she'll not only be able to rid Neith of the giant, but she'll also prove to the fane that she truly is an Artist. Persephone will have her weapons, so the Rhunes won't be defenseless. And as much as it saddens me, I understand a fight with my people is inevitable now. Respect must be earned. And if you can win a battle or two, the fane will be far more inclined to seek out a peaceful solution. That's when Suri can be the solution everyone will welcome."*

She paused, then looked directly at Suri. *"But . . . you must agree to let me teach you. No more resistance. No more fighting. Your mastery of the Art goes beyond your desire to stay as you are. You must spread your wings, for the sake of both Rhunes and the Fhrey."*

"And I'm coming, too." Persephone said. *"To negotiate for the weapons. If no agreement can be reached, then no one is doing anything. Understood?"*

"Agreed," Frost said. *"But I think when you see the giant, you'll realize death is the best way to deal with it."*

"Let me worry about that," Arion told him. *"As I said, Miralyith are trained to be creative. He's likely as unhappy about being locked up in your mountain as you are having him there. I could shrink him to the size of a mouse, put him in a bag, and return him to his homeland."*

"Uh-huh, but—"

"Quit while you're ahead. She's coming, and that's the important thing," Persephone said.

Frost nodded.

Suri looked down at Minna, and the wolf looked back. "Will you still love me if I become a butterfly, Minna?"

The wolf brought up her head and licked Suri's hand.

"It's settled then," Persephone said.

"What's settled?" Brin asked. "What's going on? How am I supposed to act as Keeper if you talk in a language I don't understand?"

"Maybe you should learn Fhrey," Persephone told the girl. "Come, I'll fill you in while I pack."

"Pack? You're going?"

The rain had disrupted life under the wool.

Even after it stopped, the ground remained soft. The beaten grass became a muddy mess, then a serious problem as poles refused to stay rooted. Moving anything heavy turned into a monumental chore. Old paths were abandoned for firmer footing, and elevation became the new standard for prosperity. A large, shallow pool had formed in the low basin midway along the wall. The Great Puddle, as it came to be known, displaced several squatters and divided the camp into East and West Puddle. Being on the incline, West Puddle was more desirable, and it was there that Habet built private quarters for Persephone. Apparently, it pained him to see his chieftain sitting on the ground with everyone else. He'd persuaded Farmer Wedon and Bruce Baker to help erect a two-chambered enclosure where they placed the First Chair, the only thing Habet had been able to salvage from the ruined lodge.

Persephone never used it.

She remained in East Puddle among the stacked baskets, bundled tools, and the people fearing more rain. There wasn't any thought in her selection, no political statement being made. Persephone had settled in East Puddle because that was where Brin, Moya, Padera, and Roan were. She had no intention of leaving them. At least not until that night.

"You're going where?" Moya shouted at Persephone while the chieftain packed.

"Across the strait to Belgreig," Persephone said while stuffing a blanket into a sack. "If Arion and Suri take care of a giant for the Dherg, then I'll get weapons for the war." She turned to Padera. "Do you think it will be cold? Should I bring my breckon mor?" She'd never been to Belgreig. For all she knew, it might be snowing there.

"Better to have than regret," Padera said, sitting in her pillows of wool and sewing together what looked to be a sack.

"Who else is going?" Moya asked.

"No one. Oh, well, except for the dwarfs, of course."

"Just you three and the shrimps?" Moya asked in a tone that suggested Persephone was insane. "What about Raithe?" she said to Malcolm, who was in the process of filling a waterskin from the large barrel.

"Hasn't said anything to me," Malcolm replied. "Does he know? This is the first I've heard." He turned to Persephone. "Do you want me to—"

"No," she said quickly.

Everyone stared.

"But he's your Shield. He *has* to go," Moya said.

"Not my Shield anymore."

"What? When did that happen?" Moya had planted her hands on her hips in an excellent imitation of Persephone's mother. The likeness would have been perfect except Moya wore a short sword slung low on one hip. She'd gotten it as a gift from Tekchin. "How did—"

"He can't be my Shield and sit as a chieftain, so I released him before the council met. And I forbid each of you from saying anything. He might insist on coming or try to chase after me. I need him to stay here and become keenig. To do that, he has to attend the meetings so the other chieftains can convince him."

"Don't *you* need to be there? You called for the clan assembly. You can't run off in the middle of it."

"Any decisions will be made by Tegan, Harkon, Lipit, and Krugen—the chieftains who still have clans. Raithe's people are all but extinct, and yet he has more say than me. He's the God Killer; I'm only the widow of a chieftain. My words have about as much impact as raindrops. But if I can bring back weapons—good ones—maybe Raithe will change his mind about being the keenig. If he does, I think the others will pledge their allegiance."

"What about Brin?" Malcolm asked. "You're taking her, aren't you?"

"No, I—"

"But this sounds like an incredible opportunity," Malcolm said. "I don't think anyone . . . well, any human . . . has ever set foot on Belgreig. You'll want her there to remember it."

Brin's expression lit up at the suggestion.

"She needs to stay." Persephone pointed at Brin. "To witness the choosing of the keenig. That's of far greater importance."

"But there are other Keepers for that," the girl said. "I can get the story from them when I get back."

Persephone looked at Brin, whose eyes were filled with eagerness. Persephone sighed in resignation. "Okay, fine."

Brin jumped up, grabbed a sack of her own, and started stuffing items inside. She gathered a stack of the slates as well.

"You aren't taking those, are you?"

Brin looked down at the three stone tablets as if they were a beloved puppy. "I mark on them."

"You what?"

"I draw memories on them. It helps me keep an accurate account. Roan understands them. Others could, too. When it comes time for me to train a new Keeper, she can just look at these tablets and know everything. I started using chalk, but it smears too easily. Now I'm making deep scratches."

"The tablets look heavy."

"I'll manage."

Persephone had finished packing and Moya gave her a scornful look. "And what about your Shield? If you dismissed Raithe, who's the replacement?"

"Nobody. Don't need one," Persephone said.

"Seph, you're going to a foreign land to face a giant . . . you need protection. For the love of Mari, you should be taking a war party!"

Persephone scowled. Moya really was sounding like Persephone's mother, which irritated and amazed Persephone, and made her miss her parents all at the same time. "We're going with Arion. She's better than fifty strong men."

"She's a Fhrey."

"So?"

"So I don't trust her to protect you."

"Moya, we're going on a ship as the guests of the Dherg, to a city where Brin and I will likely spend our time in a room doing nothing while Arion and Suri dispatch this giant.

"I'm sure Brin will have a lot to take in," Persephone went on. "But I'll likely be bored to tears."

Moya didn't look appeased.

"What?" Persephone asked. "What do you want from me, Moya?"

Moya clapped her hands against her sides. "There's no other choice. I'm going with you."

"You are?" Roan spoke for the first time, sounding concerned.

"Don't be ridiculous, Moya," Persephone said.

"You don't think I can protect you?" Moya drew the blade at her side and held it up. "Tekchin has been training me. He says I'm learning fast. And I've impressed everyone."

"Are you sure it's your fighting skills he was talking about, my dear?" Padera asked.

Moya whirled. "What's that supposed to mean?"

No one dared answer, but both Brin and Persephone struggled to suppress a laugh.

Moya glared, and then swept the blade across her body. She spun and executed an impressive downstroke, followed by a fast somersault. Back on her feet, she swept again and halted the blade just inches from Persephone's throat, positioned in a threatening manner.

Persephone jumped back and nearly fell.

No one had laughter to suppress after that.

Moya slammed the sword back into its scabbard. "I'm coming with you."

"Okay," Persephone said.

"And so is Roan," Moya added.

The ex-slave, who was on the ground fiddling with a stick and a rope, looked up, shocked.

"What? No," Persephone said. "This is getting out of hand now."

"We can't leave her here, alone."

"Moya," Persephone said sternly. Moya was well meaning, but she sometimes treated Roan like a child. "Roan will be fine. She's not alone. She'll have Padera, Gifford, and—"

Roan let out a small sound, not unlike a whimper.

"What?" Persephone asked. "What is it, Roan?"

"I took one of the little spears from one of the Fhrey," Roan said in a voice just a breath above a whisper. "I just wanted to look at it, study it, feel how it was balanced. I didn't realize that—" She started to cry.

"Roan?"

Moya answered for her. "Gifford found out, and *he* took it back. Told them that he was the one who borrowed it. He was beaten bloody."

Persephone's hand leapt to her face, and she started to leave, going in the direction where Gifford usually slept.

"He's not there," Padera said, catching her by the wrist.

"Where is he? How is he? Will he be okay?"

The old lady pushed slowly to her feet, groaning with the effort, and waved at Persephone as if the question wasn't worthy of an answer. "Gifford is like a turtle. He don't run so fast, but there's no breaking that hard shell. Got him resting up at West Puddle in that throne room Habet built for you. Gifford is lying in the lap of luxury, he is."

Persephone looked from Moya to Roan, then to Malcolm. "Isn't anyone with him?"

"He don't need much at the moment," Padera said. "Other than rest. Which is why I don't want you going up there and bothering him."

Persephone nodded and turned back to look at Roan, who sat on the ground, rocking back and forth.

Moya sat down next to Roan. "I can't help worrying about what might have happened if Gifford hadn't been there. If *she* had returned the javelin instead."

"They wouldn't hurt a woman, would they?" Persephone asked.

Moya looked back, with too many questions in her eyes. "I want to think not, but look at what they did to a cripple. Maybe to them we're only a bit above animals—almost-people. And you don't have to treat almost-people the same way as real people, do you?"

Persephone looked at Roan, who was already back to work, tying her rope to the end of the long stick that lay across her lap. *Is that how Iver had viewed Roan? As an almost-person? How else could he have been so cruel?* She imagined Roan being beaten by the Fhrey—once more beaten for being an almost-person.

"Pack light, Roan. We're not going to be gone long."

The village of Vernes was built in tiers that descended the stony hillside from the dahl to the docks in a way that reminded Persephone of the dessert Padera had made for Reglan's fiftieth birthday. Instead of wild berries and nuts, the decorations on these layers were shops and homes. Most were built of mud bricks, and several were a surprising two stories tall. The tight tiers made for narrow streets and even narrower alleys, which had the party trudging along in single file. Frost, Flood, and Rain were out front like hounds.

They left at dawn, partly because Persephone feared that the council would break up if they couldn't agree on a leader, so time was of the essence. Also, she worried about losing her courage if given a chance to think about the decision for too long. But mostly, the hour of departure was determined by the schedule of a Dherg trade ship. Frost and Flood had managed to arrange passage for them on the vessel, which would sail once its supplies were loaded. That had turned out to take most of the night.

All told, there were ten of them, counting Minna and the three Dherg. Persephone continued addressing them as dwarfs, having given up any hope of pronouncing the longer version. They didn't mind it nearly as much as being called Dherg, and her term had the benefit of beginning with the same sound. She slipped and saved herself on numerous occasions by saying, "Dher—warfs." She could see them wince at each slip, but she also thought they appreciated that she was trying. The others avoided the problem by not talking at all.

Frost led the way with Flood right behind, shouting course corrections and insults in equal measure. At that hour, the streets were deserted, and they made good time as they slipped through tight lanes and down steep, narrow stairs.

Passing a series of large buildings stained white with salt, they came upon a wooden pier and just beyond it, a row of three ships. Persephone had only ridden in boats like those used to fish on Dreary Lake, the kind two men could carry over their heads. The ships in Vernes were longer than three roundhouses, and their fronts were fashioned to look like the faces of beasts. In the center was a tall pole, and across it's middle another pole, half as long, was wrapped in cloth.

Doubt crept in. Persephone had been so fixated on getting swords that she never considered the perils of where the path might lead, or what she'd need to suffer to travel it. She looked out at the endless horizon, which appeared more infinite now.

What's out there?

She couldn't even separate sky from water.

What if we come upon the place where Eraphus swims? What if we get lost in the dark and miss Belgreig? Could we sail off the edge of the world like Brin warned about?

Rhunes never went across the sea—not anymore. She was taking them into the unknown, and she wasn't anything like Gath. She wasn't even Reglan.

They stopped on the dock while Frost and Flood spoke to another Dherg, who sported a short beard and a silver ring in his nose that matched the ones in his ears. He wore an unpleasant sneer on his lips. They spoke in the Dherg language, and none of it sounded friendly or polite.

Looking back out at the endless water, Persephone thought she should have asked Raithe after all—or Malcolm, the Killians, Tope Highland and his sons, and . . . and . . . well, everyone, really. She obviously hadn't thought this through.

She took a deep breath.

"What's wrong?" Brin asked.

"Nothing," Persephone assured her, even if she couldn't convince herself.

Moya gave her an I-told-you-so look, or maybe she, too, was scared. Persephone preferred to think she was angry. If Moya was frightened, they were truly in trouble.

They stood alongside one of the ships, which bustled with activity. Every person on board was a Dherg, but unlike Frost, Flood, and Rain, they didn't wear metal. Most were shirtless or wore only simple vests or sleeveless tunics. A wooden bridge connected the ship to the dock, and it knocked and rattled with the swells.

"It's not too late," Moya whispered. "We can go back."

"And then what?" Persephone asked.

Moya didn't reply, thank Mari. If she had given any answer, no matter how absurd, Persephone might have given up. She didn't want to get on the ship and go out into the endless void. The idea of depending on the Dherg to take them there and back was nearly inconceivable. But the most frightening thing of all was relying on Suri to defeat the giant. *Arion was right: The young mystic hadn't been ready when dealing with Rapnagar. Would Arion be able to teach her in time? And if not, would the Fhrey step in? Yes, she opposed the idea of harming the giant, but she'd defend herself and the party if necessary, wouldn't she?* Suddenly, none of Persephone's plan sounded sensible or safe.

After more negotiation than Persephone had expected, Frost and Flood waved them across the gangway onto the heaving vessel. Everyone, even Arion, paused.

"It's all right. Dent cleared us," Frost told them.

"Lipit said Rhunes aren't welcomed in Caric. That your kind might see our presence as an act of war. Are you sure this won't be a problem?" Persephone asked.

"It could have been, if there were more of you, maybe. But how could a handful of women and a couple of girls be perceived as a threat?"

"Then why did it take so long to convince that Dent fellow? He seemed quite put out by something. What was it?"

"The cargo," Flood said.

"Minna or me?" Arion asked neatly, though a bit haltingly, in Rhunic.

"Was a long war," Flood said.

"And long ago." Despite the heavy accent that clipped her syllables, Arion's dismissive tone was clear.

Flood frowned at her. "Losing leaves a bitter taste that lingers long after the sweetness of victory has been forgotten."

Arion nodded. "Well said."

"Let's go." Frost hurried across the bobbing bridge. Rain, who rarely spoke, followed him across, with Flood close behind.

No one else followed. They all watched Persephone.

She stared across the bridge, missing Reglan more than she had in weeks. If he had been there, he would've told her how foolish she was being. He'd tell her the whole idea was too risky, too strange. She'd insist, and he would take her hand, letting her squeeze it until the fear went away. Looking at the ship, her hands felt cold and empty.

Everyone waited for her.

She was only the widow of a man who had led a small clan of woodsmen, shepherds, and huntsmen, but if she didn't cross that bridge, none of her companions would—not even the Miralyith.

We'll do it together, she heard her friend Aria say once more.

She took the nearest hand she could find, Brin's, and held it tight, waiting for the fear to pass. It didn't, but she crossed the bridge anyway.

CHAPTER FOURTEEN

The Nightmare

There are many lies spoken during a war, even more before one.
That is how they start.

—THE BOOK OF BRIN

The pitcher and glasses that Mawyndulë had smashed in the council chambers had been replaced. They looked identical to the old ones, and he wondered if his father had used the Art the way The Traitor once had and just reassembled the pieces. Sadly, the Art couldn't reassemble his father's attitude—his *dusty* attitude—into something sensible. A week had gone by since Mawyndulë's outburst in the meeting, and his father hadn't said a word—no lecture, no shouting, no punishment of any sort. The lack of action didn't surprise Mawyndulë; his father was weak whether confronting his son or the murderers of Gryndal. The fane was weak, period. Everyone praised Lothian's performance in the Carfreign during the challenge, but Mawyndulë still recalled how Gryndal had dealt with Rhunes on the frontier—simply a flick of his fingers, and five Rhune died in a burst of blood. That sent a better message. His father just didn't understand.

As before, Mawyndulë slouched deep in the chair while his father's advisers sat seated around the big table. They were discussing . . . well, Mawyndulë had no idea what they were babbling about. He was trying his best to ignore them.

A fly entered the room and landed on the Miralyith banner hanging high on the wall. Mawyndulë trapped it there with the Art, holding the tiny creature frozen to the cloth. He wondered what the fly was thinking. Could it think? Did it have the concept of a god? Did it wonder if it had offended one? If he let it live, the fly might return home and tell his fellow insects of the strange experience. It would likely feel as if it had been singled out for some grand purpose by the divine. What else could it think? It certainly couldn't begin to fathom that a prince stuck in a council meeting had trapped it for a time simply out of boredom. Things happen for reasons. The fly must conclude this or else abandon all belief that it was the center of the universe. Out of pity—and the kindness born from Mawyndulë's desire that the fly and its brethren would never discover how truly insignificant they were—he pressed his fingertips together. Across the room and nine feet up the wall, a tiny fly died an honorable, yet inconsequential, death.

". . . assassins to kill . . ."

The word *assassins* brought Mawyndulë back to the conversation. When he'd last paid attention, Kabbayn had been babbling about a request from the Gwydry for more rain to help the faltering crops and a similar, but counter, request from the Eilywin for clear skies to help them meet the midsummer deadline for building the new temple to Ferrol. The latter was supported by the Umalyn, but the former—as Kabbayn put it—*isn't something you can go without*. The debate had raged in monotonous voices. Mawyndulë was almost certain there had been some discussion about revenues, but he never listened when finances were brought up. He was certain that nothing was duller. Assassins, however, weren't financial issues, unless his father was hiring some to kill Nyphron and The Traitor. Either way, they had his attention.

". . . you, my great fane," Vasek finished.

"How certain are you of this?" his father asked.

"Fairly sure, my fane," he replied. "I'm still investigating, but my sources are usually reliable."

The Rhunes are hiring assassins to kill my father?

Mawyndulë thought of the fly's family sending a killer after him. Both were equally unlikely.

"I can't believe it. This has to be a mistake, a silly rumor. Fhrey don't kill Fhrey."

No, not Rhunes. The threat is coming from within?

"If they feel justified in their belief, they might. There's a great deal of concern right now about the Miralyith legacy. The other tribes are frightened that the Law of Ferrol might be suspended and the horn denied, or the right to challenge will become pointless, given the obvious outcome."

Lothian laughed. "Seriously? These people are concerning themselves with the next challenge already? The Uli Vermar isn't for another three thousand years."

"Well, my fane . . ." Vasek hesitated with an awkward, uncomfortable expression. "Three thousand years *or your death*. And you aren't so young anymore."

Lothian scowled, then sighed. "My mother lived too long." He looked over at Mawyndulë. "But don't get your hopes up. I still have another thousand years at least."

"A continued Miralyith reign is exactly what the subordinate tribes are worried about."

"If that's so, an assassination wouldn't help anything," his father said. "Even if they were successful, Mawyndulë would take the Forest Throne, and even with his meager skills in the Art, he could easily defeat the best challenger from any other tribe. They will still be ruled by a member of the Miralyith."

Meager skills?

"Perhaps assassination would be used as a deterrent," Vasek said. "What if every Miralyith who took the Forest Throne were killed? Would Miralyith stop petitioning and leave the field to others? The horn makes all challenges a fair fight, but a goblet of poison? A knife in the back? These are difficult for even a Miralyith to survive, are they not?"

"And they would do this knowing Ferrol would reject them? That they would be cast out of the afterlife and Fhrey society? They would be isolated from everyone, even their ancestors."

"As I said, if one feels the sacrifice is worth it, if one thinks there is no other way, it is entirely possible."

"You're saying the other tribes are planning to kill my father?" Mawyndulë asked.

Everyone turned and looked. Each had the same expression of surprise, as if none had remembered he was there.

"We don't know anything for certain, my prince," Vasek said with an unaccustomed tone of sympathy in his voice.

The Master of Secrets obviously presumed Mawyndulë cared about his father's well-being, which made Mawyndulë question the wisdom of his title.

"You don't need to worry," Lothian assured him. "The tribes have no understanding of the Art. If they did, they wouldn't dream of such things. The Talwara is well protected."

"The fane's food is cleaned by a Miralyith," Vasek explained. "All doors and windows are sealed by the Art each night, and only those assigned residency may enter these walls. Besides, I expect to get to the bottom of these rumors quite soon, and then we can eliminate those responsible."

"My fane?" Vidar spoke up. He had arrived near the end of the meeting as he usually did. His only reason for coming was to learn what, if any, direction the fane might wish to relay to the Aquila. "The meeting is about to convene, your son and I—"

"Yes, yes." Lothian swept his fingers at them. "Be off. Be off."

"If I may, my fane." Vasek held up a hand to stop them. "Should these rumors prove true, the safest and easiest solution would be to calm any fears that might lead to such an act. Vidar needs to continue to assure the other tribes that they all have a voice within the Aquila and that there are no plans to change that dynamic. It may help to ease tensions until I can learn more."

The fane nodded his agreement.

"I shall do my best, as always, my fane," Vidar said to Lothian.

Then without so much as a look, Vidar walked out, leaving Mawyndulë to chase behind.

Mawyndulë's second Aquila meeting was more boring than the first, perhaps more tedious than anything could be. Makareta wasn't there. He looked repeatedly until Vidar shot him a glare. The topic being discussed wasn't the assassination possibility, but rather the drainage of the tea fields. At one point, Vidar kicked Mawyndulë's foot in order to wake him, but no matter how hard Mawyndulë tried, he couldn't keep his eyes open or his head raised. The second kick was harder than the first. The third time made him cry out.

Mawyndulë had been lost in a nightmare where an assassin was stalking him through an unfamiliar section of the Talwara, which was strange because he knew every inch. The killer had already murdered his father and was giving chase down endless corridors. The would-be butcher was a huge shadow that leapt out quite suddenly. Mawyndulë tried to scream, but couldn't. He tried to summon the Art, but nothing happened. He then resorted to running, but the killer got a grip on Mawyndulë's leg, squeezing until it hurt.

When he woke, it was less the pain of Vidar kicking him and more the terror of the nightmare that caused him to scream. Regardless of the origin, the result was catastrophic. Everyone in the chamber stopped and looked at him in shock. Vidar appeared the most surprised of all as he leaned away, his mouth hanging open, eyes wide.

"Pay attention, you little fool!" Vidar snapped.

Maybe Vidar hadn't meant to speak as loud as he did, but there was no doubt everyone in the chamber heard. Unfortunately, this included a lovely Miralyith with kitten eyes sitting in the gallery's front row. Makareta had apparently showed up too late to keep Mawyndulë awake, but just in time for his most humiliating experience since The Traitor had stopped him from ending the life of the God Killer.

Mawyndulë's castigation didn't end there. After the Aquila adjourned,

Vidar reprimanded him further. He did so far more quietly, but by then Mawyndulë wasn't concerned with volume so much as speed. He wanted to catch Makareta on her way out, and ask her if they could go somewhere before the meeting. He was hoping she would tell him where she lived. Instead, Mawyndulë was trapped, listening to a lecture from a second-rate Miralyith.

"Your father will hear about this, but that should be the least of your worries," Vidar said, and Mawyndulë realized who the shadow in his dream had been—a more frightening version of the senior councilor with fangs and claws. "You've tarnished not only your reputation in this esteemed body, but mine as well."

Vidar stepped closer and lowered his voice. "Listen, you little shite, your father might not care about the impression you make, but I refuse to be embarrassed by your behavior. While we are in this chamber, you do what I say, and that means paying attention and minding your manners."

Mawyndulë was stunned, but not so much so that he would assume a subservient role from a lesser Miralyith. He was the prince after all. "Why should I?"

Vidar smiled then, and when he did, the senior councilor really did look like the thing from the nightmare. "Politics, my boy. You might be Lothian's son, but trust me, I can ruin you. I'll make everyone in this city hate you, including your own father."

"And when I become fane, I'll have you executed."

"I'm twenty-seven hundred years old, boy. I won't live long enough to give you the satisfaction. You, on the other hand, will have to live with the soiled reputation for the rest of your long life. Think about that the next time your actions could make a fool of me."

Mawyndulë hadn't been trying to embarrass the senior councilor, but at that moment, he preferred that Vidar thought he had. The old fool walked out, leaving Mawyndulë under the great dome of Caratacus and Gylindora—the basket weaver.

When Mawyndulë turned to leave, he realized he hadn't been completely alone. Imaly was still seated in her center chair, watching him, her old fish eyes peering in a sickening fashion.

"That didn't go so well, did it?" she said, her hands clasped in her lap. She hadn't spoken loudly, but the dome amplified her voice as if she were a Miralyith using a sound-enhancing weave.

Mawyndulë shook his head.

"Vidar is an ass," she said so plainly that it stunned him. "Some aspire to these seats to better serve their fellow Fhrey. Some feel called, others obligated. People like Vidar do it for the prestige and the respect the position usually bestows. But he doesn't understand that respect isn't something you get from a position, or even from past achievements. Respect has to be earned, and re-earned, with every single person you meet. Vidar never learned that lesson, and as a result, he has never found the regard he so dearly craves, even from a pup like you. It gnaws at him, this feeling that he should be bowed to when he's laughed at instead."

"I didn't do it to make people laugh at him. I just fell asleep and had a nightmare."

"Doesn't matter. In his mind, you did it on purpose, and people have been laughing at him his whole life. They haven't, of course, any more than you intentionally tried to embarrass him. But like all of us, he sees what he looks for, and after twenty-seven hundred years he has certain expectations."

She got up and walked toward him. As she did, she glanced up toward the gallery behind Mawyndulë's head. He quickly spun, thinking Makareta might be there, that she might have come back in, but the rows were still empty.

Imaly smiled at him. "Mawyndulë," she said gently, kindly, "you're young. I know you don't think you are, but you're still very much a child. Don't take what I'm about to say the wrong way. This isn't about you personally. I think anyone under a thousand shouldn't be allowed outside without a guardian." She chuckled. "You need to be more guarded. You're the prince. You will inherit the Forest Throne, and if you survive the challenge, you will be fane. There are many people who would like to harness the power you will one day wield."

"Apparently not Vidar."

"Like I said, Vidar is an ass, but he's only an ass."

His grin grew wider. He liked it when she berated Vidar.

"There are others far more ambitious, far more sinister than he. Just remember that the one you see isn't nearly so dangerous as the ones you can't."

She looked up at the gallery once more then walked out, leaving him alone beneath the steady gaze of Caratacus and Gylindora.

Mawyndulë arrived early at the Rose Bridge and sat on a big rock at the top of the bank, near where the span met the ground. He liked it there, perched high like a hawk on a cliff's edge. Sitting in the twilight, he could see the water of the Shinara flowing by.

He rarely spent time alone. In his youth, there was a staff that saw to his needs: maids, nurses, cooks, entertainers. The older he became the smaller the staff, but he would still have had a tutor if the last one hadn't turned traitor and Gryndal hadn't died. He expected his father to appoint a new instructor, but he hadn't yet. The lack suited Mawyndulë just fine. He'd never liked lessons and enjoyed the free time, time to be alone, time to think, time to live.

A yellowed leaf floated along the river like a tiny boat, spinning in the breeze, gliding over the ripples as if weightless. Watching it, Mawyndulë felt certain there was a greater truth in that otherwise insignificant leaf, perhaps because it *was* insignificant. Everyone knew mountains and skies were majestic, and worthy of observance, but no one ever bothered to look at a leaf. Yet there was a beauty there, a simple purity. Billions of them torn free from their homes and scattered by the wind, yet each—like the one on the river—was unique, its path different from any other. What an adventure it must be having, riding the water to lands unknown. He spotted more leaves, some greener than others, traveling downstream as well. Watching them pass, Mawyndulë felt wiser, more profound, because he alone appreciated the value of a leaf drifting on a stream.

People began to arrive just after dark. That was the point. The meeting was meant to be secret. He hadn't fully understood that the first time, but things made more sense now. The other tribes were suspicious of the Miralyith and looking for excuses to revolt. An open meeting of so many Miralyith would be seen as a threat.

He didn't recognize anyone at first, just nameless faces who hauled in wine and set out blankets. Many had baskets of food to share. Mawyndulë remained on his perch. Few noticed; when someone did, he smiled and they smiled back. Most sat and talked softly among themselves, and for a brief moment Mawyndulë saw them as the leaves on the river, all unique, all adrift on powerful currents they were helpless to control. And in that instant he realized that if this were true, he, too, must be a leaf.

The thought evaporated with the arrival of Makareta.

She didn't come with Aiden as he'd expected. She was with two others whom he didn't recognize. Maybe he'd seen them the previous week, but a lot of his memory of that night was fuzzy. When she spotted him, she grinned. He hoped she would come up to his ledge, hoped that he might have her all to himself, but pivoting on her left heel, she turned and waved for him to come down. By the time he had, she was holding out a cup of wine.

"You came back," she said with a giddy, childish bounce that made him happy.

"I said I would."

"Orlene, Tandur, this is Mawyndulë, son of Fane Lothian."

Orlene was older, taller than Makareta. She actually wore her cloak and had the hood up, giving her a mysterious allure. Tandur held his cloak draped over one arm, and while his head was Miralyith-bald, he had a patch of neatly trimmed beard on his chin and just under his lower lip.

"I saw you in the Airenthenon today," Makareta said.

He cringed on the inside, expecting some comment about falling asleep, the outburst, or Vidar's reprimand, but that was all she said. He didn't know why he didn't leave it there. Mawyndulë told himself he should, but he realized he wanted to talk about it. "That whole deliberation about field irrigation was so monotonous." He rolled his eyes. "I just couldn't stay awake."

"It really was dull," she offered.

"Vidar kicked me. That's why I shouted."

"He kicked you?" The tone of indignation in her voice made him smile. "He actually *kicked* you?"

Mawyndulë nodded and took a sip of his drink, which tasted even better than the wine he'd had the week before.

"Well, no wonder you shouted. And then he had the nerve to yell at you!" She sounded outraged.

"He's always doing stuff like that. And afterward, he threatened me."

"*What?*" she exploded, those already big eyes even larger.

This caught the attention of those around them, who gathered to hear. One was Aiden, whom Mawyndulë hadn't seen arrive, but who joined their little circle, which was quickly becoming the center of the meeting.

"Makareta," Aiden said. "What's going on?"

She put one hand on her hip and pointed at Mawyndulë with the other. "Vidar kicked the prince, humiliated him in the Aquila, and then *threatened* him."

"What?" Aiden said, appalled.

"I was there for part of it," Makareta said. "I heard, well everyone heard, him call Mawyndulë *a fool*. Can you believe it?"

"He said that? In the Aquila?"

Makareta nodded so hard she spilled a bit of her wine.

More and more people gathered. Mawyndulë saw faces behind faces all looking at him, all struggling to hear what he had to say.

"He promised that he'd ruin my reputation. Guess he has connections or something."

"You're the prince!" Aiden sounded just as outraged as Makareta. "That's horrible. Am I right?"

"Yeah," Orlene said. "That's outrageous."

"Thing is," Tandur said, "Vidar is a wasted seat in the council. He wasn't meant to be a voice of the Miralyith. He was just an assistant— there to fetch water if Gryndal got thirsty. But now . . ."

"I agree with Orlene," Makareta said. "That isn't right. He doesn't know what he's doing. Last week he made an utter fool of himself and gave Imaly another victory."

Mawyndulë took a second sip of wine as people around him gathered to voice their anger at his mistreatment. Once again, Makareta was standing close, so near that he brushed her asica with his hand.

"What makes me angry," Aiden said, with a shake of his fist that appeared a bit too showy, "is that Mawyndulë was Gryndal's student, so he should be the one taking a place in the Aquila. He should be the senior councilor, not Vidar. Am I right?"

Mawyndulë wasn't certain if Aiden was really upset or just acting the part. Aiden might be the sort who would feign emotion to make himself look better.

"Vidar only got the seat because he's older. This is a travesty of timing and politics. The fane doesn't want to be seen as favoring his son, so he's forced to allow a fool to be the voice of the Miralyith in the council."

"We should do something about it," Tandur said while looking at Aiden.

As if any of *them* could do anything. Mawyndulë chuckled, hiding his laughter behind his wine cup. Did they really think he'd put up with such indignities if something could be done?

"What do you mean?" Orlene asked. "What can we do?"

Congratulations to Orlene! You win first prize for stating the obvious.

"What can we do?" Aiden laughed. "What can't we do? We're Miralyith!"

Mawyndulë got the feeling that was his answer to everything. Maybe he lived in a part of Erivan, in one of the more distant cities or villages, where the Art was worshipped. He certainly didn't live in the Talwara.

"And what are these meetings for, if not to *do* something? Each week we come and talk about the superiority of the Miralyith. Is it just talk? Do we just drink wine and complain?"

"What are you saying?" Makareta asked.

"This is our chance to do something. I mean *really* do something. Am I right?"

Mawyndulë laughed again, but noticed several of the heads in the crowd nodded, their faces intent and serious.

Makareta was nodding, too. "Like what?"

"Mawyndulë is the heir, not only to the Forest Throne, but to Gryndal's seat in the Aquila. Vidar is a disgrace to everything we stand for. He doesn't know what he's doing. He's quick to compromise because he doesn't embrace the same values we do. The values of a *real* Miralyith." Aiden's voice was growing louder, taking on a rhythm. And as he spoke, he punched the air with that fist of his, or poked his finger at some invisible foe. "He's working to diminish us to appease the lesser tribes, when he should be convincing everyone of the inevitability, and the wisdom, of a world dominated by the Miralyith."

"Instead of demonstrating how all Miralyith should be viewed as gods"—Tandur raised his own finger, pointing toward the heavens, or at least the underside of the bridge—"he only confirms everyone's belief that all Fhrey are equal. His term in the Aquila will only retard our advancement."

All around him, Mawyndulë heard shouts of agreement. Some were hopping, bouncing with excitement. A nervous energy that might have been due to the wine. By the end of the meetings, everyone always did get a little loopy.

"But what can we do?" someone else asked, someone Mawyndulë couldn't even see due to the growing cluster of people squeezing him and Makareta closer together.

"We should replace him," Aiden said. "Am I right?"

All heads nodded and there were murmurs of agreement.

"Just think," Aiden went on, "once we've replaced Vidar with Mawyndulë, we Gray Cloaks will have a direct voice in the grand council. And power to enhance our position."

People cheered, and at that moment Mawyndulë felt Makareta take his hand. "Here," she said, handing him a cloak. "You're one of us now."

CHAPTER FIFTEEN

Caric

With few exceptions, I hold no love for the Dherg. They are deceit-ful, greedy, and cruel. They epitomize the worst traits imaginable. But of all the Dherg, one stands out as the most despicable. Read on . . . I am just getting started.

—THE BOOK OF BRIN

The grunting stopped. The ship no longer jerked forward at regular inter-vals, for which Persephone was immensely grateful. Looking over the side, she saw the oars rising into the air like bony wings. They dripped seawater that sprayed in the wind. Twelve dwarf-sized sailors pulled the poles inside, sliding them across their tiny laps, and securing the handles with leather straps. Six big, dirty metal pots and five smaller ones dangled from hooks and clanged against the side of the ship. A pair of giant rudders was controlled by a single dwarf, who sat on a stool holding one lever with each arm. Persephone had counted just about everything on the ship, which turned out to be smaller than she'd first imagined, but any place became cramped when you were trapped on it.

Now that the oars were drawn in, the big sheet of cloth from the cross-beam was unfurled. It billowed and flapped as the sailors scurried to secure ties.

"Amazing," Roan said, peering up at the sail. She'd been saying that every few minutes since they came aboard. Roan was fascinated by how they steered the ship, how it broke through the waves, how the dwarfs propelled the vessel with poles, and how they stroked in unison, keeping time by singing. Roan didn't appear to mind how terrible the singing was. She even seemed stunned that the ship floated on water, as if the woman who'd invented the wheel, the pocket, the hanging chair, the pottery table, and the improved copper ax didn't know wood could float. To be honest, Persephone had her own doubts after watching them load twenty-three barrels and thirty-two crates, all of which appeared to be very heavy. "The wind is actually pushing us across the surface."

Persephone couldn't care less, so long as they got where they were going, and did so soon. All the bobbing and rolling had left her regretting the second helping of Dherg porridge from that morning. What had tasted good going down certainly wouldn't on its way back up. Arion was worse. Pale and moaning, the Fhrey curled over, hugging her legs, her bald head rolling from side to side on her knees.

The Dherg had stuffed them out of the way along with the barrels and crates, near the front of the ship, the part of the vessel that rose and fell the most. Persephone was certain this wasn't by accident. The sailors didn't like them and hated Arion. They hadn't said so, but that was part of the problem. The sailors hadn't said anything, not to them. The sailors spoke only to Frost and Flood, and only in the Dherg language. At first, Persephone thought they might not speak anything else, but she caught them sneering when Moya made a comment about one of the sailors having porridge in his beard. A moment later, the sloppy eater scrubbed it out.

Frost and Flood had reverted to their own language as well, grumbling as if the two were busy cursing every living thing.

"Oh, Grand Mother!" Brin exclaimed. The girl had been studying Arion's old bandages—the ones with the magic markings.

Everyone except Arion looked over expectantly.

Instead of explaining, Brin made some marks on one of the slates she had brought with her.

"What is it?" Moya asked, sitting with her back to a barrel, one of their blankets wrapped over her legs. Even in high summer, the morning wind on the open water was chilly. "Just realized you forgot to put out the campfire back home?" She chuckled.

Even out here, at a time like this, Moya has a sense of humor, Mari love her.

Brin held up the strips of cloth. "These aren't just magic markings or pictures. These are *symbols.*"

Everyone failed to see the significance, though Roan appeared intrigued; of course, she would be. She was also fascinated by icicle formations and the way dandelion fluff floated.

"*Symbols,* " she said, as if saying the word again with more emphasis would make them understand. "They're like what I've been trying to do." She tapped the slate with her marking stone, which clicked with a hollow sound.

Roan inched closer. "They say something?"

"Yes! They're *words*. They're a message. I'm positive of it."

"What do they say?"

Brin's bright face dimmed. "I don't know."

"Then how do you know they're words?" Moya covered her ankles with the blanket.

"Because of the way they're drawn; they make patterns that repeat. It's like what I've been trying to do. Someone else has already done it." She pointed to a circle with a line through it. "This symbol is always in front of this square one."

Everyone stared back with blank faces.

"Okay, okay, listen." She flipped over her slate and pulled out a piece of chalk. "I've been trying to figure out a way to mark down stories so Keepers can have a permanent memory of events. At first, I tried to make little pictures of things, like I did on the walls of my house back in Dahl Rhen, only it would take forever to illustrate a whole story that way, and you can't illustrate a name. That's what got me, *a name.* How do you draw a name? A name is just sounds. But what if a symbol could represent a sound?" She drew on the slate. "If this circle represents *br* and this square the sound *in,* then together"—she underlined both—"they make the name *Brin!* See? So all I had to do was make a symbol for every sound. Turns out there aren't that many. That's what I've been doing, and when you do that, these repeating patterns occur, just like on this cloth. They aren't the same as mine, of course, but they're the same sort of thing. Someone else has already done what I'm trying to do." She held up the bandages as evidence.

Persephone turned to Frost, who sat with stiffly folded arms, looking out over the water and appearing not to listen.

"Is that true? These symbols were in the rol. These are the markings of your people. Can you understand what they say?" Persephone asked him.

Frost glanced over with a miserable frown, as if she'd asked him to wash her feet with his tongue.

"The Orinfar?" Rain said.

"Is that what you call those markings?" Persephone said.

Frost nodded. "Stops magic."

"But what does it *say?*" Brin rolled up on her knees, letting her own blanket fall as she leaned forward.

Frost shrugged. "Doesn't say nothing. Just symbols. We have them for counting, too. Use them for measuring and keeping track of who owes what. But the Orinfar, we learn by rote. They were given to King Mideon near the end of the war with the Fhrey. The gift came too late to help us win. By then the elf queen had us on our heels."

Arion's head stopped rocking. One eye opened, and in a pained whisper she asked, "Who give?"

Frost thought a moment and glanced at Flood.

"Don't look at me," the other dwarf said. "You're older than I am."

"By three minutes!"

"Dee, da, dee, do, dah dah, drum," Brin muttered as she stared at the bandages. "Dee, da, dee, do, dee, dee, dee. Dee, dee, do, dah dah, dee. Dee, dee, do, dah, drum, dee, dee."

"What are you doing?" Roan asked.

"The markings repeat, and so that's the pattern these symbols would make if they were sounds . . . or something close to that."

Arion's head came all the way up and both eyes opened. Suri looked up, too. Both stared at Brin.

"What?" the girl asked.

"Do that again," Arion told her.

Brin repeated the sounds, and the Fhrey's eyes widened.

"What is it?" Persephone asked.

"Sheen hath wee hove bragen groom," Arion sang. *"Sheen hath wee hove reen, breen, froom. Sheen ahwee, hath elochments hee. Sheen ahwee hath grooms fram thee. That's the weave that I used to break Mawyndulë's control on the people in your dahl. It's what Miralyith call a* 'dampener.' *It severs an Artist's power from the source."* She looked at Persephone and added, *"Like tripping someone who's trying to run. You break their connection to the ground, so to speak."* She said all this in Fhrey, and Persephone translated as best she could—leaving out the gibberish words which weren't any language that she could tell.

"So these markings are the language of the Fhrey?" Brin asked.

Arion shook her head. "Language of Creation."

"It's the song of birds," Suri said. "The sound of wind, and rain, and rivers, the flap of wings, the rustle of grass. It's the *voice of trees.*" She said this last bit looking hard at Persephone.

"What you're talking about, this recording of sounds, is . . ." Arion hesitated. "We call it *ryeteen.*"

"Wri . . . ting," Brin mimicked her.

"Close enough. Useful for sending short messages long distances by bird."

Brin's eyes went wide. "You can do that? Can you understand this?"

Brin handed her the wrappings that had once bound the Fhrey's head. Arion studied the markings and frowned. "These aren't words. Not Fhrey words. But the sounds you made, the pattern, the rhythm . . . that was the Art. I never knew it could be painted. But the markings representing a blocking weave makes sense, as that's exactly what the bandages did to me."

"Do the sounds have meanings?" Brin asked. "Are they like words? Can *they* be translated?"

Arion and Suri both nodded. "In a way, sure. They are ideas after all." She spoke to Suri in Fhrey for a moment, asking how to say a few words. Then she softly sang in the same rhythm but using Rhunic words:

> "Shut the way of hidden power.
> Shut the way of rock, beast, flower.
> Shut away, the elements be.
> Shut away the powers from thee."

"It says all that on the cloth?" Moya asked, astounded.

"More than that," Brin said. She had followed along on the bandages with her finger as Arion sang. "There's more here." The girl laid the bandages across her lap. "So the Fhrey can mark words on cloth?"

"Some can, yes."

"Do they, um, 'write' stories?"

"Stories?" Arion shook her head. "No. As I understand it, markings are simple things with a limited number of words. In Erivan, those that *ryte* are called *scrybes*. They use the markings to . . ." She hesitated, conferred in whispers with Suri, and then continued, "Keep lists, issue simple orders, and send short reports. It takes a long time to learn. Few understand markings. Stories would be pointless."

Brin seemed to want more from the Miralyith, but Arion was showing signs of fatigue. She grimaced as if she might vomit; then she moaned and laid her head back down. The ship rose and fell across the swells, and Arion moaned again.

"How much longer?" Persephone asked.

"We should arrive before dark," Frost replied.

"*Thank you, Ferrol,*" Arion whispered three times to her knees.

"Where are your chain shirts?" Moya asked the Dherg.

Frost wasn't wearing his anymore. None of the three were. They had taken the garments off the moment they came aboard. Given how heavy they looked, Persephone guessed this was to avoid drowning should they fall overboard.

Frost grumbled something.

"Traded them for passage." Rain spoke again. He was working on the mattock-bladed end of his pick, honing it to a bright edge.

"It cost that much to be ferried across to Neith?" Persephone asked.

"With her it does." Flood nodded toward Arion.

"The rest of you didn't come cheap, either," Frost said. "Dent is a scoundrel."

The ship continued its roll and pitch, and Persephone looked for something else to count—anything to keep her mind from thinking about her stomach. Her sight settled on Roan, who was winding the length of a string around the center of her long stick. Persephone assumed Roan planned to use it as a staff since it was nearly as tall as she was. But Roan had whittled it so that it tapered at both ends and had a flattened shape everywhere except in the middle, where she was wrapping the string.

"What's that, Roan?" Persephone asked.

"It's a bow, like for starting fires, but this one isn't."

"Isn't what?"

"For starting fires."

"Huh?"

Roan thought a moment. "I got the idea for the wheel when I saw Gifford's pottery table. And I got the idea for this bow when I saw Habet starting a fire."

"But it isn't for starting a fire?"

"No."

"What *is* it for then, Roan?" Moya asked with a bit of irritation in her voice.

"Throwing things."

"Like what?"

"Remember when you were trying out that little spear, and it didn't go too far?" Roan picked up one of the shorter sticks she had in her sack. They were all very straight. and Persephone wondered how she made them so uniform.

"Uh-huh." Moya nodded.

Roan took out a thicker string, tied it on one end of the long staff, and then bent the shaft into a bow and looped the other end of the string around the opposite end. She gave the taut string a flick of her finger and listened to it ring with the vibration.

They all watched as she stood up, fitted one of the small sticks that had a notch, and pulled back. She pointed the stick out toward the water and let go. The string twanged and the force threw the stick. It shot out at a blinding speed, then spun sideways and fell into the sea.

Several of the sailors glared at them, and Dent, the dwarf with the nose ring, stomped across the deck to shout loudly at Frost and Flood.

"Don't do that again," Flood said after Dent left. "They don't like magic."

"It's not magic," Roan said.

Frost and Flood looked at each other skeptically. "What do you call it when a little one like you can toss a stick so far?"

Roan shrugged, and all she said in her defense was, "It will go farther once I weight the front with a stone or metal point, the way the javelin was weighted. A lot farther. Straighter, too."

Moya was looking out at the water in the direction the stick had flown. "If you put a point on that like a javelin, and made it fly straight . . ." She looked back at Roan abruptly and never finished her sentence, but there was an odd expression on her face, as if she was both excited and terrified.

They caught their first glimpse of Belgreig in the light of the setting sun, through a curtain of windblown rain. A gray jagged line crossed the horizon, growing higher and darker with each passing minute. Even at a distance of miles, the landscape appeared no friendlier than the sailors, and as the sun drowned in the sea, the land became a black silhouette of serrated teeth.

Persephone stood on the rainy deck, holding on to one of the million ropes to keep from falling as the ship rocked harder than ever. Soggy and dripping, they clutched bags and blankets, each longing to be free of the ship, but they were all uncertain about trading that miserable spot near the bow for the craggy shore.

How can nine of us bring back enough swords to supply an army of thou-

sands? No, not nine, only six. Frost, Flood, and Rain won't be coming. Why would they?

Across the dark, rolling swells mixed with gray rain, the world ahead didn't appear inviting. Lightning flashed, branching zigzags shone brightly, and for an instant, all the world was exposed. In that corpse-white pallor, Persephone saw a glimpse of the impossible. A rocky coast of soaring cliffs was actually a carved city. Stone towers, stone peaks, stone arches, all encased within a wall many stories high. But as monumental as the city appeared, even from that distance, she saw something hidden in the shadows behind. In that flash, Persephone spotted the hazy suggestion of monoliths too straight, too symmetrical to be mountains but too colossal to be anything else.

This is a land of dwarfs?

Thunder boomed overhead; below, waves burst white against breakwaters. A fence of blades topped the city's walls. At the corners, stone gargoyles vomited rain into the sea. *Not a friendly place. Not a welcoming town. That wall is a battlement, a fortress, a relic of an ancient age, a time before men when Dherg and Fhrey made war upon one another.* Witnessing the enormity, the stark power and militant strength of the Dherg, Persephone was dumbfounded.

These people lost the war?

She felt her heart sink. *If that's so, what chance does Rhulyn have?*

Persephone turned to look at the dark, empty sea behind them. *And how will we get home? The dwarfs traded metal shirts for passage. What do we have to trade?* Persephone squeezed the rope harder than necessary.

The sail was down and the Dherg rowed to the dock at the base of the city. Oars went up, and with hollow bumps, bangs, and curses the ship was drawn in and secured. The side of the vessel bumped against a row of barrels lashed to the dock, causing everyone to stagger. Thrown ropes were lashed to bollards securing the ship, and the wooden gangway was extended across the breach.

"C'mon," Frost told them, and led the way over the heaving plank bridge. Flood and Rain followed closely behind.

Persephone gathered the rest and sent Moya across first. Persephone came last, counting heads to make certain they all got off safely. The long plank bounced with their passage.

"Roan!" Persephone shouted.

Captivated by the walls, the woman had been looking up and not watching where she was going. Luckily, she froze at the shout. One more step and she would have fallen into the harbor. Persephone glared, and Roan sheepishly bowed her head and centered herself on the plank.

The whole line of women had stopped, each of them looking back.

"Honestly!" was all Moya said before resuming their trek.

Reaching solid ground, Persephone allowed herself a quick look up. The stone wall of the city rose so straight and high that she had to throw her head all the way back to see the top. This was higher than the walls of Alon Rhist, and the towers looked to be things of dreams. *No*, she thought, *dreams aren't built of dark stone crowned by toothy spires. This is a home for nightmares.*

They stood clustered on a dock of many moorings, hidden within a maze of a dozen ugly block buildings surrounded by crates and sacks.

"So this is Neith?" Persephone said.

"No," Frost replied. "This is Caric, the port city. Neith is behind."

"Behind?" Brin asked. "That is a mountain, isn't it?"

Frost revealed a rare smile. "What you saw was only the entrance to the great city. Neith lies *inside*." He said the last word as if it held special meaning. "Stay together now. Flood, watch the rear, and make sure they don't wander. Threaten anyone who comes too close."

"Why would—" Persephone began to ask.

"All right then, let's get moving," Frost shouted, marching them between the buildings. "Single file. Stay to the right! Stay to the right!"

The reason for this last order became apparent as teams of dwarfs with empty carts rumbled by at an alarming speed.

"Carts!" Roan exclaimed.

The first cart pusher rushed past without looking at them. The second one glanced over, and Persephone heard a gasp. The third dwarf stopped and stared in shock.

"Quickly now!" Frost ordered and began to run.

They all trotted to keep pace and soon they came to a pair of lancet-arched doors. Frost pulled them open to reveal a long colonnade: a gallery of pillars and corbels running deep into the cliff. The shadowy interior was a treasure trove of brown sacks, bright pine crates, and two-wheeled carts. Everything was illuminated by the same sort of green glow Persephone remembered from the rols.

Frost led them at a fast walk past sheaves of wheat, barley, and rye to a stone stair. Up they went without a word. Persephone and Flood continued bringing up the rear, keeping an eye on the rest. Everyone shivered in the chilled air, dripping from the wet.

At least we're out of the wind. I can thank Mari for that. Persephone felt a need to focus on the positive, lest she give in to panic. Something wasn't right. She didn't like how the dwarf with the cart had gawked, or how fast Frost was leading them. Running was never a good sign.

Pausing on a landing just past another set of doors, Minna took the opportunity to shake water out of her fur. This gave Persephone the same idea and she gathered back her hair and twisted the wet out. Flood, whose beard was running a constant drip, rushed to close and bolt the doors behind them. Once he had, Frost began the climb once more.

Moya glanced back at the bolted door and then at Persephone with a concerned look. All Persephone could do was shrug.

Roan was back to her wide-eyed fascination, staring at—and at least on one occasion touching—the illuminating gemstones mounted to the walls. Arion staggered forward, one hand covering her mouth, her skin still the color of snow. Brin's eyelids hung heavy with fatigue. Suri scowled at the walls, like she always did.

Together they climbed up past a room filled with large wooden crates, then one of barrels. When they reached a new landing, again they stopped to brace the adjoining door.

"Why are you barring the doors?" Persephone asked.

Flood looked at her with irritation. "No time to explain. We're in a hurry."

"Why is that?"

Flood looked to Frost, who smiled unconvincingly and added, "Like he said, no time to explain. Let's go!"

Climbing the stairs at such a brisk pace had burned away the chill. By the time they reached the top, no one was shivering, and Persephone felt downright hot. They passed through another set of doors, this time into a large hall with several adjoining corridors. Wooden benches and small tables formed gathering places in the corners. Long banners hung from the ceiling, looking just as large as the sail on their ship, but brightly colored in green and gold. Persephone had seen such colors of dyed cloth in Alon Rhist, but had no idea how they were created.

Frost held out a hand, silently blocking them from entering the hall. A moment later Persephone heard the echo of hard heels on stone. They waited for them to pass.

"Why are we hiding?" she whispered.

Frost didn't answer, and once the way was clear, he led them toward a corridor.

Flood abandoned his place at the rear of their procession and rushed forward to confer with Frost.

Moya once more looked back with raised eyebrows.

With a shake of her head, Persephone marched forward to speak with the two dwarfs.

Frost was shaking his head at his brother as she approached. They spoke in the Dherg language in hushed, hurried tones.

"We're not going any farther until you explain what's going on," Persephone insisted.

"Need to find Gronbach," Frost said in Rhunic.

Flood said something in the Dherg language and pointed up another, much wider, much grander set of steps that ran off to their right.

Frost bared his teeth and stomped one booted foot on the stone; the sound echoed off the hard walls. Then he responded to his brother, also in the Dherg language.

"What's going on?" Persephone demanded.

Frost ignored her and continued speaking in the Dherg tongue.

Persephone found Rain, who stood next to Moya with arms folded, waiting like the rest. "What are they saying?"

Rain looked over at the arguing pair. "Looking for Gronbach, but he's up in the Rostwell, eating. So now we're trying to think of a place to hide you until Gronbach finishes his meal. He'll be in a bad mood if he's interrupted, but we don't want to get caught before we have a chance to talk to him."

"Caught? Caught by who? Caught for what? Frost said a small group of women wouldn't be seen as a problem. Was that the truth or merely what you were hoping?"

A gasp came from behind, and Persephone turned just in time to see a plump Dherg drop a tray of stacked wooden bowls. The whole thing hit the stone with a horrible crash, sending the containers bouncing and spinning across the floor. The impact of the silver tray rang and echoed off the hard walls.

Then the chubby dwarf screamed. He continued to shriek while running up the broad stairs. Persephone doubted that this was a promising development. Clearly, some things had been left out of Frost's story.

She looked back at Frost and Flood. Neither of them moved nor spoke. Frozen, they watched the terrified dwarf run up the steps.

"What do you want us to do?" Persephone asked.

Frost looked back at her, his face pale. "Don't die. That would ruin everything."

CHAPTER SIXTEEN

Long Gone

Her eyesight was failing, her hearing poor, and she did not have a single tooth left in her head, but that old woman knew everything.
—THE BOOK OF BRIN

"Will we be going to the meeting tomorrow?" Malcolm asked. The one-time slave sat on the stack of Rhen-imported split logs to avoid the trickle of water that made its way through their corner of the camp.

"No," Raithe replied with all the willfulness of a stubborn child.

"That's three in a row. You're letting your clan down, my chieftain."

He said this with a smile directed at Tesh, who sat carving a small bit of wood into something that vaguely resembled a turtle.

The rain had returned, hindering Raithe from training the boy. The two had been spending most of their days on the beach, going over everything from proper footing to correct falling. They managed to find driftwood to approximate swords and spears. As it turned out, the kid wasn't just a fast learner, he already knew a good deal. Tesh had managed to trip Raithe twice, and the young boy had thrown the bigger man to the sand a few times. Whenever Raithe got lazy or underestimated the kid, he received a bruise as punishment. With the rain, there was little sense in sparring—too hard to see, too difficult to think. A day of rest was in order.

And so Raithe and Tesh had joined Malcolm under the wool. The three had an island of dry grass, but Raithe didn't know for how long. A sag in the overhead wool created a looming threat. The center dripped—not fast, but constantly. Malcolm had put a wooden bowl beneath it to catch the water, but it had to be emptied often, which meant they either took turns sleeping or woke up wet. That wasn't Raithe's only concern. The slow leak wasn't enough to offset the rain. The overhead pond grew wider and deeper at an ominous rate.

Malcolm held a stemless cup in both hands and sipped from it. Raithe had no idea what was in the cup and no interest in finding out. He wasn't thirsty, and while he hadn't eaten since that morning, he wasn't hungry, either. *Tired* was the only way to describe how he felt, but he'd done nothing that day to warrant the weariness. When he wasn't teaching Tesh, he had no work nor any responsibilities except being a chieftain of one. Raithe had spent a short time breaking up what little wood they had to feed their fire and had sewn up a pulled seam in his shirt, but neither took more than a few minutes. Most of his time was spent staring out at the rain. The ceaseless patter, ping, and drip drained him of all strength and ambition. Idleness created a boredom all its own. He wanted to sleep but couldn't, and he let out a sigh.

"I understand." Malcolm took another sip from his cup and began nodding. "It's indeed exhausting to sit here all day, watching your fingers wrinkle." He pulled one hand away from his cup to study it. "Captivating, not to mention gravely important."

"The rain might stop tomorrow. Then Tesh and I can do some more training."

"And if it doesn't? Will you spend another day staring thoughtfully across the field? I mean if you don't do it, who will? And it is a significantly better choice than ruling the clans."

"I don't want to be keenig," Raithe said.

"Such sentiment, some might say, is all the more reason you should take the position."

Raithe glared.

Malcolm smiled in mock innocence, then turned to Tesh. "Has he fed you today?"

The kid shook his head, and Malcolm shot Raithe a shocked expression.

"We didn't *do* anything," Raithe explained. "Don't need to eat *every day*, you know. He's fine. He's Dureyan. We don't coddle our children. You learn to survive on your own or you don't. Simple as that."

Malcolm nodded. "Might explain why there's only two of you left."

"What did *you* do today, Mister Enterprising Ball of Ambition?" Raithe asked.

"I helped out with the sheep. The flocks were getting into the crops again. Got into a little scuffle with the local farmers."

"A scuffle?"

"A shoving match."

"Who won?"

He pointed to the spear leaning against the wall behind them. "Narsirabad."

"You stabbed someone?" Raithe asked, impressed.

"No!" Malcolm said, appalled.

"But you threatened to?"

"Well, maybe . . . a little." Malcolm stirred the embers. "I also checked on Gelston."

Despite having lived in Dahl Rhen for over a month, Raithe knew few faces and fewer names. Gelston's stood out. He was Brin's uncle who had survived being hit by lightning. While most of Dahl Rhen's injured had been left at the first outer village they came to, Gelston had followed the train of people south. "How's he doing?"

"Walking around and talking but still in pain. Complains about his back and head, a ringing in his ears, and the fact that he can't sleep."

"People are calling him blessed by the gods," Raithe said.

"Don't think he would agree," Malcolm replied. "Also don't think he's ready to watch his flocks yet."

Raithe shook his head and leaned back on his hands, stretching his legs to their full length, which put his feet out in the rain. Being tall had its shortcomings. "See, there you go . . . coddling people again. A little back pain or headache shouldn't keep a man from getting his work done. His sheep could start a war. He needs to get back to work."

Malcolm nodded again. "I'm sure he would agree . . . if he knew he had sheep."

"How's that?"

"In addition to the pain, and a really exotic lesion running up his back that looks like a red fern, he has trouble remembering things. I watched him fill a bowl with water, wash his face, dump the water, and then do the whole thing over again a few minutes later without having any idea he'd done it before. Sometimes he remembers the sheep, sometimes he forgets the names of his dogs. Other times he just blanks out entirely. I suppose being blessed has different meanings for some people."

"You need to go to the council meeting today," Nyphron said.

The Fhrey was towering over him, freshly shaved, which always made him look less impressive—more boyish.

Raithe had been washing the sleep from his face in one of the clear puddles left in the field just beyond Clan Dureya's wool-roofed settlement. He'd managed a decent night's sleep and awakened on dry sod to a still smoldering fire.

Raithe wiped his eyes clear with a corner of his leigh mor. "I don't *need* to do anything. I'm a chieftain." He meant it as a joke, sort of. No one was more poorly suited to that role.

Nyphron went on as if he'd never heard Raithe speak. "They're holding the meeting inside the lodge today. I can't get in without one of you there." Nyphron seemed to recognize the absurdity of that statement, because he added, "Without causing a disturbance, that is. I don't want to brush fur against the grain, not at this point. I can be part of your retinue, the same way I did with Persephone, but that means you have to be there."

"What's wrong with tagging along with her?"

"She's gone."

"Gone? What do you mean, *gone?* Where did she go?"

"Don't know, don't care. What is important is that I missed yesterday's meeting because of her absence, and I don't intend to miss another. This is too critical to—"

Raithe didn't wait; Nyphron didn't have the answers he needed.

He started walking up the length of the wall, picking up speed and was just short of a jog when he reached the Great Puddle. Without hesitation, Raithe splashed into it, wading up to his knees before slogging out the other side. When he looked back, Nyphron was following, but walking around the pool.

Raithe dashed on and ducked under the wool where Persephone had been staying.

"Where is she?" he demanded of Padera, who was awake and already busy working a spinning wheel, a pile of twisted thread beside her. The old woman was alone. Raithe didn't know exactly how many people slept under that part of the wool, but he was certain about Persephone, Brin, and Moya. He thought Roan might stay there as well—there was certainly enough room for her—but except for the old woman, the space was vacant.

"Good morning to you, too."

"Where is Persephone?"

"Why ask me?"

"Because you know everything."

The old woman smiled at this.

"Well?" Raithe asked.

"They left the day before yesterday. You're a bit slow to inquire. Aren't you in love with her?"

Raithe stared, stunned.

"Oh, please." The old woman's smile turned into a grin. "You just said how I know everything, so don't be surprised when I do."

"But . . . oh, never mind." Raithe refused to be diverted. "What do you mean *they* left? They who? And where did *they* go?"

"Persephone made me promise not to say anything."

"Padera, you have to tell me."

"You really do love her, don't you? I don't think she fully appreciates that. Persephone sees you as a rash young man, but you're Dureyan. Your kind grows up faster than what she's used to. I doubt it's ever crossed her mind to wonder why you find her attractive—why her instead of Moya. People can be blind like that, you know?"

"Blind I can deal with; mute is a problem. Are you going to tell me?"

Padera thought a moment, both lips sucked in, both eyes squeezed shut. She looked like a gourd left to shrivel after the harvest. "Well, I guess there's no harm in it now. They've gone to Belgreig, the land of the Dherg. Moya, Suri, Brin, Roan, and that Fhrey lady, they all went. Persephone said you refused to fight because Rhune weapons are rubbish, so she's getting better ones from the dwarfs."

"How'd she manage that?" Nyphron asked. He'd just arrived from his trip around the little lake, but acted as if he'd heard the whole conversation. "The Dherg don't allow anyone but their own kind to set foot on the Belgreig shores. Quite touchy in fact. And Miralyith most of all. With Arion along, they'll be killed on sight."

"Doubt it. The Dherg invited them," Padera replied. "I'm not certain how the whole rigmarole shakes out, but Persephone is trying to get Dherg-made weapons for the war. In exchange, Arion and Suri are going to perform some service. Something to do with getting rid of a giant, I think."

"Interesting." Nyphron nodded. "I was planning to retake Alon Rhist and use weapons from its armory, but if she manages it, this could be better."

"Does that mean she'll be all right?" Raithe asked. "Because they invited her?"

Nyphron shrugged. "The Dherg are notoriously untrustworthy. Deceit is their first language and selfishness their creed, so they expect the same from others. They launched a war with my people because they thought we concealed a fruit that granted eternal life. When we told them no such fruit existed, they thought we were lying because it's what they would have done. They'll do anything to get what they want. Personally, I'd never broker a deal with them, but this is a good gamble. If Persephone succeeds, the path ahead could be much easier."

"And if she fails?" Raithe asked.

Nyphron shrugged again. "That's what makes it such a good gamble. Even if she dies, we don't lose anything of value."

For the first time, Raithe regretted leaving Shegon's sword embedded in the courtyard's pillar.

CHAPTER SEVENTEEN

Gronbach

It is funny how misleading first impressions can be. When I initially met Gronbach, I didn't like him. It took a whole week to truly despise that festering pimple on the backside of deceit, that bearded lie, that dwarf.

—THE BOOK OF BRIN

Once, long ago, Suri had made the mistake of hitting a wasps' nest with a stick. She had been about eight years old, and she didn't know what it was. Dangling from the branch of the maple tree, it had looked like a strange kind of fruit, or a weird kind of giant onion the color of mud. This was before she met Minna, who Suri was certain would have advised against whacking the odd gray puffball with the willow branch. Minna had always been the wiser of the two.

She remembered giving that nest a good sound bashing, hard enough to knock it free, and the whole ball came tumbling down at her feet—right where she'd hoped it would. Suri planned to cut it open to see what sort of treat might be inside. She loved apples and strawberries, and this was far bigger than either of those. And while the mysterious fruit hadn't looked appetizing on the outside, that didn't mean the inside wouldn't be tasty; walnuts were perfect examples of that truth.

The moment the thing bounced on the ground, she noticed an unusual number of buzzing insects swarming about, and disappointment set in. With that many bugs, the fruit was probably rotten. But still curious as to what might be inside, Suri gave the thing another good bashing. The contents poured out in a wave. A buzzing, an almost hissing sound of anger and hatred issued from the cloud of menace; even at the age of eight Suri understood the danger. Six years later, in the land of little men, Suri experienced the same sense of dread. Standing with the others at the bottom of the wide stairs, she heard the thundering of feet on stone as a horde of Dherg clamored down the steps. She hoped this encounter would be less painful.

Unlike the wasps, the crowd slammed to a halt when they saw Suri and her friends. There were about fifty Dherg, most with beards. They wore brightly colored clothes of blues, oranges, reds, and yellows. One combined all those colors in a single outfit of vertical-striped leggings and a checkered tunic, reminding her of a bird that sometimes visited the Crescent Forest in spring. Minna had agreed with Suri about that particular bird trying just a bit too hard to stand out.

The whole group stood still, staring at them. Their faces wore a mix of shock, fear, and anger. Then one stepped forward. He had the longest, whitest beard and dressed in a long yellow shirt with a dark blue vest.

"*Yons!*" he exclaimed, focusing on Frost.

Or was it Flood? She had difficulty telling one from the other.

Frost started speaking quickly in the abrupt, halting language, which reminded Suri of barking dogs. Nothing Frost said changed the expressions of those on the stairs. One of the other little people, a fellow in a dark-red shirt with a short brown beard, made his way carefully down the remainder of the steps and then moved around the room, keeping his back to the walls as if he were inching around a high ledge. When he got to the far side, he bolted down a corridor.

Frost's words had sparked sharp retorts, and by then Frost and Flood were shouting at various people on the stairs. Suri didn't understand any of the words except the occasional *elf* or *Rhune*, and once she heard Frost say *Persephone*.

The chieftain was trying to follow the exchange, and she looked back at them with a series of bewildered but concerned expressions. These indicated both *I have no idea* and *I hope we're going to be okay*. At least that was how Suri understood the silent language of her knitted brow. Minna often gave her that same look.

Loud noises came from far away. More people—all little men with beards—poured in until Suri and the others were surrounded. These new arrivals held tall poles with huge ax heads or spikes of gray metal. The same material fashioned the armor they wore, and helmets hid their faces.

"Don't do anything," Arion told Suri in Fhrey.

Suri wondered what Arion thought she might do, and why she shouldn't do whatever that might be.

Those in metal helmets with the sharp poles began using them to prod everyone into one of the side hallways. Suri and Arion had been at the rear, so this about-face put them at the front. They led the procession into a long corridor, down a set of steps, around a corner, and down another flight. Finally, they stopped before a metal door. One of the little men squeezed forward, opened it and waved them in.

Suri froze. The interior was dark. No window, no light of any kind revealed the nature of this place, and she didn't like that she was being asked—ordered—to enter. Minna didn't move, either, and the two of them pretended not to see the little man waving his arms, gesturing for them to go in. A threatening shout came from behind. Suri still refused to budge.

Arion stepped around Minna, took Suri's hand, and pulled her into the room.

Others shuffled in from behind, and the door clanged shut. Suri heard it—felt it—close, and she shuddered. She didn't like small places that she couldn't escape. The rols were bearable because she knew how to open those doors, but the first time one had closed on her, she'd panicked and thrown herself at the stone. If Tura hadn't been with her, hadn't shown her how to open the door, Suri didn't know what she would've done. Now, standing in the dark, she clung to Arion's hand, clutching it as if those five fingers were all that kept her tethered to the world.

A green glow from the corridor entered through the splinter-thin cracks around the frame, revealing close-by faces. Nothing else was visible, neither the floor nor the walls. Suri tried to imagine being in a massive space, a huge cavern. She also convinced herself the door wasn't really barred, even though she'd heard the slide of metal. *That sound could have been any number of things,* she told herself. Still, she found it difficult to breathe.

"What's going on?" Moya asked.

"I don't know," Persephone replied. "Are we all here? I can't see a thing."

"Suri," Arion's voice came out of the darkness, "summon a light."

"I don't know how to do that."

"You need to locate the strands that create light. I'm sure you saw them when trying to free the giant."

Suri knew what Arion was talking about, but at the same time she didn't. She'd had similar experiences with Tura. The old mystic would say something like, "Go to the root cellar and fetch the basket of cattails." Tura had spoken the words as if Suri made a habit of fetching cattails each day and knew all about the basket—which she didn't. She knew where the root cellar was, what cattails were, and understood the term *basket* perfectly well, but there'd never been a basket of cattails in the cellar. Finding what Tura was *actually* after was never so easy. This was what Arion wanted her to do now—find something that should be easy but wasn't. The last time she'd tried looking for what Arion wanted, she'd inadvertently killed Rapnagar, and that had been when she was outside—in the open. Besides, using the Art would mean letting go of Arion's hand. "I can't."

"It's okay, Suri." Persephone said. "Roan, are you here?"

"Yes."

"Brin?"

"I'm here."

"Frost?"

No answer.

"Flood? Rain?"

Still no answer.

Suri said, "Minna's here."

"Well, thank the Grand Mother for that," Moya said, and Suri heard Persephone sigh.

"What's going on?" Brin asked this time.

"We are . . ." Arion began, speaking in Rhunic, then paused and switched to Fhrey. *"How do you say being held in custody for a crime?"*

Persephone replied, "Under arrest? How do you know?"

"Dherg language has similarities with archaic Fhrey. I didn't understand everything, but enough."

"Why are we under arrest?" Brin again. "What have we done wrong?"

Because she stood the closest to Suri, Arion's face was the easiest to see, but in the faint glow, it appeared an eerie green. The Fhrey's brows were in a bunch as she struggled to think of the right words. Suri knew Arion was the type of person who didn't like making mistakes.

After a long while, the Fhrey said, "Dherg not . . . do not . . . allow others to come to Belgreig. Big prob . . . err . . . it is a big problem."

Suri's breathing grew shorter, and she squeezed Arion's hand tighter. *Big cavern. No sealed door. Big cavern. No door at all.* Suri didn't want to start screaming. Screaming never helped. She'd done that in the rol with Tura.

Closed was okay. Closed could be dealt with. If the door behind her now was only closed, she could open it whenever she wanted.

"So why did Frost ask us to come if foreigners are forbidden?" Persephone asked.

"Don't know," Arion said, speaking slower, more deliberately. "I think the three are guilty of something bad. Something very bad."

"The giant, right?"

"Think so."

"So are they going to let us deal with it?"

"They be . . . they *are* . . . talking, I think. So we wait. But things be good for us."

Suri heard the door rattle against the frame.

"We're trapped in a room," Moya said. "How is this good for us?"

Not trapped! We're not trapped. Even if the door is barred, Arion can rip it open. I am not trapped!

"Penalty for coming to Dherg lands is death," Arion explained. "Locked room better, yes?"

A long pause stretched between them, and then Moya replied, "Definitely better."

Suri was having a problem getting air, despite the quickness of her breath. Inhalations were shorter, and she was puffing instead of breathing.

"So what happens if they don't agree?" Brin asked. "Will they kill us?"

"Arion?" Persephone said. "If it comes to that, you'll do something, right?"

Arion hesitated. "Suri will."

Ghostly heads turned to face the mystic. Suri shook her head, and she didn't care if anyone saw.

"You can if you let yourself," Arion told her in Fhrey. *"You have the ability, and more raw talent than any student I've ever taught. You just need experience. If you tried, you could blow that door off its hinges or dissolve the walls around us."*

Suri stared at the ghostly face of Arion. *Does she know?*

"Suri, if you wanted you could put every Dherg in a mile radius to sleep. Then we could take any ship we liked and summon a friendly wind to blow us home, and in a fraction of the time it took to get here. You could do all that . . . and you will . . . you just have to spread your wings and decide it's time to fly." Arion paused then added in a softer, gentler tone, *"Suri, when you want to, you'll move mountains."*

"I don't want to move mountains," Suri said, but inside her head the response was: *But opening that stupid door would be nice.*

"I know." Perhaps it was a trick of the dim light, but Arion looked very sad then, as if she might cry. *"You remind me of Fenelyus in that way. She didn't want the gift, either. She believed that was why it was given to her. She was immune to the Art's seduction, to the addiction that touching the chords inflicts. It's a rare gift, being able to shun power. Gylindora Fane had it, Fenelyus had it, and I think you do, too."*

"I don't know any of those people."

Arion shook her head. "Does not matter. When the time comes, you will be a most beautiful butterfly."

"I'd be happy if she could just open this door," Moya said, and rattled it.

Suri cringed at the sound.

"But . . . but . . . if Suri can't save us," Persephone said, "you will, right, Arion?"

Arion hesitated for a long time, and when she finally spoke, it was in a solemn tone, like an oath. "Yes. I will do that for you."

They didn't have to wait long, Persephone realized in retrospect; it just seemed that way.

In the darkness of that little room—with their fate so tenuous—the seconds felt like days. Upon their release, Persephone estimated that they had been detained for only a few minutes—less than an hour, certainly. When the little people came for them, their attitude had changed. They didn't yell or poke at them with spears. Instead, a particularly plump Dherg with a red beard, bald head, and floor-length tunic of bright mint green announced in a quavering voice, "Please be so kind as to follow me."

They were escorted from in front and behind, but gone were the faceless, gray-armored soldiers. In their place were well-dressed dwarfs. Still, all of them were outfitted with a sword attached to their belts.

Persephone and the others were led through the corridors until she was quite lost; not that she had a good idea of how to return to the ship given their haphazard rush. She expected to be taken to some sort of throne room, like the big domed hall she had visited in Alon Rhist. Instead, they were escorted to a little study where Frost, Flood, and Rain waited.

The room wasn't big, but there were enough chairs for all. In front of the party, a beautiful fireplace, carved to look like the mouth of a beast, burned brightly, filling the room with a warm, comfortable light. A sturdy, practical desk stood to the right of the fireplace. On it was an assortment of tools, metal shavings, and old worn boxes of oiled wood, filled with a variety of metal odds and ends. The surface of the desk was marred, gouged with deep scratches. To one side was a pile of oil-stained cloths, and on the floor at the other end, was a metal bucket filled with a yellow liquid, perhaps the source of the harsh resin smell that permeated the chamber.

Flanking the fireplace were shelves upon shelves and more shelves of little drawers with small, white, polished-marble handles. Tacked up on the wall to their left was a large sheet of tanned animal skin—very thin—on which was painted a strange image. Not pretty like those Brin had decorated her home with. This was very detailed and showed hundreds of lines all interconnected in rings like the pattern found in the slice of a very large tree. A window of nine square glass panes made up the wall to their right. *Glass.* Persephone had only seen it at Alon Rhist, and she knew none of the others, except Arion, had ever seen anything like it. With the darkness outside, the material magically reflected their own images.

"Please, do sit down." The red-bearded Dherg gestured at the chairs, as the door to the room closed from the outside. Their escorts crossed the room and waited for them to comply before the one who spoke sat on a wobbly stool behind the desk.

"I am Gronbach Eyck Prigmoore, Master Crafter and mayor of Caric," he said with a strong Dherg accent that formed most of the sounds in the back of his throat before rolling them out, giving the words a sharp, hard sound. "I understand that you were invited here by these three? Is that correct?"

They all looked to Persephone, even Arion. "Yes," she replied. "We heard you were having a problem with a giant, and we've come to rid you of that menace in exchange for weapons."

"What sort of weapons?"

Persephone realized she hadn't considered what would be best. Her people had always used spears and axes, but perhaps swords and shields would be better. She looked at Frost, who sat across from them in front of the rows of little drawers looking just as nervous as she felt. "Swords." She decided. "Ones that can stand up against the Fhrey's."

Gronbach noted the exchange of glances and frowned at Frost and Flood. "Why?"

"We are going to war against them."

Gronbach's eyes widened, and immediately he looked at Arion. "This is very strange . . . very, very strange." He fumbled with a piece of shiny gray metal bent in an L-shape, flipping it over and back between his fingers. "We have treaties with the Fhrey. You must know this, severe, harshly limiting treaties."

"Do they prevent you from trading weapons?" Persephone asked.

He looked up. "Well, no, not exactly, but I'm quite certain that's because no one ever imagined . . . I simply can't see that they would . . . this is very strange." He looked at Arion again, suspiciously this time. "I think it would be best if we just sent you back home and pretended none of this ever happened."

"You can't do that," Flood burst out, giving Persephone the impression that a great deal had been discussed while she was held in the other room.

"They are our only hope," Frost told him, his tone quieter but no less dire.

"There's no reason to believe they can do anything," Gronbach responded.

"Do you think we would have risked execution if we didn't know? If we weren't sure?" Flood said. He pointed at Arion. "She is Miralyith, just like Fenelyus. We saw her open the ground, which swallowed a giant." Then he pointed at Suri. "She is her apprentice, and killed that same giant. If anyone can do something, it's them."

"You have to let them try," Frost said. He glanced awkwardly at all of them and added, "None of us have a choice anymore."

"Because of you!" Gronbach shouted. "You couldn't leave well enough alone. More than six thousand years it was contained. Three hundred of our bravest warriors gave their lives to trap it, and you . . ." He began to say more, but then stopped himself, taking a moment to breathe deeply several times.

He looked back at Arion. "We don't like each other, your kind and mine. An ocean of blood divides us. The law is clear. If I let you loose in the depths of our holy city of Neith, I will be thrown into the fires of Drumindor just as surely as these three."

"But aren't you the ruler of your kind?" Persephone asked.

Gronbach's brows rose. "Of course not. I told you, I'm only the mayor of Caric."

"Then shouldn't we be speaking to the leader of your people?" She directed her question to Frost, who made a quick shake of his head.

"We no longer have a king," Rain explained in the silence that followed. "Mideon was the last of the Belgriclungreian monarchs. When his daughter, Beatrice, died, so did the bloodline and the monarchy."

"So who is in charge?" Persephone asked.

Gronbach appeared puzzled for a moment. "Well . . . no one."

"Each city or village has a mayor or council," Rain clarified.

"It's one of the things we were hoping to fix," Frost said, while stepping forward. "We need to reclaim the Stone Throne, crown a new king, and restore the monarchy and our people to greatness. The lack of a single ruler has doomed our people to divided bickering, too many petty disputes. Every village has its own way of doing things. We can't even haul a cart from Linden Lott to Drumindor because the track of the road changes width. How can we possibly accomplish anything that way? We're no different than Rhunes now; it's impacting our crafts. We're forgetting the old ways because the tools and recipes are buried under that mountain."

Persephone addressed Gronbach, "So, if you are in charge . . . at least here . . . you can negotiate a trade, yes? If there is no one who'll stop you, then—"

"Didn't you listen?" Gronbach exclaimed. "Everyone would stop me. A mob would form and carry me to the fires of Drumindor, and they would have no trouble navigating the irregular road!"

Gronbach glared at Frost and then began stroking the length of his beard, his eyes shifting from side to side. He huffed, groaned, and finally sighed. "And yet . . ." he began. The dwarf had his jaw clenched, his mouth frowning deeply. "If we do nothing . . ."

Gronbach stood up and walked to the drawing on the wall. "Balgargarath reached the Great Anvil two days ago." He tapped on the drawing. "Echo and Khem led teams down to seal the Great Gate at Rol Berg." He tapped the drawing again, this time at a different spot. "Their efforts won't hold. We don't have long now. Khem estimates three weeks."

"Two," Rain said with conviction.

"Two?" Gronbach looked at him skeptically.

Frost and Flood both nodded.

"If Rain says two weeks," Frost explained, "it'll be two weeks."

Gronbach's shoulders slumped, his arms dangled limp at his sides, and his head hung. "We're doomed."

"Gronbach," Frost said, "if this works, all of Neith will be open again. We can finally go home."

"And if it doesn't . . ."

"Then you'll be dead even if you're not dragged off to Drumindor. They"—Frost pointed to Persephone's group—"are our best hope. Maybe our only hope. They have a Miralyith. Fenelyus created Mount Mador on the crushed bodies of the Tenth and Twelfth legions! Balgargarath will be vanquished."

Gronbach seemed to soften.

"But we'll do nothing without payment. Without weapons," Persephone said.

The mayor of Caric looked over and expelled an unhappy laugh. "If you can do this thing for us, the Belgriclungreian Nation will . . . we'll give you ten bronze swords."

"You can't be serious," Moya burst out. "Ten! This giant sounds like a threat to your very way of life, and you offer just ten weapons? Forget it. Send us home like you wanted to in the first place. You can take care of this Balgargarath yourselves."

"Moya, please." Persephone shot her a let-me-take-care-of-this look, which Moya replied to with a roll of her eyes. Turning her attention back to Gronbach, Persephone said, "I want ten thousand bronze blades."

"Ten thousand?" Gronbach's eyes widened. "Never going to happen."

Persephone firmed her jaw and stared.

"I will offer you one hundred blades," the dwarf said.

"A thousand," Persephone demanded. "That's nine thousand less than I came for."

"Perhaps, but no less ridiculous a number. I can't produce a thousand bronze blades. We don't even have the resources. We couldn't make that many if we wanted them ourselves."

"What about that?" Arion asked, pointing to the gray metal he'd been playing with.

Gronbach looked down. "This? This is . . ." He hesitated, and then hid the piece in one of the drawers. "Nothing."

"It's the same metal your weapons are made of, yes?"

"That's none of your business."

Persephone got the point. "Of course, it's the gray metal you use, so you must have stores of it. We want one thousand of *those* weapons."

"One hundred bronze swords is my offer," Gronbach said.

"Then you can take care of this giant yourselves. I can't fight a war with a hundred weapons no matter what they are made from. Give me one thousand of the weapons like your people use, or give us leave to go," Persephone said.

Gronbach tugged on his beard and looked to Frost, Flood, and Rain, who nodded encouragingly. "All right, fine. One thousand weapons, but you can't tell the Fhrey where you got them. They'll know they're Belgriclungreian blades, but they don't need to know *I* was the one to provide them. Is it a deal?"

"Agreed," she said, standing up. "We will rid you of this giant, and you'll give us one thousand gray-metal swords."

"Giant?" Gronbach hesitated and stared at her. "You realize Balgargarath isn't a giant."

"They said . . ." She looked at Flood.

"Oh, he's plenty big—so technically that's true—but he's not a Grenmorian."

"What *is* he?" Arion asked.

"Balgargarath is a demon."

CHAPTER EIGHTEEN

Choosing Swords and Shield

I have always worshipped heroes in stories. I had no idea I was surrounded by them.

—THE BOOK OF BRIN

Dawn approached, slipping in all but ignored, and Persephone found herself huddled on the bed in a small room across from another one of those amazing nine-pane windows, thinking about demons.

Now that they had hammered out an agreement, Gronbach had quietly arranged for them to stay in more appealing rooms than the cell. Hers wasn't far from the one with the huge fireplace, and she felt that was part of its appeal to Gronbach. He seemed nervous about the possibility of them wandering the corridors and offered to have whatever they needed brought to their rooms. She hadn't asked for anything—none of them had. Something warm to eat would have been nice, barley soup maybe, but that night she was just happy to have things settled. She hadn't thought to ask about food until it was too late.

The window indicated that the room bordered the outer wall, and from the emptiness of the corridors and the quiet of the place, Persephone had

the impression this portion of Caric had been emptied of its usual inhabitants. Perhaps it was because of them, because Gronbach didn't want anyone to see the forbidden Rhunes and the hated Fhrey staying down the
hall. Persephone preferred to believe Gronbach was hiding his criminal
act as best he could and that there wasn't some other reason that this area
of the Dherg city had been evacuated.

Then you'll be dead even if you're not dragged off to Drumindor.

She wondered if Frost was merely being dramatic.

Three hundred of our bravest warriors gave their lives to trap it.

Learning that Balgargarath was a demon rather than a giant certainly
gave her pause. *Can Suri and Arion dispatch something that has taken so
many lives?* Having seen Arion and Gryndal face off, Persephone would
bet on the Miralyith in a battle against twice as many Dherg. And of
course, if Arion had doubts, surely she would have said something as they
were being led out.

Persephone hadn't slept. She had a room to herself, and while the bed
was a little short, it was comfortable. Still, she had lain on top of the covers
in the dark for hours, unwilling to disturb even the blankets. She didn't feel
welcomed, or wanted, and feared the worst. At any moment, the door
could burst open, and she might be dragged away and thrown into the *fires
of Drumindor*—whatever that was.

The land of the Dherg wasn't at all what she'd expected. Because of
their bright clothes and small stature, she'd anticipated a pleasant little
world of pretty homes along a sleepy beach. This gray world of stone was
neither charming nor bright.

She may have drifted off at one point or another. If so, the sleep was
light, her consciousness skipping across slumber like a flat stone. Eventually, she sat up, pulled the top blanket off the bed, and wrapped it around
herself to stave off the chill. She tugged the blanket to her neck and stared
at the slowly brightening face of the window. Once more, her thoughts
turned to demons.

Persephone didn't know what a demon was, not really. She'd heard stories, but the tales were always vague on details. *Evil* and *powerful* were the
two traits they seemed to have in common. Persephone imagined demons

as lesser, malevolent gods, minor deities. They were the storms that destroyed the harvest, the cold that killed, and the sickness that brought fever to the dahl. There was a time when she'd believed that the brown bear known as Grin was a demon, but the beast turned out to be just a bear. Gronbach had called his demon Balgargarath, not a pleasant-sounding name.

The light from the window remained weak, just enough to cancel her reflection, but also enough to begin revealing the interior of her quarters. A small stool, the perfect size for a little man or woman, stood beside a desk similar to the one Gronbach used. The surface of this desk was clear of clutter but just as battered as the other. A device was mounted on one side. Made of metal, it had a pair of gaping jaws and a twisted piece that seemed designed to close the two halves together, squeezing anything placed between its teeth. A wide assortment of hammers was mounted on the wall behind the desk, dangling from pairs of wooden pegs.

Roan would love a place like this, Persephone thought, *although she wouldn't keep it as neat.*

A tentative knock sounded at the door.

"Come in," she said apprehensively, not at all certain what she might be inviting.

To her relief, Brin crept inside. She was also bundled in a blanket, the end of which dragged behind. "Did I wake you?"

Persephone shook her head. "Hard to sleep."

"I know." The girl stood just inside the door, shifting her weight from bare foot to bare foot.

"C'mon." Persephone scooted over and patted the mattress. "Up on the bed. That floor is freezing."

Brin trotted over and jumped up, sitting on her legs. She threw the blanket open, and then closed again, wrapping it tightly about her as she settled in like a bird on a nest. "It's still summer, isn't it?"

"Stone steals the heat, and the windows are drafty."

"Hey! You have a glass window." Brin looked across the room at the nine brightening squares with a little smile of wonder.

"You don't?"

Persephone drew a loose hair away from Brin's eyes. *How many times have I watched Sarah do the same thing and think about the futility of the effort?*

Brin shook her head, undoing Persephone's work. The chieftain reached out and pushed the hair away again.

"They put me with Moya and Roan," Brin said. "Moya snores. Did you know that?"

"Unfortunately, I do."

They sat for a time, quietly watching the early light begin to expose vague shapes beyond the panes. Ghostly forms only partially revealed themselves, shrouded behind a dim haze that Persephone finally realized was fog. She was anxious to see what this new world was like, but the temperature wasn't warm enough to burn that fog away, a disappointment. As far as she knew, they were the first Rhunes to cross the Blue Sea. Belgreig was something of a mythical place—the land of the Dherg—the once great empire brought low by the Fhrey after an epic war. It couldn't all be as dreary as what they'd seen so far.

"What do you remember Maeve telling you about demons?" Persephone asked.

Brin glanced up at her with childlike eyes, wide and innocent. Then they changed. Persephone saw the shift, the fade of the girl and the rise of wisdom. There was a legend that Keepers didn't simply memorize stories, but inherited the spirits of the Keepers who'd come before. Persephone had asked Maeve if this was true or not, but the former Keeper of Ways never answered. Looking into Brin's eyes, she wondered anew. Maybe they were all in there, a score of ancestors going back to the first days, a council of spirits who pushed forward when a chieftain posed a question. Brin looked as if she were listening to voices that only she could hear.

"Unlike spirits of nature, demons come from the same place as gods," Brin said, staring at the desk while speaking as if she were seeing some other place beyond the room. "They are eternal beings of great power that seduced women who then gave birth to the giants. Envious of the gods, they sought the destruction of all their works. They are fire and ice, darkness and despair, pain and torment. Intelligent, crafty, and wicked, they are known to change shape. They can appear as animals, fire, whirlwinds, and people. While in their true form, they are hideous creatures that can appear beautiful and thereby tempt people to act against their better natures. Their purpose is always to betray, destroy, and bring havoc upon the children of the gods, their unworthy rivals."

Brin stopped. She blinked and looked up. The girlish face surfaced once again. "You're afraid, aren't you?"

"If I wasn't before, I am now." She brushed Brin's hair away again.

Brin nodded. She swallowed hard and stared down at the bed looking as if she might be sick.

"Look," Persephone told her. "There's no reason we all need to set out. Suri and Arion are the only ones with a part to play." She thought a moment. "And I will have to go, too, of course."

"Why you?"

"I'm the chieftain. What sort of leader would I be if I didn't lead my troops into battle?" She nodded, mostly to herself, her lips firm on the subject. Most of Reglan's battles had occurred before they were married, before she was even born. But there had once been a dispute with Nadak, which she remembered. Reglan had taken down his spear and shield and marched out the gate at the head of more than sixty men, all in war paint. Forty-three returned, and Nadak never challenged the might of Rhen again. They said Reglan had led the charge and had slain the first man with a masterful thrust of his spear. The story was told many times in the lodge. Persephone never thought to ask her husband if he'd been frightened the night before. At the time, they'd only been recently married, and Reglan had yet to discover his wife was worthy of any serious conversation. She seemed to remember him lingering in the Great Hall that evening even after the other men had left. He had come to bed late, waking her when he did. He kissed her on the head—yes, she remembered that. Such a strange thing, she had thought back then. Not so strange anymore.

Another knock sounded. Before Persephone could say anything, Moya entered with Roan in tow. "Why is it so cold?"

"Stone sucks the heat," Brin said.

"Something sure sucks," Moya grumbled.

"Seph is going to leave us here and go with Arion and Suri," Brin announced.

"Like Tetlin's malformed ass, she is," Moya replied, making Brin laugh.

The girl saw Persephone scowl and stopped with a guilty look.

"She's right. You're all staying here," Persephone said.

"*I'm* not." There wasn't any jest in Moya's words this time. No attempt at bravado. She was serious. "I go where you go. Especially when facing a demon, whatever that really means."

Her hand slipped down to the handle of her little sword. The weapon was always at her side, attached to the thick leather belt that hung off one hip in a manner Persephone thought provocative. Moya could wear a grain sack and look seductive, but the low-slung belt drew attention to her hips, and the unseemly weapon declared her wild ways. Any man would be titillated by such a woman. That had been the point, Persephone thought. Moya lived to break rules, to rebel and seduce. She had flirted with the Fhrey as one more taboo, one more conquest, and the sword was a trophy.

"I don't think a sword will help against a demon," Persephone said. "There's no reason to risk your life."

"What about you? You don't even have a sword. Why are you going?"

"It's my responsibility as chieftain."

"And it's my responsibility as Shield to the chieftain."

"Shield? Who said anything about being a Shield?"

"I'm here to protect you, and I'm the only one with a weapon." She made a show of looking around. "You see someone else volunteering for the position?"

Persephone grew frustrated. Moya was being ridiculous. "You can't be a Shield, Moya. You're a woman, and not even a big one. How do you expect to defend me? This isn't a game. People could die. Be serious for once."

Moya looked as if she'd been slapped. Then her jaw set and her eyes narrowed. "*You're* a woman, too, Seph. Did you ever hear *me* say you couldn't be chieftain?"

"It's not the same thing and you know it."

"Why isn't it?"

"Because I'm not pretending to be something I'm not."

Moya's hand came off the pommel of her sword and fell limp at her side. She stood staring at Persephone for a long moment, breathing hard, pursing her lips. Then slowly she began to nod. "Okay . . . sure, so I'm not the best warrior in the world. You're right. How could I be? I've only been training for a few weeks, *and* I am a woman. And everyone knows women can't fight, right?"

Persephone didn't answer.

"Right." Moya nodded again, taking silence for a reply. "So what you're saying is that . . . that . . . I'm good for nothing."

"That's not what—"

"Yes, it is. You might not mean it that way exactly, and you'd never say those words because you're too nice, but that's the truth of it." She looked down at her feet. "You don't think I know? You think I don't hear what people say about me? Of course I do. It's why no one really protested when Konniger ordered me to marry The Stump. Because the whole dahl thinks I'm some kind of whore."

"No one has ever said—"

"They don't have to." Moya looked back up, her eyes glassy, her lower lip quivering. A tear slipped down and she pushed it away in anger. "But you know what, Seph? You're right. I'm not a man. I'm not six feet tall, and I can't lift you with one arm. I honestly don't even know . . . if it came right down to it . . . if I could really kill someone. But I know this . . ." She paused and sniffled. "I'd die for you, Seph. I'd throw myself in front of a sword, a spear, or the gaping mouth of a demon to protect you. And I wouldn't even think twice, because, as we all know, I can't think. I'm not a genius like Roan or a Keeper like Brin. I'm not a mystic or magician. All I can do—all I'm good for—is to put myself between you and harm. But isn't that what a Shield is? A *shield*? I might not be able to use a sword like Raithe, and I might not be able to wrestle even as well as Habet, but dammit, Seph, no one would fight harder to protect you. No one."

Tears were coursing down her cheeks by then, but Persephone had her own to contend with. So did Brin. Roan was the only one with dry cheeks. She had wandered over to the desk and the wall of hammers.

Persephone leapt off the bed and threw her arms around Moya and squeezed. "I'm sorry. You're right. You're my Shield."

"I'm coming, too," Brin declared through sniffles. "I'm Keeper. I have to witness, just like at the council meetings. That's why I came, isn't it?"

Persephone frowned, but nodded.

Roan was bent over, opening the drawers of the desk and rummaging through their contents.

Moya crossed the room and slammed a drawer closed. "And dear Mari, we can't leave Roan here alone. If I left a pair of shoes with Gronbach, I wouldn't expect to find both when I got back. There's something shifty and insincere about that Dherg."

"I guess everyone comes then," Persephone said. "Unless Minna chooses to stay."

"Doubt it," Moya said. "That wolf is crazy."

Suri stood near the window, looking out at the vast white of the morning fog. She didn't like being inside. The little people's stone room was better than the hut of dead trees back in Dahl Rhen, and the door wasn't bolted. That helped. She'd checked and managed to leave it open a crack, but still she missed the sun and wind. Minna felt the same way. The wolf lay with her head between her forepaws, looking up with forlorn eyes as if to say, *Do you really want to go through with this?* Suri didn't have an answer, and so she stared out the window to avoid the conversation. Minna knew what Suri was doing. The wolf always did, and Suri felt lupine eyes burning into her back.

So much had changed, and little of it for the better. This time last year she was likely swimming in the blue lake, where the falcons flew, or lying on her back in the wildflower beds of the hidden meadow. Midsummers were the best. She and Minna enjoyed exploring the Crescent Forest or naming clouds while chewing on stalks of grass.

Now, they were in a cold, dark room—far, far from home. Suri tried to pretend this was an adventure—a truly grand one. That was true, but just as a plant might enjoy swaying far to the right or left with a breeze, it was another thing entirely to be torn out by the roots. Suri felt disconnected from her home and didn't know why she had agreed to come. She was feeling sorry for Persephone, and irritated with Arion, wanting to push back. But there was more to it than that.

Why did I stay? Why didn't I leave the dahl after everything had settled down? She had planned to return to the Hawthorn Glen after Grin the Brown died. No reason not to.

Sitting in the Dherg's cold room, she imagined herself walking back from the dahl to her home, past the strawberry bushes and across the little creek. She would have used the four stones as a bridge, but Minna never did. On the far bank, she would pass the scorched mound. By then, more grass and flowers would have grown, helping to hide the burn marks of that circle, the place where Suri had said her final goodbye to Tura. Even if the forest had erased the evidence, Suri would remember. The Hawthorn Glen—that happy place of her youth—was empty. The trees were still there, the lake, the meadow, the birds and bees, but the heart had been burned to ash.

Because my home isn't where I left it.

Tura had always just been *the Old Woman.* For a time, Suri had hated her and spent a week alone in the forest as a grand act of defiance, a statement of independence. The Old Woman wasn't her mother and had no right to make demands. She believed the forest would be a better place if Tura left. Suri never thought the Old Woman would leave the way she did. She also didn't expect Tura's absence would leave such a hole. Suri's home was just a place now—a nice place, to be sure—but only a place, and one haunted by the laughter of a once carefree girl and the warmth of an Old Woman. The hole within her still ached, but Suri had discovered, with more than a little surprise, that being with Persephone and Arion took away some of the pain. They were only strangers—Arion being very strange indeed—but Tura had been only an old woman. Funny how things that shouldn't matter actually meant so much and how things as permanent as homes moved.

Arion woke not long after the light from the window reached the bed. Her deep, regular breaths quieted. Then she shifted, rolled her head, and finally opened her eyes. She peered at Suri, squinting, and then rubbed her face and pushed up on one elbow. She stayed like that for several minutes, staring at the floor.

"How do you feel?" Suri asked, speaking in Rhunic to help Arion learn.

Arion bobbed her head. "Very better. That boat and I don't agree. I fear the return trip."

Suri felt it was too early in the day to correct Arion and merely looked back out the window.

Arion sat up, stuffing the two pillows behind her back. Shifting to Fhrey, she asked, *"Have you practiced the gathering chant? The finger movements?"*

"You said those weren't necessary."

"True, but they help. Sometimes it can be difficult to concentrate. Faced with so many possibilities, it's difficult to choose. Chants can help you center, break through the confusion, and focus your mind on the task."

"Focus wasn't my problem. I focused just fine. That part was easy."

"Might need it this time."

Suri didn't reply. She peered out at the fog, which was finally thinning. She hoped to see trees, but the gray shapes in the cloud were straight, sharp, and angular.

"You should practice," Arion said in Rhunic, perhaps because it would be hypocritical to do otherwise.

"I'm afraid. I thought we were going to catch and move a giant, but Gronbach said it was a demon. What do we do with a demon? Will it need to be killed like the little men keep saying? Will I have to crush it, like I did Rapnagar? And what if I mess up again? What if I crush Persephone, or you, or Minna?"

Minna whimpered and looked at Suri, head tilted. Suri scratched behind the wolf's ears.

"I don't think it's a demon," Arion said. *"I'm not sure demons even exist. But that's all the more reason for you to train. Ferrol knows what we're going to be running into. The dwarfs certainly made it sound dire. But I'm sure there is a way to solve this problem without resorting to killing. It's the option of last resort. That's what people like Nyphron don't understand. The Instarya's first*

impulse is to kill and destroy. But there are *better ways. We both feel bad about Rapnagar. If we can take care of Balgargarath without killing, maybe we won't feel so guilty."*

Suri did feel guilty. Originally, she had blamed Arion for the giant's death, feeling angry for being called upon before she was ready. She even tried blaming Rapnagar for a time. He—and the people who'd hired him—had set the forest on fire, which made the trees scream so loudly it threatened to tear her heart open. *What kind of creature would do such a thing? Didn't he deserve to die for the death and pain he inflicted?* She hated him. He was evil and needed to die. But afterwards . . . she didn't feel the same. Afterwards, she hated herself and didn't know why. It didn't make sense, or maybe she didn't want it to. Most of all, she tried not to think about it.

"I'm just not sure I'll be able to." Suri looked up at the Fhrey. *"If I fail, will you—"* She stopped when she saw the fear on Arion's face.

Suri remembered how the Miralyith had looked in the darkened cell, her face terrified in the glowing green light. Finally, she knew why.

"You'll die if you do," she said aloud, realizing in that instant it was true. *"Every time you use magic, it hurts. It's getting worse, isn't it? That's why you're scared. You think that the next time, or the one after that, whatever is wrong with you will be pushed too far. That's why you need to teach me, because you can't use the Art anymore."*

"Maybe," Arion said. *"I don't know. But you're right; it's getting worse."* She sat up and clutched her knees, staring at her toes with a faraway focus. *"Was so bad the last time, I thought I might die. My head feels . . ."* She struggled for the word. *"Plugged, like the power is trapped . . . it fills, builds, and hurts. Feels like it might—"* She made a bursting gesture with her fingers and a silly *pfft* sound with her lips like a failed whistle. *"Maybe in time it could heal. Maybe."*

Suri looked down at her own hands and felt her stomach sink. *"I'm afraid I did want to kill Rapnagar. I was angry . . . hated him for what he and his kind did. But I didn't plan it. I didn't mean to. I . . . I don't know. It just happened."*

"*The power listens to your will, but yes, it must be your will. You were angry, hurt, scared, and didn't know what to do. It's difficult to control feelings and emotion.*"

Suri nodded. "*Still, I feel bad, even though Rapnagar was trying to kill us.*"

Arion frowned with sympathy. "*Why do you think that is?*" She asked as if she already knew the answer.

"*I don't know,*" Suri replied, hoping Arion would tell her.

"*Maybe the Art is telling you something.*"

"*Are you saying Rapnagar wasn't evil?*"

"*I'm saying that perhaps it is killing without need that is evil.*"

Suri continued to look down at her hands. She didn't like that idea at all. There had been no *need* to kill Rapnagar.

"*But what if . . . what if it happens again? Frost said if we met Balgargarath, we would want to kill it. I don't want to kill anything. But if it is a demon, if I'm angry or frightened . . . maybe I'll do it again. I don't want that. I'm . . . I'm scared, scared of what I'll do or what I won't.*"

"*I know.*" Arion leaned toward her. "*But I promise that the training will help. The best way to face your fear of failure is to find success. Now, will you let me do what I can to help? Will you let me teach you?*"

Suri looked back at her hands and nodded. "*Okay, tell me again how to do that thing with my fingers and that chant you mentioned.*"

They were treated to a fine morning meal in a private dining hall where they ate alone. The stools were short, but the food was good. Ham, sausages, porridge, breads, fruits, eggs: Persephone had never seen so fine a presentation. The group barely touched any of it. She forced herself to swallow a bit of bread soaked in gravy. That was all she managed. Stress and food didn't mix. Frost, Flood, and Rain packed what was left, placing it in leather satchels, which had been left for that purpose. Water, they said, wouldn't be an issue, as Neith had plenty of clean fountains and something called aqueducts.

An assortment of magnificent weapons was presented for their choosing. Persephone had never seen some of them before, and the dwarfs provided the names: *halberds, pikes, tridents, maces,* and *flails.* All of them were cast out of the gray metal that had been polished to a silver sheen. Looking at the array, Persephone gaped. *Such power! How could they have lost their war?* She imagined that an army outfitted with such wonders would be invincible. Persephone, however, had her doubts about the six of them no matter how well armed.

Persephone picked a shield that could be slung on her back and thought seriously about a spear, but realized she would be lugging the pole around for nothing, so she settled for a small sword similar to the one Moya wore. Brin, with her slates and marking tools, and Roan, with her sticks and ropes, had no room for more than small blades that might actually have been large daggers. Arion and Suri took nothing, and carried only food and bedding. Moya took a large silver shield, a dagger, which she hooked on to the other side of her belt, and a mean-looking spear tipped with a long, bladed point that had jagged barbs near its base. She tried on a shining helmet cast in the shape of a hawk's face—the beak forming the nose guard—but it didn't fit. None of the armor did.

Weighed down and clattering, they were escorted outside into the still, cool morning air. Gronbach and another, very nervous Dherg, who was dressed in bright yellow and orange and fidgeted endlessly with the knots in his beard, walked out with them. They must have exited the city at a higher point than they entered, as the docks were far below. They stood in the heart of Caric, in a city square complete with a stone fountain. All around them were shops and homes.

Persephone saw few inhabitants, but she did catch her first sight of Dherg females. Legend held that they were indistinguishable from males, right down to their beards. In truth, Persephone found them surprisingly cute. Without a beard among them, most of the Dherg ladies—so petite they were doll-like—had dimples, large round eyes and cheeks, and tiny noses.

No livestock was in the pens, and few lamps were lit against the gloom. Only the lonesome cry of seagulls and the ominous crash of waves pounding the cliffs masked Persephone's own rapid breaths. They were nearly alone in what she felt should have been a busy city. Perhaps Gronbach had ordered the inhabitants inside to allow the Rhunes and the Fhrey secret passage, but why empty the livestock pens?

"Just up that road"—Gronbach pointed inland—"is the gate of Esbol Berg."

Persephone stared up the steadily inclining byway toward two mono-lithic shadows, still largely hidden in fog. Initially she thought they might be clouds. They did resemble a pair of massive thunderhead anvils, and only clouds could be that large. Yet these had straight vertical sides. Look-ing carefully, she spied how the road ran directly between the huge pillars to a tall but slender gate.

"We aren't going alone," Persephone said, but she wasn't sure if it was a question or a statement.

"Of course not. Frost and Flood will guide you."

Frost snorted and tugged on his beard, and Persephone wondered if that meant something in Dherg.

"I don't see why both of us have to go," Frost said.

Flood smirked. "True, you weren't any help last time."

"And you were?"

"I fought bravely."

Flood's eyes widened. "You shouldn't drink so much so early. It rots your brain."

Frost ignored him and spoke to Persephone. "We'll lead you to Balgar-garath. After that, it will be up to you." He paused and turned around to look at Rain, who stood behind him. "No one here has a right to ask you to—"

"I'm going," the dwarf said.

"You don't have—"

"I'm going."

"The dreams again?" Flood asked.

Rain nodded.

"They're only dreams," Frost said, but Rain refused to budge.

Frost looked at Flood and shrugged.

"Rid us of Balgargarath," Gronbach told them. "And you will end generations of fear, and restore our long-lost heritage. Neith was our first home. The ruling seat of our lost king. The Children of Drome carved a life out of this mountain, and our greatest desire is to return."

Gronbach stepped forward and took Persephone's hand. He even allowed himself to look at Arion. "Do this for us, and you will have won more than the weapons you bargained for. You'll be instrumental in returning the Belgriclungreians to their home, and that will strengthen the ties between our two peoples." He turned his attention to the three. "Do this. Redeem yourselves in the eyes of your people, and all will be forgiven." He then looked up into the clearing sky. "Help them, mighty Drome, cornerstone of the world, bedrock of our hearts. Guide these would-be saviors and bless their path."

With that, Gronbach turned his back, and Frost, Flood, and Rain led the way up the desolate road.

"You were a mistake, you know," Flood told Frost as they plodded up the hill. "Mother didn't want you."

Frost shook his head. "We're twins, you idiot."

CHAPTER NINETEEN

Neith

Looking back on it, I am glad I was young. The young have no real understanding of peril.

—THE BOOK OF BRIN

The city of Neith had to be seen, and even then, Persephone couldn't believe her eyes. If at some future time she were asked what it was like seeing the twin towers of the Esbol Berg gate, she imagined she would say they were huge—no, bigger than huge—bigger than the biggest thing anyone could imagine and then triple that. Even then, the enormity wouldn't be enough. Caric, the port city that was so large it seemed to be more a home for giants than for dwarfs, was, in comparison, a tiny, humble fishing village. Neith was a home for gods, and not the man-sized Fhrey sort. This was a home for the gargantuan ones, the sun, the moon, the North, South, and West winds—but not the East Wind. The East Wind just wasn't large enough.

The trip up the road to the gate took less than an hour, but uphill as it was, it felt longer. Not that Persephone was rushing, and no one else showed any signs of being in a hurry. For once, Arion walked at the front of the party. She moved no faster than before; everyone else just walked slower.

"You've done amazingly well at learning our language," Persephone told the Miralyith after she jogged to catch up so they could walk together. "It took me years before I was capable of holding a real conversation in Fhrey, and here you've managed Rhunic in little more than a month."

"Rhunic is not a . . ." She hesitated. "Not a *difficult* language. So much is similar. For example, *lyn* and *land,* and *dahl* and *wall,* and so many others are almost the same. Also helps that I spent more than a thousand years working with sounds."

"A thousand?" Persephone said, then cringed. She was so stunned by the admission that the words slipped out. "I mean you don't look . . . you don't act . . ."

"Aren't you sweet." Arion smiled kindly. "I'm two thousand years and two hundred and twenty-five days to be exact." She paused in thought. "No, twenty-four."

Two thousand years!

"Is that old for a Fhrey?"

"It certainly isn't young," she said with a smile. "Some of us live into their third millennium, but not many."

"You look so young."

"It's the hair," Arion said, looking up as if she could see what wasn't there. "If I grew any, it would be white."

"Why don't you grow some? Nyphron and the other Fhrey have hair."

"Tangles and knots interfere with both the actuation of power and the manipulation of the Art. Even our clothes . . . what we call asicas . . . only drape. There are no ties or . . ." She looked perplexed. *"What is the word for 'button'?"* she asked in Fhrey.

Persephone stared back at her. "What's a *button?"*

Arion opened her mouth to speak then closed it. "It's a device for holding material closed, very useful for non-Miralyith." She smiled.

"Might want to introduce them to Roan," Persephone said. "She recently invented the pocket, you know."

"What's a *pocket?"*

Persephone opened her mouth to explain then shook her head. "Never mind. She can show you."

They walked on in silence, the climb making it difficult to hold a conversation. Esbol Berg—the mighty towers and gate of Neith—loomed ever larger as they approached. The fog retreated, though the sun never fought clear, leaving the sky a muted gray. The great Esbol Berg wasn't built; it was carved by nature from the face of a dizzying cliff that itself had been hewn from the steep side of the massive mountain, a façade of grandeur. Columns, piers, capitals, and plinths were sculpted into the face. The gate itself, while only twenty or thirty feet across, stood eight stories high. The pair of doors, each a vertical sliver, were impossibly tall. Persephone was pleased to see they were standing open. If not, all of them working together couldn't have pulled those gigantic slabs back. Still, she was confused.

"Why are the doors open?" she asked, looking back at the three dwarfs, who trailed along at the rear of the troop because of either their shorter legs or their better understanding of what lay ahead. She hoped for the former.

All three looked at her oddly.

"The gate." She pointed. "If you fear this demon's escape, why leave the doors open?"

Understanding dawned on the Dherg, followed by looks of surprise.

"Closing those doors would do nothing," Flood said. "They are cloth before a charging aurochs."

Persephone looked at Arion, but the Fhrey walked merrily on as if without a care.

"If such doors as these can't hold it, what did you use to trap it?" she asked Flood.

"No cage in Elan could contain *that* beast, except perhaps the one it came out of, which is now ripped open."

Frost said, "There isn't a door we could build that would contain it."

"Then how did you keep it trapped for thousands of years?"

"We didn't," Frost said. "We confused it."

"We got it lost," Flood said.

"Our ancestors spent generations upon generations digging tunnels through this mountain and down into the heart of the world," Frost explained. "There's more down there than up here, you know. Inside, we found oceans of water and seas of molten rock, caverns of crystals, chambers of salt, and rivers of metal, marvels you can't imagine, wonders of legend. There's another world beneath us, and that's where the legions led Balgargarath on a merry chase. It can sense movement, you see. The demon is like a spider in a web. It feels the quiver of stone, and travels to it. Heroes led Balgargarath deep into Elan while others placed knockers—clever devices powered by dripping water—that make a clack the same as a hammer. The knockers were spaced and timed so that just as Balgargarath got near one, another would catch his attention. Once caught in this system of clicks and clacks, Neith was declared off limits to ensure that no one disrupted Balgargarath's eternal trek."

"What happened to the heroes?"

"Why do you think we call them heroes?"

The path grew steeper the closer they came. Behind them, the view expanded with the height and the dwindling mist that by then clung only to the edges of the sea. The port city of Caric was larger than she had realized, with streets running off and intersecting at various points that were hidden to her while she was there. The city formed a large half circle that cupped an inlet where ships lay along several long piers. Looking straight out, Persephone saw a thin line of land across the sea. *Rhulyn,* she thought. So far away, and yet just seeing it, reminding herself it was there, made her feel better.

Persephone and Arion paused on the porch until they were all gathered. She felt the ground shake. Dust and dirt, pebbles and chipped rocks fell like hail. They all jumped under the lintel.

"What was that?" Moya asked.

"Balgargarath," Rain said.

"He knows we're here? Is he coming after us?" She reached for her sword.

Rain knelt down and placed an ear to the stone at their feet.

"What's he——" Persephone started, but Frost held up a hand to stop her.

After a minute or two, the quiet little man with the giant pickax stood up and shook his head. "He doesn't know about us. Just working his way up. After we pushed him off the knocker trail, he's been destroying them. Only a couple left, I think. So we don't have much time."

"Don't suppose you could do anything from here?" Frost looked at Suri and Arion hopefully.

They shook their heads, and Arion added, "Nothing useful."

Frost sighed. "Then in we go. Oh, and walk lightly."

Suri prepared for the war she would wage with herself. The door to Neith was open, and it didn't look easy to close. That was good. *As long as I can get out, I'm fine.* Suri expected it to be dark inside; caves usually were. This one was bigger and fancier than any she'd seen, so she figured it would be darker, too, though even she wasn't certain how that was possible. After all, dark was dark. Either way, Suri wasn't overly fond of caves. She wasn't happy with any place that had walls. Caves were less disturbing than buildings as they lacked doors. Doors were the real culprits—doors that sealed.

They passed through the entrance, which led immediately to a massive wall—quite the disappointment since she was expecting something grander. This cave wasn't even as big as Grin's. There was, however, a pretty picture painted on the stone: people standing in a line leading to a building and a mountain. Lots of colors and Suri liked that. She and Minna paused to stare at the picture. She almost missed seeing that Frost went left while Flood veered right, both of them disappearing through small openings. Suri wasn't the only one confused. Most followed Frost, and on the other side, it was discovered that the wall could be gotten around by going either way. Rounding it, Suri discovered how wrong she had been about everything: the size of the cave, it being dark, but most important its grandeur.

The interior of the mountain was a vast chamber lit with sunlight that streamed from shafts cut through stone. The beams struck polished surfaces and pools of water, bouncing to other mirrored planes that reflected the light again until the whole of the immense chamber was illuminated as if by magic.

"Impressive," Arion muttered in Fhrey as she stood beside Suri. *"I didn't know they could build such things."*

The room seemed to have no end. The grand hall just kept going in a series of colonnades and shafts of light entering from either side. Great sculptures of giant rams reared to butt one another over the main aisle, which was paved in gleaming silver and inlaid with gold. Every inch of wall space, and even the underside of the high, arched ceiling, had been carved with decorative designs—mostly variations on squares and circles. Great stone pillars, like the grown-up parents of the babies in the Crescent Forest rols, towered overhead, taller and straighter than any tree. To both the left and right, thin sheets of water spilled down walls to create a shimmering curtain that fell into one of the many illuminated pools.

Suri had to admit, as far as caves went, this one wasn't bad. The vast space and natural light gave her a sense of walking in a thickly canopied forest rather than being underground. The fear that usually accompanied caves wasn't in this one.

As the group spread out, moving among the statues and fountains, they wandered more than walked the long length of the grand hall. Before too long, Suri spotted doors and openings on either side and stairs leading up to balconies and additional doors. Flood and Rain had taken the lead and now headed straight to what Suri realized was their destination—a huge downward stair and an upward one as well. From the lack of elegance and unimpressive size, there was no doubt that the rising steps were irrelevant when compared with the downward ones. The city of Neith lay below.

They passed between the statues of two huge dwarfs holding up the ceiling on either side of the downward steps and began their descent.

Suri lingered at the top of the stairs, looking back the way they'd come. Wind blew across the opening that let the light in and made a mournful sound. A sharp flapping noise disturbed the wind's wailing song, and she looked up to see a shadow near the ceiling. A bird had entered one of the shafts, its nest on top of a cornice. Splatters of white and a few discarded feathers littered the floor below it. She walked over, bent down, and picked up some of the brown-striped plumes tipped in white. *Hawks!* She ran a thumb along the comb. Suri had known many hawks, good friends all. Feathers were always lucky. She slipped them into a pouch at her waist.

Frost, who walked at the rear of the party, paused with her. "After so many centuries, all manner of intruders have taken residence in here."

Suri glanced at Minna, and the wolf clearly joined her in wondering if Frost referred merely to birds. Suri didn't think so; neither did Minna.

Then they began the long descent.

They went down, and down, and down some more, passing more levels of stone opulence. By the seventh or perhaps eighth flight, the sunlight had been replaced by a new illumination. Gems mounted in the walls gave off the familiar green light, but on occasion, a blue one appeared. Minna liked them better, but Suri had no preference.

After what seemed like hours, she'd lost count of how many flights they had dropped—not that she'd really tried to count. Suri wasn't the counting sort. Roan was. Roan likely knew how many steps they'd taken. Roan likely knew how many steps they'd taken since they left Dahl Rhen.

Just as Suri's stomach started rumbling, the dwarfs called a halt.

"Stopping here for the night," Frost said. This was the first anyone had spoken since Suri and he had discussed the hawk. Aside from Arion's comment to herself, no one had said a word since entering. Even when Frost made his announcement, he did so quietly, as if they were thieves inside a carefully guarded home.

They set down their burdens and clustered on the stone floor beneath the green light of a gem mounted in the wall. Two great urns stood to either side of them, and centered beneath the gem was a chiseled picture consisting of three panels. The first one showed a dwarf hammering on an anvil. The middle panel depicted the same dwarf holding up a ball of light. The last etching showed him throwing it.

Brin was so fascinated with the picture that she stood staring, still laden with gear. She stayed there long after everyone else had settled in.

"There's no wood," Persephone said, looking around. "No way to warm our food."

Frost pulled five black stones out of his pack and stacked them on the ground. "These will burn."

Flood drew out another pair of stones and while Frost added bits of cloth and lint to the pile, Flood began clacking his stones together, creating sparks.

The sounds echoed, and Flood paused, looking guilty. They all looked out into the darkness, waiting for something awful to happen. Nothing did.

"Maybe you should let Suri do it," Arion said.

"Do what?" Flood asked.

Arion didn't answer; she simply looked at the mystic.

Suri had started fires ever since she was a young girl, and never thought anything about doing so. Requesting the fire spirit to burn wood was no more unusual than when Tura asked her to fetch water from the creek, but she knew better now. Producing fire had nothing to do with the fire spirit. Suri had unknowingly been flicking a chord, tapping the hidden power around her. Sitting deep underground, she found little warmth to draw from. The stones were cold, and the sun too far away. She sensed potential in the black rocks the dwarfs had brought, but it wasn't enough. The only source she found came from people around her.

Arion nodded. *"It won't hurt. You just need a little."*

Suri, who had made a million fires and once set a bear aflame, hesitated. Even though Arion said no one would get hurt, Suri was scared. After all, the Miralyith also hadn't expected Suri to kill Rapnagar. She looked at the faces surrounding her and realized, perhaps for the first time, that she cared for these people. The friendships had crept up on her, become important without her realizing. The idea of taking too much heat, of accidentally killing them—even the dwarfs whom she liked the least—made her shudder. And what if she killed Arion? Suri hated to admit it, but the

Fhrey had slipped into that part of her heart left vacant by Tura. The two were alike in so many ways, despite being completely dissimilar in others.

"*You can do it,*" Arion encouraged. "*I know you're scared, but you have to try. Take your time. Do it gently, slowly. It will be all right.*"

Everyone was looking, making her feel self-conscious—under too much pressure. "I can't . . . not now." She saw Arion's disapproval, and it was saddening, but killing her friend would be far worse.

Arion sighed. "It's not dangerous, but"—she held up her hands in patient resignation—"I won't push you. We both know that's not a good idea. You'll come to it when you're ready."

"So no fire?" Moya asked.

Roan unloaded her bow and one of the sticks that she hadn't put a stone point on yet, and within five minutes had the pile of tinder smoking enough so that when Frost blew on it, a flame caught.

"Thank you, oh resident wizard," Moya said.

Roan said nothing and just set to putting her things in order.

"Who is this?" Brin asked. She was still standing, still laden with gear and pointing at the picture behind them.

"That's Drome," Frost replied. "He forges the sun each morning and then throws it west, where it flies until it cools, goes out, and falls. Then after a brief rest, he does it again."

"Ridiculous," Roan said softly without taking her eyes off what she was doing. "Makes no sense. Why would anyone do such a thing?"

"To make the days," Frost said with a dash of irritation.

Roan looked up and cringed. "Did I say that out loud?"

"Frost, how far do we have to go?" Persephone asked.

Frost and Flood looked at each other, asking questions with their eyes, to which they both shrugged and then turned to Rain.

"Depends," Rain said. "Balgargarath doesn't stay in one place. He's looking for a way out."

"We'll go to where we first stumbled on him." Frost spoke as if just then deciding.

"Smart thinking," Flood said with a sneer. "Almost died doing that last time. We definitely ought to try it again."

Frost glared at him. "You have a better idea?"

"Than dying? Living springs to mind."

"Why are you always so obstinate? So against everything I say?"

"Obstinate? I'm not obstinate. But if I were, it would be because of you. When you're not around, I'm a prince of a fellow." Flood's voice grew loud. "You bring out the worst in everyone. Take Rain, for instance. He was a law-abiding, trustworthy, and honest fellow. Now look at him. The lad is a criminal with no future other than a rematch with a demon. And really, what are the odds of us defying fate a second time? You ruin everything you get near."

Somewhere in the shadows not governed by the gem's glow, they heard a stone clack.

All heads turned.

"What's that?" Moya asked in a whisper, her eyes peering into the dark. No one answered for a while.

"Well?" Moya pressed, this time looking at the dwarfs.

Frost scowled. "How should I know? Animal probably. Like I was telling the mystic, after so many centuries, all manner of things have crawled in here . . . rats or a squirrel most likely."

"Sounded bigger than a squirrel," she accused, and picked up the shield she had laid down.

"What are you doing, Moya?" Persephone asked.

"I'm going to take a look."

"Moya, I don't—"

"How is anyone going to sleep? How can we get any rest without knowing what made that sound? I'm just going to go over there and look. If it's rats, then great."

"If not?"

Moya picked up her spear.

"How are you even going to see. It's dark over there."

Rain stepped over to the glowing gem, and with the slightest tap of his pick, he chipped off a shard. He presented it to Moya. The little disk was about the size and shape of a good skipping stone and glowed in his palm.

"If you cup it," Rain said, "it'll intensify the glow."

Moya nodded, returned the shield to her back, and took the stone.

Persephone sighed and got to her feet while drawing her own sword. "Give me the light, and put your shield back on," she said, and together the two walked in the direction of the sound—into the dark.

"Whatever it is, it should be scared now," Moya whispered. "A Fhrey-trained warrior and the killer of the famed brown bear are on its path."

Persephone didn't respond, too frightened. She held no illusions about her prowess as a warrior. The tale of her battle with Grin the Brown was overblown. The exaggeration—a spark Raithe and Malcolm had ignited—had been retold by everyone until it eventually became a forest fire. They wanted to believe their chieftain was brave and capable. She wondered if Moya's interest in learning martial arts had been born from Persephone's own battle-warrior fame.

Maybe if Moya had been there and seen how pathetically I beat the trapped and choking bear with a shield while crying in terror, my new Shield wouldn't be so eager to play swordswoman. Just thinking of that moment, of the blood and the claws, invited Persephone's stomach to crawl into her throat.

She couldn't remember what the shield had felt like, but the sword she carried now was heavy. Persephone wished it were smaller—and therefore lighter—while simultaneously wanting it longer and better able to hit things farther away.

Am I holding it too high? Too low? Should I have it out at all? Yes, I should definitely have it out.

She chastised herself for not watching Reglan closer when he drew a weapon, but what need was there for a woman to know the skills of a man?

And yet, here I am. Why didn't I just send a Dherg? The thought plowed into her. *Because I'm the chieftain—and either I really am or I'm just pretending.*

The declaration sounded strong in her head, but another voice whispered: *You're being so-o-o-o stupid right now. It's just pride. You're going to get yourself, and maybe everyone else, killed because of your idiotic ego. You don't have the fighting skills of a man, but you're learning our faults fast enough.*

The voice was familiar, and it came as a shock that it took so long to recognize—it was Reglan's. Not really him, her husband never said anything even remotely similar. But in her head, she heard the same gruff bark he used during arguments when he was finally fed up and angry, his this-is-over-now tone.

Why am I hearing Reglan's voice all of a sudden? Is it because we're about to be reunited?

The two walked slowly. Despite her bravado, Moya was in no great hurry, and Persephone wondered if her friend was regretting her actions now that they were alone in the dark. To her credit, Moya walked out in front—a perfect Shield for her chieftain. Persephone held up the glowing stone, panning it back and forth, trying to light Moya's way.

Tables and chairs came into view and appeared eerily normal. Something about everyday items of people long dead bothered her.

Did anyone actually die right here? Will we find bodies—bones?

Persephone was shifting the glow of the stone at the same instant that she heard Moya whisper, "There!"

The light revealed a small animal. They both stared in fascination. The size and shape of a rather large rat, it looked like it was covered in banded plates protecting everything, including the tail.

"Even their rats have armor," Moya said. She let her shoulders relax and the butt of her spear rest on the ground. "So the dwarf was right. Just an animal."

"But Moya, it's dead." Persephone lowered the light to show the dark pool of blood that looked black in the green glow. The head was mangled, as if chewed on.

"Lucky us, we don't need to fight it. I'm not even sure where I would stab the thing."

"Moya, it's dead . . . *recently* dead. What killed it?"

"Probably fell, see?" Moya pointed up. "That was the sound we heard, this plated war-rat fell from up there. Most likely the only way to kill one of them."

Apparently satisfied, Moya started walking back. Persephone wasn't convinced.

How often do rats fall to their deaths?

She panned the light around, searching for would-be killers, but saw nothing. Looking up, she spotted the balcony Moya had indicated.

Maybe Moya's right.

Then in that brief moment that felt oddly like a victory, she saw a shadow move. What had been nothing but darkness a moment before, shifted, and Persephone spied two glowing-red eyes. The thing was man-sized, but not a man—not human, not Fhrey, not Dherg, nor even a goblin. This was lithe and lanky, with limbs too long, a body oddly twisted, and those eyes!

It's looking down at me just the same as I'm looking up at it!

"Moya!" Persephone bolted to her, grabbing the young woman by the elbow. "The rat's death wasn't an accident! It was *pushed* off that ledge."

Moya laughed. "You're saying the rat was murdered? Careful, Seph, that's a pretty serious accusa—"

"I'm serious! I saw something above us."

Hearing the fear in her voice, Moya's eyes narrowed. She gave a glance upward, and took a step back toward where the rat lay.

"No!" Persephone said. She still had hold of Moya's arm, and pulled her back toward camp. "Keep walking."

"Wait. What did you see?"

"Something."

"Something?" Moya asked.

"It's dark."

"You have the light."

"Let's just get back. I'll explain when we get to the others."

Persephone didn't think all the light in the world would've made the vision any clearer. She couldn't explain how she knew this, only that she did. The thing made her feel empty and cold. Even coming face-to-face with the bear hadn't done that. This was something else, something terrifying, and it was just a few floors above them.

Did it throw the rat down to kill it? To break its shell like birds do with shell-fish? Maybe it's trying to lure us away, separating us into groups. Is it coming down right now? Or is it running off to alert others? How long do we have before they come?

"Animal, vegetable, or mineral?" Moya asked Persephone as they re-entered the glow of the camp.

"What?" Frost asked.

Moya pulled her arm back. "Persephone saw something, and she won't say what it was."

"You saw what made the noise?" Brin asked.

"It was a rat," Moya said. "An odd thing that wears armor, a war-rat."

"We call them armadillos," Flood said.

"Are there no *short* words in your language?" Moya asked. "Having even a simple conversation must take hours."

"I thought you didn't know what Seph saw," Brin said.

Moya shook her head. "She saw something else. Something above us on one of the higher floors."

"What was it?" Brin asked.

"I don't know." Persephone realized she still had her sword out, and struggled to slip the tip back into the scabbard. "It stood on a balcony looking down at me, right above the war-rat. I couldn't even see it at first. All I saw was . . . I don't know . . . this thin shadow leaning on the railing."

"A Belgriclungreian?" Frost asked.

"No. And not human, either, and not an animal. It had bright-red eyes. Could it be the demon? This Balgargarath?"

"No," all three dwarfs said together.

"Seem pretty sure of yourselves," Moya said.

"You don't see Balgargarath and wonder if you've seen Balgargarath," Frost explained.

"Then what was it?" Moya asked.

"I have no idea," Persephone answered.

"Was the rat's face missing?" Suri asked. She was sitting cross-legged before the glowing stone as if trying to warm herself at a campfire.

Everyone turned to look at her.

"You're very odd, aren't you?" Frost said.

"No, she's right," Persephone said. "It looked like something had chewed on the war-rat."

"So you have raow here too," the mystic said to the dwarfs.

"A *raow?*" Frost asked, tugging on his beard.

Suri looked up. "Evil spirit that can take over the body of a lost person. Didn't know your kind could be turned into one, though."

"What do they do?" Frost asked.

"Lots of things, I suppose. Don't really know. But they eat faces first, always faces first. And they build nests out of bones and sleep on them as beds. They can't sleep again without adding to the pile."

"So they're bad, then?" Moya asked.

Suri nodded. "We had a raow in the Crescent the year after the Great Famine. Tura took care of it."

"What did she do?" Moya hadn't taken a seat and was looking in the direction she and Persephone had come from.

"Trapped it inside a hollow oak."

"We don't have any oaks here," Brin said.

"Can they be killed?" Frost asked.

"I would think so. Although, come to think of it . . ."

"What?" Moya asked.

"I always wondered why Tura chose to trap the raow rather than killing it. She checked the tree every day—even years later. Once when she tapped on the trunk, I swore I heard a hiss."

"And they're dangerous?" Moya still stood holding tight to her spear and shield.

"What part of 'they eat people's faces' didn't you hear?" Brin asked. "Yes, raow are definitely to be feared. Maeve told stories of how they decimated entire regions. Raow eat anything with a face, but people are their favorite food. Whole villages had to be moved or just died out completely."

"Is that true, Suri? Are they really as dangerous as all that?" Moya asked.

The mystic shrugged. "I never saw it myself. Tura made me stay home and wash the berries while she *ran an errand,* as she called it. She had funny names for things like that: *running errands, waking up the sun, bringing the rain.* None of them were remotely like the description. You never wanted to see her *bring the rain.*"

"Still," Moya said, "Tura was an old woman. Like Padera, right? I mean, how dangerous can a thing be if someone like Tura could handle it?"

Suri smiled then. Her face lit up as if for a moment she were in another place, another time, sharing a secret with someone none of them could see. "I saw that old woman drive a hungry bear off a deer-kill with nothing but angry words. She could calm a hive of furious bees, and tell ants to bother someone else's picnic. Can Padera do any of that? Can you? Tura spent almost her whole life alone in the forest. I never saw so much as a scratch on her before that day. She came back hours later, exhausted, with her cloak shredded and deep cuts on her arm and across her face. Took months for her to heal and even then there were always faint white scars." Suri looked up at them. "I can't say for certain, because I wasn't there. But if I were to guess, I'd say raow are very dangerous."

"Do you think it will attack us?" Persephone asked.

Suri shrugged. "Raow have to eat before going to sleep for the night. So I guess it depends on just how hungry it is, and how hard it is to find more war-rat thingies."

CHAPTER TWENTY

Betrayal

The Miralyith once thought themselves to be gods. I have often wondered what the gods thought about that.

—THE BOOK OF BRIN

Mawyndulë kept the gray cloak hidden. He didn't know why. The thing was just a nondescript bit of cloth, but he kept it buried at the bottom of a chest. He thought of it often, and finally gave in. After blocking the door with a chair, he fished out the cloak and put it on. Inga and Flynn weren't good tailors. The seams were uneven, and the loose stitching crossed over itself in places. The fabric was cheaper than anything Mawyndulë had ever worn. The cloak really was an awful garment, and he felt foolish the moment he had it on, and yet, he also felt something else. He put the hood up and experienced an echo, a memory of the thrill he'd had that night when they all cheered for him, and Makareta took his hand.

The door rattled, and Mawyndulë's heart stopped. For several seconds he stood frozen. *They've caught me!* Vasek and his secret guard had come to haul him away.

"Maw? What's going on?" a voice demanded. Worse than Vasek, it was his father. "Maw, what's in front of this door?"

Mawyndulë tore the cloak from his back, catching the hood briefly on his head. He shoved it in the trunk and brought the top down just as his father pushed into the room. Lothian had a perturbed expression—more so than usual. "Why is this chair here?"

"Ah . . . I . . . I just put it there. Getting it out of the way for a moment."

"Out of the way? It's right *in* the way." His father moved the chair aside, glaring at it, and then he closed the door behind him.

As flustered as he was, Mawyndulë was coherent enough to find it strange that his father had come to his private chambers. He couldn't remember the last time that had happened. Not even the year before, when Mawyndulë had a wretched illness that left him bedridden for two whole weeks, had there been a visit. The white-haired physician had come each day, looking so worried that Mawyndulë believed he was dying. But his father never stopped in to see if his son still lived.

And when Mawyndulë had failed his first attempt to pass the entrance exam to the Estramnadon Academy, there also hadn't been a visit. Treya had gone to the added effort of putting flowers in his room, fluffing his pillows, and telling the other servants, "Hush, you fools! Think of the prince. What will become of him if he can't pass the Sharhasa?" Even then, Mawyndulë's father hadn't come to him. In fact, until that moment, Mawyndulë wasn't sure his father knew where Mawyndulë's chambers were. Yes, his father's visit was strange, but what really disturbed Mawyndulë was that Lothian had closed the door. Whatever this was about, it was private.

"How have you been?" Lothian asked. The question was superficial, self-conscious, and awkward. Mawyndulë suffered the same stumbling lack of grace when he spoke to Makareta.

"Fine," he replied, inching away from the chest.

This can't be about the cloak . . . can it? But what else? It has to be.

"Vasek tells me you keep mostly to yourself."

It is. It is about the cloak! Vasek had me followed, or one of the members of the Gray Cloaks is an informant. I should have guessed. Probably Aiden, am I right?

"That's good, I think," Lothian said, and nodded thoughtfully. "Best that you keep a distance. Good not to be too familiar with the people you'll rule one day." The fane walked across the room to one of the windows, taking in the view. "That's the problem with being fane . . . being in charge of anything really, but being fane especially. You can't get too attached to people. You never know what might be required."

Mawyndulë felt his heart hesitate as his father paused at the end of the bed and took hold of the canopy post, letting his hand slide up and down, feeling the wood with thoughtful, searching fingers.

He's trying to explain why he has to lock me up. How he regrets it, but how it's for the good of the people.

Mawyndulë hadn't moved after he stepped away from the chest. He stood in the center of his room on the pretty wool carpet that Treya had given him for his twentieth birthday.

Lock me up. That's all he'll do. I can handle that. How hard, how different could it really be? Maybe other people would have a problem, but I've lived most of my life within this single room. I can handle prison.

"Your mother . . . did I ever tell you about your mother?"

Mawyndulë replied quickly, as if his father was posing a test. "You said she looked like that painting of Fane Ghika, the one in the first study."

"Hmm?" He looked up as if he'd forgotten what they were speaking about. "Oh, yes, yes. That's right. Absolutely. Very much like her. Shorter hair, though." His father paused. His hand stopped its trip up and down the bedpost.

"Is she still alive?" Mawyndulë asked, trying to cut the heavy silence, but unwilling to assist his father in getting to the point. These were his last few seconds of ignorance, his beautiful sunset that separated doubt from a future of certainty, and he wanted to stretch out that time as long as possible.

The fane pushed away from the bed, walking back toward the chair and the door. "Oh, yes, she's definitely alive," he said with a tone suggesting there was more to come, but instead, he stopped there.

Why is he meandering? Not that I'm in a hurry, but why is he dragging this out? He's only going to lock me up—or is it worse? The conjoined twin images of Gryndal's head flying free of his neck, and of his father killing the Instarya leader in the Carfreign arena, flashed in his head. *I'm his son. I'm the prince. He couldn't . . . wouldn't . . .*

Lothian reached the chair, stopped, stared at it, and then turned with a resolute expression.

This is it, the blow he's come to deliver.

"I don't want you going to the Aquila today. I'll be addressing the council, and you shouldn't be there."

"Am I to assume you are putting me under house arrest?" Every muscle in Mawyndulë's body was tight as he struggled to take the news without sobbing.

His father's expression couldn't have been more confused if Mawyndulë had just admitted to being a snowflake in disguise. "What? No! Why would you say such a thing? I just don't want you at the Airenthenon today. Some unpleasant business is going on, and I don't want you part of it."

What's he talking about?

"You're my son, and the heir apparent to the Forest Throne. I know you. You'll want to get involved, try to intervene. You'll shoot your mouth off and make another spectacle. Such outbursts are problematic in the palace, but in the Airenthenon such behavior is even more serious. I won't give Imaly *that* big a victory."

"This has to do with Imaly?"

"No, but it should make her century, nonetheless. Go do whatever you like, just stay away from the Airenthenon. Can you do that?"

Mawyndulë's body was still tense with apprehension. Unable to make sense of anything, he held still and replied, "Sure."

"Good." Lothian took a step around the chair. "And don't put furniture in front of doors where people are walking."

He's not punishing me. He doesn't know anything about the cloak, about the meetings. Terror dissolved into relief, instantly replaced with smug satisfaction. *How could he? I've been too clever for him, for Vasek, for all of them.* As his mind thawed, curiosity slipped in.

"Father?" The word came out flat, a poor note played badly from lack of practice. Now was Mawyndulë's turn to be awkward.

The fane paused nevertheless.

"Since I won't be there, could you at least tell me your plans for the war? It would save me the embarrassment of being the only one who doesn't know."

"What war?"

What war? Had his father gone senile? Or did he think Mawyndulë was too young to be trusted with such information?

"Aren't you speaking to the Aquila about your plans to invade Rhulyn? I'd just like to know what you're going to say."

Lothian smiled, a strange, unfamiliar expression, not biting, cynical, nor condescending. There wasn't even a hint of sarcasm; his father almost looked proud. "You are young and have so very much to learn. You have no idea how the world works, do you? There won't be a war. The giant's delivered the punishment already. We'll need to increase the tensions between the clans to reduce their numbers, but there is no reason for more than that."

"What do you mean?"

"I mean the Grenmorians may not have been completely successful, but the message was sent and received. That town is now deserted."

"But Gryndal's murderer is still alive. Arion is as well . . . and Nyphron."

"Yes, a great many are still alive, you included."

Mawyndulë had no idea what was meant by that or why his father included him in a list of criminals. The old man really might be losing his mind. "We have to invade, wipe them out."

"Who?"

Who? Mawyndulë physically and mentally blinked in disbelief. *He's doing this on purpose.*

"The Rhunes! They have to be destroyed, all of them."

"Why?"

Mawyndulë stood, staring in shock. "They killed Gryndal!" His voice gained volume from frustration. Maybe yelling louder would make his father understand. "They have to be punished. You can't let them get away with this."

His father's face softened. "You don't destroy an entire herd because one goat chews up an old boot. With the Grenmorians, I sent a message. Dahl Rhen is no more. They understand that defying me comes with a price, no matter how justified that defiance might appear. Arion surely understands how angry I am with her. In time, I am certain we'll have to visit that further, but I'm content to let her stew."

A boot! Did he just compare Gryndal to an old boot?

"But Vasek said the Rhunes were preparing for war."

Lothian smiled again. "You paid attention. That's good, but what you fail to see is that the Rhunes aren't an enemy to be fought. They are more like elk or deer. And it's silly to be concerned about going to war against simple animals. They have no weapons or any ability to access the Art. The only concern is a stampede, and that's why we'll increase our efforts to reduce their numbers."

Mawyndulë was furious. So angry that he almost told his father about the Rhune who'd resisted Gryndal's control. He'd purposely left that part out of his recounting because The Traitor had been adamant about telling the fane of the girl's existence. He wasn't going to play into Arion's plan. Circumventing anything she wanted was Mawyndulë's sacred duty.

He couldn't comprehend why his father was being so ridiculous, but Lothian hadn't been there. He hadn't seen the arrogance of Arion or watched the filthy Rhune slice off Gryndal's head. His father hadn't witnessed the blood, or heard the sound the head made as it struck the turf—a ghastly hollow, impossibly normal *thunk*. Arguing with his father was pointless. He didn't understand, and couldn't.

Then a question popped into his head. "Then why *are* you addressing the Aquila if it isn't about the war?"

"Something far more important has happened. It has nothing to do with you," he said, and there was that smile again.

After his father left, Mawyndulë stared at the closed door and wondered what had just happened. More important, he wondered what was about to.

Banned from the Aquila, Mawyndulë had nothing to do. He'd spent more than half his life sitting in the chair his father had just complained about, either there or on the nearby bed. Mawyndulë wasn't an *outdoorsy person*, and he'd never played sports or composed music, even though The Traitor often said he should. She also suggested painting. He'd dabbled with that a few times, but found it irritating. Still, since meeting Makareta, he'd seriously considered taking it up again. He thought he could do a few pictures and invite her to his room to see them, get her impression—one artist to another. Having her visit would make the irritation worth bearing. He imagined that if she were there, he'd never want to leave.

That day, however, it was just the chair, the chest, the table, the lamp, the wardrobe, and the bed, all poor company for a fine summer's day. He decided to go out. Perhaps he'd get some paints at the market on the Greenway. He might even set up an easel somewhere and jump right into his new hobby. The problem was that he planned on going to the Gray Cloak meeting that evening. He didn't want to have to come back, but he also didn't want to carry the cloak around with him. What if someone saw?

It's just a cloak.

He pulled a satchel out of his wardrobe and stuffed it in.

What a pain. Why have cloaks?

He slung the bag over a shoulder and went out. He spotted the dome of the Airenthenon on the far hill across the valley and wondered—briefly— what was happening. His father had the wrong impression of his son. Mawyndulë was delighted by his banishment. Not having to sit through another meeting was a gift. Resolving not to go anywhere near the Airenthenon, Mawyndulë decided to cut through the Garden. A pleasant walk, it would take him closer to the Rose Bridge. Far too early for the meeting, but he thought he might skip some stones, even go wading if he became hot enough. He'd only just entered the sunshine and already he felt uncomfortably warm.

Why is it that Ferrol made the world hot at times and cold at others?

If Mawyndulë had built the world, he'd have made it perfect. All year long, day and night the temperature would remain the same. No need for coats or cloaks—except as badges to secret societies. Mawyndulë thought about this and shook his head as he walked. Cloaks were stupid. They ought to wear rings instead. Mawyndulë made a mental note to bring that up at the meeting. He was certain rings were a great idea. She'd like that.

The guy was on the bench again, still in the dirty clothes, still staring at the Door.

People did that, Mawyndulë knew, the Umalyn especially. Priests of Ferrol sat and meditated on the Door for hours. On holy days, they came in flocks like migrating birds, all sitting there praying, clearing their minds, or asking for guidance. Maybe they just stared and thought about what they'd eat for their evening meal. Or perhaps they fantasized about someone they lusted after, or even plotted to exact revenge against a fellow priest. The Umalyn liked to act pious, but Mawyndulë figured everyone was selfish at heart. And priests probably more so than most.

He wondered if his mother had been a priest. Since his father said she was still alive, he tried to imagine who she was. Why hadn't anyone questioned her about abandoning her son? And didn't Ferrol disapprove of such behavior? Maybe she was a priest, and church leaders did what they wanted and made rules for everyone else. If he weren't going to be fane, Mawyndulë would have chosen to be an Umalyn.

"You're early," the unkempt, non-Miralyith on the bench said. He hadn't looked up, never took his eyes from the Door.

"Are you talking to me?"

"What? You think I'm talking to the stupid Door?"

Stupid Door?

Mawyndulë had never heard anyone use such sacrilegious language anywhere, much less in the Garden and in front of the Door. He was stunned to feel a sense of outrage over something he'd never cared about. He was also impressed.

"Ah . . ." Mawyndulë fumbled.

"Don't want you tarnished with the doings at the Airenthenon today, eh? Have to keep you immaculate, don't they? Can't allow that sort of stain anywhere near you."

"Stain? What are you talking about? Have we met?" Mawyndulë was certain they hadn't, but it was a polite way of getting the point across.

"You'll find out soon enough. She'll tell you when you get to the meeting."

"What meeting? And who is *she*?" He knew very well *what* and *who*, but there was no way the wretch on the bench could know anything about either.

He didn't answer, only laughed. "Okay, fine. Play it that way, if you wish. I'll not burst the bubble of your innocence. Although it's a shame really."

Mawyndulë wasn't certain, but he believed he was being insulted somehow. He stood up straight, folded his arms, bounced them once on his chest, and frowned with extreme disapproval. The mystery man on the bench never saw any of it. He still hadn't taken his eyes off the Door.

"I am the prince!" Mawyndulë finally declared when it became painfully obvious the guy on the bench wasn't going to turn.

"I know," he replied.

Mawyndulë waited a few minutes, expecting more.

Silence.

He decided to skip the insult—if in fact there had been one—what else could be expected from a blasphemer who didn't revere the sacred Door? "What's a shame?"

"You'll get over it. You're resilient. Such rich, dark soil. I can smell the fertility. From you will grow wonderfully bitter fruit. At peak ripeness, you'll harvest your crop, smash it, and distill a fine wine. Then you'll store it away, letting it ferment. A quality wine takes time, and you'll be ever so patient."

"What are you talking about?"

"Hatred. Some people get filled with it and explode. If they survive, they move on. Others just let it dribble out over the years, like a leaky bucket. One day they notice the bucket is empty, and they wonder what had been in it in the first place. Still others use hatred as a weapon, going so far as to pass it on to others—an ugly, unwanted gift disguised as a virtuous heirloom."

Mawyndulë didn't answer; he was too mystified. *Who is this person?*

The fellow on the bench continued speaking while still looking at the Door. "You're not like any of those. You're different. As I mentioned, you treat hatred like a fine wine, believing it gets better with age, never expires, doesn't go bad. But that's the thing about hatred, it *can* become rancid, and it'll turn into poison if you keep it bottled too long. Hatred will eat through any container and seep into the groundwater of a soul. Revenge is never enough to expel it because it keeps bubbling up anew. What you don't realize—can't really—is that by that time, it's all you are. You don't have the hate *in* you. The hate *is* you. When that wine is consumed, you won't ever be able to rid yourself of it. Can't vomit it up or spit it out. It'd be as impossible as escaping yourself."

He finally looked over at Mawyndulë then. "That's the shame."

Mawyndulë figured he walked farther and faster that day than he ever had in his life, and yet he never seemed to get anywhere. He couldn't even remember where he'd been. He'd just walked. He barely recalled passing the Greenway market, and thinking there was something he wanted from there, but he continued without slowing. The constant motion kept his mind from wandering, from returning to the conversation with the wretch in the Garden.

Not a conversation, he told himself, *more like a nightmare born from a fever. None of it made any sense. First my father, now this weird stranger.*

When the sun finally set, he was pleased to be rid of a strange day. Despite leaving early and having nothing to do, Mawyndulë arrived late to the Rose Bridge. He halted a few yards away, surprised by the large crowd gathered there.

Normally he would find, at most, twenty people, sometimes as few as eight. That night he saw forty, maybe fifty. A bonfire burned brightly and spark-swarms whirled toward the underside of the bridge. Dark figures danced in a circle around an enchanted blaze that changed colors and burned three times the height of a Fhrey. Laughter, songs, the pound of drums, and even the lilt of a flute drifted on the wind, although no one appeared to be playing any instruments. The usual floating lights where there, too, but that night they darted madly about like insane fireflies. Mawyndulë heard hoots and shouts, and as he drew closer, he saw that the river itself was rearing up and jumping to the rhythm of the music. His secret group had gone mad.

Mawyndulë approached hesitantly, searching the crowd for a familiar face. Everyone wore their gray cloaks, but most of them he'd never seen before.

Why is nothing normal today?

Mawyndulë was on the verge of leaving—just going home to curl up in his bed and smother the day with covers of silk—when Makareta found him.

"Where have you been hiding?" she asked. Her voice was louder than normal. She rushed up and without pause gave him a tight hug. He was caught off guard again and too disturbed by the ruckus to think. She smelled of wine. "Congratulations, Your Highness."

"Huh?" he so eloquently replied.

She smiled warmly, enough to melt his defiant refusal to be joyful. *What a face. What eyes.* Both were a tad glassy, cheeks flushed, her balance off. If he'd had as much wine as Makareta, he might have tried to kiss her and doubted she'd object. Unfortunately, Mawyndulë was thinking altogether too much. That was his punishment for arriving late. Perhaps there were always people who came later, but he never noticed the stragglers; by then he was too lost in discussions and cups of wine—not to mention her eyes—to notice.

"Congratulations!" Aiden appeared with a big-brother grin. "Did you just get here?"

"Why is everyone congratulating me?"

"Why?" Aiden appeared puzzled and looked at Makareta.

She shrugged and addressed Mawyndulë. "I . . . I don't think . . . I mean . . . you weren't at the Airenthenon today, were you? Mawyn, do you not know what happened?"

Mawyn? That's new. I'm not sure I like it.

"My father didn't want me attending. Why? What happened?"

"Of all people to be the last to know! Am I right?" Aiden shouted and clapped Mawyndulë hard on his back.

Is everyone drunk? Do I act this way when I've been drinking? Mawyndulë was pretty certain he didn't.

"Know what?"

"Vidar was found guilty of treason," Makareta said. "Your father called him out right from the floor of the Aquila. He's an assassin who was plotting to kill the fane."

"Vidar?" For an instant, Mawyndulë wondered if perhaps there was another Vidar, some evil version. Even remembering the shadow that had stalked Mawyndulë in his dream the idea still didn't mesh with the reality of the dusty old man, feeble and barely intelligent enough to feed himself. Vidar was an idiot, not a traitor.

"That makes you the new senior councilor, old Fhrey," Aiden said, clapping Mawyndulë's shoulder, harder this time, and Aiden topped it off with a little shake. "You made it. You can be our voice. We can finally be heard!"

Mawyndulë felt the gathering of people pressing around him. A pack, he thought, though he had no idea what they might be a pack of, or where that idea had even come from. Mawyndulë had never had a dog, and had only seen a single wolf. Still, they felt like a pack, a warm excited family.

Several of those gathered were grinning, and one of them placed a cup of wine in Mawyndulë's hand.

"To the new senior councilor of the Aquila!" Aiden shouted, and everyone raised glasses and drank.

"I'm so proud of you," Makareta said, pressing against him and clicking cups.

"Why? What did I do?"

"It's what you *will* do."

She squeezed his hand. Hers felt hot, and a little slickness had formed between their palms. This hidden touch, held down and out of sight from the others, excited him. He took a swig of wine.

Aiden raised a cup again. "To our first victory!"

Everyone echoed, "To our first victory!"

They drank. Mawyndulë didn't.

"Wait? How is it *your* victory?" Mawyndulë asked.

"You don't think Vidar is *really* a traitor, do you?" Aiden said with a mischievous smile and a wink.

Initially, Mawyndulë took this for an honest question. He even opened his mouth to reply, but stopped. "Wait. Are you saying Vidar is innocent?"

"I guess he could have been up to something, but it doesn't matter," Flynn said. "Your father is convinced of Vidar's guilt. Lothian locked up the ex–senior councilor, pending sentencing."

"And appointed you to replace him," Makareta said with admiration.

He felt her hand in his again. He wanted to let go, but that would be rude. He needed to think, and her closeness confused him. "But if Vidar isn't the assassin, then a real one could still be out there."

This brought a laugh from nearly all of them.

"There never was an assassin," Aiden told him.

"No, you're wrong. There was . . . or I should say is . . . one," Mawyndulë insisted. "The Master of Secrets learned about a plot weeks ago."

They shook their heads, all of them, even Makareta.

"Vasek's an idiot," Aiden said. "And his spies are so easily fooled."

"It was Aiden's idea," Makareta said.

"Yep, Vasek is always looking for conspirators so we gave him one. *You* provided the target," Aiden told Mawyndulë. "Getting rid of Vidar has allowed one of our own to assume his position."

"So the assassination plot was just a hoax?"

"Yep. A rumor we started. We planted just enough clues to make Vasek drool."

Several laughed at this.

Mawyndulë was unsure what to make of it all. He certainly held no love for Vidar, but it felt wrong to let him be punished for a crime he was innocent of. He drank his wine, still trying to work everything out.

"Vasek is such a waste. How is an Asendwayr going to do anything? I don't see why your father chose him rather than a Miralyith. I mean, what if Vidar had really been an assassin? Vasek couldn't have done anything to keep the fane safe against a Miralyith," Aiden said loudly, and elicited laughter from the crowd. "Am I right?"

They all cheered and a few of the nearest members slapped Aiden on the back.

"I don't know, I thought Vasek had some smart ideas," Mawyndulë said.

"Vasek? Smart? I don't think those two words have any place being together. What did he ever do that demonstrated even an inkling of intelligence?"

"Well, he does use Miralyith to safeguard the palace. All the windows and doors are sealed by the Art."

Aiden opened his mouth to speak, but Mawyndulë shut him down. "And only those assigned residency can even pass inside the walls of the Talwara."

There, that'll teach Aiden. He thinks others are dumb, but he's not so smart. Who is secretly holding Makareta's hand? Who has just been appointed as senior councilor? Me, that's who. Am I right? The thoughts brought a smile to Mawyndulë's face.

"The fane could still have been poisoned," Flynn pointed out.

"Nope. Wouldn't work." Mawyndulë's smile blossomed into a grin. "All food is cleaned by Miralyith as well. So, yeah, he might not be a Miralyith, but he knows how to employ them to take care of things."

Everyone was looking at Mawyndulë and nodding thoughtfully.

He felt good, as if he'd just made an exceptional stroke while sword fighting. He'd never touched a sword, but he could imagine the thrill of catching an opponent's blade at the last instant before a killing stroke, slapping it away, then stabbing out with his own assault. For once, he had all the answers, and he'd delivered them perfectly, with his lady by his side. The fast ripostes left him giddy, and he downed the last of his wine in victory.

"You're going to make a great senior councilor," Makareta said with ardor. "Who are you going to appoint as your junior?"

Mawyndulë didn't even know that was something he had input on. "I'm sure my father will find someone."

"Choice of junior councilor is the prerogative of the senior."

"Oh? I didn't know that."

"You didn't know you were senior councilor until a minute ago, so you can hardly be blamed. But who do you think you might choose?"

"I can pick anyone?"

"Yes, but we wouldn't want someone from another tribe to be the next in line," Aiden said.

"I actually think Aquila law prevents that," Inga added.

"That's true," Makareta confirmed. "Those rules were formalized in the First Quorum. But other than that, it can be anyone."

"You know a lot about the Aquila, don't you?" Mawyndulë asked her.

"I go there often. You've seen me. I think I've witnessed every meeting for the last century."

She's that old? Still, she wasn't *too* old. She might be, and likely was, only a little over a century, and there was value in age, experience, and knowledge that he didn't have.

"So do you know who you'll take as your junior?"

"Yes, I think I do."

CHAPTER TWENTY-ONE

Losing Face

The worst nightmares are the ones you cannot wake from because they are real.

—THE BOOK OF BRIN

If not for Minna, they never would have known Brin had been taken.

The wolf brought them awake with her barks, and in that fleeting moment, Persephone caught sight of the girl. She was being hauled away, a pale hand clamped over her mouth, her heels kicking weakly against unforgiving stone. Then she was gone, lost to the darkness.

"Brin!" Persephone shouted.

Scooping up the glowing shard beside her, Persephone scrambled to her feet and chased after Brin. She hadn't thought to grab a shield, and thanked Mari that she'd slept with the sword belt on, the weapon still in its scabbard. Persephone didn't remember falling asleep. She had sat up, watching over the others in case the raow came. Just a precaution, she hadn't thought it really would. There were ten of them, counting the wolf, and only one raow—at least she'd only seen one. She'd considered assigning shifts to keep watch but thought sleep was more important.

So, so stupid!

Having lost sight of everything familiar, Persephone stopped running and stood among the black-and-white squares of a checkerboard floor, completely lost.

This can't be happening. "Brin!" she screamed, her voice echoing in the vast hall.

No answer.

Oh, holy Mari, please no!

Panning the light around, she saw half a dozen corridors and archways. Brin could be down any of them. How much time did she have to find her?

Brin's voice replayed in her mind. *What part of "they eat people's faces" didn't you hear?*

Running footsteps approached, and Moya rushed into the glow of Persephone's stone. "Where is she?" Moya exclaimed, her eyes huge, her breath coming in short gasps.

"I don't know. I don't know!" Persephone yelled back, continuing to pan the glowing stone, cupping it the way Rain had instructed.

She spotted a light back toward camp. Rain had chipped another shard and was searching as well.

"We have to find her!" Moya nearly shouted.

"I know that. Don't you think I know that?" Persephone peered into each corridor for any sign, any indication about where Brin had been taken; she found nothing. Maybe if they had more light they might find clues like footprints in the dust, but Persephone didn't see any.

"Minna will find her," Suri said. The mystic trotted up with the animal at her side. "Won't you, Minna?"

The wolf was still bristling her fur and had an ugly snarl on her lips. She wasn't even looking at the corridors. Minna was growling at the stairs.

"They went down," Suri said.

That was all Persephone needed. She was running again. They all were. The wolf outpaced the rest, her nails scraping the stone as she leapt down, yipping as she went. Persephone remembered being chased by wolves in the forest, but this time *she* was the one pursuing, a member of the pack.

Persephone took the stairs three and four at a time. Moya ran alongside with her spear, but there was no sign of her shield.

Minna didn't pause at the bottom; she went right on down the next flight, and the flight after that until Persephone lost track. Finally, they reached the bottom of the staircase, and the wolf sprinted into the darkness. Suri, who was as quick and nimble as a deer, was close behind. Persephone and Moya followed. Meanwhile, somewhere behind them, Roan, Arion, and the dwarfs brought up the rear.

Persephone almost slammed into a pile of rubble, and Moya just managed to leap a toppled metal pole that looked to have been some sort of lamp. Debris was strewn everywhere: broken stone, collapsed pillars, and fallen arches. Ahead, they still heard Minna, but the wolf's barks had turned to howls and then a threatening growl.

"She's caught it," Suri announced.

Another few strides and Persephone saw the wolf. Minna was crouched, ready to fight. Suri was closing in. Ahead of them stood the raow, still holding Brin with one long hand clamped over her mouth. Persephone focused the light and saw it clearly for the first time. Pale as the underbelly of a dead fish, the thing was tall, lanky, and thin. Its arms could touch the floor with barely a bend to its back. Long, thin strands of black hair hung from a grotesque head, the locks shrouded much of its body like a brittle cloak. Just as Suri said, it had claws, sharp-pointed nails of ebony, and when it hissed at Minna, Persephone saw yellow teeth and bleeding gums.

Brin was still struggling, but she was held off balance by powerful arms. Stifled shouts and indistinguishable screams leaked through the raow's palm. The creature had stopped its flight, and with the light of her shard, Persephone saw why. Behind the raow, the floor was missing. Smooth marble tiles could be seen twenty feet beyond, but in between was the darkness of a gaping chasm. The floor, the width of the entire chamber, had broken away, leaving the raow trapped against a massive hole.

Suri stopped short and crouched beside Minna, glancing back. Beside her, Moya took a firm double-handed grip on the spear as Persephone drew her sword—no fear this time, no hesitation. She was going to kill that thing for touching Brin.

Then, as all of them watched, the raow threw Brin off the edge.

The girl screamed. Persephone stared in horror at Brin's flailing arms and legs as down into darkness she went. Her scream trailed for some time and then was cut horribly short.

Persephone stopped, as did Moya, both paralyzed in disbelief. Persephone felt as if her breath had been stolen, and she couldn't find another. The creature took several steps toward them, turned, and in a wild, running leap jumped the gap, barely catching the far side with its clawed hands. It hung there for the briefest of moments, and then pulled itself to safety.

Persephone ran forward, hit the floor, crawled to the edge, and looked down. Even with the light, she only saw darkness below. "Brin!"

"Oh, sweet Mari!" Moya exclaimed.

The others arrived. Rain joined his light to hers, helping to illuminate the tragedy below.

"Where's Brin?" Roan asked.

Persephone couldn't answer.

"What's it doing?" Arion asked, looking across the chasm at where the raow climbed a tilted pillar.

The chamber was a mess of turmoil and wreckage. Parts of the ceiling had been shattered, and a few columns, freed from their loads, stood balancing on their plinths. The raow jumped to one of these freestanding pillars and continued to climb. At the top, it braced itself against a nearby wall and the remaining ceiling and began to push with its legs.

The pillar moved. Hardly noticeable, but it did rock slightly. Realization descended on Persephone. The hole in the floor that Brin had fallen through was long and thin—the size and shape of a toppled pillar. The raow was aiming another at them. Even if it missed, the massive column of stone would take out the rest of the floor.

"Help!" Brin's tiny voice wafted up from the abyss. "Help me!"

"Brin?" Persephone looked back down, still unable to see anything. "Are you all right?"

She waited—they all did—no answer.

Across the gap, the raow shifted the pillar another inch.

With an angry glare, Moya backed up a few feet to give herself room.

For a moment, Persephone thought she was about to hurl herself across the gap like the raow had. She wouldn't make it. No human could clear that jump. Even the raow had barely succeeded. But Moya wasn't planning on jumping. She ran to the edge and when she reached it, she let her spear fly. A beautiful throw, the spear sailed straight and far but fell short, landing near the base of the pillar. The movement and noise caught the raow's attention. It grinned and heaved once more, causing the pillar to rock.

"We need to leave," Frost said.

"For once, I agree with Frost." Flood nodded while rapidly backing away.

"We aren't leaving her!" Persephone said. Then she shouted down into the abyss, "Hold on, Brin!"

Moya stood near the edge with clenched fists glaring at the raow. "You son of the Tetlin whore. You slimy—" Moya pivoted. "Roan! Roan, make your bow work."

With a nod, Roan dropped her gear and pulled out the sticks. She and Arion had been the only ones who'd picked things up before joining the chase. Even the dwarfs had forgotten their packs, although Rain had his pick secured on his back. He likely slept with it, the same way Persephone had fallen asleep with her sword.

"Suri." Arion moved forward to where the mystic knelt. "You can stop it."

Suri continued to hug Minna, looking up at the Fhrey, terrified.

"You must try." She resorted to Fhrey, but kept her words steady and calm.

Suri only hugged Minna closer.

Roan had the bow strung in seconds.

Moya took it from her. "What do I do? I put the little javelin in the string and pull back, right?"

Roan nodded.

Moya nocked the little stick. She pulled, aimed at the raow, and let go. The miniature spear flew, but it didn't travel as far as the spear Moya had just thrown.

"You need to draw it back farther, near your cheek and then let go,"

Roan explained, holding out another of her stone-tipped sticks. "Don't worry, the bow won't break. It's very strong."

Moya did as instructed, and the big bow creaked with the strain. This time the shaft shot out of the bow faster than the eye could see. It soared well over the chasm and came close to where the raow was heaving on the pillar—so close the creature looked over, frightened—but the stick drifted into a flat spin and fell away, bouncing off the far wall.

"It doesn't fly straight!" Moya shouted.

"I thought it would now," Roan said.

"Well, it doesn't!"

"Suri," Arion said more firmly. *"You need to do something."*

"This was all a mistake," Suri said, shaking her head. *"I shouldn't have come. I'm not an Artist. I can't do anything. I . . . I . . . I don't even know what you want me to do. That's not a giant over there. It's a pillar and a raow, and there's no dirt to swallow it."*

"You can hold the pillar in place," Arion said, her voice surprisingly calm, so sedate that it managed to irritate Persephone—as if the Miralyith denied everyone's peril. *"You can also paralyze the creature, or kill it. Use the chant, center yourself. You can—"*

Suri stood up, closed her eyes, and furrowed her brow. She tilted her head from side to side. *"I'm not sure what to do. There are so many choices, and so few sources to draw from!"*

"It needs a drag on the back," Roan was saying, holding the next stick up in front of her. "Something to catch the air and keep the stone tip pointed forward."

"Like what, Roan? Like what?" Moya was flashing her hands open and closed, begging for an answer. "Think, damn you. Think!"

Persephone couldn't do anything but watch. Suri remained standing, frustrated and confused. Roan dug through her bag in a panic, spurred on by Moya, who was still holding on to the bow. Arion stood next to Suri, whispering encouragement. The dwarfs were inching backward toward the stairs.

Persephone shouted down to Brin again, and there still wasn't any reply. *How could she have survived that fall?*

Persephone had thought that coming to Belgreig would be a simple thing, just a boat trip and an afternoon walk to a room where a giant was trapped. Suri or Arion would do something miraculous, and then they would be heading back with swords and maybe some shields. She'd even entertained the idea of convincing the Dherg to join them in the war. If that had happened, she would have contributed to the cause, made a difference.

On the far side, the raow finally managed to rock the pillar to its tipping point. The creature dropped deftly to the ground as the mammoth column breached the edge of its base and, just like a cut tree, began its inevitable fall. The angle was off. The tower of stone wouldn't hit them. The column would land to the left, closer to the stair, just missing the dwarfs.

Persephone realized in that late instant as the pillar fell that she never should have allowed the others to come. She should have been the chieftain and ordered Moya, Roan, and Brin to stay behind. This was all her fault, her mistake, but the gods wouldn't limit their punishment to only the one responsible. At least they were just an insignificant band of misfits: an inexperienced chieftain, a teenage Keeper, an insecure ex-slave, a troublesome beauty, a crazy mystic, and an outcast Fhrey. She wondered if anyone would even notice they were gone. *Thank Mari, I didn't bring Raithe.*

The column crashed, severing the floor just in front of the stairs. Persephone felt the ground give way beneath her, and she was falling along with everyone else, tumbling into darkness.

I'm still alive. This was the first thought that flashed through Persephone's head.

The second was that she was drowning.

She still held Rain's stone shard, and while it gave her something to focus on, it provided no answers. Its glow revealed nothing, just a light in a void of blackness. She was underwater, that much was obvious. She felt her body rise, helped by kicks and strokes until her head broke the surface. The moment she did, she felt pain as her forehead struck stone. The glowing gem revealed she was trapped under a low ceiling. The distance between the surface of the water and the overhead stone was little more than an inch, just enough to push her lips and nose up to breathe.

I just fell. How can I be trapped under a ceiling?

The answer soon became obvious. Gasping for air, she felt the surface of the stone scraping past her fingertips. She was in the grip of a strong current, moving fast, swept along a low ceiling of solid rock.

Morton Whipple!

Persephone hadn't thought of him in decades, but now she couldn't think of anything else. In the cold dark, she saw Morton's face again—just as clearly as she had at the lake.

The Whipples had farmed two fields near the forest, down in the valley by a stand of birch trees. They had six children, none of whom survived to adulthood. But back then, two of the Whipple children still lived, Morton and Allison.

Aria, Sarah, and the Whipples had joined Persephone on a trip to Dreary Lake on a warm winter's day. The snow had stopped, and the ice fishermen reported there were patches where the winds had swept the surface of the lake clear. The group had it in their heads to go sliding. When they arrived, they found the rumors were indeed true. The icy surface of the frozen lake was mostly clear and buttercream smooth. They ran and slid, dived and shoved, plowing one another into the banks of wet snow.

Before long, they were soaked from sweat and ice melt. Morton made a boastful roar, beat his chest, and ran off in an attempt to best Aria's longest slide. Unfortunately, he made the mistake of going the wrong way. He probably didn't think he'd go so far—none of them did—and they watched in horror as Morton Whipple slipped right into the hole cut by the ice fishermen. He disappeared with a barely noticeable *plunk*.

The surface of the ice was glassy, warmed by the day's sun. Persephone could see Morton's face looking up, his fingers and palms pressed white against the underside of the ice. Allison Whipple, who herself was only two years away from drowning in the White Oak River, pounded the surface, trying to break it. Four inches thick, the frozen lake didn't notice her tiny fists. Morton's mouth was open. Persephone remembered that. She couldn't understand why at the time. Later she realized that between the water and the ice there was a thin layer of air he was breathing. He was also moving. The lake was fed by streams that flowed down from the hills, and the water spilled out again at the southern end into the White Oak River. In the summer, you could feel the current; in the spring, it was dangerous; in the winter, deadly. Of course, no one ever went swimming in the winter, not until Morton Whipple fell through the ice.

Persephone had seen Morton's face looking up at her through that glassy veil for months afterward, and the nightmares returned that spring when hunters found most of his body down in the gorge. In Persephone's dreams, their roles were switched. She'd press her cheek against the cold surface, sucking air with fish lips while being dragged along. Aria and Sarah would run ahead, scrape a window in the snow so they could watch her float by, and then they'd dash off again to repeat the process. All the while Persephone could hear the dull thumps of Allison's little fists hitting the ice, turning them bloody.

The nightmare had finally come true, but instead of being trapped by ice, Persephone was under solid stone. Allison wasn't there; neither was Aria or Sarah. They were all dead. Maybe everyone else was, too. As far as Persephone could tell, she was alone.

Her fingers desperately searched for cracks or nibs to stop her drift, but the surface had been worn smooth by the water and there was nothing to grab. Even if she could have halted her passage, she had no idea what good that would do. Her only hope was that the current might take her someplace better than where she was, someplace she could crawl out.

As with all nightmares, things got worse rather than better.

The little gap between her and the rock disappeared. Terrified, Persephone was forced underwater. With the current still pulling her along, she prayed that the gap would return. It didn't. Instead, she was sucked down. Deeper and deeper she was pulled, jerked, tugged, and throttled. Just when she thought she would certainly drown, she popped up again. The ceiling was still there, but she found a greater gap, a full head's worth.

Thank you, Mari! Thank you, Mari! Thank you, Mari!

Persephone bobbed along the water's surface, one hand still holding the glowstone, the other sliding fingertips along the slick ceiling. She was moving faster, speeding up. The stone overhead flew by until her finger-tips numbed to the sensation. She held the stone out before her, hoping to spot any hanging rocks so she could duck or dodge them.

She felt herself falling again, this time through the air. For several seconds she plummeted. She almost screamed, but managed to hold it back, knowing she was likely to hit water again.

Her anticipation was realized as she plunged into another pool. Persephone swam several frantic strokes in a random direction perpendicular to the current. Her only hope was to find dry land where she could get out of the water. She was in a cavern and could hear the roar of falling water gushing and echoing. Just as she was growing tired, just as she felt hopelessness creeping in, something grabbed hold of her wrist.

Persephone jerked back, but couldn't break free. She did scream then.

"It's okay! It's me."

Persephone brought up the light and saw Brin's face.

"Brin!"

The girl pulled Persephone to a rock ledge where the two scrambled out of the water. The moment they were clear, Persephone wrapped both arms around the girl and squeezed tight. "Oh, Brin! You're all right."

Brin shivered. The air was colder where they were now, and both of them were soaked. Persephone inspected the girl with the glowstone, and found a cut near the top of her head that bled. "You're hurt!"

"So are you," Brin said. Reaching out she touched Persephone's forehead and drew back bloody fingers.

A cry cut through the water's rush. Persephone cupped the gem and searched around. They were in a small, narrow chamber that had been carved out by the underground river. Black, water-polished stone had been smoothed into wavy patterns and eddy holes. At one end was the waterfall that spilled into the chamber through a hole in the ceiling. The other end of the chamber narrowed into a drain. Searching the surface of the pool, Persephone spotted two bobbing heads.

"Hold this." Persephone gave Brin the glowing stone as she waded back into the pool to help Moya and Roan find the shore.

As she did, Arion, Suri, and Minna splashed down, and not long after came the three dwarfs, one after the other. They made a chain of hands and safely fished everyone out of the pool and up on the rock.

For several minutes, no one said a word. Few could as they coughed, spat, and labored to breathe. Whether from fear or the cold, everyone was shaking.

"I can't believe we survived that," Moya said. She was still breathing hard, her head hanging, hair dripping.

Brin nodded. "I thought I had died five different times, starting when that thing woke me. That was the raow, wasn't it?"

The others waited for Suri to answer, but she didn't. The mystic stood away from the rest, facing the waterfall.

"Yes," Persephone said. "We think so."

Brin shivered.

"Anyone else bang their head on the rock?" Moya asked, and was answered with a round of moans.

"Why didn't you do anything?" Flood asked the Fhrey, and Frost who sat beside his brother nodded. "You could have stopped that thing. Killed it in an instant. We could have died back there. Why didn't you stop it?"

"That raow, or whatever it was, is nothing compared to Balgargarath. The demon is . . . I can't even explain it, except to say the raow is a bug in comparison. We nearly died and you just stood there!" Frost shouted, his beard bristling.

Arion looked at him but said nothing.

"You're Miralyith," the dwarf said incredulously. "We saw what you can do. What happened? Why didn't you use your power, your so-called Art?"

Arion looked away as the spill of water roared off the rocks.

"Answer me!" Frost shouted.

"She wanted me to do it," Suri said.

Heads turned.

The dwarfs thought about this a moment; then Flood turned to Suri. "Then why didn't *you* do anything?"

Arion said angrily in Fhrey, *"She's learning, and that wasn't exactly a classroom setting. You don't just wake up one day able to move mountains."*

"When a creature is attempting to kill us, do you really think that's time for training?" Frost bellowed. *"You want to teach the girl, fine. But when our lives are on the line, you need to step in."*

"She needs to practice. The Art is rarely required when everything is calm and serene. Times of danger, when you must think and act fast, are the best environment for training. It builds emotion and adds power. Stress aids the process. We're talking about the Art here; it's not like making a sword or a pair of boots."

"It takes years of practice to make a decent sword," Frost argued.

"Of course. So how long do you think it takes to understand the rhythms and patterns of creation? Much of it is intuitive, but much more is not. And there isn't a formula to follow, no step-by-step process that produces the same result. It's an art, a process of intuition, trial and error. It's mastered by learning through practice, finding out what each individual can do and how they can do it. What is safe and what is dangerous. What can be altered and what kills.

"You think Suri is less capable than I, but you don't know the Art, nor can you see her potential. Trust me when I tell you that if this Balgargarath is as sinister as you keep saying it is, it's Suri and not me that you want to face it."

Arion shivered then and turned to Suri. Returning to Rhunic she said, "I am cold, and I am wet, and I am tired of explaining methods. Suri, can you please do something about that. The cold and wet part, I mean."

"There's nothing to burn," Roan said. "And even if we had anything, it'd be soaked."

"So?" Arion said, and turned to Suri.

The mystic nodded.

She raised her hands as if playing her string game without the string. She began to mumble and then hummed. Her fingers played and danced in the air for a moment. Then she paused and stopped humming. Just when Persephone was certain something had gone wrong, Suri clapped her hands, and a flame appeared. Not a campfire, just a single tongue of flame like a little person dancing on the stone.

"Over here." Arion pointed toward the center of the stone ledge. "Make it come over here."

The little spitting tongue of orange and yellow hopped and whirled to the center of the ledge. Everyone nearby drew back. Moya stumbled and nearly fell in the pool in her rush to get away. Even Minna began to growl at the dancing flame.

"Now," Arion said, "make it grow."

Suri's gaze focused on the fire, and she whispered something while squeezing her hands into fists. Slowly the flame became two and then three. They spit and sparked and fanned out. Soon it was like any other campfire, except this one didn't seem to burn anything. Still, it gave off heat, and everyone lost their fear as they gathered around it, joyous at the warmth and familiar light it offered.

The fire continued to burn, and Suri's hum changed tone as she threw out her hands first one way and then the other. When she was done, Persephone was amazed to find she was no longer drenched. Everything from the top of her head to her shoes was as dry as when she had set out. By the looks of astonishment, not to mention the dried hair, fur, and beards of the others, she wasn't the only one.

Arion nodded in approval and gave Suri a little smile. "Good. Very good."

Persephone sat beside the pool on the flat rock with her back resting against the wall. It made a fine seat, and with Suri's fire, she was warm enough to be comfortable. The light of the flames revealed the chamber to be smaller than she'd first thought. They were in little more than a pocket of hollowed-out stone, somewhere and yet nowhere, lost deep underground, disconnected from the world of light. The thought that she and the others were dead crossed her mind. This was certainly how she pictured death—dark, hard, and cold.

The spirits of warriors who fought bravely went to a place called Alysin, a green field of warmth and beauty. For the rest, there was Rel, if they were virtuous, and Nifrel—*below Rel*—if they weren't. All three realms of Phyre were underground, deep, deep inside Elan. Whether dead or not, Persephone couldn't imagine they were anywhere else. Either they had walked in through the front door by invitation or they'd accidentally slipped through an unattended crack. The result, she reasoned, would be the same. They were there to stay, but what did a person do after she was dead? The question might seem strange to the living, but was incredibly relevant to the recently deceased. She wished she had asked more questions when she was alive. She hadn't expected death to be so complicated.

After a few hours—though it was hard to tell time, if time even existed for them anymore—some sought refuge through sleep. Brin didn't try, even with Persephone's assurances that she would personally keep a vigil. Persephone could still see the image of little Brin being dragged off, that pale white hand clamped over her mouth. She wondered if either of them would ever manage to sleep well again.

Suri sat off to one side, speaking softly to Arion. Moya, Rain, and Flood had climbed up the rock toward a higher ledge to see if there was a dry path they could take. Persephone could hear them causing little landslides of dirt followed by the occasional grunt from Flood or curse from Moya. As far as she could tell, Rain never made a sound.

"Are we dead, do you think?" Persephone asked Frost.

The white-bearded dwarf sat close to the fire, his feet out toward it and his back against the cliff. He raised a bemused eyebrow and chuckled.

"Are you laughing because we are or because we aren't?"

"We are still very much alive."

Persephone wasn't sure she was willing to accept his judgment as fact, but he did sound most certain. Still, she had to admit she didn't feel dead, even though she wasn't sure what death would feel like.

"Where are we then?" Persephone asked Frost.

"I have no idea. We obviously didn't come this way before. We're down deep, though. Fell a very long way."

"It didn't seem like such a long fall."

"It wasn't just the first drop or the last. The whole trip along that sluice was most decidedly downward. Half a mile maybe, three-quarters even. Rain would know better. He's the digger. You want to know how to build a house or fortress, I'm your Belgriclungreian. You want to know about constructing a canal or a well, that's Flood. You want to know about stone, about the dark, about the passages of Neith, Rain is who you want to talk to. He'll be able to tell you exactly where we are. Honestly, I'm a fair builder, Flood is actually better . . . and don't you dare tell him I said so. But Rain . . . Rain is something special. Even among our most respected diggers, he's a legend."

"Is that why he has that gold torc?"

Frost nodded. "Grand prize at the Linden Lott competition eight years ago. All of Belgreig was there, and Rain walked away with the honor. He's amazing. The guy even dreams about digging. That's why he's really here, why he became a digger in the first place. Keeps having dreams about this lass in the dark calling to him, says she's at the bottom of the world and needs him to find her. She needs his help or some such thing. Had the dreams ever since he was a wee lad. Neith is the deepest place in Elan, so he jumped at the chance to join me and Flood as we delved down here, but I guess not even Neith is deep enough to find some things. Even though he can't find his dream lass, trust me, Rain will know where we are."

"That's good, because we don't have a lot of food. Almost all the packs are upstairs."

"The raow is probably enjoying my raisins right now." Frost frowned and shifted his feet, crossing them at the ankles. "I'm just glad I slept with my boots on."

"Frost?" Persephone said, wondering how to ask.

"What?"

"Are you scared?"

"Of what?"

It was Persephone's turn to laugh, even if the situation wasn't the least bit funny. "I'm not seeing a way out."

Frost made a *pfft* sound of dismissal. "Let me ask you this. Would you be frightened if you fell through the floor of your lodge into the root cellar?"

"Well, no, but—"

"It's the same thing. Neith is our home. This is where we learned to dig, to tunnel, to work with metals, and cut gems. This is where we became Belgriclungreians. You know, they say we were as tall as you once, but after living in the deep tunnels for so long, Drome gave us the gift of compact size to make it easier to work and get around. On the surface, you tall folk think you're so advantaged. You'll see. Down here, being shorter is better. I can't be frightened. This is my home."

"But we can't get out and we have very little food left."

"Food? There's plenty of food, just not surface food. Granted, I'm not a fan of traditional underworld fare."

Persephone remembered rumors about the Dherg eating stone. She hoped that wasn't what he meant.

"What's traditional fare?"

"Cave beetles, millipedes, crustaceans, crickets, spiders, salamanders, and cavefish. And of course, centipedes."

"Centipedes?"

Frost nodded rapidly. "Down here they grow so large, they've been spotted feasting on bats."

She grimaced.

"We could live down here forever, if we wanted."

What kind of life, or afterlife, would that be? Trapped in the dark eating centipedes. Maybe this wasn't Rel. Perhaps the gods had decided she was unworthy. This might be Nifrel. *Maybe I'm being punished.*

"The only thing I'm frightened of is Balgargarath," Frost told her. "The deeper we go, the closer we get. I suspect the water absorbed much of our shenanigans, but we've got to be close now. And I'm having second thoughts about the Miralyith."

"I can hear you," Arion said from across the shelf.

Frost frowned. "Damn their ears."

The scuffling behind them grew louder.

"Well?" Frost asked. "How does it look?"

"Nothing up there," Moya responded, despondent. "Just goes up to more rock."

"The lady wants to know where we are, Rain," Frost pointed at Persephone. "She thinks we're trapped."

The smallest of the dwarfs with the biggest of picks looked at Persephone. His eyes widened a bit and the hint of a smile touched his lips. Because he had less beard than the others, the slight curl was easier to see. Then he shook his head. "Not trapped."

"Can you tell where we are?"

He shrugged. "We're deep. Below the Rol Berg." He pointed at the ceiling. "That's the Grand Cauldron up there. I imagine it would take only a few good strokes and I could break through. Of course, we'd drown if I did." He pointed up and off to the right. "That way leads to the Deep Shaft . . . what would normally be taken to get down this far. Except . . ."

"Except we're down farther than that, aren't we?" Flood asked.

Rain nodded.

"When you were playing hide-and-seek with Balgargarath, did you ever come down this far?" Persephone asked.

"Not here, exactly, but close," Rain said.

"Are we near *it*?" Flood asked.

It? Persephone wondered. *What's it?*

Rain looked up at the cliff beside them and nodded. "That way is the Dark Fork. There's a seam I could open and that would let us squeeze through. Just beyond is the Agave."

Up until the last word, Persephone had thought that *it* was the demon, and she didn't like the idea of it being so close. But when Rain said *Agave*, the three Dherg shared looks of a most serious nature.

Is there something even worse than Balgargarath down here? she wondered.

"What is the Agave?" she asked.

The three ignored her. Frost got up and joined the other two, who had shifted off to the side. They drew closer, closing a circle with heads almost touching, speaking quietly among themselves. Persephone doubted they were trying to be secretive. If they were, she imagined they would talk in their own language.

"Any digging will alert the demon," Frost said.

"But it's what we came for," Flood replied.

"I just didn't expect to face it this deep."

"Does it matter? The question is, will the Fhrey kill it when it comes?"

"It's just that being so near the Agave—"

"What is the Agave?" Persephone asked again, more forcefully this time.

All three glared at her.

"It's the chamber," Frost said.

"*The* chamber?" Moya asked.

They all nodded and Flood said, "The chamber of the Old One." He said this with a sort of finality.

"Old One?" Persephone asked. "Care to explain?"

Frost and Flood sighed together. Then Frost held out inviting hands toward Flood who slumped his shoulders as he took a breath. "Our ancestors weren't content with the city they built inside Dome Mountain. They dug down until they found the Agave, a compartment surrounded by a wall of smooth black stone. They came upon it so deep that some believed they had reached the bottom of the world, but there was a person on the other side. They could hear him, talk to him."

"How is that possible?" Persephone asked.

"No one knows. He could have been one of us, or a Fhrey, or even a Rhune. Although your people hadn't appeared in the world yet. He said he was a prisoner and asked to be released. Our ancestors were understandably hesitant. What kind of being is imprisoned deep underground like that? Who put him there? How? Why?"

Moya sat down, looking up at the Dherg, captivated. Across the shelf, Persephone noticed Arion and Suri were also listening. Brin, too, which wasn't a surprise.

Flood continued. "It claimed to be older than the gods. Older than Drome or Ferrol."

Arion coughed.

"It said it was unjustly imprisoned and tried every trick it could come up with to escape, to persuade our ancestors to let it out. Gifts were offered, and eventually our forefathers felt pity for the Old One and foolishly set it free. For their generosity, the treacherous Old One unleashed the demon Balgargarath.

"It was believed that the Old One was guarding something of great value," Flood said. "That inside the Agave was a treasure. So naturally, after he was gone, our ancestors went inside. There, they found Balgargarath. It slaughtered hundreds, and—"

"She heard the rest from Gronbach," Frost said.

Persephone looked from one dwarf to the next. "You were trying to get in the Agave, going after the treasure. If you hadn't, Balgargarath would be merrily following his path of knockers."

"We didn't expect it would still be doing that. It's been over six thousand years!" Frost erupted. "Six thousand! It had to be dead after all that time. Nothing, not trees, not even Fhrey, live that long. We were certain that if Balgargarath had really existed and wasn't just some myth, it would have expired or left long ago. We were positive that the law prohibiting entrance to Neith was no more than a superstition. We were going to lead our people to reclaim our heritage, our birthright, to rediscover our own past."

Persephone scowled. "First it's a giant, then a demon, now we face an *ancient* fiend summoned by a being older than the gods?"

Flood looked at Frost then back at Persephone. "Okay, so we left out a few details."

"I'd say those were pretty important points," Moya said.

"Anything else you'd care to share?" Persephone asked.

"No, that's all of it," Flood replied. "In our defense, we told you what was important: It's big and has to die. Thinking it could be dealt with without killing was their idea." He pointed to Suri and Arion.

"Can it? Die, I mean," Persephone asked.

"A Miralyith created Mount Mador and killed tens of thousands of our kind. Such power must be able to vanquish Balgargarath."

Persephone miserably shook her head. "This is all too much. We haven't even seen it yet, and it's a wonder we're still alive. No. It's too dangerous. We're in over our heads. We're just going to have to go back. This isn't our fight, and I can't ask Arion or Suri to—"

"It *is* your fight," Frost said. "What do you think will happen when Balgargarath escapes Neith? Sure, it'll decimate Belgreig first, but then what? Do you think that narrow inlet will stop it? When you found us in the Crescent Forest, we were fleeing north, wondering how far away would be far enough. Balgargarath is evil, pure evil, mindless evil. The purpose of its whole existence is to destroy life: ours, yours, the Fhrey. It doesn't care. And if it hasn't stopped in six thousand years, it never will."

Persephone looked at Arion, who closed her eyes and shook her head.

"Look," Frost said, "Rain can get us back to the surface, but he'll have to dig. That will draw the demon, and we won't make it all the way out before Balgargarath is upon us. It seems to me you can either fight here or wait until it wades across the inlet and visits Tirre and Estramnadon. I would think here is a better choice."

Persephone turned to Rain. "What's the quickest way out?"

He nodded at the cliff. "Other side of that stone."

Persephone squinted at him, as if imitating Padera. "And you can cut through that?"

He nodded. "But it'll definitely alert the demon."

"It would seem that's no longer a problem," Arion conceded. The Fhrey placed a hand on the mystic's arm and said, "I'll need a little time with Suri first. Everyone should eat something, then try to sleep."

Roan nodded and dug into her bag, pulling out what she had left of the provisions the Dherg had sent with them.

"A last meal?" Moya asked.

Arion smiled at her. "Let's hope not."

CHAPTER TWENTY-TWO

The Agave

What we discovered in the Agave was incredible. We found the people we were meant to be.

—THE BOOK OF BRIN

Suri didn't know how to feel. Scared was only one of the emotions. She was trapped, and normally that would have demanded panic, but her imprisonment was a vague thing. She didn't feel cornered. No door or braced beam was between her and the surface, and she thought she could find a way out if necessary. She and Minna had explored caverns before. This was just another one. But still, the disconnect from fresh air and sunlight was unsettling. In the past, she'd been too cocky, too sure of herself, too independent. Tura had accused her of all three on many occasions. And why not? Suri was able to find rols, climb any tree, and she had to be special for Minna to love her as much as the wolf did. Such a wise and wonderful creature wouldn't fall for just anyone. But when the raow took Brin, Suri froze in doubt and ignorance. She'd found a tree she couldn't climb, one so tall it scared her.

She and Arion moved near the water to talk privately. *"What should I do?"* Suri asked in Fhrey, wanting to grant Arion the freedom to be precise.

Arion's reply shocked her. *"I don't know."*

"What do you mean? Why don't you know?"

Arion shrugged, and Suri didn't think she'd ever hated that physical expression more. *"It all depends. Everything is relative to the situation. I'm not a martial artist, but I doubt a warrior can explain how to win an upcoming battle . . . what exactly to do. Strategies can be planned, but tactics vary based on the environment and what your opponent does. We haven't seen yours, don't even know what it is."*

"Opening the ground and swallowing it up . . . is that a good tactic?"

Arion thought and nodded. *"I think so. So yes, you might look to that as a plan, but don't rely on it. Conflict is unpredictable."* Arion looked into her eyes with open honesty. *"Suri, you are very creative; that is the source of your power. That's the source of any Artist's power. Learn to trust your instincts."*

"But there are methods, right?" She raised her hands and held out her fingers. Pretending she had string on them, she performed the opening weave of a cradle. *"Things you can teach me. Established patterns?"*

Arion was nodding. *"True. There are hundreds of practiced designs adopted and refined over the centuries. But you don't have time to learn such shortcuts, and they most likely won't help."*

"Then how can I—"

Arion held up a hand. *"Who taught you all those string patterns?"*

Suri thought. Tura first showed her the game, but she only demonstrated how to make the cradle and then the diamond weave. She shrugged. *"I figured them out myself."*

"Exactly. The Art is just like that. I could show you three different ways to turn this pool into ice, and left to yourself you might come up with a fourth—one better suited to you. For example, consider the fire you just made. It's a very simple pattern, right? Draw in heat, focus it, release. But it wasn't that easy, was it?"

Suri shook her head. *"Didn't have wood, or oil, nothing to ignite."*

"Exactly. Sources I'm sure you always had in the past. So how did you do it?"

"The water." She pointed across the pool. *"The falling water. The movement had power."*

"And so you altered the weave to draw from that source. That's the creative part. That's adapting a method, and you didn't need me to explain how to vary the weave. But that's not all you did, was it? Have you ever dried water from soaked clothing in an instant?"

"No," Suri admitted.

"And I didn't teach you that, did I? So what did you do?"

"I was thinking of Rapnagar, when I could feel the dirt around him. I did the same thing with water: I saw it on the clothing and the strands of hair, and I pulled it out, separated it from everything it touched."

"An excellent approach. And now you know you can develop new weaves all on your own. Learning that lesson . . . learning to learn . . . to teach yourself . . . that's part of what it takes to be an Artist. It's the most important part. Some never learn that. They can only repeat what they've been taught, but that's not true art. Art is creating, and I've seen you do that."

Arion paused then, and a small smile crossed her lips. *"But you did something more, and you're probably not even aware that you did. Something that shows me you have great capacity. Do you know what it is?"*

Suri thought, but she didn't see what Arion was referring to. Removing the water was new, but Arion had already mentioned that, and what help would drying out Balgargarath be if they came upon him? If Suri had done something else, she didn't know what. Stumped, she shook her head.

"When you removed the water, what did the fire do?"

"Do? It didn't do anything."

"Exactly. You managed two weaves simultaneously, and so easily you didn't even notice. You're doing it now—having this conversation with me while the fire still burns. You don't have to concentrate, aren't struggling to do both at the same time. I know how hard that is. Among my kind, I'm sort of famous for performing multiple weaves at once. It's why Fenelyus dubbed me Cenzlyor, which means 'swift of mind.' I've trained students for years, but some just can't do it. Yet you juggle weaves instinctively. It's really quite amazing."

Suri didn't think it was amazing. Like Arion said, it didn't take any concentration. Still, she was happy Arion was pleased.

"Is there anything you can teach me that I can use in this fight?"

Arion nodded. *"I just did. I pointed out the abilities you already possess, and demonstrated how you figured out the answers by yourself. Yes, there are some basic formulas and some extremely powerful and complex weaves that have been worked out and handed down. I've taught those for centuries, and for lesser Miralyith it takes years, sometimes decades, to learn those lessons. But honestly, Suri, that's the hardest way to learn about the Art. The easier way is to find the path within you. Then you can do anything; you can teach yourself. I can act as a guide by pointing you in the directions that worked for me, but you must take your own journey because no two Artists ever tread the same path. Artists create. That's what it means to be an Artist, and part of that is creating your own way."*

Suri wasn't at all happy with that answer. If they came upon Balgargarath, she wanted to know more than just two simple tricks, and the best her mentor could offer was, *Do your best.* Maybe it was true, but it didn't instill confidence.

"You sure?" Suri asked in Rhunic.

Arion returned a sad but hopeful smile. "Pretty sure." Then she added, *"What you need more than anything is confidence. The more you do, the better you'll get, and the more self-assurance you'll obtain. With my experience, I can help you avoid pitfalls and dead ends. That will speed up your advancement, but you have to do the work. My best advice is to remember the focusing chant. That will help. It will settle your mind, make it easier to think, center your thoughts, and allow you to find the chords."*

"But how do I know which ones to touch?"

"How did you learn to hold your breath underwater? Did you need to be taught that?"

Suri didn't have an answer. She'd never thought about it before.

"Mastery comes with time and practice," Arion said.

"I don't have either of those."

"It'll be all right. You're just afraid. That's your biggest problem. You've touched the chords, know what they feel like. You understand the immense power residing there, and you've seen what that power can do. You're afraid that by using the Art you'll hurt someone you love. It's that fear that's holding

you back, and it's that fear you must face and overcome to gain your wings. Then you won't simply fly, you'll soar."

Arion held out her hands to calm Suri. *"I can help you. While the others rest, we'll explore the chords together. I suspect you know more about each than you realize. In Estramnadon, Fhrey come to be tested for Artistic aptitude. Then they enter a college of study where they learn to wake and develop their previously inert connection to the powers of the world."* Arion took Suri's hands in hers. *"I've watched you. Suri, you're a natural Artist. With no effort, you're better than I was after years of training. You made fire without thinking. You were born more in tune with the natural world than I could hope to achieve if I lived another two thousand years. You're a natural conduit. You merely need to take charge of that part of yourself. Suri, you really are a caterpillar trapped in a chrysalis on the verge of becoming a butterfly. Fear is your only true obstacle, and there's one other thing I want to teach you before Rain starts digging."*

"What's that?"

"How to tap the life force of those around you. Here, you had the flowing water to use as a source, but that's not always the case. At our first resting spot, there wasn't any, except for each of us. You were afraid then. Frightened that you would pull too much and hurt someone. We'll practice that now as well. Just in case it's needed. Once you find that you can do so without hurting others, you'll lose that fear."

Arion turned and started back to the camp. *"Come, it's cold, and there's no reason you can't practice where it's warm."*

The others had eaten, although not much by the look of what was still left. Suri wasn't hungry and didn't think she could eat. While the others bedded down to sleep, or try to, Arion helped Suri practice.

Tura had always taught her that stones had spirits, that they were living things, but when she searched the rock around her, Suri felt nothing but an empty void. The waterfall was a source of power, but the stone—this old, deep stone—was dead. She needed the power to pluck the chords, to instigate change, but the stone was useless. Carefully, oh so delicately, she reached out to the others, her companions and friends.

With their life force she found the needed access and reached through the veil to the chords. She instantly sensed the deep ones, huge, thick, and shimmering. Arion had warned about them. Those were the struts and pillars of existence, the instruments of gods. Their music was deafening, their power drawn from the bowels of the world and on through the heavens. They radiated heat and light and begged to be played, to have their music released, but they also required great power to pluck.

Suri turned away and focused on the smallest of chords, the little strings. Arion was right: They were all familiar. She knew the sounds each would make, the song two or more joined together would sing, and how that could change the world. The number of possibilities was infinite. There were hundreds of ways to start a fire, though only a few made much sense and the way she had done it was the most efficient. Still, she noticed other patterns that she thought would be more . . . more . . . *elegant,* maybe?

An entire bank of strings represented the stone around her. She could fold it, shatter, and shear it. She found what she looked for, and went through the practice of a weave that—had she followed through—would have opened the ground the same way Arion had done under Rapnagar. Having found it, she felt better. She stowed away the knowledge and was gladdened at knowing what to do and how to do it.

She opened her eyes. Most were asleep, but Brin and Persephone were staring at her with curious expressions.

"What?" she asked.

"You were singing," Brin said.

With a nod from Persephone, Rain pulled his great pickax from the sheath on his back. The tool looked incredibly heavy, but the dwarf handled it with ease. The way he treated it was like the care mothers took with babies. Seeing him prepare to dig, Persephone knew she was about to see the complete version of Rain.

They gathered around him at the place where the rock in the cliff had cracked, where the stratum on the right didn't line up with the layers on the left. Persephone never would have noticed it, but she imagined Rain had an eye for such things. She had no idea what was about to happen. The trick was in not showing fear. She caught Brin, Roan, and even Moya looking at her. Maybe they looked for signs of panic. No matter how she felt, Persephone had to remain calm and composed. Arion, she thought, was a master at this. The Fhrey appeared relaxed, but the serenity had to be an act. Even Minna was pacing and panting.

Rain looked over his shoulder at her with a solemn expression of expectation.

"Do it," Persephone ordered.

With a great round swing, the digger brought the pointed end of the huge pick down on the rock. Whether by some magic of the pick, or Rain's skill in knowing exactly where to strike, the wall that appeared to be so solid broke apart. Huge chunks fell away as if the dwarf were digging through sunbaked clay. Hunks came off in large fragments that slapped the ground and, in some cases, had the force to bounce and roll into the pool. The entire process took so little time that when Rain stopped she was certain he was only taking a breather, but the dwarf flipped his pick around and stuffed the handle into its sheath.

He stepped out of the way to let her see, and Persephone spied an opening in the rock, a jagged crevice that was big enough to pass through.

Rain took out his glowstone and asked, "Would you like me to lead?"

"Please," Persephone told him.

One by one, they all crawled into the black hole, each following the one in front by feel. The dwarfs did have it easier. Their compact frames appeared born to such travel. Even with his big pickax, Rain scrambled through the cramped crevasse with the nimbleness of a ferret. They went up slightly, then down. The passage grew narrower and narrower. Then with a deep inhale, Persephone squeezed out into a larger chamber. She expected to see a corridor of Dherg engineering—perhaps not the vaulted halls at the entrance, but a more compact version, something akin to the rols in the Crescent Forest. As it turned out, they were beyond the reach of Neith, deeper than the ancient city. And just as dense forest and brambles waited beyond the bounds of Dahl Rhen, here, too, was wilderness.

Dripping stone spikes hanging from a toothy ceiling greeted Persephone. Wrinkled rock formed uneven, sloping walls. Another natural pool—this one larger, with irregular edges—played a lonesome music of *plinks* and *ka-plunk*s as calcified fangs from overhead let stony saliva slip, making elegant ring patterns on an otherwise glassy surface. At the base of the cavern snaked what appeared to be a woodland deer path of packed dirt. Persephone surmised it was a dry underground stream. She could see all this by the light of luminous lichen whose bluish glow turned the chamber into a strange fairy wonderland. For all its grandeur, the Dherg halls of Neith could not surpass the raw magnificence of this natural cavern. Nor had Neith provoked such a sense of dreadful awe. The world they found themselves in was no longer one of measures and weights, no longer a tamed realm.

They followed Rain's lead, scooting down the steep slope to the trail. Looking both ways, Persephone saw a long zigzagging path disappearing into darkness.

"Which direction?" Frost whispered softly. The place demanded a quiet reverence.

Rain nodded to the left.

"How far?" Flood whispered even softer.

"A hundred yards, maybe."

Eyebrows rose as the answer rocked the two dwarfs. They looked to each other, sharing excited expressions.

"It's like we're at the bottom of the world." Moya's head was up, eyes large, examining the jagged ceiling.

"No, not the bottom," Rain replied, and Persephone believed him. At that moment, Persephone would have believed anything he told her.

Brin was the last down to the path. The girl had sallow cheeks and shadowed eyes.

"Are you all right?" Persephone asked her.

Brin nodded.

Persephone didn't believe it. Brin, the once happy-go-lucky girl of Dahl Rhen, had lost her parents, her home, and nearly her life—face first—*eaten* by a creature from a nightmare. Brin wasn't all right. None of them were. But like the rest the girl continued to move, still pushing forward. Not a single complaint had passed her lips.

Thinking about it, Persephone realized that none of them had complained. They had suffered sickness on a ship filled with hostile Dherg; faced imprisonment in Caric; volunteered to fight a demon; and nearly drowned while falling through cracks into depths so deep it seemed doubtful they would ever get out. But, not a word of protest had been uttered. No one whined, and there were no grumblings, no tears.

Although men were strong like rocks, any stone could crack. Women were more like water. They nurtured life and could shape the hardest granite through unrelenting determination. Persephone had always felt the women of Rhen were a tough lot, more durable, more resilient than its men. They were the ones who carried on, who picked up the pieces whether the battle had been won or lost. Watching Roan, Moya, Suri, and Brin march down the dry riverbed, Persephone felt an enormous sense of pride.

Rain led them down the path, and when it forked, he stopped. At that point, Persephone saw evidence of Dherg activity. A narrow stair led down to a short path, which ended at a vast wall. In the rock face, a twisted crack ran from ceiling to floor. This great fissure disturbed Persephone in a manner she couldn't sum up in rational thought. Just a crack and yet, it *felt* ominous. Some primordial instinct warned her away. The longer she looked at it, the more she noticed how unnatural it was. This gap in stone wasn't a crack at all; it was a tear. Here, the world had ripped open.

"That's the Agave," Rain said, pointing toward the crack.

Frost and Flood stared at the dark entrance in awe. "It's so close," Frost said excitedly.

"Rain, do you sense Balgargarath? Can you feel him coming?"

The dwarf put an ear to the ground, and then rose and shook his head.

"Please," Frost begged. "I *have* to see what's inside. To come so close only to turn aside . . . I'll surely regret it for the rest of my life. You can start heading out if you want, but I can't go, not yet."

Persephone's curiosity was certainly piqued. And Roan, Moya, and especially Brin looked from the Agave to Persephone and then back to the crack. They were all thinking the same thing. They, too, wanted to know what was inside.

She nodded, and Rain led them down the path to the left.

When they reached the crack, Rain held up his glowing stone, offering it to any who wanted to enter. To Persephone's surprise, neither Frost nor Flood took it. The two dwarfs hesitated, and in that moment of second thoughts, Moya stepped forward, took the stone, and walked in. The rest followed.

Despite all the anticipation, the interior of the Agave was nothing but a small cave. An uneven stone floor was broken up in several places where minor digging had clearly taken place. What had been excavated was stacked near the center of the cave. Some of the stone was used to make furniture: a chair and a table. Thinner slabs were stacked in a neat towering pile several feet high.

The cave appeared to go on into darkness, but Persephone couldn't see where it went.

"Place is empty," Moya declared.

Using Rain's glowstone, the three Dherg started to explore the depths. Persephone watched their bobbing light as they walked as far as they could, which wasn't far at all. "This can't be all there is," Frost said.

Brin took Persephone's light and began studying the stack of slabs. Reaching up, she took some off the top. Persephone hoped she wouldn't topple them onto herself.

In the distance, toward the back of the cave, she heard a clacking sound. The dwarfs were doing something. Rain was swinging his pick, grunting with effort and then grumbling in frustration.

Moya gestured toward the opening. "You think *it* made that hole? Balgargarath, I mean?"

Persephone looked back. The glow from the lichen just outside provided enough light to see the edges of the great crack—the rip.

Persephone shrugged.

"You're just a wealth of knowledge, aren't you?" The tone was playful, no sign of reproach. That Moya could find levity when trapped under the world while a six-thousand-year-old demon searched for them was comforting in a way Persephone couldn't quite put her finger on.

"Want answers?" Persephone said. "Talk to Roan. I'm just here for the food."

The comment brought a smile to Moya's lips, but then her brows furrowed. "Speaking of Roan." She looked around, nervously.

Persephone looked as well, and spotted the young woman creeping along in the dark near the wall opposite from the wandering dwarfs.

"Roan!" Moya called and swung her arm in a big arch to coax her over.

"You don't have to nag after her like that," Persephone said. "She's a grown woman."

"You know how she is. I don't want her getting lost down here."

"You don't want *her* getting lost? Tell me exactly, where are we?"

Moya frowned. "You know what I mean. What if there's another one of"—she gestured at Brin—"those *things* out there? Or the same one still following us. Could you imagine *Roan* being grabbed?"

Persephone hadn't thought of that. As awful as it was to see it hugging Brin, it could have been worse. She mimicked Moya's gesture with a bit more authority. "Roan, this way. Come over here and work on that spear thrower of yours. There's enough light coming in from the crack."

Roan nodded and came back to the pair. She sat down and unrolled her bundle.

Arion, Suri, and Minna joined them as well, while the three dwarfs, marked by the moving glowstone, continued their trek. Suri and Minna flopped down on the floor, but Arion remained standing. Suri ruffled the fur around the top of Minna's head, then lay down, using the wolf as a pillow. Minna didn't appear to mind. She curled her body around and rested her head on Suri's shoulder, the two nuzzling each other. Arion's serenity had faded. Persephone noted twin furrows between her eyes, all the more noticeable because of her bald head.

"Something wrong?" Persephone asked.

"We shouldn't stay here," Arion replied.

"Why?"

"The walls," she said, looking around the interior.

"What about them?" Moya asked.

Suri looked over and nodded. "This place is a dead zone."

"Dead zone?"

"Like the rols," Suri explained. "Well . . ." She looked around, puzzled, and then focused on Arion with a question in her eyes. "Not exactly. Is it? It's different but also the same somehow."

Arion nodded. Everyone else looked baffled.

"The Art needs power," Arion said, "The sun, trees, plants, animals, wind, rain, currents are ah . . ." She groped for the appropriate Rhunic words.

"They give us the power to do magic," Suri finished for her.

"None of those things are here," Arion said.

"So you can't do magic inside the Agave?" Moya asked.

Both Arion and Suri nodded.

"Bad place to face Balgargarath then," Moya said.

"Has there been a good place?" Persephone asked.

"Out there"—Arion pointed past the tear—"by the pool, there are some sources to pull from. Not much, but droplets do fall and there is the lichen. It's something at least."

"We'll leave as soon as they come back." Persephone gestured toward where the dwarfs had disappeared.

Everyone except Brin and Roan turned to watch the slow progress of the glowstone. It stopped. They were probably speaking privately. Brin was still taking the carefully stacked column apart, and Roan was studying her little spears. Persephone found it strange how the two could be so single-minded even in that place. *Like children,* she thought.

"I need something to catch the wind, something light," Roan said. "Something to help it fly." She had a habit of talking aloud to herself, which was why Persephone, Brin, and Moya usually ignored her. But Suri looked over.

"Like a feather?" the mystic asked.

Roan's eyes brightened. "Feathers, yes. Feathers would work perfectly, I think."

Suri reached into her bag and pulled out the handful of hawk feathers. Roan grinned. "Wonderful."

Frost and Flood finally approached, with long faces and slow steps. Frost was tugging hard on his beard, and Flood watched his feet, looking as if he might cry.

"There's nothing here," Frost said wearily. "The cave goes back some, but then . . ." The dwarf stopped with a perplexed look.

"Then what?" Persephone asked.

"Stops . . . sort of." Flood said. "There's an opening, but we can't get through."

"Rain tried chipping it away, but nothing happened," Frost said. "He's still sitting there trying to figure it out. It's like . . . it's like the world ends here."

"So much effort, so much risked, and all for nothing," Flood whimpered. "There isn't any treasure."

"Yes, there is," Brin declared. She had managed to disassemble nearly half the stack of tablets, carefully placing each on the ground, where she examined them with the glowstone. "This is it. *This* is the treasure."

The dwarfs looked at her more than skeptically—they shot her looks of irritation as if she'd made a joke at a funeral.

"Those are just pieces of stone, Brin," Moya said.

"No they aren't," the girl said. "These are tablets. Just like I was making." She held one up and positioned the gem below it so they could see chiseled markings on its surface. "These are words. This is a story. It's marked down in the same language as the rol symbols. And . . ." She looked up excitedly. "I think I can understand some of it."

The dwarfs, who had never lost their frowns, began to scowl and shake their heads in disgust.

What did they expect? Persephone thought. *Gold, diamonds? Well, certainly not etched tablets.*

"What do they say?" Roan asked, already working to add the feathers to her little spears. She made a split along the wood's shaft and slid the straightest feathers through it.

"I've been trying to work that out." The girl was all smiles. She pointed to the first tablet. "This one is actually a key."

This caught Frost and Flood's attention. "A key to what?" Frost said.

"To this language—like the one we're speaking. These symbols are abstract ideas. This first tablet is a map to work out how to understand the others. Don't you see? Whoever did this wanted the people who came after to understand. They were trying to communicate."

Brin paused, seeing the blank stares, and sighed. "Whoever was sealed in here left a message that I can hear by using these tablets. Understand?"

Frost looked at Roan, then Arion, Brin, and finally Persephone. "Are all of you witches?"

"It's not magic," Brin said.

"You can hear the voice of someone who was here thousands of years ago using hunks of stone, and you don't call that magic?" Flood said.

Brin started to answer when Arion stopped her. "Give up now. Explanations will only be a waste of time. Just accept that to them, it's magic."

The Keeper looked as if she was about to debate the point, but then something seemed to dawn on her. For a moment, she and Arion shared a revelation that left Brin wide-eyed. In that exchange, Persephone felt a twinge of envy. The girl had learned a cosmic truth—had gained a rare glimpse into the wondrous world of gods and had received some divine gift of understanding not meant for mere mortals.

"The one who was here . . ." Frost began, "was an Ancient. He predated the gods." He reached out as if to touch the tablets but stopped short. "You're saying these contain his words?"

Brin looked down at the tablet in her hand and nodded. "I suppose so."

"What does it say?" Persephone asked.

"I'm still working that out, but I think it's about the creation of the world. It speaks of Drome, Ferrol, and"—she looked at Persephone and smiled—"Mari."

"Mari? *Our Mari?*"

"I think so."

"What about that?" Suri asked, gesturing to the table.

The mystic and Brin moved toward it. "I'm guessing this is where the Old One made all the markings."

The Dherg, weighed down by disappointment, sat on the stony floor. Moya took the pause to lie down and relax.

Everyone's attention was elsewhere, which was why only Persephone noticed when Minna's head came up off the floor and looked intently toward the entrance. An instant later Arion looked in the same direction.

"Suri," Arion whispered.

Minna began to growl.

"Suri, it's time."

CHAPTER TWENTY-THREE

The Gula-Rhunes

If all the stars had fallen from the sky and gathered into three groups, it would have mimicked the arrival of the Gula-Rhunes, or at least that's what I've been told.

—THE BOOK OF BRIN

The rains had stopped. The chieftains' meeting was held outside again, and Raithe was back. His entourage had grown, and behind his chair was Malcolm, his senior adviser; the boy Tesh, his Shield; and Nyphron, whose official capacity was explained as foreign affairs adviser.

Four people representing a clan of two. Raithe looked at the boy, who was still dressed in tattered clothes that were cinched tightly around his waist, revealing a starved body. *Well, one and a half.*

Raithe hadn't planned to return to the council. He had no real idea what he intended to do after his dramatic exit. That was supposed to be his farewell to the world of politics, his final word on the subject of keenig. Most of what he'd said was addressed to Persephone, and she wasn't there anymore.

They've gone to Belgreig, the land of the Dherg . . . With Arion along, they'll be killed on sight.

Raithe stole a glance at the empty chair where Persephone should be sitting. None of the other chieftains had even asked where she was.

Persephone had been gone for only a few days. Raithe didn't know whether that was long enough to cross the Blue Sea. Walking from Dahl Rhen to Tirre had taken the refugees nearly a week. Crossing a sea seemed like a bigger feat.

Persephone said you refused to fight because Rhune weapons are rubbish, so she's getting better ones from the dwarfs.

The whole idea of fighting the Fhrey was absurd. No Rhulyn clan had ever lived by the sword as fully as Dureya, and he and Tesh were all that remained. That should be more than enough evidence to anyone curious about the virtues of war. If his father hadn't been stubborn, if he'd handed over his weapon when Shegon demanded it that day by the river, Raithe wouldn't even be in Tirre. They could have left, then circled back after Shegon, Malcolm, and the other slave had left. Instead, his father had fought, and died, leaving Raithe adrift.

He looked at the other men seated in the circle. They all planned to fight, to go to war. Raithe was no genius, but he knew how that venture would turn out. The smart thing to do was disappear, walk away. In the turmoil of the conflict, the Fhrey wouldn't be watching the frontier. It'd be easy to slip across the Bern and Urum rivers and vanish forever into the wilds of lush fields and abundant game. And yet . . .

Raithe glanced at Tesh, and then again at the empty chair and wondered where she was.

"I crushed your father's warriors at the narrows near Greenpoint," Tegan said in a raised voice to Harkon, who sat red-faced for reasons Raithe had missed.

"You weren't even there!" Harkon shouted at him. "Sile Longhammer led that attack."

"On my orders!" Tegan said in a raised voice "My wisdom succeeded in—"

"Getting your best and brightest killed?"

Lipit stood up. "This is foolishness. It's obvious who the best keenig choice is." He stared at Raithe.

"But he refuses," Krugen said. "You still do, don't you?"

Raithe nodded.

"There, you see? Instead of arguing among ourselves, why don't we focus on how to convince him to serve?" Lipit stamped his foot in frustration. "Raithe must be keenig. He is the only one capable."

"Not the only one," Nyphron said from behind Raithe's chair. This was the first time he'd spoken since the initial meeting, and once more he stepped inside the ring of chairs. "There's another qualified and more capable choice. Someone who has vast experience leading warriors into battle. Someone who has never known defeat. Someone privy to the secrets of the Fhrey, their strengths and weaknesses, and who already has a perfect plan to defeat them."

This got their attention and each leaned forward.

"And who is this secret savior?" Tegan asked.

"Me," Nyphron said. "You'll find no one better in a war against the might of Estramnadon, I can assure you. From birth, I was trained to lead skilled warriors. My father was the chieftain of Alon Rhist, the most powerful stronghold in all of Avrlyn. I have led battles against giants, goblins, witches, and dragons. My name, and that of my Galantians, are legends to my people. I could train you, teach your men to wield spears and javelins as we do, to fight in formation, to wheel and pivot. I'll show you how to use terrain to your advantage, to make your enemy fight where and when you want. I can show you how to befuddle, divide, and conquer. I know every weak point, every back door that can be broken."

Tegan opened his mouth to speak, but Nyphron went on. "I know you wonder why I would do such a thing. Why I would turn against my own kind. The answer is I'm not. Those in Estramnadon, the fane and his cohorts, are nothing like the Instarya. They are no longer even Fhrey. They have been taken over, seduced by magic that has worked as a poison to my people. I hope to cut out that toxin the only way I can . . . by removing it.

"My father tried. He fought for leadership of the Fhrey, battled in one-on-one combat with the ruling fane, and was killed. Not because he was weaker, but because the fane cheated in what should have been an honorable duel. I'll lead you across the Nidwalden and we'll take Estramnadon."

"What about your law against killing your own kind?" Raithe asked.

"True, I can't be out in front with a weapon, but that's not what you need me for. You require someone who isn't so much a warrior as a planner. Your commander doesn't have to be on the battlefield. Your best choice is someone with the ability to achieve great things, a person with confidence in themselves and the people they lead, a strategist who can see what needs to be done, and who is able to put a plan into action to accomplish it. More than anything, your leader should be someone with conviction who is willing to sacrifice everything to succeed."

"But we can't appoint a Fhrey as keenig," Lipit said.

"Of course you can!" Nyphron said. "Think about it. As a Fhrey I am outside the petty politics that you are mired in. We have no history or grudges. I will make my decisions fairly and without the prejudice that none of you can hope to avoid. My impartiality is just another reason why I'm so well suited to the task."

"You don't understand," Harkon said. "We *can't* have a Fhrey keenig."

Nyphron slapped his side and spun. "I know it's unusual, but if you really want to win this war . . . if you want to continue *existing* . . . you need to set aside your petty prejudices and realize I am the best one for the task."

"Lord Nyphron," Lipit said, "your offer is . . . very impressive . . . and appreciated." He looked around, Harkon and Krugen at least nodded. "But making you keenig is impossible."

"How is it impossible?" The Fhrey held up his hands. "You just declare me as keenig and it's done. That doesn't seem at all difficult."

"My lord, what you are failing to see is that, in the same way that your law requires that Fhrey cannot kill Fhrey, ours demands that the keenig be from one of the Ten Clans. A Fhrey cannot be keenig. Your failure to know this underscores that you aren't one of us, and displays exactly why you are fundamentally unsuited for the task."

Nyphron stood silently, his jaw clenched tight. The Fhrey was difficult to read, but Raithe was certain the Galantian was fuming. Still, he did well to hide it, and without another word, Nyphron walked away.

As he left, a horn sounded—three crisp blasts, harsh and shrill in the morning air. Everyone around the circle looked to the walls where one man was waving his arm.

"What is it?" Lipit called.

"They're coming!" the watchman shouted.

"The Fhrey?" Lipit said, his eyes fearful.

"No. The Gula."

"I suppose that answers the question of whether they got the message," Raithe said, reaching the top of the wall with the other chieftains. A horde was gathered at the top of the hill, and more could be seen on the hills behind that. If the entire expanse was filled with Gula-Rhunes, and there was no reason to think that wasn't so, there had to be thousands.

At that distance, they didn't look like men, but rather tiny things—an army of ants. The swarm of humanity spilled from the highlands, funneling into the valley much like a wash of dark water, the host so numerous it appeared to be a great flood, a deluge certain to drown.

"Couldn't they just have sent emissaries?" Tegan asked, disgusted. The Warric chieftain sounded cavalier, but there was fear in his voice.

"They've brought all three clans," Raithe said, spotting the tri-colored banners held high on poles. "Erling, Strom, and Dunn, they're all here." Then he added with a dry chuckle and a slight shake of his head, "Udgar and his banner men are out front. Nothing changes."

"You know them well, do you?" Lipit asked. Their host stood with one hand on the guardrail as the other wiped sweat from his brow. The summer sun was warm, but not that warm.

Raithe shrugged. "I haven't faced the Gula myself, but it was all my brothers ever talked about. My family made a career fighting them. Most Dureyans do . . . did," he corrected himself. That one word—*did*—felt too final, as if he were lighting the pyre beneath his people. He'd found Tesh, there might be others. A fine line divided acceptance from giving up.

"You should speak to them," Lipit said with an eager expression. His other hand came up to help the first in getting the sweat out of his eyes.

"Why me? This is *your* dahl."

"I don't know the Gula-Rhunes. None of us do, right?"

The other chieftains nodded—a long line of bobbing heads and hopeful faces.

Raithe's father had had little respect for chieftains, and none for the leaders of the southern clans, who'd grown fat on green pastures. *Their wealth is their wool, and like all sheep they fear being sheared*, he used to say. Raithe had believed that his father, like all Dureyans, was jealous of the southerners. Plenty to be envious of as they had everything—everything except courage.

"He's right." Tegan stepped forward and threw an arm around Raithe's shoulders. The action was probably meant as a fatherly gesture, or what passed for one in places like Warric and Tirre. Tegan had no clue the sort of gestures Dureyan fathers extended to their sons. Hugging wasn't among them. "This meeting is dangerous." Tegan looked out at the army descending on them. "It has to be handled carefully. The slightest misstep and we could be facing disaster."

Raithe laughed.

The others looked at him, shocked, but he couldn't help it. The irony was too much to bear. Somewhere the spirits of tens of thousands of Dureyans were laughing along with him. "You want a Dureyan to speak as your ambassador because you *don't* want trouble?"

Tegan pulled his arm back and scowled enough to show teeth. That was the sort of fatherly gesture Raithe knew well. "Who would you suggest?" Tegan asked, his tone reproachful—another Dureyan father–son tradition. Tegan was finally hitting all the right notes if his intention was to appear Dureyan-paternal. All he lacked was a solid cuff across the side of Raithe's head.

"Lipit?" Tegan answered his own question. "It *is* his house, but forgive me, dear host, you are far too civilized to deal with *their* lot. The Gula-Rhunes will sense weakness and see an opportunity for a winter home by the sea."

Lipit's eyes went wide as his head began to shake. "Oh, no. No, we don't want that."

"Indeed not," Tegan said. "And what about Harkon here? Melen is known for poets and musicians, and if the Gula were the sort to be impressed with a ballad, I'd be the first to shove him onto the field. As for Krugen . . . he could . . . well, he could try to bribe them, but it's impossible to entice a thief with jewels he can take for himself."

"You're right," Krugen said, rubbing his rings. "Nothing I could offer would appease them."

"There's always Alward," Tegan went on, casting a hand out to the new leader of Nadak. They all turned their attention to the willowy man in rags who blinked back at them as his mouth formed an appalled and fearful O. "Perhaps not," Tegan agreed.

"*You* seem capable enough," Raithe told him. "Smart, even."

"You're right; I'm *very* smart, smart enough to know I'm not the man for this. I've never seen a Gula-Rhune until this moment. My ignorance could be our undoing, but the little I do know about these northern men is that they are fighters, and the one thing that a warrior respects is another warrior."

Raithe squared himself in front of the Warric chieftain, fixing Tegan with a steady stare. "I'm not the keenig."

Tegan sighed. "I don't care, not right now. Look out there!" He waved his arm at the ant army creeping down the hill. "You don't have to be keenig, but if you don't make them think twice about marching on these walls, we won't need one."

This brought a small moan from Lipit, who by then had resorted to mopping his head with a sleeve.

Once more, Raithe noted the three banners rising above the approaching horde: Erling, Strom, and Dunn. These were the three Gula clans, violent sons of continual warfare. Raithe had more in common with them than with those beside him on the wall. That's what Tegan was saying, but Raithe wondered if the chieftain of Warric knew that.

"Okay," Raithe said. "I'll go, but I want to point out, it was your idea to send me. Whatever happens is your fault, not mine."

"What could be worse than them attacking?" Tegan said, prompting another chirp from Lipit.

Raithe shrugged. "Who knows? But I once met a Fhrey named Shegon, and look where we are now."

This raised Tegan's brows, and he nodded. "Fair enough. I'll go with you."

At midafternoon, Raithe walked uphill through the tall meadow grass. The waist-high shoots, with green tops and straw-brown stems, had gone to seed. The whole of the field lay over, brushed to a permanent western lean by a tireless ocean wind. True to his word, Tegan walked alongside. Malcolm joined them as well, along with Tesh, who was treating his responsibility as Shield with the excessive seriousness of a boy tasked with his first adult duty. None of them wore weapons. This was Raithe's decision. He'd heard his father speak of battlefield meetings, and how weapons were left behind to indicate a peaceful talk. He hoped this practice would be honored and wasn't just one of Herkimer's tall tales.

They walked to the top of a small rise halfway between the walls of Tirre and the vast horde that was the Gula encampment. The four waited on the windswept knoll.

The Gula-Rhunes had spread out on the high ground, taking each major hill in a half circle around Dahl Tirre. Raithe could hear the clang of metal, the thump of wood, the shouts of orders in their odd dialect, and laughter. The Gula laughed well—deep hearty howls and hoots, the sort only men who'd faced death on a regular basis managed without sounding insane. And yet, a few of the laughs went on too long, were too high, and Raithe suspected some of the Gula—maybe a lot of them—were just like his eldest brother.

Heim had grown to love the killing. Hegel and Didan reported that he had taken to bathing in the blood of his adversaries. Heim said it made him stronger, but his father insisted his oldest son just liked wallowing in death and relished the killing. For Heim the carnage was always over too soon. Maybe that wasn't considered crazy in a band of men who repeatedly charged into walls of spears. His father certainly never forbade the practice, never even chided Heim as far as Raithe knew. Herkimer considered it unusual, but what passed for normal in the lives of soldiers would horrify the likes of Farmer Wedon or Heath Coswall. Once more, Raithe wondered if they had a clue what Persephone and her talk of war was getting them into.

The Gula-Rhunes made them wait.

The sun passed the midpoint and slipped down toward the west, crafting shadows that elongated the dahl as if it were melting. Seabirds' shadows skimmed in circles on the grass. Bees droned; wind blew; gulls cried.

"Maybe they don't know we're here," Malcolm suggested.

"They know," Raithe said.

"What makes you so sure?" Tegan asked.

While not tall, Tegan was a big man, and he had the look of a stone that was heavier than mere size suggested. He was also dark: dark-skinned, dark-haired, and dark-eyed, his black curly beard just making the turn toward gray. Another foot shorter and Tegan could have passed as a Dherg.

"They've taken position on every hill but this one," Raithe answered.

"It's not much of a hill," Malcolm pointed out.

"It's closest to the dahl." Raithe stared at the Gula horde. "They haven't taken it because they left it for just this purpose."

"They're like locusts, aren't they?" Malcolm said.

Tesh raised his arm and pointed.

They followed his gesture and saw that a band of three had separated from the crowd and was walking their way. Each wore only a leigh mor, swept up and pinned over one shoulder, each garment a different color and pattern. Raithe was more interested in what they weren't wearing—no paint, no shields. None of the three held a spear or an ax. Raithe's father had been right; the old man was far wiser in death than he'd ever seemed in life.

If Raithe hadn't already met Grygor, and his less cordial relatives, he would have described the one out in front as a giant. It wasn't just that the man was tall—he had to be a full foot taller than Raithe—but he also looked Grenmorian. His red hair was a wilderness of ratted curls that joined seamlessly with an even wilder beard. Bushy brows shaded fierce eyes. Thick hair, more akin to fur, covered his shoulders, his arms, and the backs of his hands. Across his face lay an ugly scar that ran at an angle from his left cheek to the right of his chin. The wound had taken off the lower part of his nose, giving him a ghoulish appearance. Another injury left a long gash across his chest from shoulder to nipple, lined by holes where the wound had once been stitched.

Each of his companions was smaller, but equally scarred. The one on the right was missing an eye, the one on the left lacked a hand. In its place was a beaten copper spike.

Raithe had never considered himself civilized. He'd lived most of his life in a dirt hut, breathing the smoke of a dung fire, but he felt conspicuously cultured in comparison to the Gula.

"I am Udgar, son of Holt, chieftain of Clan Erling," the redhead declared with all the musical eloquence of chopping wood. "We received an invitation to a council to be held here."

"I am Siegel, son of Siegmar, chieftain of Clan Dunn," said the pale one with the gaping eye socket. Now that they were closer, Raithe noted that a serpent tattoo curled up the man's right forearm. The serpent was well done, despite the burn mark across its middle. "It is said that this council will pick a keenig for all the tribes."

"I am Wortman, son of Rothwell, chieftain of Clan Strom," said the one with the spike for a hand, who spoke with an odd softness. "This keenig . . . it is said . . . will bring war upon the Fhrey."

They all respectfully nodded.

"That is the plan. I am Raithe, son of Herkimer, chieftain of Clan Dureya." Raithe hadn't actually witnessed a truce meeting and had no idea if there was protocol involved, like clasping forearms or spitting, but since they hadn't done anything, he didn't, either.

At first, Raithe thought he'd messed up; perhaps he ought to have made some sort of gesture, praised the gods, or done something more obscure. All three glowered at him and stepped back, anger on their faces.

Siegel felt at his side for something not there. Wortman cringed. Even the redheaded giant Udgar flinched.

Tegan hesitated, then said, "I am Te—"

"Son of Herkimer?" Udgar burst out, pointing a big finger at Raithe. "That's not possible! All the sons of the Coppersword are dead. I slew Didan myself on the Plain of Klem!"

"*You* killed my brother?" Raithe asked.

Beside him, Tegan tensed, his eyes growing wider.

Udgar pointed to the scar on his face. "Didan gave me this before I hacked his head from his shoulders."

"The Coppersword took my hand." Wortman growled out the words from behind clenched teeth.

Such a beautiful set of heirlooms my family has left me! Raithe thought. He looked to Siegel. "And did my father, or maybe Hegel, or Heim, take your eye?"

"No." His upper lip curled into what might have been called a smile. "My wife did that with a hay rake while I was sleeping. But I did help kill Heim at Eckford, in the High Spear, me and thirty-eight others."

"So the Coppersword had another son," Udgar said, his eyes studying Raithe. "Kept you hidden. You must be his favorite."

Raithe let slip a smile as he suppressed a laugh. *Oh, yeah. Dad adored me, he did.*

Udgar took the grin as confirmation and nodded. "Why'd he send you to meet with us?"

"He didn't. My father's dead."

The three shared grins of their own.

"Who killed him?"

"A Fhrey named Shegon."

Eyes widened, then narrowed.

"*You're* the God Killer," Udgar said, and then looked to Siegel.

Siegel nodded. "The God Killer is the Coppersword's favorite son. His secret treasure."

That's right. Herkimer left me to die from starvation with his wife and daughter, because he treasured all of us so much.

"So you're the keenig who wants to lead us in a war against the gods?" Wortman said. "The son of the cur that stole my hand?"

"I'm not the keenig." Raithe turned to his right. "This is Tegan, chieftain of Clan Warric. He can—"

"Where are your warriors?" Udgar asked, and all three looked around.

"Hidden in the buildings?" Siegel asked.

"On ships?" Wortman suggested, pointing toward the beach.

"Behind us somehow." Udgar stared back toward the hills. "Yes. That would be the plan, to trap us against the sea. We should have known!" He glared at Raithe. "Your father isn't dead. He's behind us preparing the attack."

Udgar spit at Raithe, then howled like a wild thing. He squeezed his great fists and raised one at the Dureyan. "We won't die easily. We'll take you with us, so help me Mynogan!"

"It's not like that at all. You *are* invited to take part in the council."

"Ah-hah! Hear that!" Siegel shouted. "That's their vile plan. They'll take us into the dahl and slit our throats."

The three were backing away.

"No. No, that's not it. I'm telling you the truth," Raithe assured them.

"I will kill you when we meet again, son of Coppersword. And we will!" Udgar declared.

Raithe and Tegan watched the Gula chieftains retreat into the swarm of bodies, and soon they heard the sound of horns.

Tegan turned to Raithe. "You were right. Lipit would have been a better choice."

CHAPTER TWENTY-FOUR

Balgargarath

Some things are simply unimaginable right up until you are look-
ing at them, and even then, you might not believe. Love is that
way; so is death. Balgargarath was, without a doubt, in that lim-
ited assortment of the impossible, but then the name should have
been a clue. When something sounds like a giant vomiting up a
dwarf, you should not expect sunshine and daisies.

—THE BOOK OF BRIN

Something is coming.

Persephone couldn't hear anything, but she knew what was happening.
A force of nature was on its way, and she sensed it like a rising storm.

Arion took Suri's hand, and said, "We have to go out near the pool.
Everyone needs to come. She might need your strength as well." The
Fhrey looked calm, not at all frightened. This made Persephone feel better. The Fhrey was Persephone's standard of measure, and so long as she
showed no concern, Persephone felt hopeful.

They followed Arion without question, without a word. Everyone understood somehow that the final moment had arrived, and it deserved re-
spectful silence. By the time they returned to the cavern, Persephone could
hear it. A sound came at them from far in the distance. The noise was faint
but attention grabbing, a harsh shrieking like the desperate wail of a child
or the tearing of stone.

They crossed through the glowing blue chamber until Arion and Suri stood beside the pool. No longer still as glass, it quivered. Rings rippled out to the edges, then rebounded, running to the center again.

"Everyone stay back," Arion shouted over the noise, her voice small in that vast place. "Give us room."

"Why are we here?" Flood asked. "What do you expect us to do?"

"Just stand there."

The sound was getting so loud Persephone could feel it, the shriek of shearing stone. Overhead, stalactites shook, ringing like wind chimes. One fell and shattered on the path ahead. Two more broke free and crashed with such violence that Persephone and all the others jumped.

Then the rear wall of the cavern exploded.

Rocks burst out at them. The force blew Persephone's hair back and pelted her with pebbles. Out of the ominous cloud of billowing dust, a giant hoof like that of a great goat struck the ground hard enough to stagger those watching.

Dust fell away, and in that eerie blue glow Persephone finally saw Balgargarath. The demon's lower body was that of a giant goat, with hooved feet and shaggy legs. Its upper body was that of a powerful man, but its head was too grotesque to be believed. Withered, leathery skin wrapped muscle and bone the way a sheet stretched over a corpse. Twin horns, twisted and curled, jutted out from either side of its barren skull where a piggish nose with flaring nostrils divided two tiny yellow eyes. A huge mouth hung open, displaying rows of pointed teeth behind glistening lips.

The behemoth paused, its little yellow eyes focusing on them. Then, drawing up to its full height, so that its horns scraped the ceiling, Balgargarath let forth a deafening roar. Two more stalactites fell, but if their shattering made noise, Persephone never heard it over the magnitude of its roar.

Persephone froze, not by conscious thought, nor by a magical spell; she simply couldn't move. Fear seized every muscle in her body. She'd even stopped breathing. *How could I have ever imagined the Fhrey were gods when something like this was in the world?* Of course, who could have dreamed such things existed at all. *Demon* didn't do it justice. Perhaps there was no word that could. This was the nightmare that made nightmares wake up screaming.

"Use the movement, use the dust, use the vibration of the sound," Arion shouted at Suri, who stood beside her. Both of them were well ahead of the rest—two tiny bugs at the hooved feet of a horned mountain.

Suri was singing—singing to Balgargarath! Persephone knew how it was supposed to work, she'd caught on that magic was somehow wrought by vocalizing melodic sounds, but she didn't understand how anyone could stand before such a thing and sing. Even Minna had retreated several feet, her hair up and teeth bared.

Still, Suri sang. The tune was similar to the one she'd performed before, only louder this time, shifting in rhythm and melody like someone tuning an instrument. The tiny eyes of the beast focused with some effort on the two ants before it, and it took a step forward. The ground shook with its motion. Persephone felt the tremor, and saw bigger ripples in the pool. The massive hooves dragged, slowed. The beast roared again and Persephone saw it then. Balgargarath was sinking.

The stone appeared to melt at the demon's feet, turning into tar in much the same way as the dirt had when Arion trapped Rapnagar. This was more dramatic, a suspenseful bubbling up of viscous rock, and the sluggish descent of the hapless victim. The behemoth roared with anger and frustration as it struggled to claw forward.

"Now!" Arion ordered.

Suri's arms went out to either side then she brought them together in a clap of her hands. As she did, the walls at the far end of the cavern mimicked her. Persephone couldn't believe what she saw. Solid stone walls, the size of cliffs, hurtled at each other. Then an instant later—whether as an additional act of magic, or the mere result of moving the walls—the ceiling came down, teeth and all. Everyone rushed back, retreating up the path toward the Agave.

A cloud of dust and a rain of tiny rocks showered them as they ran.

"You did it!" Arion praised Suri in Rhunic. "I knew you could. It is—" She stopped and then spun around. She shook her head slowly from side to side as disbelief painted her face.

Persephone never understood the phrase *to feel as if someone is walking over your grave.* It didn't make sense that someone alive could have a grave. But at that moment, as fear rose on Arion's face, Persephone's heart sank, gooseflesh rose on her arms, and she understood.

"Impossible," Arion said in Fhrey.

"What's happening?" Persephone asked.

Arion continued to look back into the collapse of the cavern in shock. *"It's still alive . . . only . . . it isn't. It's not alive at all. It never was. I think. I think it's . . ."* The Miralyith's face blanched. *"Oh, holy Ferrol, that's not possible!"*

"What isn't?" Persephone asked, though she didn't need the answer. Everything was made clear by Arion's words. They were buried a mile or more beneath the roots of a mountain, across a foreign sea, and their one lifeline had slipped back into speaking in Fhrey because she was terrified.

Brin, Roan, and Moya stood oblivious to what was being said. They looked at Persephone for answers. She had none.

The dwarfs had heard, and they understood.

"But you're Miralyith," Frost said, bewildered.

"Miralyith are only good at killing Belgriclungreians," Flood snapped. "Now she's killed three more."

"What?" Moya asked. "What's going on?"

"It's not dead," Persephone said.

"What do you mean it's not dead?" Moya stood with a hand on one hip, the other pointing at the rubble with conviction. "Suri crushed it three different ways and buried it. What makes you think it isn't dead?" She sounded angry. Like everyone else, she wanted it to be true.

Then they felt the tremor.

Moya rolled her eyes. "Oh, by the rotten heart of the Tetlin Witch. You—are—kidding—me!"

Moya shouted at Roan to run just as Persephone found Brin's hand and the four began their retreat, chasing the three dwarfs back up the path.

"What do you want me to do?" Suri's small voice asked Arion.

Persephone expected some complicated magical jargon, something about gathering, and focusing, and summoning, and harmonizing. Instead, Arion shouted, "Run!"

Brin pulled—nearly dragged—Persephone along. Together they plunged back into the Agave. Once inside, they stopped and caught their breath.

Will it follow? Can it squeeze in the doorway? Of course it can! This is where it came from!

"What are we going to do?" Brin asked, her voice shaking as if she were freezing to death.

Struggling to catch her breath, Persephone managed to get out, "I don't know there's anything we can do."

Moya followed Roan in and, turning back to face the opening, drew her sword. As pointless as it seemed, Persephone loved her for it. Taking another round of deep breaths, Persephone drew her own weapon and joined Moya. With tears slipping down her cheeks, Brin swallowed, and she, too, drew her blade. Roan glanced at her own side, appearing surprised to find that she also had a sword. She pulled it free of its scabbard.

"Keep the tip up but hold it back like this." Moya demonstrated, raising the weapon level with her face. She held her arm cocked and close to her body, the point aimed forward.

"Do you honestly think it matters?" Persephone asked even as she imitated Moya.

"If we're going to do this, let's do it right."

Persephone nodded. "Sure . . . okay . . . good point." She was babbling out of nervous fear but what did it matter? What was there to care about anymore?

"Keep your left foot in front," Moya shouted. "And when that thing comes at us, step forward with your right as you swing or thrust."

"Which is it? Should I swing or thrust?" Roan asked.

Moya swallowed. "Ah . . . I don't know. Whatever feels good at the time, I guess. Just try to hit it."

"This metal is amazing." Roan marveled at the weapon in her hands.

"Not now, Roan! Focus!"

Suri, Minna, and Arion flew through the opening, nearly running into them. Persephone couldn't help noticing Arion was rubbing her head again.

"Where is it?" Moya asked.

"Still buried," Suri replied.

Arion looked at the swords. "What do you plan to do with those?"

"Whatever we can." Moya challenged the Fhrey with a glare. She was in a fighting mood.

Arion simply nodded.

"Why aren't you doing anything?" Frost said to the Fhrey. *"You had no problem in the forest. Quit relying on this girl. She doesn't know what she's doing. You need to finish it."*

"Is that why it didn't work?" Suri asked Arion. She had a desperate, guilty expression. *"Is it because I—"*

"It's not your fault," Arion said. *"I couldn't have killed it, either. Balgargarath can't be killed, because it isn't alive."* The Fhrey glared at the dwarfs.

She looked back at Suri. *"Didn't you feel it? Didn't you see it?"*

"It looked . . . bright," Suri said. *"Like . . . I don't know. Almost like . . . a chord."*

"That's because it is. It's not solid, not natural, its form isn't made, it's cast. It has its own song, its own pattern. It is the Art manifested into corporeal form. I've never seen anything like it. I would have said such a thing is impossible, but I tried to push against it and nothing happened, as if it weren't really there, as if it were smoke."

She switched to Rhunic and continued. "Neither you nor I can harm it." She looked at the naked weapons. "I don't think anyone can."

"Then it's over." Frost's mouth hung open, his arms dropped limply to his sides.

"We should have kept going north when we were in Rhulyn." Flood's hands came up and grabbed the sides of his head.

"Not over yet." Arion looked to the dwarfs. "Seal the opening."

"That won't do anything. The rock here is brittle. It won't stop that thing," Frost said.

"I'm going to help," Arion replied.

"You said you couldn't hurt it," Persephone said.

"I can't, but I should be able to slow it down. Stop it even." She made fists with both of her hands and butted them together, knuckles-to-knuckles. *"The Art doesn't work against itself, understand? So I can do nothing to Balgargarath. I'm hoping it works both ways. We just need to create a barrier between it and us."*

They all felt the ground shake. Everyone looked out the opening at the distant blue light that was the remaining half of the cavern.

"And hurry," Arion said. *"It's breaking free."*

True to their word, Frost and Flood were superb builders. Using stone they found in the rubble, and what Rain broke up for them, they rapidly chipped, fit, and stacked a tight stone wall that filled up the crack.

As they worked, the tremors grew stronger and more frequent. It wasn't long after the last few stones were placed that Balgargarath could be heard breaching the surface of the cave-in.

Arion didn't wait for Suri this time. The Fhrey started her own little song.

"What are you doing?" Suri asked, worried. Although Persephone didn't understand why the mystic would be so concerned.

"It's okay, this is small." Despite her words, Arion sat down slowly.

A moment later the beast reached the door. They all felt the quake as it slammed against the pile of stones. Arion stumbled backward with the jolt. The barricade shifted slightly but held. Another shudder shook the chamber, then two more. This time the rocks didn't move at all.

Suri crouched beside Arion, but the Fhrey waved her away. "Fine. It's fine," she said.

"So it's holding?" Moya looked around. "We're safe then. As long as we stay in here, right?"

"How long before it gets tired and leaves?" Persephone asked the dwarfs.

"I don't think that will *ever* happen," Suri said. The mystic faced them with a miserable expression. "Arion is right. It's not alive. It's a weave of some sort. It won't ever leave. It'll struggle for eternity to get through those stones."

"Well, thank Mari," Moya said. "We're fine then."

"We don't have enough food and water for eternity," Roan pointed out.

This one truth was evident to all as they stood in a circle with long faces and unfocused eyes peering into a bleak future. Persephone felt someone walking over her grave again . . . and this time they must be directly overhead.

Suri saw a bloody tear slip down from Arion's nostril. The Fhrey didn't notice until the droplet hit her upper lip. She wiped it away, leaving a rosy smear.

"*It's killing you,*" Suri said. "*Holding it off is too much.*"

Arion looked at the blood on her fingers. Her hand was trembling.

"*Let me do it,*" Suri told her. "*Show me how.*"

Arion shook her head. "*It's trickier than it seems. Balgargarath is a clever conjuration. It's stopped just beating and is looking for gaps . . . trying to pry the barricade open. It requires my constant attention. I need to keep shifting the shield to stop it from ripping through. It's not easy. I told you, part of my training was learning how to split my thoughts, to do two, even three, things at the same time. It's what I'm good at, and what takes me just a little effort might be quite difficult for you.*" She allowed herself a little smile. "*It's funny. Just before I left Estramnadon, I was trying to teach the prince how to split his thoughts, do more than one thing at a time. That seems so long ago . . .*"

Arion's expression was so sad it just about broke Suri's heart. "*And I left my home in such a mess. I told myself it wouldn't take long to deal with Nyphron and that I'd clean it when I got back.*"

Even though Arion had said it wasn't her fault, Suri knew it was. The guilt threatened to consume her. Failing to defeat the monster, Suri had let everyone down. No. She'd done worse than that. She'd killed them. This wasn't like forgetting to gather firewood or eating all the strawberries.

Minna must have known how Suri was feeling, for she came over and laid her head in the mystic's lap. Such a good and wise wolf. Minna always knew how to make Suri feel better, but not even Minna could lift her spirits this time.

"*How long can you keep the shield in place?*"

"I'm not sure." She waited for several minutes before saying, *"Tell me about death."*

"What?"

"We live so long that death is a rare thing. But being short-lived you must have seen it often. Haven't you? Is it awful? Gryndal's and Zephyron's deaths were both violent and horrible. Is it always such a terrible, awful thing?"

Suri thought about all the people in Dahl Rhen, Magda and the other trees, and animals like Grin the Brown and Char the wolf. Mostly she thought of Tura and Maeve. When Tura died, Suri hadn't been there. She'd found Tura lying in the garden, facedown in the freshly dug soil. But she had been with Maeve. Suri had been touching her, talking with her, when she passed on. *"I don't think so,"* Suri said, trying to remember how it was. The old woman just closed her eyes, and she died with a big smile on her face. *"Seems a lot like going to sleep, except that you never wake up."*

Arion nodded. *"Sleeping doesn't sound so bad. I like sleeping. I wish I could sleep now."* Arion reached out and took Suri's hand. The Fhrey had long delicate fingers. They wrapped Suri's and squeezed tightly. *"Remember. None of this is your fault. It's mine. The Art, like anything, has good aspects and bad. Nothing can be wholly good. It's impossible. Creation gives birth to all things, positive and negative, or what we think of as good and evil. Like all life, the power of creation seeks to exist. The Art's greatest problem is its ability to seduce, telling you what you want to hear. It's easier to believe the most outlandish lie that confirms what you suspect than the most obvious truth that denies it. Fenelyus taught me that. Arrogance . . . narrow-minded arrogance. It comes with power, and the Art is power. I thought . . . I believed . . . that even if you couldn't defeat this Balgargarath, I could. I never doubted it, not for a second. I made the same mistake I once condemned Gryndal for: I imagined I, too, was a god. I'm not."* Her lip trembled. *"If I hadn't been so confident, I would have insisted we start up the trail to the surface the moment we arrived in that chamber out there. I wouldn't have let us delay. And maybe we wouldn't have gotten out, but we would have had a chance. Now . . . well, now . . . I'm so, so, sorry, Suri."*

Arion began to sob.

The ground shook. The stones placed in the crack rattled, and they all heard the thunder of the beast throwing itself against the barrier.

Arion gritted her teeth and pursed her lips. *"See!"* she said, wiping her eyes. Another tear of blood ran from her nose. *"It's always looking for a way in."*

Frost, Flood, and Rain snored.

Roan had always enjoyed the sound of a crackling fire, laughter, and a good deep snore. Iver snored when he came home drunk and lay flat on his back, a deep throaty roll. When the snoring stopped, that's when Roan worried. Then Iver would cough, roll out of bed, and spit. From that point until he fell asleep again, she had to be prepared. For that reason, Roan liked to stay up late or wake up early. Spending her few safe moments sleeping was such a waste.

Moya also snored. Most people wouldn't think it by looking at her, but she did. Roan wondered if she, herself, snored, and pondered how she might sound and what caused it. Most people who snored did so when exhausted and while lying on their backs with open mouths. Roan was a light sleeper and preferred to sleep on her side, but she spent a week on her back trying to catch herself snoring. She never did. Either the sound didn't wake her, or she didn't snore.

The three Dherg that Persephone called dwarfs, but who Roan collectively thought of as the little men, most certainly snored. Dahl Rhen's gate horn wasn't much louder than them, and she couldn't understand how they managed to sleep through the racket they produced. What drew her attention, besides her usual interest in all things snoring-related, was that they made a specific pattern. Each repeated the same sound, the same pause, the same inhale, and then the same riotous, rattling noise. She focused on this because her mind was working on repeating sounds, and because her brain had a habit of drifting to similar events when she was working out a problem. She got many good ideas that way. A leaf spinning on the surface of a pool gave her the idea for Gifford's pottery table, which later gave her the idea for the wheel. Roan was hunting something more elusive this time—how to draw language.

What had begun as Brin's obsession had become a puzzle for Roan as she sat on the floor looking at the stone table. From that angle, she could see the underside and found it was gouged and chipped. The quizzical expression she must have had on her face attracted attention.

"Just leave her alone," Moya whispered to Persephone. "That's what she does, and believe me, right now we need her doing it."

Roan ignored them and continued staring at the table. Normally, when she wanted to focus, she chewed on her hair. When that wasn't enough, she pulled on it hard until it hurt. This time she went to the extreme of lifting the strands, forcing the hair against the grain. Making the pain worse helped her concentrate, always had. Roan got her best insights when Iver beat her. In the worst of times, Roan's mind learned to block the world out. Iver, the house, the pain, the fear: It all faded into a background haze as her thoughts converged on a single point. Focused in such a fashion, she could endure anything, and brilliance was often the result.

The little men are snoring. No, the snoring isn't important. It's the space between.

The pauses coincided with their breathing. Breathe in, snore, breathe in, snore—a pattern. People paused when speaking, too, but not always to breathe, rarely to breathe. Pauses occurred before and after words, and greater breaks when changing ideas. When drawing words, the lack of sound would be a lack of drawing. The gaps between the marks were those pauses. Words were divided by gaps. New line—new thought. What wasn't there was as important as what was.

Brin had already worked that out. The girl's system of writing sounds based on symbols took this into account. Genius really. Each mark was a sound. A series of marks became a word. Gaps between, delineated one from the next. Using this concept, Brin had already begun deciphering the markings on the tablets. All this was fine and good, but what about snoring?

And what about the table? Because . . .

"It's not a table at all," Roan muttered to herself.

Persephone, who was still sitting in the stone chair looking at her, said, "It's not? What is it?"

"It's another tablet," Roan replied. "I can see markings on the bottom."

Moya and Persephone bent down and looked.

"It was set up this way to work on," Roan explained. "Easier when you can sit in front of it and slide your legs underneath. I can't imagine it's easy to chisel all those marks—harder if you're forced to crouch down on your knees. As this is the only one propped up, this would be the last thing worked on."

"Why is it upside down?" Persephone asked.

Roan shrugged. "Maybe to make more markings on the back, or . . . to hide what's on it."

Moya and Brin turned the stone over. Nearly all the rock of the Agave's floor was shale, a layered rock made from mud that easily broke and split into leaves of surprising thinness. The tablets were all about the thickness of Moya's thumb and not too terribly heavy. They were also soft enough to allow the markings to be scraped rather than chiseled. Once the stone had been turned, Moya and Persephone glanced at it with disappointment. Brin left the stack she was working on and, holding up the glowstone, took a moment to study the new markings.

"Can't understand it," she declared with a scowl. She ran fingers lightly over the symbols. "I've worked out a lot of the words using the key and the Orinfar. A few phrases, too, but this . . ." Brin frowned at the table tablet. "I don't recognize anything here." She paused. "Well, I do. I mean the symbols are the same, but I can't make out any of the words."

Roan nodded, and that's when it all made sense. At such times, it was like a flash of light, an instant of perfect illumination. For that one moment, the whole world was revealed and she could see it down to the purpose of every grain of sand. Then the light went out and all she took with her was the afterimage.

Roan pointed toward the snoring dwarfs. "Can you understand what they are saying?"

Brin looked at her puzzled. "They're snoring, Roan. They aren't saying anything."

"But their mouths are open and they are making sounds."

"But the sounds aren't words. They're just sounds."

"Exactly," Roan said. "What if that's what's on the table tablet . . . just sounds."

"I don't understand." Brin leaned over the table, looking at its marred surface.

"I do," Suri said. The mystic had been sitting, petting Minna; now she got to her feet and walked over to the table tablet. "Tell me what it says."

"It doesn't say anything," Brin insisted.

"But you understand the symbols?"

Brin nodded.

"And they make sounds?"

"Sure, but not words."

"Show us. Make it snore," Roan said.

"What?" Brin asked, confused to the point of bewilderment.

"Make the sounds."

Brin shrugged. She looked down at the surface of the stone. "I don't know all of them. I guessed at quite a few, so they're probably wrong." She placed a finger on the stone, using it as a placeholder, dragging from left to right across the symbols as she made noises.

Suri shook her head after Brin had only gone down three lines. "That's wrong."

"What do you mean it's wrong? What's wrong? How do you know it's wrong?"

The mystic shrugged. "It just is."

"Read from the top down," Roan suggested.

"But I learned from the tablets that the words are marked left to right in lines."

"Try anyway."

Brin began making sounds again, this time dragging her finger down the tablet.

Again, Suri shook her head.

"Try right to left," Roan prompted.

"I don't understand," Brin said. "What are we even doing?"

"Read it right to left." When she did, Suri's eyes grew wide and a smile formed on her face.

Suri listened to Brin as she started making the sounds again, this time running her finger from the right of the symbols to the left. The tones were elongated and awkward, like someone singing a song they didn't know, in a language they weren't too familiar with, but she heard it. As distorted as it was, the tune was there.

Arion heard it, too. "That's a weave," she said from across the room.

"What's a weave?" Brin asked. "You mean it's a spell? So if I were to finish this, I would make something magical happen?"

"No," Arion said. "You have no power."

"You're just making patterns with string between your fingers," Suri said, realizing for the first time how that piece fit. "But if you were an Artist and could draw from a source, you could weave with the real strings, the strings of creation—create the music of the world and alter its tone."

"Yes," Arion said. "Exactly."

"How is this helping?" Moya asked. "Is this helping?"

"This is the last thing the Old One was working on before leaving this room," Roan said.

"Wonderful, Roan," Moya said. "How does that help?"

"It's a magic spell," Roan said.

"A what?"

"It's not just a spell," Suri said. "This is the weaving pattern that created Balgargarath."

Suri had known what it was the moment she'd heard the drawn-out sounds Brin was making. The symbols scratched on the stone were like stages in a string game, and she could see the process: the steps and the patterns. The whole method had been worked out in preparation for the attempt. In doing so, it left a path behind, a map that pointed to the chords of creation. The mystic was still learning, still a novice, but she knew enough to understand that whoever had created this had been at least a little crazy, and quite possibly a full bowl of nuts.

The pattern, the way it wound deeper and deeper, indicated that the creator was playing with the giant chords, the monolithic base elements rooted in the abyss. When Suri had killed Rapnagar, when she was touching the strings, she had noticed the drop-off, the same way someone might notice a draft or a whisper. The presence was just as irresistible and just as disturbing.

What's down there? The question had haunted her ever since.

Now that you know . . . now that you've seen what it's like, you've had a taste and are hungry for more. Now that you've touched the chords, you can't help wanting to fly.

Arion had been right about that. Having seen, having touched, she was infected by the possibilities. Suri felt as if she'd spent her whole life on a little hill, content and happy. Then one day she glimpsed the truth, that the hill was actually the nose of a great beast. Not easy to sleep after that. Knowing about the chords, realizing she could alter the world, made ignoring the possibilities intolerable. She was wearing a shirt with a loose thread and was dying to pull it—if for no other reason than to make the desire go away, to make it stop distracting her.

If it had just been the thin, high strings, she might have put the whole thing out of her mind. Fire was made by plucking the light strings, and she'd done that for years. The abyss was what drew her. The chasm out of which grew the great chords, the supports, the foundations of the world. That was a forest of trees whose roots held the universe together.

What would it be like to pluck one of them? What would they sound like? And what would happen if I did?

The person who created Balgargarath had touched those chords. He had stroked them and wrought a monster.

Suri looked toward the sealed crack. Using the Art to passively tap into the nature of the world, she could sense the creature just on the other side of the stacked stones. A gigantic, brilliant mass of light. Pure power. In contrast, Arion's sliver-thin shield coating the stacked stones—the enchantment that prevented Balgargarath from reaching them—appeared as dim as moonlight glinting off the sheen of a frozen lake. The veneer was all that was needed, but Suri suspected it was all Arion could manage.

"How did he do it?" Suri asked. The words weren't directed at anyone; they just spilled out.

"How did who do what?" Moya asked.

Suri looked up surprised. "What?"

"You asked—"

"Oh, I was just wondering . . . the Old One . . . if he was trapped in here, how did he create Balgargarath, where did he get the power?"

Arion's head turned away from the doorway. "Such a thing would require an enormous source."

"If you found it," Persephone said, "could you get us out of here?"

Arion nodded. "With a source that strong, Suri could pick up this entire mountain and just toss it aside."

"What about you?" Persephone asked. "I know you've been trying to teach her, but, like the dwarfs, I think things have gone far beyond lessons. Our lives are at stake."

"She can't," Suri answered. "The injury to her head . . . in the dahl when Malcolm hit her with the rock . . . it damaged her. Every time she uses the Art, it hurts. Even holding the door is killing her. Doing anything that big would be suicide."

Persephone's eyes widened. "That's why you've been leaving everything to Suri. That's why you didn't stop the demon."

"It is why I rely on Suri; but even if not hurt, I couldn't stop it. No one can."

"But wait," Persephone said. "You're keeping that thing from coming in. What source are you using?"

Arion gave a guilty look. "You."

"Me?"

"All of you. Feeling tired? I stealing power. Mostly them." Arion nodded toward the dwarfs, who were still snoring. She smiled. "Keeps them quiet."

"Won't that eventually . . ."

Arion nodded.

"How long?"

Arion tried to form a reassuring smile. "Not to worry." She wiped at her nose. "I'll die before you do." She swallowed and winced as she did, then looked at Suri. "I think I need to teach you to do this."

"There's always a better way," Roan muttered.

Suri looked at Roan, who stood staring back at her as if she wanted to say more but couldn't, or maybe she didn't know what came next.

The way Suri saw it, they were standing on a path that had three forks. The problem was that each trail led to the same awful place. Arion could fail to hold the demon and they would be killed. They could die of thirst or starvation. Or Suri could take over for Arion and eventually use up everyone's strength. Then she would be without a source and Balgargarath would enter and kill her.

Roan was right. There had to be a better way.

Suri turned to Brin. "Show me how to sing what is on the table tablet."

"Suri," Arion said. "There's no power."

"The one who made Balgargarath found power in here, I just have to discover where it's hiding." She faced Brin again. "Teach me."

CHAPTER TWENTY-FIVE

Makareta

Everyone thinks their adversary has an easier time than they do. They believe that all their opponent's schemes work out exactly as expected, while their own plans constantly suffer setbacks. It is a funny notion, especially since you can't have an adversary without being one.

—THE BOOK OF BRIN

As Mawyndulë and Makareta walked into the Airenthenon together, he knew this would be the greatest moment of his life. Despite being the crown prince, his life up until that point was a disappointing one. He'd never done anything noteworthy, and aside from his one ill-fated trip to Rhulyn, he'd never gone anywhere. No laws prevented him from leaving the palace, but he felt the disapproval when he did.

His father rarely left the Talwara. As fane, people came to him. Monthly visits to the Temple of Ferrol were acceptable, but mingling in the marketplace wasn't. Mawyndulë's life mirrored his father's, and most days were spent in his room. Everyone thought he was meditating, developing his Art. He did that, but mostly he did nothing. He spent hours lying on his bed daydreaming, which was a challenge as he had so little raw material to work with. His fantasies had become more specific over the last few weeks, but that day—that glorious afternoon—several became reality.

Gryndal had been the senior councilor for the Miralyith, and for years, Mawyndulë had longed to imitate his hero. But with Vidar as his tyrannical master, he'd grown to hate the dull sessions. Yet that day, just like in one of his wonderful dreams, Vidar was simply gone. Convicted of treason, his former master had been locked away. In his place walked Mawyndulë, with the beautiful Makareta by his side. His father hadn't questioned her appointment. Vidar's sentencing was distracting the fane so thoroughly that he didn't seem to care who was picked. For once, everything was working the way it should. The old had been wiped away, and this was a new start. Yes, the start of a new life, a better life. Mawyndulë imagined he was entering the Airenthenon again for the first time. It certainly felt that way.

Not until they had taken their seats—when he sat in the senior councilor's place—did he feel the guilt.

You don't think Vidar is really a traitor, do you?

Mawyndulë had avoided asking questions about Vidar's fate, mainly because he didn't want to know what his father planned to do, but also partly out of concern that Lothian or Vasek might grow suspicious. The fane had already been watching him. *Vasek tells me you keep mostly to yourself.* But they didn't know about the Gray Cloaks.

What if they did? What if Vasek discovers Vidar wasn't a traitor after all? And worse yet, what if he finds out I knew but didn't say anything? He would certainly be in trouble, which he felt was completely unfair. After all, he hadn't done anything. He was more innocent than Vidar, who, in a way, deserved his punishment. *And what could I have done? Told my father everything?* Then Makareta and Aiden would be locked up, possibly killed. He couldn't let that happen, not to her.

The whole matter was in the past. He wasn't certain why he was even thinking about it. He'd made his choice, and it was a sound one. Vidar was old, while he and Makareta had their whole lives ahead. If someone needed to be sacrificed, let it be the dusty, bitter old Fhrey.

The speaker beat the staff on the tile and called the session of the Aquila to order.

Hemon, senior councilor of the Gwydry, was the first to speak, saying something about a shortage of indigo resulting in a lack of blue dyes. Mawyndulë tuned her out after the first three sentences, focusing instead on Makareta's thighs. Since it was a warm summer's day, she wore a short asica, and seated on the benches as they were, the hem of her garment inched up well above her knees. Her right thigh touched his left—bare skin to bare skin. She didn't seem to notice, but to Mawyndulë it was as if he'd stepped off a cliff. His stomach rose and hovered somewhere just below his throat. Breathing was difficult. Filled with a nervous energy, he squeezed his hands into fists. Closing his eyes, Mawyndulë tried to calm himself. But that only brought forth random images of the two of them together.

Arion—The Traitor—used to say he had a great imagination, and she would laud the ability as an advantage in the practice of the Art, but it could also be a torment. He couldn't turn it off. He saw them together on his bed, in that quiet place where he was always alone, her presence transforming his prison into paradise. He imagined them lying side by side, facing each other, talking. She was still wearing the short asica, her bare thighs close to his, and he would reach down and feel her smooth skin. She would smile, sigh contentedly, and in that exhale would be an invitation.

Opening his eyes, Mawyndulë bit his lip, trying to slow his heart and relax his breathing.

His daydreams had never been this powerful before, but his fantasies were also never this close to becoming a reality. He'd already decided to make his feelings known to Makareta. After the meeting, he planned to walk with her down by the river to the eastern glade. If she protested, he would insist. He could do that now that he was senior, and she junior, councilor. A bench sat near the water and despite the lovely view, few people ever went there. They would be alone.

He wondered if he should ask first or just kiss her. He was likely to fumble the words, but how many ways could he screw up a kiss? After that, what need would there be for words? She might slap him, might think he was too forward, too presumptuous. But he was the prince, the heir to the Forest Throne, and the senior councilor for the ruling tribe in the Aquila; he should be confident, strong, assertive. Asking for permission might appear weak, might disappoint her. It hardly felt romantic or dashing to explain in painful detail how he had trouble breathing at the sight of her bare thighs.

He couldn't help staring. Her legs were beautiful. Perfect. Not too thick or thin, and smooth without any blemishes, not a freckle or pimple. Touching her would be—

He was still staring at her legs when she stood up.

"I would like to propose a motion that henceforth the Aquila be divided into two houses." Makareta spoke to the assembly in a loud, clear voice. "An upper house, to be composed entirely of Miralyith, and a lower house to represent the remaining tribes, which will be presided over by a Miralyith administrator. The lower house will submit suggestions to the upper house, who'll be tasked with considering if any proposal warrants being passed on to the fane. In addition, the upper house will create and submit its own advice for our leader. In this way, the lesser tribes will retain their voice in government, but it will no longer be a hindrance to the progress of our society."

When Makareta stopped speaking the Airenthenon was silent. Everyone stared, first at her, then at him.

Mawyndulë was paralyzed. He couldn't believe what had just happened. He would never have dreamed of making such a blatant statement on his first day. She hadn't even discussed it with him. What was she thinking? She just stood up and spoke.

"Everyone," Imaly said, standing as usual in the center of the ring. She extended an arm in their direction. "Allow me to introduce the new, and apparently very eager, *junior* councilor for the Miralyith. Makareta is so unfamiliar with her task, she's not aware that junior councilors have no voice in the Aquila."

"I'm aware of the *old* rules, Imaly. It is you who are ignorant of the new rules."

Imaly looked at Mawyndulë, then back at Makareta, and sighed. "You're embarrassing yourself, dear. Not to mention the shame you are bringing to your senior councilor and your tribe. I hope it is an embarrassment you will learn from."

"As you are of the Nilyndd, Imaly, it is you who must understand your place in the new order. You should be quiet and listen to your superiors."

A gasp rose from the other councilors.

Imaly's brows rose. She focused squarely on him and said, "Mawyndulë, as senior councilor, please muzzle this whelp of yours, or I will be forced to find you both in contempt."

Mawyndulë cringed in embarrassment; given another second he would have stopped Makareta. He would have told her to sit down and be quiet. Only that second never came.

"*Whelp?*" Makareta exclaimed. She made a motion with her hand, one that Mawyndulë recognized but couldn't believe he was seeing. The Art was never used in the Airenthenon, even Gryndal—

Imaly flew across the chamber, slamming into the far wall where she collapsed to the floor.

"How dare you speak to a Miralyith with such irreverence."

"Makareta!" Mawyndulë shouted in shock.

She ignored him and faced the rest of the assembly. "The days of equality are over. We Miralyith are your betters. This fact can't be changed any more than you can alter the rising of the sun. The gods are divine, and we now join them. You will bow before us, or be muzzled like any ill-behaved animal."

"Makareta, sit down," Mawyndulë whispered, even as he realized things had already progressed beyond her merely resuming her seat.

Across the chamber, Imaly was still on the ground. She was moving, thank Ferrol. She was still alive.

The chamber exploded with angry shouts.

"How dare you!" Cintra of the Asendwayr yelled.

"Blasphemy!" Volhoric declared.

Mawyndulë was lost. Between hurried breaths, his wonderful daydream had shifted to his worst nightmare. The transition left him dazed, struggling to catch up, to make sense of it all, and thinking was very nearly impossible. All the councilors, seniors and their juniors, as well as the spectators—of which there were far more than usual—were on their feet, stomping and yelling. He heard the chant of *"Miralyith, Miralyith!"* coming from the gallery.

What's happening?

"Today is a new beginning," Makareta said, using the Art to amplify her voice so that it boomed. "Today the Miralyith take our rightful place in the pantheon of gods."

"The fane will not allow this! This . . . this . . . this . . ." Nanagal shouted, unable to locate a single word that could encompass his outrage.

"Your new fane sits beside me," Makareta said, placing a hand on his shoulder. A touch that for once brought no sense of delight. "And he agrees with me."

"What are you talking about?" Mawyndulë said. "I'm not the fane."

Makareta finally turned to face him and smiled. "In a few minutes you will be."

"I don't understand. What's going on? Why are you doing this?"

"For us." She touched his cheek. "For all the Miralyith, and for you."

"Okay, back up, *what* are you doing for me?"

"This was all your idea. You're a genius."

Maybe he was dreaming. None of this could be real. Wasn't that always the way? Nightmares start out as pretty little dreams, and then before you know it, Imaly is thrown across the room and the world falls apart. "Stop talking and make sense, will you?"

Makareta giggled. In another time and place—in his bedroom perhaps—that might have been cute, but surrounded by an angry mob, she just sounded mad.

"Explain what's going on!" He was shouting to be heard over the growing din.

She nodded. "We're just following through on your suggestion. Well, not precisely, but you provided the stepping-stones."

The councilors were struggling to flee the Airenthenon, but the doors appeared to be locked. Someone threw a clay cup that shattered on the wall near the steps. The ceremonial guards, whom Mawyndulë had previously believed to have the most boring duty in the world, attempted to restore order, but they were tossed aside in the same manner Imaly had been.

"Makareta, please. Make sense," he begged.

"You told us that Vasek had taken precautions against the actions of an assassin, or even a full-scale attack on the Talwara. That was helpful. Aiden and I had been planning variations on both, but you saved the day. The solution was simple once you pointed out our mistakes."

The councilors were pounding on the doors. Some were openly crying. In the gallery above, Mawyndulë heard howls of laughter from a dozen spectators. Among them, he recognized Inga and Flynn.

"What solution?"

"It's far too risky to kill the fane in his palace. But he can't plan for the unexpected, for chaos. Even Vasek couldn't anticipate that we would lure him here."

Kill the fane? Kill my father?

He stared at Makareta, his mind unable to get past those three words.

She must have seen something in his face, because hers softened, and a sad smile appeared. "You do understand that your father must die. He's far too weak. I know it's not his fault, but we can't wait for a natural death. That would take too long. His biggest deficiency is being a product of his time, growing up when the tribes were considered equal. But that era has passed, and we can't wait for the throne to pass to you. This generation . . . our generation . . . will see the ascension of the Miralyith, and the world will be a very different place . . . a better place."

"Makareta, please. You can't."

Again, she laughed. "Don't worry. Everything will be fine. We don't need to fear the wrath of Ferrol. Not us, not the Miralyith. The laws of one god can't apply to other gods. And that's what we are now. I know it doesn't feel that way just yet, but wait until we have our own worshippers. Then it will all make sense."

Worshippers?

Mawyndulë couldn't think anymore. His brain locked up and he just sat down.

"The fane is coming!" someone from the gallery called and Mawyndulë thought it sounded like Aiden.

"Have to go," Makareta said. Then she paused, pivoted on her left heel, and bent down to pat his hand. "We understand if you don't want to join us for this part."

With that, she left him on the bench beneath the dome where Gylindora Fane and Caratacus stared down.

CHAPTER TWENTY-SIX

The Challenge

The Gula-Rhunes are a lot like rattlesnakes. Both enjoy lying in the sun, and both make a lot of noise before a fight. The difference is that the Gula are bigger, they are meaner, and sometimes you can reason with a snake.

—THE BOOK OF BRIN

"What now?" Malcolm asked, as he climbed the ladder that creaked under his slight weight.

"I wish people would stop asking me that," Raithe replied. He leaned over the wall, his elbows resting on the stone slab that teetered to whichever side he placed the most weight. "I'm not the keenig."

"You're Dureyan. Troublemakers in times of peace become heroes in times of trouble."

"I'm not a hero."

Malcolm shrugged and looked out over the wall to the north. "Too bad. Looks like we could use one."

In the dark, the Gula-Rhunes' campfires covered the hills, making the countryside look as though it were plagued with a swarm of fireflies. And the northerners had a fondness for drums. Raithe's father and brothers began all their stories with them. *We were woken by the beat of the Gula's drums; the night before the battle we slept to the rhythm of the drums; we charged into battle to the pounding of their war drums.* Raithe had never fought the Gula-Rhunes. Despite what Udgar thought, Raithe was just too young. He would have gone to the High Spear the next time the Fhrey called for troops, but that time never came. The sum total of Raithe's combat experience came from fighting his brothers and fellow Dureyans, which—in a land where food was scarce and spears plentiful—provided him a sound education. War would be different. He wasn't certain how, just a gut feeling—and the stories.

"Do you think it's the same guys?" Malcolm asked. "I mean, do the drummers take turns? They have to switch, right? The same set of people can't keep beating them like that all night."

"Seriously, there are times I'm amazed by how your mind works."

"What? I think it's a perfectly reasonable question. I mean the drumming never stops."

Raithe sighed. "At least Persephone isn't here."

"She'll be back." The statement was said with so much confidence that it made Raithe wonder if Malcolm had heard some news about the negotiations with the Dherg.

"If she's smart, she'll stay away."

Malcolm was shaking his head in that same self-assured manner, his Fhrey-look. "Persephone lives for her people. I would have thought you understood that by now. They mean more to her than anything. She'll never abandon them. Not out of fear of war, nor the love of a man. Kind of tragic, actually. You two are like a pair of ill-fated lovers in the tales of old."

Raithe gave him a sour look. "You don't know anything about me, so don't pretend you do. You lived a pampered life in Alon Rhist, like a prized pig. I lived—"

"In Dureya, I know," Malcolm said. "An arid, windblown plateau of rock, dirt, and thin grass where there was little food and even less compassion. You hated your father, while somehow still managing to maintain an unwavering respect for the man. You also hated your three older brothers and didn't particularly care for your clansmen, either, I suspect. The only ones you ever really loved were your mother and sister, and now Persephone. I think the reason you fell for her, fell so quickly and so completely, is because she reminds you of your sister or mother . . . maybe both." Malcolm held his spear, Narsirabad, with two hands, tip up as if he planned to churn butter. Neither man looked at the other, both simply staring out at the multitude of campfires. "You never told me how they died, your mother and sister."

"And I don't plan to."

"You were with them, weren't you? They died, but you lived. Traumatic, I would think. And so fitting with the corollary of the stories of old. I'm guessing you suffer feelings of guilt."

The ex-slave had a terrible way of irritating Raithe with conversation. He'd never met anyone who liked to babble as much as Malcolm. "Talk about something else."

"I'm just making the point that, for you, Persephone is some sort of second chance. That's why you keep asking her to come away. To save her because you couldn't save your mother and sister."

"Looks like that won't be an option."

"I told you, she's coming back," Malcolm assured.

"Well, if she does, I hope it's after this is over. They're going to kill us, you know."

Malcolm didn't say anything for a while, then shifted the grip on his spear and sighed. "They haven't attacked yet."

"They will."

"The chieftains' messengers got out. Help will be coming."

"They won't arrive in time."

Malcolm clapped the butt of his spear on the stone walkway. "Quit being such a damned optimist."

Raithe looked over. They exchanged a smile that was one-part smirk and two-parts truce.

"What if something's happened to her?" Raithe asked.

"Oh, well, you mean like being besieged by thousands of angry warriors? Something awful like that?"

"Yeah, something like that."

"Wherever she is, I can't imagine it could be worse than being here."

Raithe nodded. "There is that."

"And does it help? Knowing that you drove her away in time to miss all this fun?" Malcolm had an impish look on his face, as if he'd just performed some magician's trick.

"Actually it does."

"Then can you answer my question about what we should do now?"

Raithe nodded. "We wait."

In the dark, Gifford inched his way along the wall, his right hand feeling the stacked stones. He wondered how the people of Tirre got so many and how long it took to place them. He held his other hand against his chest, fingers splayed as if he were taking an oath. Oddly, his ribs hurt less when pressing on them. Just breathing caused stabs of pain, little jolts that caused him to suck in more air, which in turn caused another pang. Gifford was usually a believer in the adage: *If doing that hurts, don't do it anymore,* but if ever there were an exception to a rule, this had to be it.

"Where are you off to?" Padera asked, her voice coming out of the dark like some ghostly spirit. The old farmer's widow had returned to camp faster than he'd expected. Gifford could never determine if it was a testament to her youthful vigor or his crooked back that made Padera his rival in the slowest hundred-yard sprint. "Hurts to breathe don't it? You shouldn't be on your feet for a week at least."

"I'm looking fo' my cwutch," Gifford said.

Padera waddled out of the gloom to the path that hugged the wall. In recent weeks, it had become the main thoroughfare for all things Clan Rhen. Much of the trail lay under the wool, but this section was between East and West Puddle—no-man's-land.

The ancient woman carried a bundle of wool on her back. Both she and Gifford were hunched over—a pair of ugly trolls meeting in the dark. "Crutch? You're looking for the wooden stick? Or the one who made it? The latter is gone."

"What do you mean *gone?*"

"They went across the sea to the land of the Dherg."

"Woan's gone?" He had to ask because the old woman had stopped making sense. The trip to senility was one race he didn't mind losing to her. "Woan went on the sea?"

Padera nodded. "So there's no reason to be out dancing the way you are."

Dancing? Maybe Padera had won that particular race already. "What makes you think Woan went anyplace?"

Padera gave him one of her famous squints—her way of letting him know she didn't like having her word questioned. With god-like knowledge came god-like irritation when doubted. "Persephone went with the three Dherg to get weapons from their people, and Moya tagged along to protect her. Moya took Roan so she didn't get into any more trouble."

Padera smacked her mushed-melon mouth, looked at his hand pressing against his ribs, and she said, "So what's your plan? Hop down to the dock while trying not to pass out? Then fight your way onto a Dherg ship? Force their captain to take you to Caric where you'll track her down by sense of smell? Or no. Love, that's what you'll use. Yes, that's it. Somehow, love will direct your twisted feet, and you'll find her. Of course you will, because that's how the world works, you know? She'll be in some pit just about to be eaten by a wild animal. You'll batter the beast to death with your crutch, assuming I'm kind enough to fetch it for you, which I'm not. And you'll save her. Then you'll take her up in your arms, lifting her with your mangled excuse for a back, and return home, walking across the surface of the sea, no doubt."

Being beaten unconscious by the Fhrey didn't hurt half so much as her words. Gifford hesitated a moment then took a deep breath, letting the pain rack him. For once, it felt good. "Why do you hate me?" he asked. "You always nice to ev-we-body but me. You the long-lost mommy to all the people in the clan. Why—" His voice hitched, and he stopped himself, taking another breath. "Why do you have to be such a witch to me?"

The old woman stared hard at him with both eyes—*both eyes*. That had to be a first. She rumpled up her mouth like a poorly rolled rug, her frown reaching new lows. Not a happy face. Not a friendly face, either. Very slowly, she began to speak, "You know the story about how you were born, yes?"

He nodded. "My ma died giving me life."

"That's right. Aria was . . ." Padera chewed her lips and dragged in a breath. "She was courageous. Always had been. People talk about her like they knew, but they didn't. Few did. Now I'm the only one alive who remembers."

"Memba what?"

The old woman fumbled with her lower lip as it began to tremble. "She knew." Padera backed up and leaned her shoulder against the stone wall of Dahl Tirre, easing the weight of her bundle, or just needing help to stand while she said the words—words that seemed too heavy for her. "It's common for young mothers to seek out the mystic to ask the future of the children they carry. When Tura cast bones, most of the prophecies were what you'd expect: *Your daughter will be beautiful and marry well; your son will be a great hunter.* Though some were surprising. The prophecy she gave your mother was one of those. You had a great destiny she said, but it would come at a price. The cost would be Aria's life."

Gifford's eyes widened.

"Yes, she knew." The old woman sucked her lower lip tight, but still it shook. "She could have stopped it. Stopped you. I knew how. But your mother . . . she . . ." The old lips folded again, quivering and chewing. "We loved Aria, the whole dahl, because she was special. Everyone knew it. She was smarter, kinder, braver and just plain better than the rest of us. We cherished her." Padera sucked in a breath. "And when you came out, it was too much to bear. Aria had sacrificed everything for you because you were going to . . . going to . . ."

"What? What did the mystic say about me?"

Padera peered at him. She was back to one eye, but that eye could have cut stone. "She said you would run faster and farther than any man ever had, and that the fate of our people would rest on the outcome of you winning that race."

Gifford felt as if she'd hit him, and not lightly, but a good stiff fist in the gut. He really had killed his mother.

"Seeing you come with that twisted back and shriveled leg, we knew Tura was wrong. Your father refused to accept that Aria had died for nothing, and he took care of you. Maybe he was willing himself to believe you'd get better, because he couldn't bear the truth. He died broken-hearted. So I raised you."

"No you didn't."

"Didn't I?" Padera gave him a wicked grin that wasn't at all wholesome. "I made your life a living pit of despair every chance I could. When you were six, who do you think put the burr under those boys' belts to pelt you with stones? Who do you think urged them to beat you bloody when you were twelve? Who gave them the idea to call you "the goblin"? And who made certain Myrtis hated you?"

Gifford couldn't believe what he was hearing. Padera, the kindest woman in Rhen, the one who made pies and cookies for the kids, and who selflessly healed the sick, was the Tetlin Witch in disguise. Though as he thought about it, perhaps it wasn't much of a façade. "Why would you do that? Punishment? Vengeance? You've been vicious to me my whole life because my ma wouldn't kill me and live—"

"Don't be stupid. Of course not!" She scowled, and, being better equipped for it than anyone, Padera did it well.

"Why then?"

"Tura is dead. Your mother is dead, and so is your father. All the people who knew about that prophecy are gone. Everyone sees you as a cripple who makes pretty cups. But I still remember the promise Tura made to Aria. I may be a fool, but I still believe. I have to. Your mother was special, and you're supposed to be special, too. And by the Grand Mother, you're *going* to be or I'll kill you in the process. The day is going to come when you have to run a race. And you won't win it by being weak. I've made you take beatings so you'll know how to endure pain. And I've taught you to fight. To fight when every single person around you would walk away. I've taught you to strive for the impossible because that's what you'll have to do. You'll have to accomplish the inconceivable, Gifford. One day you'll have to run faster and farther than anyone has because that is the only thing that will save our people. It's why your mother died, and I won't let her death be in vain."

Padera hoisted her bundle to sit more centered on her back, turned, and walked away.

Gifford could barely remain standing. He leaned against the wall, staring into the dark. He was halfway between East and West Puddle, feeling as lost as if he were in the darkest of forests. Across the water, he could see the lights of the Gula-Rhunes, scattered on the hillsides. War was coming. Being outside the walls, he and the rest of Rhen would be the first to die. All he wanted that night was to find Roan, to tell her he was all right. He knew she would be upset, that she would blame herself for his beating. Gifford didn't want to die without first having absolved her of the crime she didn't commit. And he wanted to clear his own conscience for having hurt her, for not having been strong enough to take the beating and still return and explain that it was okay, that it was his choice, that she didn't do anything wrong.

As it turned out, he was a long way from a clean conscience, from absolution.

Gifford placed his back against the wall and let himself slide down until he was sitting.

"I'm sow-wee," he said to the night, because he couldn't say it to the ones he loved.

Nyphron entered the lodge with Sebek at his side. He had no right to be there, but judging from the look on his face, Raithe knew he wasn't going to be stopped, and Lipit's men wouldn't try. The Galantian leader crossed the length of the room and stood before the council, who were once more seated in their ring of chairs—one chair still empty.

"What's going on?" Nyphron demanded. "What did the Gula messenger say?"

"The Gula-Rhunes have chosen Udgar to be keenig of the north,"

Tegan said. "He's challenging the keenig of the south to battle. The victor will be the ruler of the Ten Clans."

"So they aren't going to attack?" Nyphron asked, surprised.

Tegan shook his head. "Maybe they realize that reducing our numbers with infighting would weaken our ranks and hamper our ability to defeat your people. The Gula apparently have more confidence in the cause than we do, but they won't have Raithe as keenig. Making the challenge is their way to ensure that. It seems they hate him . . . his whole family."

Nyphron exchanged a look with Raithe.

"They expect we'll put forth Raithe and are confident Udgar will kill him."

"He would. Udgar killed my brother," Raithe explained. "And Didan was bigger and a more experienced fighter than me."

"What did you say in return?" Nyphron asked.

"We asked for two days to choose our champion, and we sent runners to the nearest Rhulyn villages," Lipit replied.

"And what will happen in two days?"

"That's what we're trying to decide." Tegan folded his arms. "We don't have enough men to offer a serious challenge. The Gula-Rhunes have close to twenty thousand. Twenty thousand! Who knew there were so many?"

"I did," Nyphron said. "And that's just a fraction of the number who still wait in the High Spear Valley."

Tegan frowned. "And did you also know they would bring so many to the meeting? Lipit's warriors number only three hundred. Rhen brought only two hundred able men. We might boost our numbers another four or five hundred from the nearby villages. We have walls, but not everyone can fit inside the dahl. And our runners will take too long to return, assuming they get through at all."

"I say we accept the challenge," Harkon said. "This might be the best way to solve the problem. The old ways are best."

"Yes, we should let the gods decide," Lipit said.

"The only problem is that Raithe is convinced he can't prevail," Tegan added.

"I'll fight him," Nyphron said.

"We've already told you that's not possible. A Fhrey can't be keenig," Tegan replied.

"I don't care about your silly laws!" Nyphron exploded. He threw up his hands and began to stalk about the hall. "This is war—war with my people—people who are superior to you in all ways except numbers. It isn't some stupid inner-clan skirmish or a game. If we lose—we lose everything. We have no time for foolishness. The Fhrey are the best in the world. Estramnadon exacts tribute from the Dherg only because they *chose* not to extinguish them. They keep the goblins in their holes and the giants in their caves. What chance do you think you have without me?"

He wiped a hand over his face, trying to calm down. He took a breath, let it out, and then drew another. "There's no greater power in the world than he who sits on the Forest Throne. But we can win, and we can win for two reasons. First, because the fane doesn't expect sheep to wage war. And second, because you have *me*. I can teach your people to fight, and I can lead your people to victory. Without me, without my leadership, all of you will die."

"My lord Nyphron," Tegan intervened. "Even if all you say is true, consider this from our perspective. How can we place our people under the rule of a Fhrey when we are risking our lives to cast off the Fhrey's influence? How could we even explain that to our people? I'm afraid that despite all your good intentions your role can never be more than as a valued adviser."

Nyphron gritted his teeth but said nothing else.

"Which brings us back to who should answer the challenge," Tegan went on, looking to all those in the ring. "One of us will need to step forward."

The Rhulyn chieftains faced one another in silence. For days, they had done nothing, but they still looked exhausted: shadows beneath their eyes, shoulders slumped, and dull expressions. Worry and fear had beaten them before the battle began. Still, they all had weapons. Belt daggers mostly, but Tegan had an ax next to his chair, and Harkon had his spear by the door. No one trusted the Gula-Rhunes not to attack without warning.

Alward stood to speak. "Would it be such an awful thing to have a Gula keenig?"

"The Gula are an unforgiving people," Raithe said, "who have always hated the Rhulyn-Rhunes. If by some miracle you defeat the Fhrey, you may find life under the rule of the Gula is worse than you have now."

"And yet you doom us to this by your refusal to fight," Krugen said.

"I'm not dooming you to anything. I'm merely stating a fact. I can't defeat Udgar. If you want victory, I'm not your man. You'll have to choose someone else."

The chieftains looked around at one another. Resignation filled their faces, the bleak, joyless acceptance of inevitable defeat. Krugen looked down at his lush robe and his hands as if he would soon need to say good-bye to both.

Krugen huffed, not having it in him to laugh. "Does anyone here honestly believe they can beat Udgar in battle?"

No one spoke for a long time. Eyes shifted from face to face, but in the end, they all looked at the floor.

Tegan leaned forward to the edge of his chair. The chieftain appeared to be the same age as Raithe's father had been. "You must do it," he said to Raithe with a finality to his words. "There's no other choice."

"The Gula-Rhunes have more skill and experience in battle than the Dureyans," Raithe replied. "Udgar looks to be a fine warrior. He's seen many more battles than I, and if he killed my brother, then I really have little chance."

"Perhaps not, but little is better than none. Besides, you need to avenge your brother."

"I hated my brothers," Raithe said, and sighed. "Dead for three years and they're still trying to kill me."

CHAPTER TWENTY-SEVEN

Facing the Demon

You never know what you are capable of until you are so desperate as to try anything. You might be pleased or disappointed, but always, always surprised.

—THE BOOK OF BRIN

Roan woke up in the blackness, wondering where she was. Usually she saw the orange glow of the slumbering coals in the center of the roundhouse, but it was dark. Iver wasn't snoring. Waking to silence always frightened her. Doing so meant that her nightmares had followed her into the waking world. *Nightmare, not nightmares,* she corrected herself. Roan only had the one.

She heard a sound, some kind of movement. Roan prepared herself, held her breath, and turned her head. It wasn't Iver. In the glow of the green light, she saw Persephone, Moya, and Arion sitting near the center of the stone chamber. Everything came back. She wasn't at home; she was trapped in a foreign land a mile beneath the world in a stone tomb with no water and little food, and there was a demon who would soon break through their barricade and kill them. *Oh, thank you, Mari! Thank you!* She sighed in relief and relaxed.

The little men were also awake, sitting together a few feet away from Persephone, Moya, and Arion, two trios gathered like sets. The larger glowstone lay on the ground between them. Roan spotted the light of the other farther away, near where the desk and stack of tablets lay. She figured that was where Brin, Suri, and Minna were.

Roan found it odd that she had fallen asleep. She hadn't planned to, hadn't even remembered lying down or closing her eyes. Most of all, it wasn't like her to sleep so easily. Most nights she struggled, tossing and shifting. Iver used to collapse and pass right out. Moya, Roan discovered, slept well into the morning, even in the winter when nights were long. Usually, when Roan managed to sleep at all, it was only for three or four hours. The slightest sound woke her, and once up, she was completely awake with no hope of returning to slumber. Roan found it strange to discover she was still tired, groggy, weak, and bleary-eyed.

Maybe I'm sick.

Roan was rarely ill, but when she was, it was horrible. She thought back to the last time and realized her mistake too late.

Gifford.

She saw his face in the darkness, smiling at her the way he always did—with his lopsided grin, the one that made the boys call him goblin. When she was bedridden from the fever, he had made her soup. Perhaps the best soup she'd ever tasted, which meant he didn't make it by himself. Gifford was many things, but he was not an especially good cook, and soup that wonderful could only have been made by one person. He had gone to Padera. Gifford *never* went to her. They didn't get along, which Roan always found odd, as those two had to be the nicest people in the world.

Gifford was always doing things like that, sacrificing himself on her behalf. He gave her his best pottery. Once, when he was trying to get honey for her birthday, he'd been stung nearly to death. And because of his leg, hunting copper for her in the pits near the river wasn't just agonizing but dangerous. She wished he wouldn't do it. Sweet as it was, he made her feel guilty. The worst part of getting sick was knowing how much it would hurt Gifford.

Right now, Gifford is lying under the wool, battered and bloody because of me, because I couldn't stop thinking. And yet I didn't think. She never thought *the right way.* People like Persephone could always reason things out so much better than she. Others understood not only what to do but how and when to do it. Roan always had problems with things like that. Moya said it wasn't her fault, that Roan hadn't lived a *normal* life, but Roan knew that people—the nice ones—made excuses for her, too many excuses.

Gifford didn't make allowances; he refused to see her faults and failures. And she had plenty of both: like the leg brace that threw Gifford in the dirt or the spear thrower that proved to be useless. Gifford saw only the good in her, and that was the problem. He had been beaten because he couldn't see what was so obvious to everyone else.

You're nothing, Roan. Iver's voice always groaned from the back of his throat the way most people sounded only in the early morning. *That's what 'Roan' means . . . 'nothing.' That's why your mother picked that name. She knew you would never amount to anything. You were a burden to her, and you've been a burden to me, and you'll be a curse to anyone who cares about you. That's what you really are, Roan, a burden and a curse.*

She used to pretend it wasn't true, but how could she keep believing when there was so much evidence to the contrary? What had happened to Gifford was a prime example. She could still see his bloody, beaten face.

You'll be a curse to anyone who cares about you.

"Roan?" Brin said, her outline blotting out the light from the small stone. "Are you awake?"

She nodded, realized that was stupid, and said, "Yes."

"Oh, good, I came over before, but didn't want to wake you. I wasn't quite done anyway."

"Before? How long was I sleeping?"

"Don't know. But a good while. Long enough for me to decipher quite a few tablets. I think I know what happened. I'm going to tell everyone, and I want you to hear, too."

"Okay."

Roan sat up straighter and scrubbed her face with her palms, trying to drive the grogginess away. The stone floor had sucked away her body heat and left her chilled. When she was done with her face, she rubbed her arms and thighs. Feeling a bit warmer, she got up and walked to where the others were gathered. She felt heavy, as if she'd gained weight, and was relieved to sit back down between Moya and Persephone, who smiled weakly at her.

Arion didn't look up. She faced the stoned-up crack. The bald Fhrey lady sat hunched over, her legs crossed, her hands in her lap, eyes closed almost as if sleeping. Just in front of her crossed ankles, dark dots marked where blood had dripped from her nose to the stone. They all looked exhausted. Persephone and Moya had dark circles under their eyes, and it seemed that even sitting took quite an effort.

"Have a good sleep?" Moya asked.

Roan thought about it and shook her head. "Still tired."

"Yeah, I think Arion has been needing more energy to keep the door closed," Persephone said.

"Perhaps she'll put us to sleep when the time comes. Might be better that way," Moya added.

"There's no point in thinking like that," Persephone said. But Roan wondered if their chieftain really believed her own words.

Brin came over, holding one of the tablets. "So let me explain what I've learned." The girl placed the stone on the ground in front of them and sat beside Roan.

"What about Suri?" Persephone asked.

"She knows this already."

"Where is she?"

"Memorizing the table tablet." In the green light, Roan could see dark circles around Brin's eyes, too. The girl's normally round face drooped, but she seemed buoyed by the thrill of telling what she'd discovered, revealing a secret.

"So I've been studying the tablets as best I can. I still miss a lot of the words. They're in reverse order, meaning that the first tablet is on the bottom and the last one that was created is on top. So I started the story backward."

"Story?" Persephone asked.

"The tablets are about the person who was imprisoned here."

"The Old One?" Moya asked.

"Except he didn't call himself that. As far as I can tell, his name was The Three. He was killed by his own brother, I think. A dispute over a woman. Both were in love with someone who was . . . real? Something like that. There's a whole lot about this woman that I skipped over, but—"

"Killed?" Moya asked. "How could he be dead and here as well? That doesn't make sense."

"Yeah, I know." Brin made an embarrassed face and shrugged. "But just listen anyway. So this Three person—the Old One—was trapped, sort of like us, okay? He couldn't escape."

"But he did," Roan said.

Brin nodded. "The dwarfs made that possible. According to the tablets, The Three heard their hammers and shouted for help. They came closer, but they wouldn't open the prison. He begged them, but they were afraid. They thought he was Uberlin."

"Who's that?" Moya asked.

Again, Brin shrugged. "Someone bad, I guess."

"The Evil One," Flood spoke. "Ancient lore speaks of one who brought wickedness into the world. Uberlin is the great enemy of everyone and everything."

Brin nodded. "It fits. So, The Three apparently knew many things and offered to give the dwarfs a powerful gift if they let him out. He had learned that they used only stone tools and he offered to share the secret of a metal called copper."

"Wait," Moya said. "The dwarfs didn't know about copper? Isn't that what Roan made her ax out of?" She looked at Roan, who nodded.

"This was a very long time ago," Brin explained.

"Humans didn't even exist then," Flood said.

"Oh, no. We did," Brin said. "I saw references to the Three Peoples."

"The what?"

"The Children of Ferrol, the Children of Drome, and the Children of Mari."

Persephone smiled when Brin said that last word.

Brin smiled back. "I have a feeling there's a lot more about that in the other tablets that I've yet to go over. There's so many of them. Must have taken decades to make them all."

"How many did you decipher? How many have you gotten through?" Persephone asked.

"Just two. And I helped Suri work out the table tablet."

"So, to get back to the story . . ." Moya paused to yawn, and then she looked in Arion's direction. "You were saying that this prisoner asked the dwarfs to set him free and . . . ?"

"Right," Brin said. "The dwarfs said they needed to test the gift, and they went away for a long time. When they returned, they said it wasn't good enough because copper is too weak."

Roan nodded. "It's true. You can't do much with it."

"So The Three offered a better gift, the secret to making bronze. Again, the Dherg went away for a very long time. When they returned, they complained that copper was too scarce, and the gift was worthless."

"Bronze is made from copper?" Roan asked excitedly.

"And tin, apparently. The whole formula is right here." She pointed to the tablet that lay between them. "You see now why I wanted you to hear this?"

Brin's tales were usually good, but Roan had to admit this one was particularly interesting.

"Bronze wasn't good enough?" Persephone said with a smirk, looking at the dwarfs.

"We weren't there," Frost reminded her.

"Anyway," Brin went on, "The Three was getting irritated by this time, thinking he was being used by the dwarfs."

"I know how he feels," Moya said, and Persephone nodded with her, making Frost and Flood frown.

"But he offered them one more gift if they absolutely guaranteed to let him out. He then gave them the secret of something called Eye-run."

"Iron," Frost said.

"Iron?" Brin looked at him thoughtfully.

"Is that in there too?" Roan asked, staring down at the flat stone at Brin's knees and daring to touch the engraved marks on the surface "How to make it, I mean?"

Brin nodded. "Just like bronze. I think it might be the gray metal we saw."

"Happy birthday, Roan," Moya said.

Roan looked at her confused. It wasn't her birthday, at least she didn't think so. Roan's mother, Reanna, lived until Roan was eleven, but never celebrated the day her daughter was born. Iver told her Reanna called it "the worst day of her life."

"Anyway . . . so, the dwarfs went away again, okay? For a very long time. And when they came back, they said it's still not enough. They wanted more. The Three then promised the key to immortality, which is to eat the fruit of the First Tree. He explained that he had a seed, and if they planted it, they could have all the fruit they wanted. This was very clever because the other gifts were just knowledge, but the seed was a physical thing and they would have to open a tiny hole in the stone for him to pass it through. The dwarfs went away again to think about it. By then The Three knew he had tempted the dwarfs with something they couldn't resist."

Frost and Flood made huffing sounds and grumbled. "What a pile of silt."

Brin pretended not to hear. "The small hole was all The Three needed to get out. But by then he hated them so much for their greed and treachery that he couldn't bear to let them get his treasure, the tablets and the wisdom they contained. So, he determined how to create Balgargarath, but he didn't call it that."

"Balgargarath is our word," Flood said.

"The Three used another name."

"A shorter one, I hope," Moya said.

Brin shook her head. "Sadly, no. And I have no chance of pronouncing it. He also referred to the creature as *almost alive*. The sentinel would live forever and prevent the dwarfs from accessing the tablets. He gave it rein to roam all of Neith and permission to punish the dwarfs should they enter."

"Oh!" Frost exploded. "He curses us? Claims it's our own fault?"

Moya shook her head. "You told us yourself that you came here in search of riches. Your habits don't seem to have changed."

"Quiet, the both of you," Persephone said, raising her voice. "Go on, Brin."

"The Three forbade his creation from going beyond this mountain, to prevent it from becoming a curse on the rest of the world."

"Wait. What? It can't leave Neith?" Frost said.

"Not according to this."

"Well, that's something," Persephone said. "At least we don't have to worry about it coming to our shores."

"So what happened next?" Moya asked.

Brin shrugged. "That's all there was. This last tablet was never finished. I think because the prisoner left. It spoke about his sacrifice, and how he would escape and create Balgargarath."

"How'd he get out?" Persephone asked.

"I guess the dwarfs returned and made that small hole."

"And that was enough?"

"It would appear so."

"Arion wants you," Brin told Suri, who had been going through the enchantment one last time. "I think . . ." Brin sat back down with the tablet pile. "I think I won't have time to study all of these."

Her expression was one of the saddest things Suri had ever seen.

Suri nodded and gave the girl a sympathetic smile. Then she and Minna walked across the stone chamber to where Arion sat.

The Fhrey hadn't moved in hours, and she wasn't looking good. Her skin had become nearly gray, her breathing was labored, and the trickle of blood was dripping from both nostrils. "I'm almost done, Suri."

"Want me to take over?"

"Won't do any good. Have you memorized the weave from the table? If you had a source, do you think you could cast it?"

"Maybe. But . . ." Suri felt horrible. Since leaving Tirre, she'd failed at everything. And she hated disappointing Arion. No one except Tura had ever pushed her to be more than she was. No one else ever had faith in her. Without realizing it, Arion had become Suri's replacement for Tura—part teacher, part parent, part friend. And Suri discovered she wanted to please her, to make her proud, to prove she was worthy of Arion's faith. But so far, all she'd been was a failure. "I can't find a power source. One big enough to reach the deep chords."

"I know."

"I'm sorry," Suri said. "Maybe there are some caterpillars that never get to be butterflies."

"No, not like that," Arion told her. "You will fly, but not without payment. You were right about that."

"What payment? What do you mean?"

Arion shifted to Fhrey, which she always did when there was something important to say. *"I thought of a source, and I think it is a powerful one. You see, all life generates power. Power that can be tapped like I'm doing now. And emotion heightens that energy. Fear, hate, anguish—these feelings are like blowing on a fire or pumping a bellows. They make the blaze hotter, more intense. I'm thinking death might provide a similar effect. I sensed a release of energy when Zephyron died, and I felt it again when Gryndal was killed. Maybe when the spirit frees itself from the body, there's an explosion of sorts. I suspect that if the death is also a sacrifice, especially of someone loved, then . . . well, the combined power would be enormous. While short-lived, it might be enough to move the deep chords."* Arion reached out and took Suri's hand. *"I can give you that power."*

Suri was already shaking her head.

"You need to kill me and—"

"No."

"Suri, listen to me."

"No. I can't."

"I would kill myself, except it wouldn't be as powerful . . . the emotion you

would feel would only be one of loss. If you killed me, if my death was by your own hand, then——"

"I won't do that. I can't."

"You have to or everyone dies."

"I might mess it up. I might . . . no wait!" Suri smiled with delight. *"You can do it! You can kill me!"*

Arion pointed to her head. *"I can barely hold the door. I could never survive using the deep chords. Besides, you're the important one, remember? Not me. Your existence is the key to saving everyone. You can bring peace and understanding to our peoples. That's why I came here. And if by my death you can blossom into an extraordinary Artist, then it's an insignificant price."*

"I can't kill you."

"You must."

Suri shook her head harder. *"You're practically dead already, how much power could you possibly generate?"*

"A power equal to how much you care for me." Arion looked into Suri's tear-filled eyes. *"Do you think that would be enough?"*

Suri began to shake. They were speaking in tones too low for the others to hear, but Minna noticed. She drew close, nuzzling Suri.

"What are you asking? For me to slit your throat?" Her words were breaking up, her jaw shaking, lips trembling.

"That would work."

"No, it wouldn't. No, it would not." Suri sucked in a sluggish breath. *"You're like . . . you've become . . . How can I . . . ?"*

"I know." Arion patted her hand. *"And that's why it has to be me, don't you see? You're the only one who can make the weave, so the sacrifice must be someone who you care deeply for, and we've grown close haven't we? Killing me will be a sacrifice. Your own explosion of emotion will fuel the weave, and the sorrow that follows will give you the ability to play the deep chords. That's how he must have done it. This Old One sacrificed something. Something very dear. That's what you need to do, Suri. Kill me, harness the power, and weave your own Balgargarath. Send it to fight for you, and then run for the surface."*

Suri clutched Minna with both hands. She was crying. She couldn't help it.

"*Go on,*" Arion told her. "*Do it now. The longer you wait the worse it will be for you.*"

That was a lie—didn't even make sense. If what Arion said were true, then drawing out the process would heighten the emotion, produce more power. Suri could see the real reason in Arion's face, in those sky-blue eyes that were glassy with tears and the lips that trembled. *The longer I take the harder it is for* her. *She's terrified and doesn't know if she has the courage to go through with it. She thinks if I kill her fast enough, she won't have time to reconsider and won't try to stop me.* Arion didn't understand death. For Fhrey it was an alien thing, and for a Miralyith it must be their single remaining horror.

"*Just get a dagger and kill me.*"

"*But I can't.*"

"Suri." She sounded stern, shifting to Rhunic. "You have to."

"*No! There has to be another way.*"

"*Suri, listen. You aren't starting a fire or making an earthquake. Doing this, creating a creature, is something I've never heard of. It's not even something I thought was possible. The power required is massive. To create an independent being, you will need to do more than touch or pluck the deep chords. You'll have to hit them hard, strum them loudly and with world-shattering force. Such a thing requires massive strength, and you just don't get that from the movement of water. Think about it. Balgargarath is self-sustaining! Not even Avempartha can generate that kind of power. This must come from within and without. The pain you will suffer will make it possible. It has to be you, and it has to be now. Get a dagger, Suri, and become the butterfly you were meant to be.*"

Suri stared at her. She was shaking.

"*Do it!*" Arion ordered. "*I can't hold on much longer.*"

Slowly Suri stood up and willed herself to walk. She moved toward Brin, staying away from the light so no one would see her face. Brin had taken her sword belt off. The blade the Dherg had given the girl lay on the ground near the table. Suri picked it up, clutching the weapon and holding it close as she moved back into the dark. She wasn't just shaking; her whole body rattled, racked with anguish, fear, and dread. She felt cold. Suri wiped her eyes and sat down alone in the blackness to think. She laid the weapon beside her and covered her face with both hands.

I can't do it. I can't! But how can I fail her again?

All Suri wanted was to go back—back to the Hawthorn Glen, to her little home. She never should have come to Dahl Rhen, never should have spoken to Persephone, never set all those horrible stones rolling. She should have stayed silent, happy, and content. Happy and . . .

She wept.

There has to be another way. Oh, dear Grand Mother of All, there has to be another way.

As she sat in darkness rocking slightly and trying to find the courage to pick up the sword, she once more felt Minna. The wolf placed her head in Suri's lap, and the mystic hugged her, burying her face in Minna's soft and comforting fur.

Persephone was falling asleep again.

Whatever Arion was doing exhausted her. Just sitting felt as taxing as climbing stairs. She felt heavy. *Dead-tired* was how her father used to describe it, *all strung out* was what her mother used to say. Persephone was pretty sure she was both at once and then some. She couldn't ever recall being this bone-weary weak. The dark stillness didn't help. Everything demanded she surrender.

Then suddenly the weariness was gone.

Something snapped; something broke. The accompanying sound didn't come from outside, so the barricade wasn't breached. Persephone didn't know what had happened, but she felt the weight fall away. All at once, she felt light, awake, and as energetic as if an adolescent again. The grogginess was gone; the stupor she had wallowed in—for how long she couldn't tell—simply vanished.

Just in time for the end. The thought brushed Persephone's mind with ironic—just short of insane—laughter as she first heard, then saw, the formidable stack of stones blocking the doorway burst. Rocks skipped across the floor, clacking and breaking, and the blue light of the cavern lichen floated in with the dust and debris. Following the course of one hurtling stone, which came uncomfortably close, Persephone spotted Arion, whom the stone had barely missed. Seeing the Fhrey told the story. Arion lay sprawled across the stone floor of the cave.

This is it, the end.

Somehow, Persephone had expected more warning. She figured Arion might have made an announcement or alerted them in some way. Why she hadn't, Persephone didn't understand. The Miralyith could have given them time to say farewell or pray. Maybe it was just a matter of Arion's inability to hang on any longer. Or maybe the creature had done something unexpected. Persephone found it strange that in those last minutes of her life she had the time, and empathy, to feel sorry for the Fhrey. Persephone felt even a little stab of guilt for dragging her—all of them—into that mess.

Balgargarath broke into the cave, scraping through the crack on its goat's knees, grunting as it did. The demon hadn't changed. Twin horns twisted like knotted rope and the awful visage of its face was dominated by sharpened teeth and tiny, mad eyes.

This is truly the face of death. Does everyone see what I'm seeing, or something like it, when they die?

"Seph, get behind me." Moya pulled Persephone back. Even then, Moya was holding firm to her role as the chieftain's Shield.

In the face of Balgargarath, Persephone didn't think other Shields would have stood as courageously as Moya. The Stump certainly wouldn't have stayed at Konniger's side, and Konniger would have left Reglan's in an instant. Yet here was Moya, making a living shield of herself. The woman, previously known only for her good looks, remained intent on protecting her chieftain from a twenty-foot goat-legged demon. Courageous hearts weren't banned from the breast of women.

By the Grand Mother, how I love you, Moya!

The great beast drove forward through the opening. Balgargarath drew up to its full height and roared so loudly Persephone involuntarily covered her ears. Then she, too, drew her blade. *Why, in the name of the Tetlin Witch, shouldn't I?*

To their credit, Frost, Flood, and Rain lined up beside them. The first two held their swords, Rain his pickax. They all stood shoulder to shoulder, two diminutive women and three even smaller dwarfs. By accident or some act of providence, they all raised their weapons in perfect unison, as if they had trained together for years.

I'm going to die. The thought rang through Persephone. With one well-placed hoof, at least two of them would perish. She ought to be terrified, but her mind was a volatile mix of emotions, and fear wasn't one of them. *I'm not frightened. Not even slightly.* She found that strange, but fear had no place once all hope had fled. Looking up at the malevolent mountain that even a Miralyith magician couldn't stop, Persephone hadn't the slightest thread of hope. If anything, she was exhilarated. She felt alive as if for the first time. Freed from the mire of quasi-existence that Arion's cloud had wrapped her in, she'd burst into a state of living beyond anything she'd ever known. Her heart thundered; her breath heaved. She felt the placement of each finger on the handle of the sword, registered how it lay in her palm. She smelled the cold, damp air and heard the remaining stones come finally to their rest.

Balgargarath took a hooved step forward. Persephone and Moya both shifted their weight to their back heel, ready for the charge. Then from behind Persephone came a deafening roar.

The only illumination emanated from the two stones, and the blue light of lichen entering from the other chamber. The roar had come from the deep dark of the cave's interior. A large, inhuman sound. In the darkness, something huge was moving.

Are there two now?

Balgargarath took another step, and this was one too many as a giant shape from the shadows flew out of the darkness and slammed into the demon with a terrible force. The two hammered the wall near the door, putting a new crack in the surrounding stone, and then they broke free of each other.

Persephone picked up the glowstone and cupped it to create a beam of light. Balgargarath faced off against another giant, this one on all fours with a long neck, tail, claws, and leathery wings.

"A dragon?" Moya said. "Where'd the dragon come from?"

Persephone looked to Arion. The Fhrey still lay on the ground; she looked dead.

"I don't know," Persephone replied. "But . . . but . . . I think it's on our side."

Moya responded with a wry smile.

The two titans slammed together again. This time the dragon raked with fore and rear claws while at the same time biting with a rack of teeth lining a long snouted mouth. Balgargarath slammed the dragon with its hooves. The sound of their clashes hurt Persephone's ears. Balgargarath got hold of the dragon around the neck and slammed it against the wall, creating more cracks in what was previously believed to be impenetrable stone.

"Brin!" Suri screamed.

Not a shout, not a yell, this was a true scream. Never before had Persephone heard such a sound from the mystic. Moya screamed all the time, so did Brin, but not Suri. Nothing usually bothered the mystic.

Out of the darkness Suri walked toward them, covered in blood.

"Oh, Mari!" Persephone gasped.

Suri's face was drawn and pale. She was crying, hitching, gasping for air. "I need Brin. I need Brin. I need her, right now!"

Near the door, another terrible boom echoed, followed by unworldly howls.

Brin arrived seconds later, materializing out of the dark into the halo of the ghostly green light emanating from Persephone's hand. "What's wrong? What—"

"The name!" Suri shouted at her. "You have to mark down the name."

"What name?" Brin asked, her eyes growing in horror as she looked at the mystic. "Suri, what happened? Where . . . where did all that blood come from?"

"Not mine. Not my blood," Suri said in a shuddering voice, that barely sounded like her.

The mystic was shaking all over, her head jerking, her breathing a staccato series of sucks.

Boom!

The chamber shook and everyone except Suri jumped. Tiny bits of stone fell to the ground, sounding like a sprinkling of rain.

"Brin." Suri crowded the young girl, until the mystic stood near enough to touch noses. Even so, her voice was loud, a borderline cry. "I need the name of Balgargarath on a sword."

"On a sword?" Brin asked, flustered and frightened. She glanced at Persephone in desperation. "I . . . I don't know how to write *Balgargarath*."

"Not *Balgargarath*! The thing's *real* name, the one on the tablet. Just copy it. Copy it!" Suri pointed toward the stack of tablets. "Repeat what you see on the tablet onto a sword. Just do it! Do it! Do it!"

The mystic went on screaming *do it,* over and over, her blood-covered hands out in front of her, fingers fanned as she shook them.

Brin looked scared to death.

"Suri, stop!" Persephone ordered. She gave a quick glance at the two beasts battling near the front of the cave. They were still going at it. "Tell us why? What does it matter? And where did the dragon come from?"

Suri began making and unmaking fists in rapid succession. She tried to speak, but nothing came out.

"Suri!" Persephone grabbed her by the shoulders. "Calm down! Calm down. Just tell us what happened."

"*I* made the dragon." Suri spoke in very deliberate words, as if summoning each one was a great task. "I used the weave from the table. When I did, I found it had to have a name. All things have names. That's the secret. It's the seam, the point that binds and unbinds. Balgargarath has a name and Brin knows what it is. The Old One carved it into the tablet. It's part of the binding."

Suri was a bundle of nervous energy. She couldn't stand still. She was rising on her toes then dropping back to her heels. "If I had only known. If I'd realized the seam could be torn open. Then I wouldn't have . . . I wouldn't have . . . No, no, if I hadn't I wouldn't have learned the truth. I wouldn't know the importance of the name, and what it can do."

"Suri, you're not making any sense—"

"It's the seam. The seam! Don't you see!" Suri shouted at all of them in frustration. "The . . . the . . . the *knot* in a weave. The point that keeps it together. That keeps it from unraveling. If you stab Balgargarath with its name, it'll cease to exist!"

"It will kill him?"

"Yes! Yes! Yes!"

Moya turned the handle of her sword in a remarkably sophisticated spin. She held the pommel to Brin. "Put it on my blade. I'll do it."

From the door, they heard a screech and then another roar. Persephone looked over, but the behemoths had moved into shadow.

"She's not going to win." Suri sobbed. The tracks of her tears made clean lines on her blood-splattered cheeks. "You have to hurry."

"How can I mark a sword?" Brin asked, frantically, looking to all of them for an answer.

"Scratch into it," Moya said.

"With what?"

"I don't know." Moya looked at the dwarfs. "You have tools, don't you? Metal tools?"

Frost was shaking his head. "The blades you were given are too hard. Scraping into it would take"—he looked over toward the sounds of fighting—"longer than we likely have. And that is if we had etching tools, which we don't." He looked around him. "Nothing in here is likely to mar those blades."

The quiet figure of Roan inched over. She was coming out of the darkness to join them. No one wanted to be alone while the dragon and Balgargarath fought.

"Does it have to be a sword?" Roan asked barely above a whisper.

"Yes! It needs to enter Balgargarath's body."

"But does it have to be a sword? Could it be something else with the name on it?"

"It doesn't matter. It doesn't matter. The name is all that's important. Just the name . . . it has to penetrate . . . it has to get inside."

"What are you thinking, Roan?" Moya asked.

"My little spears are made of wood. It'd be easier to mark on them."

"Will they work?" Persephone asked, bending slightly to stare deep into Roan's frightened eyes. "Did you fix them? Will they work now?"

Roan nodded. "Yes. I think so. Maybe."

"Which is it, Roan?" Moya shouted, making the girl jump.

"Calm down, Moya!" Persephone snapped.

"They . . . they . . . they should," Roan said. "I put feathers on two of them, but I haven't tested either. Haven't really had a chance."

"So you have no idea?" Moya stamped her foot.

"Moya, be quiet," Persephone told her through clenched teeth.

Persephone stepped closer to Roan, being careful not to touch her, but close enough that she filled the girl's vision. "Look at me, Roan. Look into my eyes. Do *you* think they will work? The way you have them now. The way they are right now. Do *you* believe they will work?"

Roan thought a moment, then said, "Yes."

Persephone turned away. "Good enough for me."

"How do I do it?" Brin asked. "How do I mark on a spear?"

"You could paint it with the blood Suri's dripping," Moya said.

At first, Persephone thought Moya was making a horrible joke, but one look at Moya's face showed she was quite serious.

Still, Suri shook her head violently. "Can't. It will smear. Has to stay perfect all the way in."

Another cry came from the front of the chamber. The boom that followed was close, and Persephone aimed the glowstone to reveal the dragon on its back not far from the center of the room. The dragon had lost ground and nearly landed on Arion, who still lay in the same place despite the giants' continued battle.

"Moya." Persephone handed her the glowstone. "Take Frost, Flood, and Rain and get Arion out of there. Move her near the table. Roan, devise a way for Brin to make permanent marks on the shaft of one of your little spears. Carve or burn the name, whatever it takes. Brin, you have the other glowing shard, use it to find the tablet with the name."

Everyone raced to their tasks—all except Persephone and Suri.

The mystic was down on her knees by then. She had her hands over her face, spreading more blood without care or notice. She rocked forward and back, sobbing.

"Suri?" Persephone spoke softly as she took the mystic's hands in hers. "Suri, what happened. Whose blood is that?"

"I killed her," Suri said. "I killed her. I killed her. I loved her and I killed her. Arion said it was the only way to reach the deep chords, and it was, and it did."

Persephone stole an awful glance at Arion just as Moya and the dwarfs knelt beside her body.

Persephone put her arms around Suri and held her tight, rocking with her. The mystic reached out and squeezed back, burying her face in Persephone's chest. She wept and wailed, her body jerking violently.

Then she paused, took a breath. "I had to . . ." Her face still buried, her voice muffled. "It had to be a sacrifice. That's what Arion told me. I . . . I . . ." She fell back into sobs.

Moya came running back, searching for the two of them with the glow of the stone.

"Over here," Persephone called.

Moya ran over breathing hard. "The dragon isn't doing as well as before. Balgargarath tossed it a couple of times like a basket of leaves. I hope this name thing works."

"What about Arion?" Persephone asked, bracing for the news.

"Not sure," Moya said. "She's weak, real weak. Unconscious, but I think she'll live. She's exhausted, you know? Blown out. The dwarfs are carrying her over." Moya paused and looked down at Suri. "How is she?"

"Bad."

"What happened to her? Where did all the blood come from?" Moya asked.

Suri jerked at the sound of Moya's words. "She loved me. She loved me, and I loved her. I loved her, and I killed her."

Moya's eyes narrowed. Then she looked around, shocked. She focused on Persephone and mouthed the word, *No.*

Persephone nodded.

"She was my best friend," Suri cried, "my sister, and now she's gone."

Suri started a fire, and everyone placed the tips of their metal weapons into it, heating the blades. Brin lay on the floor with the tablet to one side and the wooden spears to the other. With her hands wrapped in cloth, she burned symbols onto the shafts—delicate work, requiring care to prevent the wood from catching on fire.

"Thank Mari, the name is just one row," Brin said. Holding her tongue between her teeth, she finished the last symbol.

Roan took the shaft and compared the markings with the ones on the tablet. Then she ran a finger over the four feathered flights mounted near the rear.

Even before Roan nodded her approval, Brin busily worked on the next spear.

With the brilliant light of the fire and the eerie gleam of the glowstones, the two behemoths were clearly visible. They battled at the doorway. Balgargarath had been shoved out, and the dragon guarded the entrance. The demon's attacks were fierce, and on two occasions, the dragon had been driven back into the Agave, but each time she managed to push Balgargarath back out.

Earlier, Persephone had thought the two creatures were mindless beasts, each obsessed with the destruction of the other. But there was no doubt the dragon was working to protect them. She found it impossible not to notice the familiar way the dragon dipped her head and hunched her shoulders. When she did, the great beast's wings would rise slightly, like fur, then the dragon would roar and pounce. Once, when Balgargarath came too close, the dragon flew up and sank all four sets of claws into the goat-legged beast, biting at the back of the horned monster's neck. When she had a good grip, she hauled the demon away with great gusts from her wings and then threw Balgargarath out through the crack once more. Yet for all the combat, for all the strikes and blows, Balgargarath displayed no wounds and didn't appeared any weaker.

The dragon was a different story.

By the time Brin finished putting the symbols on the first spear, the dragon was favoring her right side, and one wing drooped lower than the other.

The weave might be indestructible, but it could fray.

"Is that all the spears we have?" Persephone asked.

"Yes," Roan replied.

Including the little wooden javelins, Roan had everything she carried nested around her knees in neat piles for quick retrieval. Persephone noted a ball of twisted plant-fiber string, another ball of thread twisted from wool, and two tiny blades of sharpened knives held together with leather that Roan called clippers. Beside them were several strips of willow bark—the sort that fever tea was made from; a bone needle; three leaves—one oak, two maple; a handful of shriveled berries; a hat Roan never wore; three round stones; a bit of black charcoal; a short stick burned on one end and beaten on the other; and one stunningly beautiful glazed clay cup with delicate loop handles on either side. How it hadn't been broken was a mystery to ponder on another day, assuming Persephone would see one again.

Of the six little spears, four had feathers, and two of those had rows of finished markings. The other two lacked any improvements, being just small, wooden, stone-tipped spears. The dwarfs stood beside Persephone and Moya, fixated on the battle across the room, while the mystic and the Fhrey sat together oblivious. Arion lay with her head resting on Suri's lap. She was still breathing, but that was all.

With a vicious punch, Balgargarath knocked the dragon aside and lunged once more into the chamber. Everyone flinched, and both Frost and Flood staggered backward and nearly fell. The demon managed only two massive steps before the dragon was on it again. Teeth bit into an ankle, and the dragon jerked the demon back toward the door the way a dog might play with a rag.

"We need to hurry," Persephone said. "Brin, how much longer?"

"Almost done."

"Suri." Persephone turned to the mystic. "If this doesn't work, we'll have to make a run for it. Do you think you can . . . is it possible to talk . . . can you tell Minna to draw Balgargarath away from the door?"

At the sound of the name, new tears slipped free of Suri's eyes, but she held herself together. Suri shook her head. "Maybe. I don't know. I can try."

Persephone nodded, and picking up the two blank, nonfeathered shafts that lay beside Roan, she handed them to Moya, who already had the bow strung. "Here, looks like you're only going to get four with feathers, so practice with these."

No one questioned that Moya would do the shooting. She was the most athletic, and the bow was too tall for the dwarfs' height and the draw too long for their shorter arms. She was also the only one with experience.

Moya nodded. Fitting the first spear, she drew it back across her chest. She made an unpleasant face, adjusted the position of the shaft on the string, and did it again—letting the tip of the spear rest on the thumb that held the bow. "Hand me Roan's charcoal."

Moya took it and made a mark on the string where the shaft needed to be placed to keep it level when drawn. She tossed the charcoal away, refit the little spear, drew it back, and aimed at Balgargarath.

"Don't!" Persephone yelled. "Not yet. Shoot somewhere else. I don't want it to know."

"Are you serious?"

"We have no idea how smart it is. Let's not give it any warning."

Moya nodded and drew the bow back again until her arm was quivering. She aimed at a trio of big stones toward the rear of the Agave and let go. As expected, the little spear flew erratically, turning sideways, losing speed, and falling before it even left their sight. Moya looked at the fingers that had pulled the string and licked them. She also adjusted the hand that held the bow, sliding her grip up a bit. Then she took the second featherless shaft and tried again. The little spear flew just as awkwardly, but Moya muttered, "Better."

Another loud crash shook the ground. Balgargarath had slammed the dragon down and was holding her pinned with one hand around her neck. The dragon shrieked as she tried to rake with her rear legs. The sound caused Suri to bury her face in her hands.

"With the dragon down like that, Moya has a clear shot," Frost said.

"How long, Brin?" Persephone asked.

"Almost done with this row."

"Seph?" Moya looked to her with questioning eyes.

Persephone nodded. "Go. Do it. Take the shot."

Moya took a breath, looked at Roan, and said, "Give me a rowed shaft."

Roan handed up a spear with four flights of feathers and a row of burned-in marks. Moya took it with careful fingers and gingerly fit the notch into the string.

"Does she need to get closer?" Persephone asked.

"Not if it flies straight," Roan said.

All but Brin and Suri watched as Moya arched her back and bent the bow. With a whispered twang, the string flashed and the shaft flew. A cry of delight came from each of them as they saw the little spear travel fast, far, and true. So much so that it flew right past both the dragon and Balgargarath and right out through the crack.

"Tetlin's ass!" Moya yelled.

Persephone didn't know if it was their shouting in unison or the little spear that had just missed its mark that caught Balgargarath's attention, but something did. The great monster lifted its ugly head from the pinned form of the dragon to look their way. No doubt about it: The beast focused on Moya.

"Close," Persephone said. Hope was back, and with it came fear. "Try again."

"That wasn't my fault. That cul of a stick went off target," Moya said, her voice more than a little shaky. "At the last second I felt a kick."

Balgargarath continued to stare, then took a step toward them.

Moya held out her hand, rapidly opening and closing it. "Roan! Give me . . . the . . . ah . . . I need another one . . . another one with a row. Give me another row. Hurry up!"

Roan handed it to her, and watched as with shaking hands Moya had trouble fitting it in the string. She aimed and let the shaft fly. Again the little feathered stick flew straight, but again it went wide to the left and out the door.

"Mother-filling son of the Tetlin whore!" Moya yelled.

"You've really nailed shooting through the crack," Persephone said.

"It's not my fault," Moya yelled back. "That should have been perfect. I was right on."

"Did it kick again?" Roan asked.

"Yeah."

Persephone watched the demon. Balgargarath looked out the open door. When he turned back, he focused all his attention on Moya and roared. "Oh, Grand Mother!" she exclaimed as the demon let go of the dragon and charged.

"Give me another row! Give me a row! A row, a row!" Moya screamed.

Persephone passed her the last marked shaft.

"No!" Roan snatched it away.

The cavern shook as Balgargarath pounded his hooves into the floor, leaving chipped ruts and kicking up shards of rock. The monster closed on them, and was only a few strides away when the dragon downed it with a swipe of her tail.

Bits of stone sprayed them as the wind from the collapse blew by.

"Roan, what are you doing?" Moya shouted. "I need it. Now!"

Roan ignored the demand and tore off one of the flights. "Fit it with the missing feather against the bow staff."

Looking desperate and exasperated, Persephone wondered if Moya had heard.

Balgargarath kicked at the dragon and got to its feet.

Moya drew back the bow and let the shaft fly. This time it didn't waver, didn't hitch. The spear flew with perfect precision and an ever-so-slight arc that Moya had managed to account for. The bolt punched into the center of Balgargarath's chest. It couldn't have been a better shot.

"Yes!" Persephone cried out.

The beast looked down at the shaft sticking out of its dead-corpse skin.

"Isn't it supposed to be dead?" Frost asked, almost pleaded.

Suri looked up confused.

Roan had the answer. "It didn't go deep enough. Not all of the name is inside."

"I need another one," Moya said. "I need another arrow."

"Almost done," Brin said.

"No," Roan told her. "Start over on the other side. Make the markings closer to the point."

"We don't have time," Moya said.

True enough. Balgargarath snapped the stick off its chest, and with a horrible growl, it began to charge.

"I'll just pull back farther. Give me the arrow!"

Brin looked to Persephone. "Do it!"

Moya took the arrow and started to fit the shaft. "Dammit!" She put the feathers to her mouth and tore off one of the four.

Rain flung his pickax at the charging demon with both hands, causing it to flip end-over-end three times before the point glanced off Balgargarath's leg. The dragon made another lunge, but missed.

The giant horned monster with its beady eyes, sharpened teeth, and bulbous head shook the ground with its last few strides, cracking stone as it drove forward at an astounding speed. Nothing could stop it. The forward momentum would propel Balgargarath through them and past the wall beyond.

Moya nocked the arrow and hauled back on the bow until the notched end of the shaft was at her ear.

In the instant before the arrow flew, Persephone saw Moya standing alone in the path of the giant—a perfect sight. She wasn't shaking, never flinched, didn't cower even though a ghastly mountain was charging at her. Moya was a true hero. And as she let go of the string, Persephone overflowed with pride.

That's one damn fine Shield!

The arrow's trip was short by the time Moya loosed it. Given the size of Balgargarath, she couldn't possibly have missed. Persephone never saw the shot land, as the moment Moya let go she and everyone else were blown flat on their backs. The massive gust of wind ripped Persephone's torc off her neck and scattered the stack of stone tablets. The table was thrown over. The explosive blast slammed their swords, packs, glowstones, and all of Roan's worldly possessions into the walls, and the fire that Suri had made was snuffed out.

CHAPTER TWENTY-EIGHT

Death by Steps

How many tears must we weep? How loud must we cry? How many farewells must we say, for the dead to hear goodbye?

—THE BOOK OF BRIN

From out of the dark Frost asked, "Anyone else alive?"

Persephone heard a cough that sounded like Brin.

"You're not rid of me yet," Flood replied. "Rain?"

"What?" the third of the trio asked.

"Never mind."

"Moya? Moya?" Persephone called.

"Still here," the woman said with a labored breath. "Got him that time, didn't I?"

"Roan? Brin? Suri?" Persephone called out, and in turn they all answered that they, too, survived whatever it was that had happened. Arion was the only one who failed to speak, but Suri declared her no worse than before.

Persephone spotted the muffled light of one glowstone buried under debris, and crawled to it. Digging the stone out, she held it up. The room was still there although a scorched spot marred the floor where Balgarga-rath had been. Smeared marks of blackened stone flared out in all directions from that point. Everything else in the room was plastered against the outer walls, including each of them.

Persephone noticed a throbbing in her head. She reached up and felt a lump on the back of her skull. She must have hit her head on the floor or wall, but had no memory of doing so.

"Suri, can you make a fire?" Persephone asked.

A short pause, a faint humming sound, a clap, and then a bright flame appeared. The brighter light revealed the rest of the cave. Everything that had been in the middle of the cavern was scattered, thrown away in equal measure from the center point that had been Balgargarath. Brin had an ugly cut across her forehead that bled into her eyes. Moya, who still held on to the bow, sported a scrape on one cheek and a set of bloody knuckles as if she'd been in a fistfight. The three dwarfs and Roan had only minor scrapes. Being so far away and close to the wall, Suri and Arion showed no injury; Persephone knew better.

The dragon was still there as well. In the light of Suri's fire, she turned around three times before lying down. The great beast tucked her serpent tail around herself and lowered her head between two great claws. Her open eyes focused on Suri.

"You did it," Frost said to Moya. "You killed Balgargarath."

He spoke in a disbelief mirrored by his fellow Dherg. "That creature has denied us access to our hallowed halls, our first and most ancient home, for six thousand years. Warriors, great heroes, and kings fought with magic swords and armor and died trying to do what a small band of witches did with sticks and a string."

Moya bent down and picked up one of the practice arrows that had been gathered with the rest of their things near the side of the Agave. "You really want to call us names while I'm holding this?"

Flood took a step back and held up his hands. "Good witches . . . of course. Wonderful, wonderful ones, really. Witches don't have to be bad, right?"

Moya stared at the dwarf for a moment, pursed her lips, and nodded. "Fine."

Persephone knelt beside Suri and Arion. "How is she?"

The Fhrey looked better than she had. Some of her color had returned, and the bleeding had stopped, leaving only the telltale sign of a dried and flaking crust on her upper lip. She was breathing easily, eyes closed. Suri held Arion's bald head in her lap, stroking her gently, not unlike how she used to pet Minna.

"I took too long." Suri sucked in a ragged breath. "I just took too long, and now they're both . . ." She shook her head rather than finish.

Persephone took Suri's hand and gave it a strong squeeze. "You saved us. You know that, don't you? We'd all be dead if you hadn't."

"*She* saved us . . ." Suri looked up across the room at the dragon. A hand fluttered to her mouth.

"Yes," Persephone agreed. "You're right, of course, but *you* did, too. You need to remember that." She watched the mystic struggle to breathe. "You know, I remember seeing a white wolf throw herself at another wolf, a bigger and meaner one, because that other animal was going to hurt you. I think, Suri . . . I think if you could have explained what you were doing, Minna would have agreed. She was a very wise wolf."

Suri cried.

They ate what food they still had and prepared to leave the cave that had been their refuge for . . .

Suri had no idea.

She didn't care.

The others struggled with complications arising from the fact that Arion was still unconscious. The little men suggested leaving her and coming back with more help. Brin offered to stay. She wanted more time with the tablets. Persephone refused. "No one is remaining here. No one left behind."

Suri sat in the dark, watching them pack. Persephone and Roan gathered their things into bags and a pile. Brin struggled with the tablets, but the stones were heavy and she could only manage to take a few. Moya rounded up the arrows and practiced with the bow while two of the three little men worked on constructing a sling to carry Arion using Persephone's breckon mor. Rain, having found his pickax, went out to clear a path to the stairs that the dwarfs referred to as Death by Steps.

Suri watched the activity in the privacy of the dark beside the body of a wolf. After seeing her sit down next to the still form, the dragon left the Agave and went out to the lichen-covered cavern.

"I'm sorry," Suri said.

She had spoken to Minna every day since the white wolf came into her life. They'd held endless conversations concerning the stars and the flight of bees, but now this was all she could think to say. Other words refused to come, her throat tight. She brushed her fingers across the familiar fur.

"I'm sorry," she repeated.

Suri's hand found a paw. Her lifelong friend lay beside her, and in the dark, she could imagine Minna was only sleeping, except for the limpness of that foot. Her sister, companion on countless adventures, wasn't sleeping. Minna was gone.

"I'm sorry," Suri whispered, rubbing her thumb along Minna's leg.

She stayed with her in the dark until Persephone called for them to leave.

Suri stood up then, and raised her hands. She placed them together palm-to-palm and began to slowly rub them in a circular motion, moving them faster and faster.

"I love you, Minna. I always will."

In the quiet of the cave, the loud clap caught everyone's attention and they all turned to see the burst of fire erupt where once there had been the wisest of all wolves.

Death by Steps was, as one might imagine, a steep and endless series of stone blocks. Suri, who was used to trotting up cascades, shouldn't have had trouble bounding up the steps, but she was tired. No, more like drained, as if some part, an important part, had been poured out. The others needed to pause frequently, and on one occasion, they fell asleep. Suri sat in the dark on the bottom step behind them, her legs curled up, arms folded—so cold without Minna. She laid her head down and closed her eyes.

"You need to be careful," Tura had said. The old woman was crouched on the floor of their home, sorting the ripe berries from the green. "That's a wolf pup."

"She's cute," Suri said.

"She is now."

"You didn't leave me in the woods." Suri tried to steal a berry and got her hand slapped.

"That was different."

"How?"

"One day, one day soon, she'll weigh more than you, run faster for longer, and have teeth and jaws that can rip flesh that will provide her all she needs to eat. Minna won't need you then; you'll just be a nuisance."

Suri looked down at the bundle of white fur with the black nose and the curled tail. "Minna would never hurt me."

"She's a wild thing. She listens to the wind and to the will of Wogan. If a situation calls for it, she could turn."

"What kind of situation?" Suri asked.

Tura shrugged. "Life and death. If the two of you were starving in a cold winter, she could see you as nothing more than a tasty rabbit."

Suri smirked as she played with the little pup, whose needle-sharp teeth pulled at her belt bag until Suri lost her balance and fell over. "Minna would never hurt me, not even then."

"How do you know?"

"Because she loves me, just as I love her."

"Maybe. But if I were starving . . . if you and I were going to die . . . I think I might consider what wolf meat tastes like."

"That just proves Minna is better than you. You hear that, Minna? You're wiser than old Tura. You must be the wisest of all wolves."

Suri tried again and this time managed to steal a berry. She popped it into her mouth before Tura could stop her. The old woman frowned.

Suri grinned and chewed, but the berry had been a green one, and tasted bitter.

Suri woke up with a crick in her neck, one still-sleeping leg, and an aching sense of loss. The blissful dream broke apart, leaving only traces of joy that rapidly dissolved in the acid of reality. The others were getting to their feet and Suri joined them, struggling with the pins and needles in her lazy leg.

She heard it then, such a familiar sound—panting.

Suri snapped her head around, looking behind her, but the glowstones were both up ahead, and all she saw was black. She peered into the void but saw nothing.

"Minna?" she whispered.

No response—even the panting had stopped.

She waited until the others were far ahead. She wanted it to be true. Flashes of her dream came back. Images of a wolf pup rolling on a floor.

"Minna?" she called louder.

Silence.

"I miss you," she said. Then she turned and followed the others.

By the time they reached the top of those stairs, even Suri was exhausted—and still they were far from out. Instead of reaching sunlight, they entered a large hall in the city of Neith. Suri's legs throbbed, feeling tight to the point of snapping. She lay down with the rest of them, the cold stone feeling good against the heat of her back.

"We're only to here?" Moya said in agony.

Tilting her head up, Suri noticed that the hall was vaguely familiar. Pillars lined the open space except a large section where the floor had fallen away.

"Is this . . . ?" Persephone started.

"This is where we fell," Moya confirmed. "We still have all those wide stairs left to go."

"Is there really no more food?" Brin asked.

"I'd be happy with water," Moya said. "I'm sweating like a rat in a cat's mouth."

"Water on the level above us," Rain said.

"Then I say we head up, have a long drink and a rest before we go any farther," Persephone declared.

"Okay," Moya said, but she took her time getting up.

Nevertheless, everyone had moved off toward the stairs except the mystic, who remained seated. She waited, looking back down the dark hole of the steps.

"You okay?" Persephone called back.

"No."

"Right, stupid question. Sorry." Persephone came back to her. She sat down, pulled her knees up, and offered Suri a sympathetic smile. "When my husband, Reglan, died it was just a few days after my last son's death." She shook her head remembering. "I felt all alone in the world. Empty. Lost. Angry, too. Lots of anger really, hate even. I had plenty of that. I hated the world, myself, even Reglan for dying, as if he'd done it just to hurt me."

Persephone was trying to be comforting, but she wasn't helping. Her loss was nothing like Suri's. Minna hadn't died. She'd been murdered by her best friend.

"Want me to leave you alone?" Persephone asked.

Suri nodded, though she wasn't really sure. She didn't feel like talking, or listening, but silence didn't help, either. Nothing helped.

"Okay." Persephone started to walk away, then stopped. "Here," she said, holding out the glowstone. "We'll be at a fountain one flight up. Don't take too long. You'll make me worry."

Suri listened to the shuffle of Persephone's feet until they faded away and she was alone again.

She set the glowstone down, hugged her legs, and watched as the others, marked by their bobbing light, climbed the steps and disappeared.

Then Suri waited.

My imagination. That's all it was.

She sat as still as she could, listening. So strange to be alone in that silent dark. Suri strained to hear anything, but not a creak, not a rodent scuffling, not even the drip from some unseen pool disturbed the quiet. Suri sighed and stood up. Partway to her feet, she froze.

Panting.

The sound was close—very close—right behind her.

Minna?

Suri started to turn, but before she could, an icy, damp hand clamped over her mouth.

Persephone began recognizing things and realized they were nearly out.

The hardest part of the trip was over. Already Persephone began wondering: *Have they appointed a keenig? Is it Raithe? It has to be him, who else? Certainly not that limp bit of a man, Lipit, or the skittish Alward.* But maybe Raithe had remained adamant in his refusal, or maybe he had simply left—gone with Malcolm to his hill past the Bern River to build a new life. Maybe the chieftains had given up. *Have they disbanded the Council of Tirre, gone their separate ways, leaving the question unresolved? Or have the Fhrey attacked?* This last one frightened her more than any of the others. Although she was surprised to discover that not seeing Raithe again came in a close second. Now that she was heading back, Persephone was seized with fear and worry that she'd be too late, had taken too long. She saw faces in the dark: Padera's mushed-melon frown, Gifford's lopsided smile, Habet's boyish grin, even Tressa's scowl. What if while she was gone the Fhrey had killed them all?

"Where's Suri?" Brin asked.

They were gathered alongside a stone fountain. About the size of Brin's old roundhouse, it had a basin like a shallow bowl, partially sunk into the floor. In the center, was a statue of three dwarfs standing back-to-back, though they could hardly be called dwarfs given they were at least seven feet tall. At the feet of each sat a bucket, partially tilted and spilling water into the basin. When Persephone arrived, the others had already drunk their fill, and some, like Moya, splashed their faces and wet their necks.

"Just downstairs," Persephone replied. "Wanted to be alone. She'll be along in a little while."

"What's the big deal?" Flood made a disparaging sound. "It was just an animal."

Persephone whirled on him. "Don't say that again! Not ever. Do you hear me?" She flashed a glare at the rest of them. "Not any of you."

"You'd be taking your life in your hands, that's for sure." Moya was nodding. "If Suri hears you say that, you'll be a grease spot."

"That's not it at all." Persephone lowered her voice but not her tone; if anything there was more heat in her words, more condemnation than ever. "That wolf . . . Minna . . . she meant everything to Suri." Persephone fixed each of them with a hard stare. "If it were just the two of them down there, if just Suri and Minna were trapped in that cave, they'd both still be there. Suri sacrificed Minna for *us*. Don't you *ever* make her regret that. Do you hear me? Even for a minute, or Mari help me, I'll . . ." She continued to stare until she had garnered a nod from everyone, short of Arion, who still lay unconscious in a sling that looked very much like one of Roan's hanging chairs. Then Persephone took a breath and calmed down. She shrugged. "And there's what Moya said, too."

Persephone looked back down the stairs. The glowstone below didn't give off enough light for her to see clearly.

"Suri's been known to forget about time," Moya said. "Her idea of *a little while* could range anywhere from a minute to a month."

"Let's give her a bit longer," Persephone said.

After another few minutes, she called down. "Suri?"

Silence.

She got up and walked to the edge of the stair. "Suri, we really should be pushing on."

More silence, but she could see the glowstone right about where she'd left it. Fear gripped her stomach as she descended the stairs. As she got closer, her eyes told her what her heart already knew. The glowstone was still there but Suri wasn't. She picked it up, panned it around, but still nothing.

"Suri!" she shouted. Her voice echoed. "Suri, can you hear me?"

The panic in her voice brought others. When they reached her, Moya had her sword out, as did Brin and Roan.

"Suri!" Persephone yelled once more while pulling her own sword. "Suri, where are you?"

Persephone's voice bounced back, and then . . .

"Lost another little one?" A voice came out of the dark, speaking skewed Rhunic, a cold haunting voice with a rasp and a high, taunting lilt. "It's ours now. We have the small one in the dark where you can't find us. Your dog is gone, and you can't track where we are."

The voice was right. Persephone struggled to determine where the voice came from; echoes confused her. The words came from everywhere and nowhere at the same time.

"Suri can do magic," Moya whispered to Persephone. "She can defend herself, right?"

Brin overheard and looked at both of them, horrified. "She needs to make sounds. To do her singing. And she needs her hands to wiggle her fingers. It covers your mouth and holds your wrists with long, clammy hands and a grip that's so strong. You can't get it off."

Persephone took a step, but didn't know where to go. The stone floor spread out into darkness in all directions, running under a forest of pillars that eventually disappeared into the dark.

"She has a lovely face," the voice teased.

"Oh, dear Mari." Brin shuddered.

"Suri!" Persephone screamed.

The only answer, besides the echo, was a horrible little laugh.

Persephone looked to each of them, but there were no answers to be found, and no time to find one. "Let her go! Let her go, or we'll kill you. We've already killed Balgargarath."

Another chilling laugh. "You are all flies in my web. All little children to be swallowed. Please come look for me. Come into the dark and search for—" The voice paused.

They waited.

Then a wind rose, blowing so hard that Persephone had to steady her stance.

From beneath, they heard a rhythmic beating: *thrump, thrump, thrump.*

This was followed by a crack of stone that jarred all of them off their feet. Persephone fell, her sword and the glowstone clattering onto the floor. She felt the spray of pebbles and finally heard a deafening roar. She knew that roar. Trapped in the Agave, she'd heard it over and over, until it had hurt her ears. Then she heard a scream, a high, raspy, gurgling scream. This was followed by a *snap, crack, crack,* and *snap* as if someone were walking over brittle branches on a cold winter's day. The screaming stopped. The thrumping of the wings halted.

Persephone had the presence of mind to scoop up the glowstone. Cupping it, she searched the area. Across the vast room, the light revealed the dragon lying down, tail curled, head tilted. They rushed down, crossing the room until they spotted Suri. She stood beside the dragon, rubbing the bridge of its massive snout.

"Good girl," Suri said. "What a good girl you are."

CHAPTER TWENTY-NINE

Aftermath

The seeds of unrest in Estramnadon were planted long before Grandford. By the sound of things, they had grown ripe and were harvested prior to our first real battle.

—THE BOOK OF BRIN

Mawyndulë stood bewildered beneath the great painted dome of the Airenthenon. Outside, he heard explosions. The prince wasn't alone. Huddled around the walls, the other members of the Aquila cowered in terror. The gallery had emptied. The Miralyith who had filled it joined with Gray Cloaks who had waited outside. That's where the battle raged, on the front steps of the Airenthenon.

They planned it.

The Gray Cloaks were trying to kill the fane.

Makareta planned to kill my father.

Mawyndulë was still trying to make sense of how any of it could be real when he heard someone crying. Hemon of the Gwydry huddled beneath one of the stone benches, staring at him in horror. They all were. Even Imaly watched him with concern as she sat with her back propped against the wall where she had been so inelegantly tossed by Makareta.

The Aquila's Curator clutched one arm, and there was a patch of blood staining her forehead. Only an abrasion, a scrape, but it looked terrible. Mawyndulë hadn't seen many wounds. Blood bothered him, and, once again, he remembered Gryndal's beheading.

Is that what they are doing to my father?

Mawyndulë started toward the doors.

He managed to take a total of two steps before the building began to shake. He staggered as the ground shifted, tilting and rocking. Hunks of plaster and stone broke free from the ceiling and fell, smashing with great bursts of white where they hit the marble floor. The fluted stones that formed the pillars of the colonnade moved, shifting out of alignment, making the dome itself slide. Larger parts of the ceiling fell, exploding on the floor—lethal hail.

One of the councilors screamed as part of the gallery balcony collapsed. Mawyndulë thought the councilor had been hit, but only two tri-legged braziers were crushed.

Mawyndulë was terrified.

All around him was weeping, crashing, and blood. He had no idea what was happening and didn't want to. What he wanted was to be back in the Talwara, in his room, on his bed, with Treya bringing him cider and tarts.

As more of the ceiling came down, he thought to run out, but was too scared to move.

I need to get out before—

Another huge stone hit the floor, bursting only three feet away. Bits of debris pelted him.

Horrified that another rock was on its way down, he reacted. Mawyndulë drew in power and pushed out. He felt for the building around him, grabbed it, seized every pillar and stone and held fast, binding each block and pebble, weaving a web of defense. All that marble was his shield, and he wasn't letting it go anywhere.

Outside, the world was a terror, filled with screams.

Inside, Mawyndulë supported the roof, weathering a storm he'd rather not see.

The exterior of the Airenthenon had been blackened with scorch marks. On the east side, the steps were gone; nothing of them remained. One of the great trees—the old sacred ones that had shaded the square since the days of Gylindora Fane—had been severed in half. Cut clean, the great elm laid its leafy head and broken branches over the stalls of the marketplace.

Standing on the steps outside the Airenthenon's doors, Mawyndulë expected to see blood—lots of it. A grotesque splatter of red stained the market, but it was only paint. A war between Miralyith produced great carnage but little gore.

A member of the royal guard found Mawyndulë after the battle and informed him that his father had survived. The fane and his troops had chased the last of the rebels through the streets of the city. In the distance, Mawyndulë heard the occasional shout.

"What will you tell your father when he returns?" Imaly asked. The Curator stood beside him, both staring out at the changed landscape.

"That I wasn't involved." He faced her. "I wasn't, you know."

"Oh, I believe you, and I'm sure he will as well."

She was still clutching her wounded arm, cradling it across her stomach. She winced with pain, and he noticed that she limped each time she took a step with her right foot. The old Curator slowly moved down what was left of the western steps, one at a time, always taking the dip with her left foot. Mawyndulë took hold of her good arm, lending what support he could.

They paused at the first landing, where the fountain miraculously continued to spout water, though the upper half of the stag was missing, leaving just a set of four spindly legs. Mawyndulë took that moment to look back at the Airenthenon. For the first time, he spotted the crack splitting the surface and leaving a horrific scar through the ancient pediment.

"Would have been much worse if not for you," Imaly said. She sported her own wound as the scrape on her head continued to seep blood that dripped down the side of her face. Some of her hair was matted to it, drying like glue. To Mawyndulë, Imaly appeared as a living personification of the ancient order; both had been assaulted, hurt, and scarred.

"I didn't do anything."

"It's still up, isn't it?" She turned and looked back, then nodded. "Yes, the Airenthenon is still there, just that crack. Don't think it could have survived without help, do you? All that shaking, all those attacks. No, I think it would have been destroyed."

"I didn't do it to preserve the Airenthenon." It felt good to say so out loud. "I didn't even do it to save you or anyone else." He looked down. "I wish I had. I wish I could say I did it for some noble reason, to protect our heritage and the people cowering inside, but that's not true." He sighed and shook his head. "I did it to save myself. When the building started to come down, when it cracked, I was terrified. I didn't know what else to do. I'm not very good with the Art."

He would never admit that to anyone, not even himself. He didn't know why he told her, except maybe because she was the only one he could tell. More than anyone, Imaly seemed to understand him. To her, he wasn't the prince, or a son, and not even a Miralyith. To Imaly, Mawyndulë was just a young Fhrey, well meaning but inexperienced. He told her because he needed someone to know.

"Maybe," she said.

"Maybe? Oh, no, it's true." He nodded at her. "That's what happened."

"I believe you, and I'm certain that's even how you remember it, but that doesn't mean it's true. Not the whole truth."

"Of course it does."

Imaly gave him a wise smile. "Mawyndulë, you could have run out of the Airenthenon. Almost everyone else did. Why didn't you? I'm not a Miralyith, but I imagine there were easier ways to protect yourself than preserving the entire structure of that building. That had to be more difficult than putting some sort of shield around just your body. You had a number of options, but you chose the one that preserved our great heritage and saved the lives of all those around you." She took another painful step and then paused again. "A lot can be determined by the choices we make, even if the action is initiated by self-preservation. Many . . . no, most . . .

of our choices are driven by fear: fear of death, fear of humiliation, fear of loneliness. But it's how we respond to fear that matters. It's what defines us. What makes us who we are. So maybe in your mind you acted selfishly, but I'm alive because of the choice you made. So I'll remember it as an act of kindness and, yes, even bravery."

She nodded then, as if coming to a conclusion, and by the look in her eye, it was an important one. "There you have it. Two realities to choose from. In mine, you acted heroically, risking yourself to protect the lives of the entire Aquila. Yet you remember it as selfish because you're uncomfortable with the idea of being a hero. You feel guilty, don't you? You think you didn't do enough and therefore don't deserve an honorific for failure. Heroes, you are certain, don't feel guilt. Personally, I like my reality better, but you pick whichever you like. Just don't share yours with anyone else."

"What? Why?"

"You're the prince. One day you'll be fane. People prefer to see their leaders as renowned, something larger than themselves. This hierarchy makes society possible. It's so much easier to humble oneself before greatness, to obey someone universally known to be superior in every way.

"But . . . but . . . I don't think I am, not really."

Imaly turned and smiled warmly at him. "That's why you are. You're a good person, Mawyndulë. You've been warped a bit by an insular life and the powerful influence of a few dominating people, but deep down you're still a good, decent person. That's why you feel guilt. It's when you no longer feel that nagging sense of doubt, that pain of regret, that it's truly over for you. But you aren't there yet. You can still be salvaged."

"What do I have to do?"

"What do you plan to tell your father?"

"The truth."

"And what is that?"

"That I didn't know anything about the rebellion. That I went to the meetings a few times where they got me drunk, but never told me what their plans were. That I was used."

Imaly shook her head. "No, don't do that."

"No?"

"Absolutely not." She took another step and winced.

"We should get you to a doctor."

"It's a broken leg. I'm not dying, and this is more important."

"What is?"

She looked at him, peering into his eyes as if trying to find something hidden. "Mawyndulë, do you understand what just happened, and what will happen now?"

"Some people . . . people I sorta knew . . . tried to murder my father."

"That's one way to see it."

"How do *you* see it?"

"Do you realize that except during the Uli Vermar, no Fhrey has ever attempted to harm a fane. Ever. Just as until today, there had never been violence inside the Airenthenon. Do you know why?"

"Because it's wrong?"

"Because until today, it was unthinkable. The very foundation of our society is grounded in tradition, the observance of rules. Those rules have been challenged, and the result will be catastrophic."

"How so?"

"Let me ask you this. What do you think your father will do now?"

Mawyndulë had no idea. Like she said, what had happened was unthinkable. What his father would do was equally so. "I don't know."

"He was just attacked by his own people, the Miralyith, those he trusted the most. They very nearly killed him, and did kill many of his friends. How do you think he feels? Angry?"

Mawyndulë nodded.

"Frightened?"

He had a harder time with that one. He couldn't imagine his father scared of anything.

"How did you feel in the Airenthenon when the battle was just outside? You were scared. You just told me so. There you were, surrounded, while people around you died . . . no . . . were killed. No one, on either side, wanted to hurt you, and yet you were rightfully terrified. Imagine how the fane feels. They were trying to kill him, and like I said, most choices are caused by fear. The question is, will your father choose to hold the building together or save himself and let it rip apart? You could make the difference."

"Me?"

Imaly hopped on one foot, and this caused a sharp grimace. "Let's sit down." She pointed to the fountain with the severed stag legs, and he helped her lower herself to the rim of the basin. In the water, he spotted a shoe.

"A lot of people died today."

Mawyndulë nodded. He didn't know about Makareta, but from the doorway of the Airenthenon, he had seen Aiden's body. Rinald, Inga, and Flynn were also dead, and he'd seen faces of other Gray Cloaks who had died. Several of his father's personal guard were dead, along with three of the seven members of the Aquila. There had also been bystanders who lost their lives in the square. Most of them had worked or shopped in the marketplace, as they had on any other day.

"Your father needs to respond to this, for the sake of maintaining his authority to rule, but he'll also want revenge . . . retribution against everyone who harbors any drop of dissent toward him. He won't be satisfied until he has dug deep and found the source of this poison. What is that source, Mawyndulë, can you tell me? What was it that caused this?"

"The Miralyith want more power."

She nodded. "A division between the tribes. Do you know why there is a fane? Why we have the Horn of Gylindora and the Uli Vermar? It's because we used to war among ourselves. We are our own worst enemy. In ancient times, the tribes slaughtered one another until the coming of Caratacus, who brought Ferrol's horn to Gylindora Fane. She was just a simple basket maker back then. She didn't think she was a hero, either. The tribes had nearly annihilated one another through constant battles for dominance. Gylindora and Caratacus changed all that. They gathered those of like mind from all the tribes and came here. They built this place and established laws, unbreakable rules, to make certain such infighting would never happen again. These have protected us, served us well. Once in a generation, the ruling line can be challenged. Even then, the choice is made by *single* combat. Not by war, not by the death of thousands. We have peace . . . at least within this forest. But what now? What happens when the rules are broken? What does the fane do when he feels the old ways aren't working anymore?"

"He makes new ones."

"Yes." Imaly rested her injured arm on her injured leg to brush a lock of hair back from her face. "He tightens his grip, punishes large portions of his people. Do you think this will make them love or hate him? Do you think the Miralyith will thank him? Or now that they have been shown that rules can be broken, will they try again? What if they do so with larger numbers and better planning? Mawyndulë, we are facing civil war. We are taking our first steps back to our old destructive ways. A path that will eventually lead to our destruction."

"I don't see what this has to do with me."

"You were there. You attended the meetings. You are at the fork in this path, and we need you now. More than we've ever needed anyone before. Your father will ultimately decide which way to go, but you have the power to influence that decision. To change history before it happens."

"I still don't understand."

"You can tell your father that a large number of his people, of his own tribe, tried to kill him because they want more power, and that will send him down the path of civil war. Or . . . you can tell him they were manipulated. You can say the Gray Cloaks were controlled, coerced, and seduced by someone else . . . someone external. With your single pointed finger, you have the power to unite us all against a common enemy and preserve the Forest Throne, or we can turn to infighting, which will ultimately destroy us."

Mawyndulë thought of how Vidar had been set up, falsely accused of something he had no part in. He didn't think he could do that to anyone. "I couldn't lie about something like that."

"Are you sure? One little white lie to save your people? And it isn't like I'm suggesting you accuse an innocent."

"Who, then?"

"The one person the fane would believe." She paused.

Mawyndulë was frightened by who she would name. *Will it be me?*

"Nyphron of the Instarya," Imaly said.

Relief washed over him. The moment she said the name, Mawyndulë knew it was the answer. An instant later he wondered if perhaps it might actually be true. How hard was it to believe that the outlaw, and maybe even The Traitor, would seek to destroy all of Fhrey society by pitting them against one another? *Divide and conquer. Isn't that a military axiom?* And here it had nearly worked.

"Once again, just like in the Airenthenon, we are threatened. What will you do? Save yourself, or stand and use your influence to protect your people and preserve our heritage? This is your chance to be a hero, Mawyndulë. The salvation of our people is up to you."

The itch was worse, almost maddening, and while harming the flora or fauna of the Garden was greatly frowned upon, Imaly resorted to breaking a slender twig. She snapped an offshoot free, sat down on one of the benches, and plunged the stick down inside the plaster cast that encased her leg. For several insane seconds she struggled desperately, and then in one glorious moment, she reached the itch. In that instant, she could have died happy. In ecstasy, she melted on the bench and wallowed there limp and lazy, the branch still sticking out of her cast.

"Hello."

She opened her eyes. Before her stood a person she'd never seen before. He was so unkempt and disheveled that for a moment she couldn't be certain if he was Fhrey. Though who else could he be, standing in the middle of the Garden in the very heart of Erivan.

"Hello," she replied.

"May I join you?"

She nodded, pulled herself together, straightened up, and scooted over to give him room to sit.

"You don't come here often," he said. "I come every day, and I've never seen you."

"No, not often. I'm very busy, you see, and—"

"Of course, being Curator is a very demanding position. You're Imaly, yes?"

The question was disconcerting. She wasn't as prominent as some, even those in lesser positions, and yet it wasn't unusual for a stranger to know who she was. Still, there was something unsettling about *him* knowing her, while she was clueless about who he was—or what he wanted.

"Yes, that's right, and you are?" she asked.

"Trilos," he said. "Pleased to meet you. That's an excellent position to hold. Influential, yet in the shadows."

"And what is it that you do? What's your occupation?"

He smiled at her. "Mostly I sit here, look at the Door, and ponder mysteries."

"You're Umalyn, then? A priest of Ferrol?"

"No, I can't say that I am."

She was about to ask which tribe he was from when he spoke first. "Things worked out quite well, wouldn't you say?"

"Things?"

"I was concerned Erivan might slip into old habits. I was certain the Miralyith were going to start eating their own for a while."

Not Miralyith at least.

"But that doesn't look like it will happen. Not now, not after the prince told his father the whole thing was orchestrated by Nyphron. It appears the fane will take his rage out on the rebel, his Galantians, and the Rhunes who support and harbor him. I've heard he's set plans in motion to build an army. The first time that's happened since the Dherg War. I don't think he trusts the Instarya to handle such matters. I do have a question, though. One that I'm surprised hasn't crossed Lothian's mind."

"And that is?"

"How did he do it?"

"How did who do what?"

"Nyphron. By all accounts, he is hundreds of leagues away, just him and a handful of Galantians, living in rough, remote, places with the natives. How did he manage to cause a Miralyith insurrection?"

"Many of those killed—those who called themselves the Gray Cloaks—

were, as I've heard the tale, friends of Nyphron. Apparently he planned this whole thing out in advance, setting it up when he and his father were allowed back for the Uli Vermar."

Trilos nodded with a smile. "Yes, yes, I've heard that, too. And Mawyndulë learned all about it during his visits to the meetings under the bridge."

"I do believe that's what he said, yes."

"Odd, don't you think? How is it that the son of the leader of the Instarya, who hadn't set foot in Estramnadon for centuries, had so many friends here, and in the Miralyith tribe, no less? You would think, given his father was killed by one, they wouldn't exactly travel in the same social circles. But what do I know?"

What indeed, Imaly thought.

"Oh, well, circumstances can make odd bedfellows. Isn't there a saying like that? Still, we should be grateful, I suppose. Everything worked out in the end, unexpected, but very convenient, very tidy."

"Who are you? And what is this really about?"

Trilos gave her a surprised, innocent look, one she didn't believe in the slightest, even though it was excellently played.

"I told you. I'm Trilos, and as I said, I'm pleased to meet you, Imaly. Anyway, where was I . . . oh, yes, as I was saying, I don't think the war will be."

"Will be what?" she asked, confused.

"Tidy," he said. "Wars never are. Wars are chaotic and full of surprises, most of them unpleasant."

"I suspect it won't be much of a war, more of a hunt, really. And I don't expect it will last long," she said. "The Miralyith have ways to locate who they are looking for, and they can be very efficient in getting what they want. Now, who are you? Who are you really? I know almost everyone in Estramnadon, but I don't think I've ever seen you before."

Trilos stood up. "No . . . no, you haven't. A pity, I think. But I'm so glad we were able to bump into each other this fine day. And I do believe that from now on I'll be watching you."

CHAPTER THIRTY

The Nature of Dwarfs

I have already mentioned my disgust for the vile creature that is Gronbach. If given the opportunity, he will lie, cheat, and deceive to get what he wants. He is everything that is evil in the world condensed into a despicable little fraction of a person.

—THE BOOK OF BRIN

They never found any trace of the raow. While no one had actually seen it happen, the consensus was that the dragon had eaten it. Persephone liked to believe it was so and that the dragon had started with the raow's face.

From that point on, the dragon followed the party. Large as it was, it had no trouble doing so. The stairs of Neith, while built by a diminutive race, were wide and the ceilings high. The passages were big enough to accommodate giants, a pretension the dwarfs likely regretted after the appearance of Balgargarath. The raow attack put newfound energy into the group, and they pushed on without pause, climbing flight after flight until they reached the remains of their first camp. Their shields, blankets, and food bags were still there. Starved, they paused to eat and rest, but little was said. Moya found energy to practice once more with the bow and the arrows they had salvaged. With a dragon escort, Persephone didn't think

Moya was concerned for their safety. The woman had simply taken a liking to the device, and she reveled in her own ability to use it.

Once done, Persephone called for them to push on. Nobody wanted to tempt fate by sleeping there again. When they reached the top of the final stairway, Suri and the dragon hung back. Persephone stopped the group, returning to find out why. The others followed.

"What's wrong?" Persephone asked.

"I don't know," Suri replied, looking at the dragon, who sat on her haunches. "She won't go any farther." She addressed the beast. "Come. That's a good girl, come on."

The dragon put her head down.

Suri stared, confused.

"She can't go any farther," Roan said.

"Why?" Persephone asked.

Roan looked ahead of them. "We're almost out. She can't leave Neith. Suri used the table spell from the Old One." She looked at the mystic. "Did you change anything?"

Suri shook her head. "Just the name."

"Balgargarath couldn't leave, either."

"That's right," Brin said. "The creature would live forever, denying the dwarfs access to this place and preventing anyone from entering. He gave it rein to roam Neith, to punish the dwarfs, but denied it the freedom to go beyond so it couldn't become a curse on the rest of the world."

Moya pointed at Frost, Flood, and Rain. "How come she didn't eat them? Wouldn't she have to? I mean, if she was following the same rules?"

"The rules apply to the nature of its existence, not its actions: what it was, not what it did. Or maybe she would if Suri wasn't around," Brin said.

Frost tugged on his beard, pulling harder than usual, his face twisted in frustration. "So we destroyed one monster just to make another?"

"She's not a monster!" Suri raised her voice. Her harsh tone caused Frost to retreat a step.

Moya sent Frost a big-eyed glare—silently shouting at him. The others stood by, waiting and watching the mystic.

Just a fourteen-year-old girl, Persephone reminded herself. *Maybe fifteen by now.* Sometimes it was easy to lose track of that fact, hard to believe that Suri was so young. Even harder now. The mystic hadn't grown an inch. Physically she was the same girl who had come with them into Neith. But in every other way, she was different. Her eyes were no longer as bright, not as sunny. The same with Brin. Both of them had lost their brilliant bounce of childhood innocence. In its place, Persephone saw the hard-won maturity of two people who understood that dreams came with a price. Survival meant learning to live with setbacks, disappointments, and heartache. She had no doubt that when the need arose, these two would be willing to push on, to overcome, and to help those around them do the same. Persephone was looking at women, and she couldn't be prouder of them.

Suri petted the dragon on the nose. "She's not a monster, and she would never hurt anyone."

"Made short work of the raow," Moya said. After a sharp look from Suri, she added, "Given half a chance, I would've done the same. Well, maybe not *eaten* it, but you know what I mean."

Persephone said, "But what *will* she do? I mean, if Suri's not here? Would she hurt the dwarfs if they tried to return to Neith? I don't think we can be certain. We don't really know, do we?"

"I do." Suri ran her knuckles up and down the bridge of the dragon's nose. "She killed the raow to save me, because that's what Minna would have done, and Minna never had a problem with the little people."

"Maybe you should tell her to go back down anyway," Persephone said. "Just to be safe."

"No." Suri shook her head, and when she turned around they could see she was crying. "I can't leave her alone . . . forever in the dark. I can't do that to her. Minna hates being alone. I won't leave her that way. I can't. I just can't."

"You can't stay with her," Brin said as she, too, started crying. "She'll live forever, but you won't. Eventually she will be alone."

Suri didn't seem to hear; she was sobbing too hard.

More than a dozen well-armored dwarfs were waiting outside the gate to Neith. With pointed spears and rounded helms, they were lined up in three rows, shining a brilliant silver in the morning sun. Persephone wondered if Gronbach had received reports of their progress in the same manner that he had known about the general whereabouts of Balgargarath, or if he had ordered guards stationed there since they'd entered. Knowing Gronbach, even as little as she did, she guessed both.

The leader of the troop spoke directly to Frost in their language. Frost replied, and the soldier appeared shocked.

"He asked if it was dead," Frost volunteered to Persephone, but she'd already guessed that much.

The soldier looked them over, taking particular interest in Arion, who remained unconscious in her sling, carried between Flood and Rain. The Fhrey's condition hadn't changed. She continued to breathe, but her eyes hadn't so much as flickered.

Once more, the soldier addressed Frost.

"He says we're missing one."

"Tell him he's wrong. We're missing two."

Persephone looked back into the dark gate of Neith. Suri was still inside. They hadn't been able to convince her to leave—not yet. Persephone hoped that given a little time, Suri would accept the need to leave Minna. After reporting to Gronbach, Persephone would return and fetch the mystic while the dwarves loaded the weapons on the ship. She no longer had any concern for Suri's safety. The girl had a dragon for a watchdog.

Frost relayed Persephone's message. The soldier accepted it. She knew he would. Easy to think they'd suffered casualties. What would be difficult to accept is there had only been two. The hardest thing to believe would be that they had succeeded. She saw that on the soldier's face as well, an amused little smile wreathed in mustache and beard that proclaimed, *"Sure you did."*

The group's leader insisted they follow him back to Caric, though *follow* was less than accurate; his squad of metal-clad warriors surrounded them for the entire journey. The downhill trip took no time at all—or at least it felt that way to Persephone who spent the walk marveling at the warmth of the sun and the feel of the wind. They had only been underground for a few days, but in more than one way, Persephone felt risen from the dead.

Gronbach received them in the great hall they called the Rostwell. Before being allowed inside, their loaned weapons were reclaimed. A studious dwarf inspected each for wear. Moya had a disagreement with a guard over her bronze sword until she pointed out it was Fhrey-made. A second look ended the argument, although the dwarf still insisted she leave it outside the hall. Arion was taken to a room with a bed, where Roan—never one for crowds—volunteered to stay with her.

Inside the Rostwell, tables had been shoved aside and stacked up, along with scores of little chairs. Everything had been cleared out to make room for their arrival. The Master Crafter and Mayor of Caric occupied the only remaining seat, which had been set up on a box, apparently so he could look down at them. He wore full battle dress, with a heavy silver breastplate and a pointed helm that appeared a size too large. Surrounding them were another dozen dwarfs in armor, holding pikes and shields. Persephone hoped the amount of metal in the hall was in honor of their victorious return. The stern looks beneath the helms gave her doubts.

"I have been told you destroyed Balgargarath," Gronbach said, leaning forward. "Is this true?"

"It is," Persephone replied, and nodded respectfully.

"And the Fhrey? How is she?"

"Wounded. I don't know how severe. Time will tell, I think."

"I'm told she is unconscious, barely breathing."

"That's true."

Gronbach nodded. She didn't see any hint of concern in those flinty eyes, but at least he didn't smile.

"Have you finished making the swords we agreed upon?" Persephone asked.

Gronbach pushed back in his chair, an irritated grimace squished his lips, and she knew bad news was coming.

When he remained silent, she asked, "So you haven't started? How long will it take?"

"What swords are you speaking of?" Gronbach steepled his fingertips. His face took on a forced expression of innocence that appeared as awkward on him as a smile on a snake.

"What swords?" Moya asked, stunned, and Persephone knew she wasn't done.

She stopped Moya by holding up a hand. "We had a bargain, sir. One thousand gray-metal swords in return for killing your demon. We killed Balgargarath. Now we—"

"Do you have his head?" Gronbach made a show of lifting himself on the arms of the chair and stretching his neck. "I don't see one."

"He burst into dust and air."

The dwarf leader settled back on the cushion of his seat and looked at her with a skeptical, pitiful shift of his brows. "Now isn't that convenient."

"Are you accusing me of lying?"

Gronbach did smile then, a horrible, dismissive grin. "Three Rhune women, two Rhune girls, a Fhrey, and three criminals go into Neith . . . it sounds like the opening of a joke, doesn't it? You go after a demon that has effortlessly destroyed armies of well-armed, well-trained Belgriclungreian heroes. Then you poke around for a few days, and then come out with this . . . this story . . . this claim that you destroyed something invincible." Gronbach held his hands out and made a show of dusting them off. "He's dead, you say. Balgargarath is vanquished, you proclaim. All done, all taken care of, no problem." He leaned farther forward with a smile of amused condescension. "Do you really expect me to believe that?"

She pointed at Frost, Flood, and Rain. "Your own people will confirm what I say!"

"Of course. Criminals will say anything to stay alive. Besides, we had no bargain, you and I, no *deal*. I am not in the habit of giving dangerous weapons to foreigners. There's a law against that."

"What law? You have no king. In Caric, you're the law."

"Yes, I am." Gronbach grinned. "As such"—he raised his voice, speaking to the room—"I hereby decree, by the power vested in me by the Caric Crafters' Association and the citizens of the City of Caric, that these Rhunes and the Fhrey with them, as well as the felons Frost, Flood, and

Rain, be executed for the high crime of unlawful trespassing on Belgri-clungreian lands and the defiling of our most sacred city of Neith. Sentence to be carried out immediately."

"What? You can't be serious!" Moya erupted, advancing on Gronbach, who jerked back in his chair. "We killed that thing. I did it myself. Arion nearly died. She may yet. Suri lost Minna in the battle. We can take you down there right now and show you that it's—" Two dwarfs grabbed Moya by the arms, pulling her away.

"He's lying, Moya," Persephone said as she, too, felt the hands of dwarfs upon her. "He knows we killed it."

"The bastard is just refusing to keep his end of the bargain!" Moya shouted.

Persephone struggled to break free, but the hands of the dwarfs were as strong as their metal. "You never had any intention of giving us those swords. And now that Arion is hurt, now that she's no longer a threat, you think we're helpless."

Gronbach smiled. "I'm pleased you understand the situation so well. Take them to the yard. Have Kirn put shackles on. We'll toss them back into the sea from whence they came. Better that way. Less mess, and if anyone asks, we can honestly say they drowned."

The dwarfs hauled each of them toward the exit. Moya put up the best fight, kicking one of the two holding her to the ground and nearly getting clear of the other before she was grabbed again.

"Break their arms if they resist!" Gronbach shouted as he stood up on the edge of his box.

"You still have a problem," Persephone shouted. "A big problem. A *dragon* problem."

This caught Gronbach's attention. "What? Did you say *dragon*?"

"I did." Persephone was hauled toward the door. "In our fight against Balgargarath, Suri, apprentice of the Miralyith, created a dragon. It's still in Neith and is just as formidable as Balgargarath."

"You're lying."

"Send a runner. It's easy to find. The dragon is right inside at the top of the stairs. It's on guard there with the ninth of our party, Suri. The dragon does as she commands. Do you think we are so foolish, so naïve as to trust you and your ilk? If we don't come back, Suri has orders to come down here with the dragon and find out why. I'm not sure you'd want that."

The dwarf pulling on her stopped. Persephone didn't think most Dherg understood Rhunic, but it appeared the majority of those in Caric—or at least those in that room—did, as with no comment from Gronbach, the efforts to force them out the door ceased. The dwarf holding Persephone still gripped her elbows, forcing them behind her back and keeping her off balance, but he no longer made any effort to drag her away.

Gronbach nodded to a dwarf near the door, who ran off.

The Master Crafter slowly sat back down. He looked at each of them, making a study of their faces before coming back to Persephone, whom he studied the longest.

Can't tell if I'm bluffing, can you, little worm.

"Assuming there is a dragon," Gronbach began, "what do you propose we do about it?"

"I'll get rid of it for you. Destroy it."

"In return for what?"

"For one—" Persephone jerked against the hands restraining her, then glared at Gronbach.

The Master Crafter nodded, and the hands let go.

Persephone took an irritated breath, rubbed the marks on her arms, and reclaimed a step back into the hall. "For one, you will not treat us poorly. In fact, I would say it's in your best interest to provide us with the finest rooms, baths, food, and drink. Doing otherwise would make the dragon sad. You *don't* want that."

"Is that all?"

"No. We'll require safe passage back to Tirre. A ship with a good crew and irrefutable orders to transport us safely."

Gronbach pursed his lips and thought a moment. "The *Calder Noll* is scheduled to leave for Vernes soon, isn't it?"

"At dusk tomorrow." The answer came from behind Persephone.

"Will that do?" Gronbach asked.

"I also want them." She pointed at Frost, Flood, and Rain, who were still being held. Rain had a dwarf on each arm and one with a hold around his neck.

This caught Gronbach by surprise. He shifted his gaze between the three dwarfs and Persephone with a puzzled look. "Why do you want them?"

"Do you really care? And if you give them to me . . . sending them into exile . . . we'll leave this place. Wouldn't that be nice?"

"What about the swords you wanted? Aren't you going to ask for them too?"

Persephone shook her head. "No. You won't give them to me. Even if I threatened to lay waste to all of Caric with the dragon. It's not a matter of stubbornness. It's fear. And I can't persuade you with one threat when you see the alternative as worse. You're afraid the Fhrey will learn that you gave us weapons. And they terrify you more than a dragon in your house."

"The elves nearly erased us," Gronbach said. "They wanted to; they still do. Our only hope is to give them no cause."

Persephone nodded. "I've heard that argument before."

Rain spat on the floor and said something to Gronbach that made the mayor scowl.

"Do we have a deal?" Persephone asked.

"How will you get rid of this dragon?" Gronbach asked.

"The same way we got rid of Balgargarath. And in case you have any ideas about going back on your word again, you'll face worse than a dragon. Betray me again, and I'll wipe out all of Caric. You can kill the few of us, but if you do, you'll sign the death warrant of every single person here. Understand?"

Gronbach nodded. "So you say."

"Now, we will require one thing. To destroy the dragon, we'll need a sword."

"I'm told this one has her own sword." Gronbach pointed at Moya.

"True, but to slay the dragon we need a special sword. It will have to be made. Show him the tablets, Brin."

The girl was still being held and couldn't move.

"Let them go," Gronbach ordered with a frustrated groan.

Brin looked to Persephone.

"Show him," she said.

Brin had used her breckon mor to make a sling for several of the Old One's tablets. She unwrapped them and laid them out for Gronbach to see.

"We found these in the Agave," Persephone explained. "On these stones are markings that tell how to make the sword that can kill these monsters. Brin and Roan will need access to metal and tools to forge such a sword."

Brin's brows rose in shock, but thankfully she held her tongue.

Equally fortunate, Gronbach wasn't looking and didn't notice. "These stones say how to forge a magic sword?"

"Yes," Persephone said with an even tone and a blank face.

"What about the sword you used to destroy Balgargarath? Where is it?"

Persephone had expected the question. "Consumed along with the demon."

"I see." Gronbach peered at the tablet Brin held. His pink tongue licked his lower lip, causing the hair below to bristle upward. "Very well. You will give us this stone, and my smiths will forge the needed sword."

Persephone was prepared for this, too. "It will do you no good. You can't decipher it."

"But I doubt"—Gronbach peered across the room—"this girl, Breen, and the other woman can wield a hammer well enough to forge a sword."

"Her name is Brin."

"I don't care what her name is. She's nothing more than a child, and she can't swing a hammer!"

Persephone forced herself to wait before replying. She wanted to give the appearance that she was thinking the proposition over. Finally, just as Gronbach began to frown with impatience, she nodded. "You're right. Roan and Brin will work *with* your smiths to create the sword."

"Yes, that could be arranged."

"Good," Persephone said. "Tonight the sword will be made, and in the morning, we will return to Neith and destroy the dragon. Once it is dead, all of us, including Frost, Flood, and Rain, will board the ship and leave. Agreed?"

Gronbach hesitated.

"If you'd rather, Suri can tell the dragon to lay waste to Caric."

Gronbach wasn't moved by this and continued to stare at her. Persephone held his glare, refusing to blink, to shift, to show any weakness. This was a battle of wills. Buying from the Dherg traders in Vernes was always a battle of offers and demands, but this time the stakes were beyond high.

"Well?" she asked after several moments had passed.

"Assuming there is indeed a dragon, I will agree on one condition." He looked back at Brin. "You must hand over the tablets you stole."

"What? No!" Brin said.

"They're from our mountain. They belong to us."

"But . . . but," Brin began in disbelief, "you can't even understand them. What good are they to—"

"Those tablets are part of our heritage. They belong here. There's no deal without them."

"Fine," Persephone said.

"Seph!" Brin shouted.

"I said fine!"

"You're an evil little dwarf," Brin seethed.

"They are our treasure, not yours. And I'm a Belgriclungreian, not a dwarf, nor a Dherg, and no more evil than anyone else."

"Yes you are," Brin said, "and I'll make certain everyone knows it."

Gronbach looked puzzled.

"I'm the Keeper of Dahl Rhen, and your treachery will be passed down to all the Keepers and everyone who comes after me. You'll be reviled throughout the world by future generations as the very face of evil."

At that, Gronbach laughed. "Little girl, the history of the Belgriclungreians is long, longer than the existence of the Rhunes, and will continue well after the Rhunes are wiped out by the Fhrey. No one will remember what you say about me or anyone else."

"That's where you're wrong," Brin said. "I'm going to write it down."

"What are you doing, Seph?" Moya asked the moment they were alone.

They had been escorted to the room where Arion lay on one of three beds. Then Roan and Brin were taken to the smiths to make the sword. Roan appeared more puzzled than frightened, and Brin promised to explain things to her. After the two left, Moya and Persephone were sealed in. She had no idea where Frost, Flood, and Rain were. That didn't bother her too much. Gronbach wouldn't kill them, but he would want to question them in private—probe for holes. She just hoped they didn't say anything stupid.

"Seph, Brin and Roan don't know how to forge a magic sword!"

"Keep your voice down." Persephone pulled Moya away from the door. "They don't need to know."

Moya's eyes narrowed. "I don't understand."

"Look, I want Roan in there when the dwarfs make the sword, so she can see how it's done. Brin will mark down all the details. The smiths won't even know what she's doing. They'll think it's magic or something, just like Flood did . . . part of the sword's enchantment."

"But Seph, you promised to *destroy* Minna."

"It's not Minna, and you know it."

"I do, sure, but I'm not the one you have to convince, am I?"

Persephone sighed and ran her hands through her hair. "One thing at a time, Moya. One thing at a time, okay? For the love of the Grand Mother, I'm doing my best to keep us alive!"

Persephone fell onto one of the vacant beds. "I hate that little bearded bastard! I'd like to strangle him with his own whiskers! We nearly died down there!"

Her voice took on a mocking impersonation, *"What swords are you speaking of?"* She punched a pillow across the room, where it landed on the spare bed. "Miserable little son of the Tetlin Witch!"

Moya stood with brows high and an amused smile on her lips as she stared at the pillow. "I like this side of you. Let's see more of it in the future."

"If there is one."

Moya looked confused.

"A future," Persephone clarified, then she turned her thoughts to next steps. After a while, she said, "In the morning, I'll need you to stay behind with Arion."

"Me? But I'm your Shield. I have to go with you."

"I'll need Roan and Brin to mark the sword, and I can't risk leaving Arion alone . . . not here. It will be your responsibility to make sure everyone is on the ship and ready to sail by the time we get back. I'm counting on you for this. Don't let me down."

Moya nodded. "I won't, but who will . . . you know . . . kill it?"

"I guess I'll have to." Persephone gathered the blanket from the bed and hugged it on her lap. She looked at the door and then over at Arion as she lay so very still. "Moya, I'm scared."

"I know."

"Are you scared?"

"I'm too stupid to be scared."

"You're not stupid, Moya."

"I'm not smart." She sat beside Persephone. Then Moya took one of Persephone's hands and held it in both of hers. "I could never have done what you just did in there. If left to me, we'd be at the bottom of the sea right now."

"All I did was lie."

"But you did it so well! That was impressive. Even I believed you." Moya laid her head on Persephone's shoulder. "You're the best chieftain Rhen has ever had."

"If this doesn't work, I might be the last."

The next morning was clear and hot as Persephone, Roan, and Brin walked under escort up the long sloped road to Neith. Gronbach went with them this time, still dressed in armor. Persephone didn't try to fight the guilty pleasure of watching Gronbach sweat under the blistering heat. By the time they reached the entrance, the Master Crafter was soaked.

He stopped at the gate, as did the escorts. None of the dwarfs were willing to enter with the dragon slayers, which was more than fine by Persephone.

As she, Brin, and Roan entered the cool interior of Neith, Persephone took further pleasure in knowing Gronbach would bake until she decided to return. No one rushed.

"Any trouble making the sword last night?" Persephone asked as soon as they were beyond the decorated wall and out of Gronbach's hearing. For reasons known only to Roan, she had wrapped the weapon in a blanket, as if it were sacred. Perhaps it was.

Brin shook her head. "They asked what we wanted them to do. So I found the part I'd already figured out on the tablet and said a few things about heating iron in a charcoal furnace to melt out impurities that would settle to the bottom. The smiths already knew that, I guess. Then later on, I prattled on about folding layers of carbon and iron. I had no idea what it even meant, but they did. I don't think I told them anything they didn't already know. They had this system and just worked through it. After a while, they ignored us. I'd nod and say, 'That's right' or 'Good' every once in a while. Don't know if they even heard me."

"It was amazing," Roan muttered.

"Were you able to see everything, Roan?"

She nodded.

Of course, she did, Persephone thought. Sending Roan to the smith's workshop was like sending a dog to a butcher's house and wondering if the animal noticed the meat.

Before long, they came upon the dragon. She was lying down, but her head was up and looking at them. Persephone didn't see the mystic. "Suri?"

The girl's head popped up. She'd been lying on a blanket, her head resting on the side of the dragon, its long tail encircling them both. An absurd image, this wild, barefoot mystic with her ruddy cloak and tattooed body, lying snuggled up with a fearsome giant, all claws and scales, wings and teeth—a girl and her loyal companion.

"I was wondering if you'd return."

"I told you I would be back. I'd never leave you behind."

Suri smiled, a sad one, but a smile nonetheless.

"Suri, I need to talk to you about Minna—" Persephone started, but she was cut off by the mystic.

"She's not Minna, not really."

"No, she isn't."

Suri placed a hand to the dragon's neck. "Still, I think there's a part of her in there, something trapped inside. I can't leave her here like this."

"I don't want you to." Persephone looked at Roan and nodded.

Stepping forward, Roan laid the bundle down then unfolded the cloth, but never touched the sword. The blade was the most amazing thing Persephone had ever seen. The metal was brilliant silver, but around the edges where the shadows pooled, she saw a blue tint. The blade tapered elegantly, every line straight, and the handle was built out of the same metal, making Persephone believe it was all formed from one solid piece. Not nearly as decorated as Raithe's sword, or even as stylish as any of the Galantians', this was perfection through simplicity. In the same way musical accompaniment failed to add to, and often distracted from, a great singer, the Dherg had mastered their craft to such a level that any change would have been a flaw.

Roan pulled out a small bag and unrolled it. Inside were a tiny hammer and half a dozen little etching tools.

"I'll need to know her name," Brin said.

Suri nodded.

"Show me." And the Keeper gave the mystic a piece of chalk.

Suri drew the symbols on the floor.

The three of them went to work etching the blade as Persephone and the dragon watched. *Does she know?* Balgargarath had appeared to understand when Moya shot the first arrow, but the dragon either didn't understand or didn't care. Her eyes were open but empty. *Maybe that's what Suri saw—the emptiness.*

When they were done, Suri got on her knees and, using a glowstone, ran her fingers along the blade where the marks were etched. "It's her real name. I called her Minna because that's what a songbird was singing when

I found her. I thought the bird was telling me her name. But that wasn't her *real* name. This is." She tapped on the blade. "This is what it looks like. I found it in the weave." She wiped her face and began to shake. She got up and looked at the dragon. "I can't believe I have to do this again. Can you leave us?"

"Suri, if you want, I can——"

Suri shook her head. "It has to be me."

Persephone nodded.

Roan gathered up the tools and bag, and together the three of them started back toward the gate. As she walked away, Persephone looked back and saw the dragon watching Suri as she picked up the sword. For a moment, fear gripped her. *What if she's sensing her death? Will she attack?*

Suri held the sword in her hands as if it equaled the weight of Elan. The dragon continued to watch the mystic, and then Persephone saw it. Just a glimpse, just a flash, but it was there. Those large forgiving eyes that were far too familiar even to Persephone. She felt her own tears crest, slip, and fall.

"Minna." They heard Suri's soft, fracturing voice. "Minna . . . remember the time we came home and found Tura lying in the garden . . ."

Persephone led Roan and Brin back outside to where Gronbach waited with his soldiers. He looked at them suspiciously. "Is it done?"

"Almost," Persephone said.

The release of power threw the great gates of Neith back to their full reach, as if they were nothing more than a pair of bedroom doors.

A cloud of dust blocked out the sun for a moment, at least for those near the entrance. Everyone stared at the opening, waiting. Several minutes passed, and just when Persephone was about to go in to make sure Suri was okay, the mystic walked out. She was covered in a fine powder of dust, except on her cheeks where rivulets glistened untouched. Sobbing, Suri clutched the blade to her chest with both hands.

Gronbach stared at the mystic in disbelief. He glanced at his soldiers, then back at Suri as if not quite able to accept what he was seeing. Suri didn't fit anyone's expectation of a dragon slayer. He gestured to one of his men, who ran inside to verify that the dragon wasn't there. It didn't take long for him to return and nod.

Then Gronbach gestured, spoke something in the Dherg language, and once more Persephone found herself restrained by the little dwarfs.

"Are you really such a fool?" she shouted at him. "We've killed Balgargarath *and* a dragon. And you *still* aren't honoring your word?"

Gronbach chuckled. "You're the foolish one. If I lied before, what makes you think I wouldn't again? It's best you die, as you are obviously too stupid to live." Noticing the sword Suri held, he added, "And I see you lied about the magic sword being consumed."

He focused on the blade with greedy eyes and held out his hand. "Give it to me."

Suri looked at Gronbach, as if noticing him for the first time. "It has her name on it." She tilted the blade so he could see the markings.

"I don't care whose name is on the thing, little girl. It's mine."

"But it has her name on it," Suri repeated, louder this time.

Gronbach rolled his eyes. "She's simple, is she?" He shook his head and reached out, grabbing hold of the pommel as Suri clutched the blade even tighter. As they struggled in their tug-of-war, the ground began to shake.

A giant slab of rock, one of the pair that formed the gates of Neith, slipped free and fell, exploding in a burst of dust. The towers of Esbol Berg began to shudder and teeter. Stones slipped free of their ancient moorings, and a giant block the size of a roundhouse plummeted, crashing down the hillside.

Gronbach let go.

The moment he released the sword the shaking stopped.

He looked at the place where the stone had crashed and then up at the towers.

"It has her name on it," Suri repeated, oblivious to the earthquake that had nearly brought the ancient city of Neith down around them.

Gronbach looked from the great edifice of the Dherg's ancestral home to Suri. He stared deep into the mystic's eyes, then shook his head. "That's not possible."

He reached out again.

"Gronbach, don't!" Persephone shouted. She tried to stop him, but couldn't break free of the hands holding her.

He was more forceful the second time, and wrenched the weapon free of Suri's little hands, giving her a shove backward in the process.

Overhead, thunder cracked, and dark clouds covered the sun.

Suri glared at the dwarf. She was muttering, her fingers flexing. To anyone who didn't know better, they might think she was merely angry, that she cursed him under her breath.

"Gronbach, give her back the sword! Now! Hurry!"

He ignored Persephone as he studied the weapon.

The wind rose. Dust and dirt swirled.

"Suri, don't—" Persephone started to say.

The jolt was so abrupt that Persephone had to lean on the dwarf holding her just to keep standing. "Oh, blessed Grand Mother!" she exclaimed as snaps, cracks, and loud booms escaped from the open gate of Neith, deep painful groans issuing from that ancient mouth.

What had survived thousands of years of warfare, erosion, and the presence of a demon named Balgargarath didn't survive the retribution of a teenage girl. In minutes, the legendary Belgriclungreian city of Neith fell. Weakened pillars, unequal to the task of supporting so grand a roof, broke, and the weight of the mountain came crashing down. They felt the shudder and jolt through the ground, the collapse of hollow places beneath their feet. To either side, the great towers of Esbol Berg listed, staggered, then fell. One dropped toward the sea, where the top destroyed one of the docks and raised an enormous wave that lurched ships, slamming some so hard they shattered against the docks. The other great tower imploded, collapsing in a huge plume of dust and bursting stone. The cloud of debris blew out over them. The gust of wind and shower of pebbles shoved Persephone to the ground, and the dwarf behind her let go.

The world disappeared into darkness, a hazy cloud of fragments. Persephone couldn't see Suri, Brin, or Roan, all of whom had been right beside her. She pulled up the sleeve of her dress to breathe through and covered her eyes. "Suri! Stop it! Suri! Suri!"

The ground settled. The shaking stopped, and for a long moment, there was silence. Not a voice, not a bird, not a bee broke the hush. The only sound was the soft pattering rain of tiny stones. By the time the wind drove the dust to the sea, the sun was shining again. A coating of powdered rock covered them. Brin coughed, struggling to wipe her eyes clear.

The soldiers who had escorted them were gone. Persephone saw the sunlight glinting off their armor as they ran down the slope. Gronbach himself remained exactly where he had been. He still held the sword, his face a display of disbelief.

"It has her name on it," Suri said for the fourth time. "You can't have it." The mystic held out her hand.

"For all the gods' and everyone else's sake, give . . . it . . . back," Persephone said.

Gronbach continued to stare in shock. Maybe he was too frightened to move. Persephone could understand that. She was a bit on the terrified side herself. But she knew Gronbach by now. *He doesn't want to lose.*

"Give it back, and we'll get on a ship and leave. And Mari help you if any harm has come to Moya or Arion; Suri's even more fond of them than she is of that blade."

Gronbach looked to Persephone and nodded. He handed the sword to Suri who clutched it to her chest.

"Unlike you, I'm a woman of my word. It's time we left," Persephone said as she walked past Gronbach down the road toward Caric.

A strangely silent crowd came out of their homes and lined the docks as Persephone's party climbed on board the *Calder Noll*. They gathered in the streets and squares weeping and wailing. A few whispered to one another in their own language, and for once Persephone was happy she couldn't understand.

The captain said nothing to them, neither did the crew. Persephone took charge and directed everyone to the cargo space toward the front of the ship. Standing there as the lines were cast off and the little ship was rowed away from the docks, Persephone looked back at Neith. The full face of the sun shone on what was left of the mountain. The great gate was gone, the towers missing. The majesty that was Neith had vanished, and the road up the slope led only to a battered memory and a broken dream.

On this trip, the crew of the *Calder Noll* avoided them much as the first ship's crew had. Arion was wrapped in blankets, her face pale, but she was still breathing. Persephone took that as a good sign. She thought that if the Miralyith were going to die, she would have done so by now.

They all gathered around the prone Fhrey, blocking the harsh sea winds and taking turns cradling her head as the deck pitched.

"Don't suppose you managed to bring the tablets?" Brin asked Moya.

She shook her head. "They stopped treating us well the moment you left. I thought we were off to our deaths when a group of Dherg came and led us down to the dock.

This brought nods from Frost and Flood as well.

"You're alive," Persephone told Brin. "And going home. That's enough; be grateful."

"I know, and I am. It's just . . . well . . . I didn't get a chance to decipher hardly any of them. I was going to study them last night, but I . . . I . . ."

"She fell asleep," Roan said.

Brin cocked her head at Roan. "Didn't *you?*"

"No, I never sleep when there is something to work on, and last night I had a lot to do." Roan smiled. "It's okay, really it is."

Brin nodded. "I know. I just wish I had time to study them."

"No, I mean it's okay. I fixed it."

"Fixed what?"

Roan opened her bag and drew out a thin, rolled tube. Brin inched toward her as Roan untied a string and unrolled what had been inside. "The little men call this *vellum;* it's made from sheepskin. It's the same thing they use to make maps and diagrams. Very thin and light. It's great at holding something they call *ink*. Of course, I didn't have any of that."

On the interior of the vellum were markings. Markings that looked exactly like the ones on the tablet.

Brin stared in amazement. "How did you do that?"

"I laid the vellum on the tablets and rubbed the charcoal from the furnace over them. It made this image."

Brin reached out.

"Careful," Roan said. "It will smear."

"You're a genius," Brin said, and eagerly took a seat beside Roan.

Watching the two studying the scroll, Persephone felt her lips rise into a smile that lingered until she noticed Suri. The mystic still held on to the weapon, a faraway look in her eyes.

"It's a beautiful sword," Persephone said. "Roan, do you think you could make others now that you've seen how it's done?"

Roan nodded.

"And is this one strong?"

Again, Roan nodded. "I think I'll be able to make the next one even better. If I could—"

"But is *this one* strong? Is it as good as bronze?"

"Stronger."

"You sure?"

Roan nodded again.

"That's good enough for me." Persephone squinted at the markings on the sword's blade. They were different from those she remembered on the shafts.

"What does it say?" she asked Suri. "What was her real name?"

The mystic didn't reply.

Brin glanced at Suri cautiously. "It's . . . it's hard to pronounce."

Persephone nodded her understanding as Suri watched them. Her eyes were red, cheeks flushed and blotchy.

They rode the waves that rose and fell, and Persephone was glad Arion wouldn't suffer the sickness that had plagued her on the first trip. Hours passed in silence. When Suri finally spoke for the first time since leaving Belgreig, she said, "Her real name was *Gilarabrywn*."

Persephone offered her a little smile. "I like Minna better."

"So do I," Brin said.

"Me, too," Suri agreed. She looked down at the sword and raised it over her head.

"Don't!" Persephone shouted. "What are you doing?"

"I feel like it should be put to rest, too," Suri said.

"If you're just going to throw it away, could I use it first?"

"For what?"

"To change the world."

Suri looked down at the blade, puzzled.

"It's a magic sword, Suri. Minna made it so."

"You know it doesn't have any *real* power." Suri held the sword out to Persephone.

"Trust me, Suri," Persephone said, feeling the weight of the weapon in her hands, "this sword will change everything."

CHAPTER THIRTY-ONE

The Keenig

Some things you never see coming. I remember this whenever I think of Udgar.

—THE BOOK OF BRIN

The other chieftains were trying to be kind, but their actions only helped to remind Raithe that he had only hours to live. He'd spent the night in the lodge on Lipit's bed. The evening meal found him feasting on a succulent pig—a prized animal Harkon had brought for a celebration feast. Krugen offered his best wine, but Raithe didn't drink. His father had taught him to keep a clear head before a fight. Drinking came after.

Lipit also offered him women. Raithe turned them down as well. Herkimer had said women drained men of their vitality. Of course, Raithe knew a lot of his father's "sage advice" was crap, like how best to raise a family, and how a sword and a reputation meant more than anything. But there was another reason even more substantial. He wasn't interested. It wouldn't mean anything, and that night, of all nights, he needed it to mean something.

Raithe had no doubts that Udgar would kill him.

One of the pillars of combat was confidence. To win, a fighter had to believe he would. Raithe knew—absolutely *knew*—he wouldn't. While he was a good fighter by Dureyan standards, Udgar was great by Gula reckoning, and even his father had admitted that the Gula-Rhunes were better in battle. Desperation did that to a people, hardened them, and the only people on the face of Elan who had it tougher than the Dureyan were the Gula. For centuries, the Fhrey had ordered attacks against them, and warfare was an integral part of their way of life. They had to become battle masters just to exist.

"You're going to kill him, right?" Tesh asked, as he opened the windows to let the morning light in. The boy had slept on a mat at the foot of the bed, stunned by the luxury of the room.

"Sure," Raithe replied. "I'm the God Killer, right? A Gula-Rhune has to be easier than a Fhrey."

"Then you'll be keenig."

"That's how it's supposed to work."

"Your word will be law over all the clans, over thousands and thousands of people."

"That's the idea."

The boy crossed to the seaward side of the bedroom and continued opening shutters. The kid was still skinny as a bag of bones, but he did have better color. And for the first time, Raithe noticed a fine haze of hair sprouting on his chin and upper lip. A pang of disappointment stabbed him as he realized he'd never see the man this kid would become. Despite his earlier reservations, Tesh had grown on him, as had the idea of shaping his future. Tesh wanted Raithe to teach him to fight, but Raithe wanted to teach the kid so much more—all the things Herkimer had failed at. "I suppose you'll choose a new Shield, then. As keenig, you'll need a real Shield."

"You are a real Shield."

"You know what I mean."

Raithe was going to die in a few hours, what difference did it make? "Listen, you're the only Dureyan besides me. Sure, you might be a bit on the small side now, but you're good stock. You'll grow, fatten up, build muscle, train hard . . . harder than any of them, and one day you'll be the best warrior in the world, mostly because you're Dureyan." He picked up a boot and pulled it on. "But . . ." He hesitated, stomping his foot into place.

"But what?"

"I can't teach you what you want to know. No human can."

"You're the God Killer. Of course you can. You—"

"And I told you I was lucky. I survived by sheer accident, and because Malcolm has a fixation with rocks and people's heads. The point is, there isn't a human alive that can teach you how to fight as well as they do." He shook his head. "The way you learn how to kill someone is to have *them* teach you. You learn how they fight. Discover their strengths and weaknesses. Uncover their secrets, and never let them see yours. You want to learn how to kill Fhrey? You learn from them. And yes, they may hide their weaknesses, but you have to see through their deceptions."

Tesh opened his mouth to object, but Raithe cut the boy off. "And don't tell me you don't like them," he said when Tesh started to frown. "Did you like your village? Did you like the rocks and snakes? Did you like freezing in winter because there wasn't enough dung to burn? Did you like going days without food? Did you like drinking that muddy water that tasted of metal? I know I didn't. And no one I knew who was Dureyan ever has. But we still got up every day, still drank that water, dug those rocks, and burned that dung, because Dureyans are survivors, and we don't complain. So, if you want to learn how to kill elves, you learn from them. Do what you're told. Listen to what they say. That's how you beat them."

"What are *elves*?" Tesh asked.

"They're what you want to kill."

The boy looked puzzled.

"Do you think they deserve to be called *gods*?"

Tesh smiled. "I *have* been watching them, going to the practices, seeing what they do. They have different fighting styles. Did you know that? Each of them is a master in a different skill. Sebek uses two small swords and a very aggressive attack. Tekchin relies on a long, light blade and uses a lot of footwork, very complicated. Eres is all about throwing things, spears and javelins mostly. Anwir uses a sling, a net, and a cleve that he spins. Grygor uses a gigantic sword, big even for him. In close quarters, he grabs it partway up the blade, where he dulled the edges for a handgrip. That means he can use the blade as a sword and spear. And Nyphron uses a sword-and-shield combination, sort of like you." The kid thought a moment. "If I join the practice sessions, let them teach me, I could learn each of the different techniques."

"Good plan."

The boy watched Raithe pull his other boot on. "You *are* going to kill him?"

"We just went over this."

"It's just . . . he's really big."

"Yeah, he is."

"But he carries it easy. He's got great balance, and he's naffing light on his feet."

"Naffing?"

The boy shrugged. "My father used to say it a lot."

"What does it mean?"

"It's what he used to do to my mother first thing after coming home from the High Spear, but I guess it means different things at different times because he used to say our sheep were lousy naffs, and Haden Woolman was a crazy naffer." The boy paused, thought a moment. "Then again, maybe not."

Raithe laughed; it felt good. *Probably the last time.* The kid continued to impress him. Not with his mastery of language, but the fact that he was dead-on about Udgar. *How can a kid his age see so much? He has a real gift.* Maybe he really could be a great warrior, assuming he lived long enough.

Raithe stood up, slamming his heels into place. He grabbed up his leigh mor and looked for the piss pot. "Where's . . ." he started, when he saw Tesh leaning out the window so far that his feet were coming up off the floor. "What are you looking at?"

"You can see the docks from here. One of those Dherg ships is coming in."

The Gula keenig had already arrived. Raithe spotted Udgar and his lieutenants in the courtyard. That's where the fight would be held, a good enclosed space where spectators could sit up on the walls and watch. They weren't scheduled to begin blows until midday, but already the parapets were filling. The big event had arrived.

This was the inevitable fate of all Dureyans, try as they might to avoid it. The Mynogan couldn't be denied their blood. Unlike his father, who offered sacrifices before each fight, Raithe had little use for the Dureyan gods of war. Yet it seemed they had a use for him.

His death would have a grand audience, at least. How many could say that, unless they were the guest of honor at a hanging, beheading, or burning. A lot of people died in unremarkable ways, choking while eating, frozen on a hillside, or drowned in a river. When he and his father had crossed to the west, Raithe was certain he'd exit life because of a stupid accident. He would break his leg somewhere in the wilderness, and being alone, he'd slowly starve. Death by Udgar was better. Udgar was a professional. He'd make it quick.

Once again, Raithe recalled the words of his father, *the worst that can happen is you'll die. Might even be a step up.* Everyone died. Raithe had already outlived his whole clan.

He hadn't made a career out of killing like his father and brothers, but he wondered if this one battle would grant him entrance to Alysin. It sounded nice, but if that meant he'd spend eternity with the likes of his brothers, then Rel would be good enough. That's where his mother and sister would be anyway. *What kind of mess is the afterlife when vicious killers are rewarded through eternity for being cruel?* His mother and sister were just as brave, just as courageous, and never vicious. They didn't kill anyone, and for that, the pair were relegated to a lesser reward. *Doesn't make sense.*

Since there didn't seem any point in waiting until midday, Raithe walked out of the lodge. He intended to challenge Udgar right then, just to get it over with, but that was before the three women entered the gate.

Roan and Moya followed Persephone into the courtyard of the dahl, having come directly from the docks. She had instructed Brin, Suri, and the dwarfs to take Arion to Padera. Something important was obviously going on, the place was filled with people. All the chieftains were present and dressed in their finest. They sported torcs and fine leigh mors, assuring everyone of their importance. The Galantians clustered on the grass to the right of the gate, and around them remained an open space, an invisible barrier, as no one dared come too close.

Among the sea of faces gathering on the walls, she spotted Heath Coswall sitting next to Hanson Killian. They were with the Bakers and old Mathias Hagger. Their bare feet dangled, sawing back and forth like a giant centipede. Down on the ground near the empty feed bin, she saw Farmer Wedon with a hand on the shoulder of Shepherd Gelston, who looked confused and pale, as if he hadn't seen the sun in months, but at least he was standing. Even Tressa was inside the walls; she stood alone. Gifford leaned on his crutch and Habet's left shoulder. Persephone's heart ached when she saw the bruises, but Padera had been right. Gifford could endure blows better than anyone.

At least they are all here, still alive, still safe.

Persephone spotted Raithe coming down the steps of the lodge. He had a huge grin on his face, and his eyes were wide with relief as he rushed toward her at a trot. He didn't stop. He grabbed hold of her with both arms and lifted her off the ground.

"I missed you," he whispered as he swung her in a circle. "I feared you'd never come back." He pressed his cheek to hers, his black beard scratching her face, a feeling she didn't mind in the least.

"Of course I was coming back!"

He let her slip down, and she struggled to plant her feet on dirt again. The welcome was appreciated, but she had work to do and needed to be taken seriously. Being flung in a circle like a new bride didn't project the image she was trying to portray.

When he finally let go, she asked, "What's going on? Has a keenig been chosen?"

"Not yet." Raithe sounded giddy and kept staring at her with a big smile.

She sighed. "So you still won't do it? You won't lead us because we lack weapons?"

"Well, it's complicated. You see——"

"Never mind, I have an announcement. I think you'll want to hear this." Persephone smiled. "Everyone! Listen to me!" she shouted to the crowd. "I am Persephone, of the House of Gath, chieftain of Clan Rhen."

Persephone already had a sizable amount of attention after the dramatic embrace Raithe had given her. She spotted Tegan, Harkon, Lipit, Krugen, and Alward standing near one another by the well and focused on them. "Before I left, there was doubt about our success when facing the Fhrey. We had the numbers, but lacked proper weapons. The Fhrey's swords and armor were considered too advanced."

She turned. "Moya! Roan!"

The two rushed forward. Moya carried the bow, while Roan carried a blanketed bundle.

"I've traveled across the sea to the land of the Dherg, to the ancient city of Neith, and I've returned with hope for our future."

The courtyard was silent except for the bustling of people shifting to see what was wrapped in the blanket. Taking the bundle, Persephone lifted the sword above her head. A communal gasp was followed by a deep silence. The morning sun glared off the mirrored blade. Persephone walked in a circle, displaying the weapon to wide eyes and gaping mouths. She ended her circle at the post where Raithe had embedded Shegon's sword. The blade was still there, extending out like a tree branch.

Persephone pointed at the bronze blade. "This fine Fhrey sword was placed here by Raithe of Dureya, the God Killer. It's capable of cleaving any of our weapons. It's been argued that we stand no chance of fighting the Fhrey because they possess swords like this. Because their metal is so strong."

She glanced at Roan. The woman stood with hands clasped before her. Persephone took a deep breath and said a quick prayer to Mari. Wielding the sword with both hands, she raised it high and with as much strength as she could summon swung it in a great overhead chopping motion. The shock jolted up her arms, nearly breaking her grip, but she hung on as the dwarf blade struck the Fhrey's just above the hilt. She felt it give. When she looked up, only half of the bronze blade remained in the post. The handle lay in the dirt near Raithe's feet.

The crowd gasped, and Persephone breathed again.

Like everyone else, Raithe stared at the shimmering sword in awe. "How many did they give you?"

"Just this one." She couldn't help but smile.

"One?" Raithe looked at her puzzled. "But . . . just one sword? You can't outfit an army with a single blade." She watched his smile fade, his shoulders droop. "Even if they'd given you a thousand, it wouldn't be enough."

"Exactly. Which is why I didn't return with shipments of swords. Tell him, Roan."

Roan, who was still folding up the blanket after having started over three times, froze at the sound of her name.

"Tell him," Persephone insisted.

Roan said something, but with her head down and her hair hiding her face, her voice didn't carry.

"Louder, Roan," Moya said.

Roan lifted her head. "I . . . I can make them."

"*You* can make them?" Raithe asked.

She nodded far too timidly.

Persephone shouted to the crowd while pointing at her. "This woman knows the secrets to making swords like these!"

Roan jumped at the volume of Persephone's voice and visibly cowered. She took several steps backward, leaving the open space of the courtyard and joining the crowd.

Persephone handed the sword to Raithe.

He stared at the weapon, then at Roan.

The girl drew up her shoulders as if she were a turtle trying to hide, but somehow she found the courage to say, "I can make better ones."

Raithe glanced at the post. "This one destroyed Shegon's sword."

"I know, but I can do better. I . . . they . . . didn't follow the steps right. But then they didn't know how to figure out the markings on the stones. Only Brin knows how to do that. In fact, they didn't even know about the tablet until we brought it out of the mountain. So, they just did what they've always done. The Old One's way is better. More carbon makes it harder, less flexible, and a bit more brittle, but it will hold a sharper edge and be lighter, so much lighter. I could make a sword twice this length and it will weigh half as much. Well maybe not half, a third less perhaps. I don't know. I have to try some things."

The other chieftains approached. "Is it magic?" Tegan asked, watching the blade in Raithe's hands as if he held a dangerous snake.

"No," Persephone said. "Which means Roan can teach others to make them as well." Persephone stepped before Raithe. "I didn't bring back a thousand swords. I brought back a thousand swords a month."

"More than that . . ." Roan spoke up again. The girl was a mouse except when it came to talking about how things worked. "Once I get everything figured out, we could work in batches. The real problem is getting the material." She reached into her pocket and pulled out the reddish rock. "This is iron. Well, sorta. I took this from their workshop. They had plenty."

The chieftains drew closer to look at the silver-speckled rock.

"Will the Dherg let us have it?" Krugen asked.

"For a price, maybe," Lipit said, his tone disapproving. "The Dherg are vicious traders."

"Don't count on that," Moya told them. "I doubt they would part with an ounce regardless of the price."

"Then what good is it if we can't—"

Gifford pushed his way through the crowd, using his crutch like a shepherd's crook to clear a path. "I've seen that be-foe," he said, elbowing his way in.

"Gifford!" Roan shouted. Dropping her carefully folded blanket, she rushed over, stopping just short of touching him. "You're all right! You're better!"

"You can look at me and say that?" He grinned.

"I just thought . . . I thought . . ."

"I thought the same about you."

"Where have you seen it?" Harkon demanded.

Gifford refused to take his eyes off Roan, so when he spoke he appeared to be talking to her. "I dig fo' stuff to make glazes. Woan and I've found all kinds of metals. But I couldn't do anything with that, so we didn't use it."

Roan smiled. "You have to heat it until it's very hot. You use this huge bag that blows air. It's called a bellows."

"How common is this?" Lipit asked.

"Very, I think," Tegan said. "In Warric we mine for copper in the hill near the Galeannon River. Not much copper, but there's a lot of this rock."

"If we get the iron, we can make more than just swords," Persephone said. "We can fashion armor, too, shirts of metal rings like the Dherg. They will be light but stop the sharpest blades. And we can make shields that won't shatter. Given time, we can outfit an army with better weapons and armor than the Fhrey."

Raithe took Persephone by the shoulders. He was biting his lower lip as he grinned, his eyes staring as if he'd never seen her before. "You did it," Raithe said in awe. "You really did."

Persephone grabbed hold of his arms and squeezed. "So you'll accept? You'll be keenig?"

He stared into her eyes. "No."

"No! But . . . do you realize how difficult it was to—"

Raithe turned to the other chieftains and interrupted her. "I never got a chance to name my nomination."

This brought a look of puzzlement from everyone.

"You didn't need to," Tegan said. "Persephone already nominated you."

"Not me. *Her.* I nominate Persephone, chieftain of Clan Rhen, to be our keenig."

Persephone displayed the most shock of anyone. "Raithe. No. I—"

"I agree!" Moya said, a huge grin on her face.

Raithe smiled at her, and then spoke to the chieftains, who looked less than convinced. "For days we've sat here arguing and accomplishing nothing. While we talked, while we worried, Persephone risked her life crossing the sea, and she's returned with the answer to our problems. And did she take an army? Did she wield sword and spear in battle? No. She took the best minds she knew, and that's how she succeeded, by using her head rather than muscle. Could you have done that, Tegan?"

The Warric chieftain shook his head and looked at Persephone with different eyes—serious eyes.

"What about you, Lipit? You live here at the foot of the sea, right across from the Dherg. You trade with them daily. Why didn't you manage to obtain the secret of this magic metal?"

Lipit didn't answer. He, too, stared at Persephone, his eyes shifting from her face to Raithe's hand and the shimmering sword.

"Truth is, none of you could. I know I couldn't." Raithe raised his voice to a shout. "How about you, Udgar? Could you do what this woman has done?"

Persephone turned to see a huge, ugly man standing at the far side of the courtyard. He was missing parts of his nose and was covered in thick red hair.

"Persephone, chieftain of Dahl Rhen"—Raithe motioned to the giant man—"meet Udgar, keenig of the Gula clans."

"*You* are a chieftain?" Udgar spoke in a deep, brawny voice.

"Yes," she said, looking nearly straight up at the hulking brute. "So the Gula-Rhunes got my messages."

"*You* called us here? You invited the Gula?"

"All of this was her idea," Raithe said. "She was the first to see the threat coming; the first to believe we could win. She called this summit. Persephone is the one who suggested the appointment of a single leader. And when we needed better weapons than the Fhrey's, she made that happen, too. I've never believed in the impossible. I've never believed that one person could make a difference. Persephone has proved me wrong. I haven't believed in much, but . . . I believe in her. Persephone has done the impossible, not just once but over and over again. Look at Udgar. The leader of the Gula-Rhunes is standing inside Dahl Tirre taking part in the appointment of a keenig for *all* the clans. Lipit, did you think that would ever happen?"

The chieftain shook his head.

"Neither did I, but Persephone thought so, and saw the need, and she made it happen. When I didn't think there was any way to beat the Fhrey's weapons, I gave up. A keenig doesn't give up. Persephone didn't give up. Look what she's done with a handful of women and a couple of young girls. Imagine what she could do with the full might of the combined clans!" He shook his head and his eyes settled on her. "Persephone, I can't be keenig. You already are." Then he fixed his gaze on Udgar. "And not just the keenig of the Rhulyn-Rhunes. She needs to be the keenig of *all* the clans!"

"You can't be serious!" Nyphron broke into the clearing of people where Persephone and Raithe stood. When he spoke, those close by backed away, including Udgar who glared at the Fhrey. Only Persephone and Raithe held their ground. This didn't go unnoticed.

"When you put forth your name for keenig," Raithe told Nyphron, "you said it wasn't necessary for the keenig to swing a sword, remember? You said the keenig doesn't need to be on the battlefield. You said what's required is someone who sees what needs to be done and can put a plan in place to accomplish it. I'd say obtaining the knowledge of Dherg metal certainly qualifies, wouldn't you? You also said we need someone who believes in the cause and is willing to sacrifice everything to succeed. Persephone lost her husband, her son, most of her clan, and her dahl. None of those setbacks stopped her. She never gave up. And she isn't merely *willing* to sacrifice . . . she already *has*."

"But what does she know about combat?" Nyphron asked. "How could she possibly—"

Moya smirked and stepped forward, addressing the Fhrey as bravely and boldly as always. "They didn't just hand us the recipe, you know. Give us their most sacred traditions with a smile." She stood leaning on Roan's bow that, unstrung, looked like a thin staff. "We had to fight for it."

"*You? Fought?*" Udgar chuckled. "What did you fight, little girl? Did you defeat the Dherg's kittens?"

Moya smiled up at him. "What I killed would consider you a bug. Balgargarath was a hundred times scarier than your ugly ass."

Udgar grinned at her. "You don't think I'm scary?"

As casually as if she were courting, Moya flipped back a lock of hair. "After what we've seen? You're a floppy-eared puppy."

Udgar's grin disappeared. "Enough. Do you think me such a fool? That I would be so easily tricked by this staged act. The deceit of the southern clans is legendary, but I see through your false claims. It's time to fight." Udgar glared at Raithe. "It's time for the son of Coppersword to die."

"What's going on?" Persephone asked.

"The Gula-Rhunes picked their candidate for keenig. Now they want to decide the matter by combat. The winner will be keenig of all the clans," Raithe told her.

"Why does everything need to be decided by fighting?" Persephone shouted.

"To see who is greater!" Udgar shouted. "To see who is worthy to lead. Now get out of the way and let men finish this."

Udgar conferred with a group of other Gula, all big, all clad in fur. One held out a spear and shield to him.

"I'll fight." Raithe looked to the chieftains. "But it will be as champion for Persephone. If I win she is keenig, agreed?"

"Can you beat him?" Persephone asked quietly.

Raithe didn't answer.

All around the courtyard, people became excited. The show they'd come to see was about to begin. Those nearby backed away. Those far away leaned forward, and the courtyard became a hum of whispers.

"Raithe? Can you?"

He looked at the sword and then into her eyes. "I don't know. I didn't think it was possible, but with this . . ." He looked to the sword. "Maybe with this I can."

When Udgar turned back, Raithe stepped between him and Persephone.

"Well? Who will it be?" Udgar asked. "Do you accept the son of Coppersword as your champion? Or do you prefer to fight me yourself? Or maybe the pretty one with the big mouth." He laughed wholeheartedly. "It doesn't matter. Whoever I fight, I'll kill, and then I'll be keenig. Who do you choose? Who will face me?"

"Me," Raithe declared.

"No. Not him," Persephone replied quickly, moving out from behind.

Raithe spun to look at her. "Don't be insane. He'll kill you."

"No, he won't."

Raithe was stern to the point of anger. He took her aside and whispered, "Udgar is probably the best warrior in all the clans. All the clans . . . Gula and Rhulyn both."

"Better than you?"

Again, Raithe didn't answer.

She squeezed his hand. "I don't need you to act as my champion. I have a new Shield."

"What? Who?"

Persephone pulled away from him and faced Udgar, who stood with shoulders back and chin up. His awful scarred face highlighted his self-important sneer. She looked to Moya, who nodded slightly. "If you must have a fight to decide this, Moya will act as my champion." Persephone gestured in her Shield's direction.

"The little girl with the mouth even bigger than her eyes?" Udgar looked at Moya, nodding with amusement. "Oh, I see. You think I won't kill a pretty girl. That I will concede the fight and make you the keenig. You are wrong. I've killed many pretty girls. I accept this challenge."

"Is that so?" Moya said.

"Wait!" Tekchin rushed to Moya's side. The Fhrey had a vicious look on his face. "I'll do it." He peered at Udgar like a hungry mountain cat eyeing an abandoned baby. "I'll fight in her place."

Lipit turned to Tegan. "If I'd known there would be so many champion volunteers, I would have pushed harder to be keenig myself."

"The Fhrey aren't a part of this," Udgar declared. "We are choosing a keenig. The killing of the Fhrey will come after."

"Moya," Tekchin pleaded, but she refused to look at him.

"This is insane," Raithe told Persephone. "He'll kill her. Moya will die."

"And then the Gula-Rhunes will rule over all of us," Lipit pointed out. "This isn't just her life at stake."

For most of the trip back, both inside Neith and on the ship, Persephone had watched Moya practice with the bow. On the boat, she'd refined her technique, tweaking Roan's invention until she could repeatedly hit the forward stanchion from the rear of the hold. The ship was too small for any long-range exercises, but Udgar wouldn't be that far away, and he was wider than a stanchion. Still, a wooden post wasn't a man and Persephone looked to Moya for reassurance.

The woman leaned on the bow and offered that disarming smile of hers. Then Moya jerked her head at Udgar and silently mouthed the word *puppy*.

If she weren't so genuinely concerned, Persephone might have laughed.

"If you truly believe that I should be keenig . . ." Persephone looked at Raithe. "If you think I can lead our people to defeat the Fhrey nation, then you must believe I can defeat a single Gula. I know you think it's impossible. But you just said I proved the impossible is achievable. I'm asking you to believe that I know what I'm doing. Do you, Raithe? Do you *truly* believe what you so eloquently said? Do you believe in me?"

"But Moya—" Raithe said.

"Just answer the question. It's a simple question."

A long silence, and then . . . "Yes," Raithe said.

She didn't want to, but she couldn't help leaking a little smile. Raithe was in love with her. He'd admitted as much on the beach and in Dahl Rhen, the first time he'd asked her to come away. He'd do anything to protect her. This one word proved more than his love; it proved he trusted her, even when reason told him he shouldn't.

She looked at the other chieftains. "Well? Do you agree? Do you appoint me to represent the Rhulyn-Rhunes? Do you give me the authority to choose my champion? And if my champion prevails, will you accept me as the leader of all our clans?"

"Win this battle, and you will win my undying loyalty," Tegan told her.

"Does that go for the rest of you as well?" she asked, and they nodded.

"It's decided!" she shouted. "Moya will represent me in battle against Udgar for the position of keenig!"

The crowd came alive. Shouts of "Gula!" and "Udgar!" came from the small but loud fur-covered contingent. Shouts of "Rhulyn!" came from the rest. No one cheered Moya's name.

Persephone walked to Moya as she bent the staff to string the bow. "Are you scared?"

Moya looked over her shoulder at Udgar, who was flexing his arms and cracking his neck. "Of him?" Moya said, sounding insulted.

Persephone watched Moya fit the string. Her hands were steady, her movements fluid.

Is she really so confident?

"No pressure, Moya. Just the future of every Rhulyn-Rhune, and maybe even all of humanity, is in the balance. So, nothing to *really* worry about."

Moya glared.

"Seriously, though . . ." Persephone hesitated. "It's just . . . he isn't a demon. Does that bother you? Killing a person, I mean?"

Again, Moya looked at Udgar. "Not him it doesn't."

Persephone nodded. "Okay, then."

The mob drew away, pressing toward the walls, giving the two plenty of room. Raithe moved close to Persephone as they both backed up to the edge of the crowd.

Persephone said a silent prayer to Mari as Moya pulled five feathered shafts from her belt pouch. One without feathers had been lost and the other one had been fixed by Roan during the boat trip back.

"Sticks? You fight me with sticks?" Udgar laughed at her. He hefted his spear and pounded it against the face of the shield secured to his arm, making a mighty *whump!* "Come get me with your sticks, little girl."

Moya held all five arrows in her pull-hand, fitting one in the string. "Don't need to."

Udgar raised his spear and took one charging step forward. Moya drew back, bending the bow. Just as with Balgargarath, she made a fine image—straight and confident.

She loosed the arrow. A sound like the whisper of a small bird taking flight issued, and across the courtyard the Gula champion stopped his charge and collapsed to the dirt.

In the wake of his fall, there wasn't a sound. The courtyard remained silent. No cheer, no shouts of anguish. Bewilderment infected every face as the crowd continued to lean forward with anticipation for a battle that had already ended.

Udgar thrashed on the ground, clawing at his neck, a spray of blood forming a pool. His legs kicked, and an awful gurgling sound bubbled from his mouth along with a wellspring of blood.

The spectators still stared.

"What's happening?" someone asked, as confusion held everyone in shock.

Finally, Udgar stopped moving altogether. The pool continued to spread, soaking the dirt. Still, there was a shaking of heads, a narrowing of eyes, questions whispered.

One of the Gula-Rhune clansmen approached Udgar's prone form and examined him. Everyone waited for the explanation to the riddle. When the man stood, he had a look of shock on his face. "Udgar . . . Udgar is dead."

Still, no one cheered. This wasn't the answer they had expected. If not for the blood, they might have thought Udgar was faking. Trying to lure his opponent closer, so he could strike. Not even their own eyes were enough to prove that a petite woman had killed the Gula giant. That she had done so in the span of a single breath, made it even more unbelievable.

Raithe looked at the fallen warrior, and then at Moya, who was already unstringing the bow. "You did it." He turned to Persephone. "She did it. She actually did it! That was . . . that was amazing."

"You all right, Moya?" Persephone asked.

Moya nodded, but there was no smile, no flippant remark. Instead, Moya wore a grim, serious expression—the look of a warrior.

"By the blessed hand of Mari," Lipit muttered as he took a hesitant step forward, struggling to believe. He stared at the prone form of Udgar facedown in the dirt. Then the chieftain of Tirre looked at Persephone with awe. "You really are the keenig."

Tegan nodded. "You are the keenig." Then the chieftain of Clan Warric upstaged Lipit by kneeling before her.

"Yes, you are the keenig," Harkon affirmed as he also took a knee.

So did Krugen and Alward, making it official.

"I'd pledge my sword," Raithe told her, "but all of mine are broken."

"I'll make you a new one," Roan told him. "A good one. One that won't break . . . ever."

Tekchin ran to Moya. "And here we thought you couldn't throw a spear! That was amazing! I've never seen anything like it. Didn't even see it fly."

She whirled on him. "No? Well, trust me, you will if you ever hurt anyone I love again!"

Tekchin pulled back, confused.

Moya leaned in, jabbing a finger at him, her eyes filled with far more fury than she'd showed Udgar. She pointed at Gifford. "If you *ever* do that, I swear to Mari, I won't hesitate to—"

Tekchin threw his hands up in defense. "I didn't—"

"But you didn't stop it, either. I mean it, Tekchin! I'll drop you like the poisonous snake you are. You or any Galantian." She stared fiercely at Eres. "And I'm pretty sure I could do so at more than a hundred yards."

"Moya," Gifford said, "it's all wight."

"No, it isn't!" Moya glared at Tekchin. "You could have done something, but you just stood there and watched . . . watched while he . . . he . . ."

"I didn't like what happened, either," Tekchin said.

"But you didn't stop it! Why didn't you stop it? *Why?* You stood there like everyone else, just watching. You heard Gifford's cries; you heard his screams. And what did you do? Nothing!"

She was sobbing.

"Moya, I—"

She held up a hand in front of Tekchin, wiped her tears away, and then slowly walked over to Gifford. She couldn't look him in the eye; instead she stared at the potter's feet. "Gifford, I'm . . . I'm . . . sorry. I'm so very, very sorry."

Gifford let his crutch go, hopped a step, and put his arms around her, hugging her close. "It's okay."

She shook her head against his chest.

"Moya, you just saved us fum Udga the Tewible. I absolve you."

"Absolve?" Moya asked.

Roan looked over. "He means *forgive,* he just can't pronounce the *r*."

Gifford smiled. "I might even owe you a few mo' snapped bones. You did so much."

While Gifford held her and Moya cried, Tekchin started to walk away, his head down.

"Wait!" Moya called when she noticed. She gave Gifford a kiss on his forehead. "Thank you," she whispered. Then she turned toward Tekchin. "You're ugly. You know that, right?"

Tekchin nodded. "You've mentioned it once or twice."

Moya shifted her weight to the hip that carried her sword. She folded her arms roughly and gave him a scowl. "Well, in case you forgot, or thought you might have improved while I was gone, I wanted to let you know you haven't. You're still uglier than Tetlin's ass on a bad day . . . but . . ."

"But?" Tekchin tilted his head to one side. His eyes narrowed and his lips parted just slightly as he studied her. "But what?"

"But it doesn't mean I want you to leave."

The Fhrey smiled.

"Don't go grinning at me," Moya said.

Just then a scuffle broke out among the Gula-Rhunes in the small group across the yard.

"It's the law!" one of the Gula yelled. One shoved, and the other pushed back.

A fist was thrown, then another. Two more men jumped in. Then a spear was thrust and one man fell. The one with the spear glared at Persephone with hate-filled eyes. Jerking the bloody weapon out of the man's body, he ran across the courtyard at her.

Raithe, who'd gone over to Tesh after the challenge to show him the sword, moved to intercept. Moya did, too, drawing her sword as she ran. The Gula-Rhune was faster than both and rushed to within a foot of Persephone, where he halted. Not as big as Udgar, he was nevertheless terrifying: crooked yellow teeth, an empty eye socket, and the tattoo of a serpent curling up his forearm. His huge hands were soaked in blood where they gripped the spear.

Persephone didn't move. She was too terrified to even blink, but slowly, very slowly, she tilted her head up and looked into his one eye.

A cyclops, she thought. *I'm going to be killed by a cyclops!*

"I am Siegel, son of Siegmar, chieftain of Clan Dunn."

Tilting her head was as much as Persephone could manage. She kept her jaw tight and her eyes focused on that one eye. He appeared puzzled for a moment, then moved back one step and looked her over. "You are nothing to look at." He began to nod, his lower lip protruding in grudging approval. "But you are brave."

Just too scared to move! Persephone thought.

The cyclops—who hadn't appeared to notice either Raithe or Moya— paused to look behind him at the other Gula-Rhune, then faced her again. "You can show us how to do that?" He pointed at Moya. "To do that to the gods? Kill them from a distance?"

"They aren't gods," Persephone said. "They're just Fhrey. And yes, Moya will teach you. And Roan will give you swords of iron that will break bronze weapons. And shields with markings that will stop their magic."

Siegel grinned, his mouth filled with crooked teeth. He nodded once more, then turned to Raithe. "Son of Coppersword, you accept this? You believe she can lead us to victory?"

"Udgar would have killed me," Raithe said. "We both know that."

"Yes."

"And yet I would have fought. I would have died; died for her. No one else . . . only her."

Siegel looked back at Persephone. "And it was you who invited us?"

"I need you to win," she said. "You need us to survive. Together we can be free."

He grinned, then raised his voice so everyone could hear, "She has killed Udgar. The gods have chosen. Persephone of Clan Rhen is keenig. The keenig of Rhulyn *and* Gula."

Siegel reached up to the blade of his spear and dragged his palm across the chipped jade edge, cutting a long slice. Then he held out his bleeding hand.

Raithe walked over and offered the edge of the iron blade to Persephone, nodding at it.

She looked at her soft white hand, and with a quiver in her stomach and a clenched jaw, she extended it over the blade. Raithe put his on top of hers, pressing her skin to the sharp edge. Raithe made it quick. She felt the pain like a burn across her palm.

She didn't want to look. She was afraid to see what the sword had done. Instead, she reached out. Siegel, still grinning, took her hand and squeezed. It hurt but she imagined he could have broken every bone if he wanted. She continued to grit her teeth, and Siegel continued to grin.

"You are the keenig," he told her. Letting go and grabbing her by the wrist, he shoved her arm up, nearly wrenching it from her shoulder. He shouted to those behind him, "She *is* the keenig!"

He let go, and Persephone clutched her throbbing hand to her chest as blood ran down to her elbow. Raithe was ready with a strip of cloth that he wrapped around the wound. She turned away from Siegel, who was walking back toward the others at the gate. She looked at Moya and mouthed the word, *ouch!*

"Roan, get Padera," Moya said. "Tell her to bring bandages and a needle. No offense, Raithe, but the Keenig of the Ten Clans deserves the best."

"Sharp, right?" Roan asked with a big smile.

"Very," Persephone managed to say through gritted teeth.

"Roan . . . Padera . . . now! Go!" Moya barked, and Roan ran off.

The chieftains ordered wine to be brought and spits to be loaded for the first ever Rhulyn–Gula celebration.

"You okay?" Moya put her arm around Persephone.

"Hand hurts, but yeah. I guess I am."

Moya gave her a hug. "You know what else you are?"

Persephone nodded slowly. "I'm the keenig."

CHAPTER THIRTY-TWO

The Plan

And that is how it all happened. It is how Persephone became the keenig of the Ten Clans, and Moya became her Shield. It is also the story of how Roan invented the bow and how Suri mastered the Art. For my part, I learned to write. I think each of us believed our adventures were over, and that under Persephone's guidance, men like Raithe and Fhrey like Nyphron would take over and finish what we started. We certainly did not expect what came next. I am not sure anyone would have.

—THE BOOK OF BRIN

"What now?" Nyphron asked, shaking his head. "Everything was going so well until . . . Why didn't you know about this stupid rule where only Rhunes can become keenig? You're a Rhune. Why didn't you know?"

Malcolm didn't reply. The two walked the beach just back from the surf. He didn't look the least bit apologetic or even concerned. The ex-slave of Nyphron's father offered the hint of a smile and then turned to look out at the sea.

"More Rhunes are coming, you know," Malcolm said. "Thousands are already on the march from Warric, Melen, and Menahan. The army you wanted, the one you dreamed of having, is on its way. And Persephone has provided you with the means to equip them. All that remains is your training."

"That's not *all* that remains," Nyphron growled. "It's not *my* army because *I'm* not the keenig! You botched it. You were so confident, so certain that . . ."

Nyphron grabbed Malcolm by the shoulder and turned him around. "Wait. You did know. Didn't you?"

That hint of a smile again.

"Actually, I didn't. Being enslaved in Alon Rhist didn't lend itself to learning all the ins and outs of Rhune custom and tradition. Still, I suspected they wouldn't trust one of your kind in that role. Especially not when fighting your people for survival."

"So why the smug smile? What am I missing?"

"I'm surprised you haven't come up with it yourself. Law prevents you from becoming the keenig, but nothing stops you from marrying one. As husband, you'd rule alongside Persephone."

Marry? A Rhune? Little wonder Nyphron hadn't thought of it. He'd never been married, and hadn't planned on it. Marriage was a waste of time. After so many years, people inevitably grew apart. His father had never wed his mother, and that worked fine for them. The idea of marrying a Rhune was even more absurd. "Don't be ridiculous."

"She needs you to train her troops, help plan strategies, and indicate where the Fhrey are weak and how best to exploit their vulnerabilities. Without you, those thousands of iron-wielding warriors will be little more than a bunch of skittish farmers. They'll run at the first Miralyith earthquake."

Malcolm allowed himself a full smile. "Presented at the right moment and in the proper light, it could work. Even if Persephone doesn't find you appealing, I believe she'll see the wisdom of a union. She's a very practical woman and entirely dedicated to her people."

Nyphron looked back at the dahl. The Rhunes were gathering supplies. They had a new leader, new hope, and spirits were high for a better future.

"And, of course, you'll outlive her and any children she bears," Malcolm went on. "After enough generations, people will only remember what you want them to . . . about Persephone . . . about the war . . . and about yourself. I'm positive that one day you will be known as Nyphron the Great and your empire will be regarded as the most impressive in the world."

"Can you do anything for her?" Suri asked the old woman.

Arion was probably twenty-five times older than Padera, but the Fhrey didn't have the look of wisdom that came with wrinkles and white hair. Padera had enough wrinkles to be the sage of sages; and according to Maeve, she wasn't white-haired, she was bald under her head wrap. Tura hadn't looked even that old, and Tura could fix anything.

"Hmm," the old lady intoned, sucking in her lower lip, rolling it like a curl of dough as she walked around the Fhrey.

Separating from Persephone at the gate, Suri, Brin, and the three dwarfs had carried Arion around the wall of Dahl Tirre and laid her in their old camp under the wool. Padera had been the only one there. The old farmer's wife sat in a pile of wrinkled clothes, two deft hands stitching a hole in a shirt far too large for her.

Padera heaved herself to her feet and laid a hand on Arion's forehead. Her insanely malleable lips shifted around thoughtfully. The old woman put her thumbs on the Fhrey's eyes and bent over, as if to kiss her. Then she clutched Arion's throat, fingers kneading into the soft hollow of her neck. Nodding, she let go and waddled over to the cooking pit. She placed two logs on the coals, blew on them until they caught fire, and then suspended an animal-skin bag above the flames.

"Well?" Suri asked.

"We'll see." Padera poured water from a gourd into the bag. "Not totally here, is she? Not gone, but not here, either."

Suri sat down beside Arion the way she had during most of the boat ride. The Fhrey looked pale, almost white, not that she had looked all that robust before. Suri hadn't noticed it in the cave, or even on the ship, but when upon familiar grass and dirt, she saw how colorless Arion had become—how dead she seemed.

"She's not dead," Padera said.

The mystic blinked in surprise, thinking the old woman had heard her thoughts.

"No, not dead, but very close. She's teetering. Seen it a thousand times. Usually with the fever. They sweat, they wail, they see things that aren't there. Then they calm down, just lie quietly . . . and they teeter. It's as if they're trying to make up their minds about leaving or staying."

"Is there anything we can do to convince her to stay?"

"Not really," the old woman said, pulling leaves from a jar and tossing them into the boiling water. The moment she did, Suri smelled the scent of feverfew. "You have willow bark on you?"

Suri nodded.

"Figured you would. Hand it over."

The old woman took the bark, broke it up, and added it as well. "If she wants to go, she will, and there isn't a thing we can do. But . . . if she wants to stay . . . we can make it easier for her to come back."

Suri hung her head.

"Guess things didn't go so well in the land of the Dherg?" Padera asked. "Did you at least get what you wanted?"

Suri didn't answer.

"Where's your wolf?"

Brin, who had been unpacking her bag, froze. "I don't think that—" the girl started to say.

"I killed her so Arion could live," Suri said.

The old woman sucked on her lip again and nodded. Then she reached out and took hold of Suri's hands. "Stop blaming yourself. That won't do either of you any good."

Suri's throat tightened, making it hard to swallow.

Padera rubbed Suri's back and then walked away. Turning her attention to Brin, she said, "And what are you doing back there?"

Brin, who had been digging through the supplies stacked at the back of their shelter, said, "I saw a map hanging on a wall in Caric. Made of treated animal skin that was soft like cloth. They drew on it with something called ink. It's a dye made from a chalky stone, but Roan says she could make something better. There's a tree called a book pine. She says she can make a resin from its syrup. Apparently, when you cook it, the stuff becomes really dark."

"It does do that."

"She also thinks a hollow straw, feather, or reed would hold the resin and make it easier to control the marks. I'm looking for some feathers that I think are back here."

"And why do you want all this?"

Brin looked up with bright eyes. "I'm going to write the history of the world. I'm going to put all of it down on soft, cured animal skins so they're light, easy to carry, and will last forever. Centuries after I'm dead, people will still be able to understand them and know what happened. Even if the Fhrey win this war, even if we are all killed, this will remain. And it will be the truth, the truth about all things. No one will be able to lie or change the story, or forget. Everyone will know there was an evil dwarf named Gronbach, a terrible monster named Balgargarath, a mighty warrior named Moya, a brilliant leader named Persephone, and a genius named Roan." She looked over at Suri. "They'll also know about a powerful mage named Suri, a wise Fhrey named Arion . . . and a brave and beautiful wolf named Minna . . . the wisest wolf in the world."

"Thank you," Suri whispered.

"And I'll write about my parents, too, so they will never be forgotten. In a way, they won't really die. Anyway, I'm going to mark it all down, so no one will ever forget us, or them. I'm also going to include what I learned from the tablets. It will be the most complete story, the best story ever, and it will never be forgotten."

"What will you call this story?" Padera asked. "*The Tale of Clan Rhen?*"

Brin shook her head. "It will be about more than just our clan. More than only Rhulyn or the Gula. It will be about everything." The young girl paused and thought. "I know. I'll call it *My Book Pine Markings*. That's true enough."

"A century from now do you think anyone will know who *My* is? Maybe you should use your name. Call it *Book Pine Markings of Brin*."

"I like it. Yeah, I'll call it that." Brin smiled.

Padera brought a bowl of the brew over and spooned a little into Arion's mouth. The Fhrey moaned, but she didn't cough or choke. The medicine went down.

"Padera," Brin said, "isn't there anything else you can do for her?"

"This will help. It's the best I have to offer."

"Suri?" Brin asked. "What about you? Can *you* do anything?"

Suri looked up confused. "Like what?"

"Mystics aren't healers, child," Padera explained. "Tura knew some of the healing arts. They understand herbs and such, but that's not their calling."

"No, not as a mystic," Brin said. She took a step closer, glancing nervously at Padera as if she was uncomfortable speaking around the old woman.

Brin focused on Suri and said, "What you . . . what you did when we were leaving Belgreig, and the other things, when we were down in Neith. Well, if you could do all that . . . couldn't you . . ." Brin glanced at Arion. "I don't understand how it works or what's possible, but it seems like you and Arion can do just about anything, as long as you aren't trapped in a prison and cut off from . . . sources. And here you aren't. I was just wondering . . . is there anything that *you* can do? I mean, have you tried?"

Suri hadn't. The thought had never crossed her mind. The moment it did, the second Brin said it, she was gripped by both excitement and fear. She had no idea how to go about healing someone, no clue at all. She might make things worse, but holding Arion's cold hand, looking at her pale face . . . *Is worse even possible?*

"If you *can* do something," Padera told her, "do it soon. She's teetering, and more often than not they fall on the far side."

Suri's hands trembled. It wouldn't be like opening and closing the ground, and it wouldn't be like creating a dragon from her best friend. She didn't have a weave carved in stone to follow or a mentor to whisper in her ear. She would have to guess, and guess, and guess all the way through, blindly groping for a path that might not even be there. She would be starting with a single loop of string and trying to make a specific pattern, one she'd never seen before. If she failed, Arion might die because of her. *Can I live after killing them both?*

Suri sat, unsure of what to do. Leaving things alone had to be the wiser choice. If she did nothing and Arion died, at least *that* death wouldn't be on her hands.

Brin and Padera watched her expectantly. She couldn't take their stares and closed her eyes to block them out.

You're just afraid. That's your biggest problem. You've touched the chords, know what they feel like. You understand the immense power residing there, and you've seen what that power can do. You're afraid that by using the Art you'll hurt someone you love. It's that fear that's holding you back, and it's that fear you must face and overcome to gain your wings.

She rubbed Arion's hand. It felt so cold, so dead.

What should I do? Tura, Minna, Grand Mother of All. Please, help me decide. What should I do?

"Look at that," Padera said. "First one I've seen down this way. Thought the sea winds would be too strong for them. Fragile, you know."

"It's beautiful," Brin said.

Suri opened her eyes and caught a flicker of movement to her right as a butterfly fluttered in under the wool. Big, beautiful wings of green and gold were outlined in rich black. The visitor made no sound, just hovered for a time. In all her years, Suri had never seen one like it. Then as they watched, the butterfly turned and fluttered out again.

"Just stopping by to say hello, I guess," Padera remarked.

"I don't think so." Suri took a deep breath, raised her hands and said, "Hold on, Arion. I'm coming."

Glossary of Terms and Names

Agave: The prison of an ancient one deep in the heart of Elan, discovered by the dwarfs about six thousand years in the past.

Age of Lothian: The time during which Lothian ruled as the fane of the Fhrey people. Lothian's reign began following the death of Fenelyus and after he prevailed in an Uli Vermar, when he was challenged by Zephyron of the Instarya.

Aiden (Fhrey, Miralyith): One of the leaders of the Gray Cloaks, a secret Miralyith society.

Airenthenon: The domed and pillared structure where the Aquila holds meetings. Although the Forest Throne and the Door predate it, the Airenthenon is the oldest *building* in Estramnadon.

Alon Rhist: The chief outpost on the border between Rhulyn and Avrlyn. Staffed by the Instarya, the fortress acts as a bulwark preventing the

Rhunes from crossing into the Fhrey lands. It was named after the fourth fane of the Fhrey, who died during the Dherg War.

Alward (Rhune, Nadak): The new leader of Nadak, one of the two clans destroyed by the Fhrey.

Alysin: One of the three realms of the afterlife. A paradise where brave warriors go after death.

Amphora: A delicate storage vessel with an oval body that tapers near its base. It has two handles near its top.

Ancient one: A being whom the Dherg claim predates the gods of Elan. He was found by the Dherg, locked deep underground in the Agave.

Anwir (Fhrey, Asendwayr): Quiet and reserved, he is the only non-Instarya Fhrey member of Nyphron's Galantians. He has a penchant for knots and uses a net for a weapon.

Aquila: Literally "the place of choosing." Originally created as a formalization and public recognition of the group of Fhrey who had been assisting Gylindora Fane for more than a century. Leaders of each tribe act as general counsels, making suggestions and assisting in the overall administration of the empire. Senior council members are elected by their tribes or appointed by the fane. Junior members are chosen by the seniors. The Aquila holds no direct power, as the fane's authority is as absolute as Ferrol Himself. However, the Aquila does wield great influence over the succession of power. It is the Curator and Conservator who provide a challenger access to the Horn of Gylindora.

Arion (Fhrey, Miralyith): The former tutor to Prince Mawyndulë and one-time student of Fenelyus. Also known as Cenzlyor. Arion was sent to Rhulyn to bring the outlaw Nyphron to justice and was injured when a Rhune named Malcolm hit her in the head with a rock. She fought Gryndal, a fellow Miralyith, when he threatened to destroy Dahl Rhen and kill all its residents.

Art, the: Magic that allows the caster to tap the forces of nature. In Fhrey society, it's practiced by members of the Miralyith tribe. Goblins who wield this power are referred to as oberdaza. The only known Rhune to possess any Artistic ability is the mystic known as Suri.

Artist: A practitioner of the Art.

Asendwayr: The Fhrey tribe whose members specialize in hunting. A few are stationed on the frontier to provide meat for the Instarya.

Asica: A long Fhrey garment similar to a robe. Its numerous wraps and ties allow it to be worn in a number of configurations.

Atlatl: A device used to extend the distance a spear can be thrown.

Aurochs: A breed of large ancient cattle.

Avempartha: The Fhrey tower created by Fenelyus atop a great waterfall on the Nidwalden River. It can tap the force of rushing water to amplify the use of the Art.

Avrlyn: "Land of Green," the Fhrey frontier bordered on the north by Hentlyn, and by Belgreig to the south. Avrlyn is separated from Rhulyn by the east and south branches of the Bern River.

Balgargarath: A creature residing in Neith who prevents the Dherg people from returning to their home city.

Battle of Grandford: The first official battle in the war between the Rhunes and Fhrey.

Battle of Mador: During the Belgric War, the battle between the Fhrey and Dherg when Fenelyus first used the Art, crushing the Tenth and Twelfth Dherg legions under a pile of rock that subsequently formed Mount Mador. The battle turned the tide of the war by stopping the Dherg advance.

Belgreig: The continent to the far south of Elan where the Dherg people reside.

Belgriclungreians: The term Dherg use to refer to themselves and their kind in the years after settling in Belgreig.

Belgric War: A war between the Fhrey and Dherg. Also referred to as the Dherg War and the War of Elven Aggression.

Bern: A river that runs north–south and delineates the border between Rhulyn and Avrlyn. Rhunes are forbidden from crossing to the west side of this river.

Black bronze: A metal alloy whose recipe—known only to the Dherg—utilizes gold, silver, and copper. It's especially important in the making of sculptures.

Blue Sea: The body of water due south of the known lands and east of

Belgreig. It's believed by some to be endless; others think it marks the boundary where the world ends.

Book of Brin: The first known written work chronicling the history of the Rhune people. It dates back to the time of the first war between the Rhunes and Fhrey.

Breckon mor: The feminine version of the leigh mor. A versatile piece of patterned cloth that can be wrapped in a number of ways.

Brin (Rhune, Rhen): The daughter of Sarah and Delwin, Keeper of Ways for Dahl Rhen, and author of the famed *Book of Brin.*

Brown, The: Known as Grin the Brown by Tura and Suri. A ferocious bear who terrorized residents of Dahl Rhen. She was responsible for the deaths of many residents, including Mahn, Persephone and Reglan's eldest son; and Maeve, the dahl's Keeper of Ways. The beast was eventually killed by Persephone.

Caratacus (Fhrey): The sage adviser who brought Ferrol's horn to the first fane, Gylindora Fane. Creator of the Forest Throne.

Carding: The step that comes between shearing and spinning wool. Combs are used to detangle, clean, and intermix fibers, turning them into a continuous aligned web.

Carfreign Arena: A large open-air field in Estramnadon where contests and spectacles are held. It was there that Lothian defeated Zephyron in a particularly gruesome Uli Vermar challenge.

Caric: The Dherg port city across the straits of the Blue Sea from the Rhune village of Vernes. It was built just outside Neith, the Dherg home city.

Cenzlyor: In the Fhrey language, the term means "swift of mind." A title of endearment bestowed by Fane Fenelyus upon Arion, indicating her proficiency in the Art.

Clempton: A small village of Dureya, home of Raithe (the God Killer).

Cleve: A simple and practical type of short sword, favored by the Instarya tribe of the Fhrey.

Cobb (Rhune, Rhen): A pig farmer and gatekeeper in Dahl Rhen.

Conservator of the Aquila: The keeper of the Horn of Gylindora and, along with the Curator, one of the two Fhrey most responsible for administering the process of succession. The Conservator is also responsible for picking a new Curator when needed.

Coppersword: A moniker for Herkimer (Raithe's father). It was bestowed upon him by his enemy, the Gula-Rhunes, because of the unusual weapon he wielded.

Council of Tirre: A meeting called by Persephone to bring all the Rhulyn clan leaders together with the purpose of appointing a keenig to rule over all the Rhunes and lead the battle against the Fhrey.

Crescent Forest: A large forest that forms a half circle around Dahl Rhen. ·

Crimbal: A fairy creature that lives in the land of Nog. Crimbals travel to the world of Elan through doors in the trunks of trees. They are known to steal children.

Cul: A Rhunic profanity often used for a despicable person.

Curator: The vice fane who presides over the six councilors of the Aquila, elected by a vote of senior members. The Curator leads meetings of the Aquila in the absence of the fane, and chairs the Challenge Council, which decides who gets the right to blow the Horn of Gylindora. Together, the Conservator and the Curator are the Fhrey most responsible for determining the succession of power and administering the Uli Vermar challenge process.

Dahl (hill or mound): A Rhune settlement that is the capital city of a given clan and is characterized by its position on top of a man-made hill. Dahls are usually surrounded by some form of wall or fortification. Each has a central lodge where the clan's chieftain lives, along with a series of roundhouses that provide shelter for the other villagers.

Deep Shaft: The passage in Neith that leads to the bottom of the city.

Delwin (Rhune, Rhen): A sheep farmer; husband of Sarah, father of Brin.

Dherg: One of the five humanoid races of Elan. Skilled craftsmen, they have been all but banned from most places except Belgreig. They are exceptional builders and weaponsmiths. The name is a pejorative Fhrey word meaning "vile mole." The Dherg refer to themselves as Belgriclungreians.

Didan (Rhune, Dureya): One of Raithe's brothers.

Door, the: A portal in the Garden of Estramnadon that legend holds is the gateway to where the First Tree grows.

Drome: The god of the Dherg.

Drumindor: A Dherg-built fortress located on an active volcano at the entrance to a large strategic bay on the Blue Sea. Two massive towers provide protection from any invasion by sea.

Dunn: One of the three Gula-Rhune clans. The other two are Erling and Strom.

Dureya: A barren highland in the north of Rhulyn, home to the Rhune clan of the same name. The entire region and all but two of the clan members were destroyed by Fhrey Instarya. Before their destruction, they were the most powerful warrior clan of the Rhulyn-Rhunes.

Dwarfs: Any flora or fauna of diminutive stature (as in *dwarf wheat* or *dwarf rabbits*). Also, the name Persephone gives to Belgriclungreians, as it is easier to pronounce than *Belgriclungreians* and not taken as an insult as *Dherg* is.

East Puddle: The less affluent area of the Rhen settlement in Tirre.

Eilywin: Fhrey architects and craftsmen who design and create buildings.

Elan: The Grand Mother of All. God of the land.

Elf: The Fhrey word for "nightmare" and a derogatory term used by the Dherg to insult the Fhrey people.

Eraphus: The sea god of Dahl Tirre.

Eres (Fhrey, Instarya): A member of Nyphron's Galantians. His main prowess is with spears and javelins.

Erivan: Homeland of the Fhrey.

Erling: One of the three Gula-Rhune clans. The other two are Dunn and Strom.

Esbol Berg: The massive towers and gate at the entrance of Neith.

Estramnadon: The capital city of the Fhrey, located in the forests of Erivan.

Estramnadon Academy: The school where Miralyith are trained in the ways of the Art. Entrance to it requires passage of the Sharhasa, an aptitude test.

Eten: The former chieftain of the Nadak clan. He and almost all his people were killed by a Fhrey Instarya attack.

Fane: The ruler of the Fhrey, whose term of office extends to death or to three thousand years after ascension, whichever comes first.

Faquins: Practitioners of the Art who can't draw power directly from the forces of nature and must instead use physical elements as a crutch to harness that power.

Fenelyus (Fhrey, Miralyith): The fifth fane of the Fhrey and first of the Miralyith. She saved the Fhrey from annihilation during the Belgric War.

Ferrol: The god of the Fhrey.

Ferrol's Law: The irrefutable prohibition against Fhrey killing other Fhrey. In extreme situations, a fane can make an exception for cause, or can designate a person as exempt. Breaking Ferrol's Law will eject a Fhrey from society and bar the perpetrator from the afterlife. Since it is the Fhrey's god that will pass judgment, no one can circumvent Ferrol's Law by committing murder in secret or without witnesses.

Fhrey: One of the five major races of Elan. Fhrey are long-lived, technologically advanced, and organized into tribes based on profession.

Fhreyhyndia (killer of Fhrey): A Fhrey word sometimes used by Nyphron when referring to Raithe. Also, the name that Tesh of Duryea would like to adopt.

First Chair: An honorific for the chieftain of a dahl.

First Minister: The third most important person in Fhrey society (following the fane and the Curator). The primary role is the day-to-day administration of the Talwara. The present First Minister, Kabbayn, replaced Gryndal upon his death.

First Quorum: The group that developed the foundations of the Fhrey society. Notable members included Caratacus and Gylindora Fane.

Five major races of Elan: Rhunes, Fhrey, Dherg, Ghazel, and Grenmorians.

Flood (Dherg): One of three Dherg found by Persephone, Arion, and Suri in a rol of the Crescent Forest. The twin brother of Frost.

Florella Plaza: A large public square with an elaborate fountain outside the Airenthenon in Estramnadon.

Forest Throne: The seat of the fane, located in the Talwara in the capital city of Estramnadon. It was created when Caratacus intertwined six trees as symbols of the (then) six tribes of the Fhrey.

Frost (Dherg): One of three Dherg found by Persephone, Arion, and Suri in a rol of the Crescent Forest. The twin brother of Flood.

Furgenrok (Grenmorian): Leader of the Grenmorians, the giants of Elan.

Galantians: The Instarya party led by Nyphron and famed for legendary exploits of valor and bravery. Exiled from Alon Rhist for disobeying orders to destroy Rhune villages, they remain outlaws living in Dahl Rhen.

Garden, the: One of the most sacred places in Fhrey society, used for meditation and reflection. The Garden is in the center of Estramnadon and surrounds the Door, the Fhrey's most sacred relic.

Gath (Rhune): The first keenig, who united all the human clans during the Great Flood.

Gelston (Rhune, Rhen): The shepherd who was hit by lightning during the Grenmorian attack on Dahl Rhen; uncle to Brin.

Gifford (Rhune, Rhen): The incredibly talented potter of Dahl Rhen whose mother died during his birth. Due to extensive deformities, he wasn't expected to live more than a few years.

Goblins: A grotesque race feared and shunned by all in Elan, known to be fierce warriors. The most dangerous of their kind are oberdaza, who can harness the power of elements through magic. In the Dherg language, they are known as:

Ba Ran Ghazel (Forgotten Ones of the Sea)
Fen Ran Ghazel (Forgotten Ones of the Swamps)
Fir Ran Ghazel (Forgotten Ones of the Forest)
Durat Ran Ghazel (Forgotten Ones of the Mountains)

God Killer: A moniker given to Raithe of Dureya, who was the first known Rhune to kill a Fhrey (Shegon of the Asendwayr tribe). While staying in Dahl Rhen, he killed another Fhrey (Gryndal of the Miralyith).

Grandford: A stone bridge over the narrow gorge of the Bern River that separates Dureya from Alon Rhist. The first official battle of the Fhrey–Rhune war takes place there.

Grand Mother of All: Another name for the goddess Elan (the world).

Gray Cloaks: A secret society of Miralyith who believe they have ascended to a higher state of being than other members of the Fhrey society.

Great Famine: A year of unusually harsh conditions that destroyed most of the crops of the Rhunes, leading to mass starvation and many deaths.

Great Puddle, the: A large pond formed outside the walls of Tirre during unusually heavy rains. It divided the Rhen camp into two distinct living areas: West Puddle (the more affluent) and East Puddle (the less desirable).

Great War: The first war between the Fhrey people and the Rhunes.

Grenmorian: The race of giants who live in Elan.

Grin: The name Suri and Tura gave to The Brown, a ferocious bear of the Crescent Forest.

Gronbach Eyck Prigmoore (Dherg): The mayor of Caric and Master Crafter of that city.

Grygor (Grenmorian): A member of Nyphron's famed Galantians, and the only giant of the group. Known for his love of cooking and the use of spices.

Gryndal (Fhrey, Miralyith): The former First Minister to Fane Lothian. Respected as one of the most skilled practitioners of the Art, Gryndal was killed in Dahl Rhen by Raithe, the God Killer.

Gula-Rhunes: A northern alliance of three Rhune clans (Dunn, Strom, and Erling) that have a long-standing feud with the seven southern Rhulyn-Rhune clans. Historically, the Fhrey have pitted these two sides against each other and fostered their mutual animosity.

Gwydry: One of the seven tribes of Fhrey. This one is for the farmers who are responsible for raising crops and livestock.

Gylindora Fane (Fhrey, Nilyndd): The first leader of the Fhrey. Her name became synonymous with *ruler*.

Habet (Rhune, Rhen): The keeper of the flame of Dahl Rhen, responsible for ensuring that the braziers and the lodge's fire pit remain lit.

Harkon (Rhune, Melen): Chieftain of Clan Melen.

Hawthorn Glen: Home to Suri and Tura.

Hegel (Rhune, Dureya): One of Raithe's brothers.

Heim (Rhune, Dureya): The most ferocious and skilled fighter among Raithe's brothers.

Hentlyn (land of mountains): An area to the north of Avrlyn, generally inhabited by Grenmorians.

Herkimer (Rhune, Dureya): The father of Raithe, killed by Shegon.

High Spear Valley: Home of the three clans of the Gula-Rhunes.

Horn of Gylindora: A ceremonial horn kept by the Conservator that was originally bestowed on Gylindora Fane by the legendary Caratacus. The horn is used to challenge for leadership of the Fhrey. It can only be blown during an Uli Vermar (upon the death of a fane or every three thousand years). When blown at the death of a fane, it's the fane's heir who is challenged. If the fane has no heir or if it is blown after three thousand years of reign, the horn can be blown twice, providing for two contestants.

Imaly (Fhrey, Nilyndd): A descendant of Gylindora Fane, leader of the Nilyndd tribe, and Curator of the Aquila.

Instarya: One of the seven tribes of the Fhrey. Instarya are the warriors who have been stationed on the frontier in outposts along the Avrlyn border since the Belgric War.

Iver (Rhune, Rhen): A woodcarver and abusive slave owner; the former master of Roan and her mother.

Jerydd (Fhrey, Miralyith): The kel of Avempartha.

Kabbayn (Fhrey, Eilywin): The current First Minister, who replaced Gryndal after his death.

Keenig: A single person who rules over the united Rhune clans in times of trouble. There hasn't been one appointed since the days of Gath. The Council of Tirre has been formed to select a new keenig to see the Rhune people through the approaching war with the Fhrey.

Keeper of Ways: The person who learns the customs, traditions, and general memories of a community and is the authority in such matters. Keepers pass down their knowledge through oral tradition. The most famous Keeper is Brin from Dahl Rhen, who created the famed *Book of Brin*.

Kel: The administrator of a prestigious institution.

Knots: Known to disrupt the natural flow of the Art, knots often create difficulty in communication and prevent consensus building. Once a knot is unraveled, so, too, are arguments unknotted, leading to eventual agreement.

Konniger (Rhune, Rhen): Shield to Chieftain Reglan of Dahl Rhen and husband of Tressa. Konniger ruled Rhen for a short period of time between the reigns of Reglan and Persephone after assassinating the former. He also tried to kill Persephone and was inadvertently killed by Grin the Brown.

Krugen (Rhune, Menahan): Chieftain of Clan Menahan, the richest of the seven Rhulyn clans.

Krun: The patron god of Clan Melen.

Leigh mor: Great cloak. A versatile piece of fabric used by Rhune men that can be draped in a number of ways, usually belted. A leigh mor can also be used as a sling to carry items or as a blanket. Usually, they're woven with the pattern of a particular clan. The female version, known as a breckon mor, is longer, with an angled cut.

Linden Lott: The chief Dherg city after the fall of Neith. It holds an annual contest to determine the best in various endeavors valued by the Dherg people, such as building, forging weapons, and digging.

Lion Corps: Personal bodyguards to the fane.

Lipit (Rhune, Tirre): The chieftain of Dahl Tirre.

Lothian, Fane (Fhrey, Miralyith): The supreme ruler of the Fhrey, father to Mawyndulë, son of Fenelyus. He came into power after an unusually gruesome challenge in which he defeated Zephyron of the Instarya in a humiliating and cruel display of power.

Maeve (Rhune, Rhen): The former Keeper of Ways for Dahl Rhen and mother of Suri; she was killed by Grin the Brown.

Magda: The oldest tree in the Crescent Forest; an ancient oak known to offer sage advice, including information that was instrumental in saving the village of Dahl Rhen when it was targeted by First Minister Gryndal of the Miralyith.

Mahn (Rhune, Rhen): The son of Persephone and Reglan. He was killed by a ferocious bear known as The Brown.

Makareta (Fhrey, Miralyith): A member of the Gray Cloaks and the object of Mawyndulë's first romantic crush.

Malcolm (Rhune, honorary Dureyan): The ex-slave of Zephyron and former resident of Alon Rhist. After Malcolm attacked Shegon with a rock, he and Raithe became companions. He is also responsible for attacking Arion in a similar manner.

Mari: The patron god of Dahl Rhen.

Master of Secrets: The adviser to the fane who is responsible for Talwara security. Vasek is the current holder of that title.

Mawyndulë (Fhrey, Miralyith): Prince of the Fhrey realm; the son of Lothian, grandson of Fenelyus, and former student of Arion and Gryndal. He was present at Dahl Rhen when Raithe killed Gryndal. He's currently representing the Miralyith in the Aquila as the junior councilor.

Mehan: The patron god of Clan Menahan.

Melen: A Rhulyn clan known for its poets and musicians.

Menahan: A Rhune dahl known for its wool, ruled by Chieftain Krugen.

Mideon, King (Dherg): A key player in the Belgric War between the Dherg and Fhrey. The last monarch of the Dherg race.

Minna: A wolf and the best friend of Suri, who dubbed the animal the wisest wolf in the world.

Miralyith: The Fhrey tribe of Artists—people who use the Art to channel natural forces to work magic.

Morton Whipple (Rhune, Rhen): A childhood friend of Persephone.

Mount Mador: A mountain conjured by Fane Fenelyus during the Belgric War, which killed tens of thousands of Dherg.

Moya (Rhune, Rhen): A beautiful young woman of Dahl Rhen known for her fiery spirit and loud mouth.

Mynogan: The three gods of war worshipped by the Dureyans and other warrior tribes. They represent Battle, Honor, and Death.

Mystic: An individual capable of tapping into the essence of the natural world and understanding the will of gods and spirits. Both Tura and Suri are mystics from the Hawthorn Glen.

Nadak: A region in the north of Rhulyn that is home to the Rhune clan of the same name. It was destroyed by the Fhrey Instarya, and most of its residents were slaughtered.

Narsirabad: A large spear from the lodge of Dahl Rhen used by Malcolm. Its name is Fhrey for "pointy."

Neith: The original home of the Dherg in Belgreig. Neith is a huge underground city and the most revered place in the Dherg culture.

Nidwalden: A mighty river that separates Erivan (the land of the Fhrey) from Rhulyn (the land of the Rhunes).

Nifrel: Below Rel. The most dismal and unpleasant of the three regions of the afterlife.

Nilyndd: The Fhrey tribe of craftsmen.

Nyphron (Fhrey, Instarya): The son of Zephyron and leader of the famed Galantians. After attacking the new leader of Alon Rhist, he was declared an outlaw. He and his Galantians found refuge in the Rhune village of Dahl Rhen.

Orinfar: Ancient Dherg runes that can prevent the use of the Art.

Padera (Rhune, Rhen): A farmer's wife and the oldest resident of Dahl Rhen, she is known for her excellent cooking ability and for being the best healer in the dahl.

Persephone (Rhune, Rhen): The chieftain of Dahl Rhen and widow of Reglan. She killed Grin the Brown.

Petragar (Fhrey, Instarya): The lord of Alon Rhist, appointed by Fane Lothian after the death of Zephyron.

Phyre: The afterlife, which is divided into three sections: Nifrel, Rel, and Alysin.

Pithos: Extremely large clay urns used to store crops for long periods of time.

Rain (Dherg): One of three Dherg found by Persephone, Arion, and Suri in a rol of the Crescent Forest. An even-tempered Dherg who wields a large pickax, Rain is perhaps the best digger of his people and the grandprize winner at the Linden Lott competition.

Raithe (Rhune, Dureya): The son of Herkimer; also known as the God

Killer. He killed Shegon (a Fhrey Asendwayr) in retribution for his father's death, and Gryndal (a Fhrey Miralyith) when he threatened the people of Dahl Rhen.

Raow: A feared predator that eats its prey starting with the face. Raow sleep on a bed of bones and must add another set before going to sleep. A single raow can decimate an entire region.

Rapnagar (Grenmorian): The leader of a raiding party sent by the Fhrey to destroy Dahl Rhen and kill Arion, Nyphron, and Raithe.

Rasra: The patron god of Clan Nadak.

Reglan (Rhune, Rhen): The former chieftain of Dahl Rhen and husband to Persephone. Killed by Konniger in an attempt to usurp his power.

Rel: One of the three regions in the afterlife.

Rhen: A wooded region in the west of Rhulyn that is home to the Rhune clan of the same name. It was formerly ruled by Reglan; his wife, Persephone, now rules the region.

Rhist: Also sometimes referred to as the Rhist, a shortened name for Alon Rhist, the Fhrey outpost.

Rhulyn: The "Land of the Rhunes," bordered by the Fhrey's native Erivan to the east and the Fhrey outposts in Avrlyn to the west.

Rhulyn-Rhunes: The seven southern clans of Rhunes: Nadak, Dureya, Rhen, Warric, Tirre, Melen, and Menahan. The Rhulyn-Rhunes have been in constant conflict with the northern tribes of the Gula-Rhunes.

Rhune: One of the five major races of Elan, the race of humans. The word is Fhrey for "primitive," and for some, it is seen as derogatory. This race is technologically challenged, superstitious, and polytheistic. They live in clusters of small villages, and each clan is governed by a chieftain. There are two major groups of Rhunes, the Gula-Rhunes from the north and the southern Rhulyn-Rhunes. The two factions have warred for centuries.

Rhunic: The language spoken by the humans who live in Rhulyn.

Roan (Rhune, Rhen): An ex-slave of Iver the woodcarver. An incredibly talented, emotionally scarred inventor.

Rol: A small Dherg fortification. Rols were created throughout the frontier to provide shelter during the Belgric War. Most have a hidden door that opens and shuts via a series of pulleys and gears and are lined with Orinfar runes to protect those inside from magical attacks.

Rol Berg: A gate deep in the heart of Neith.

Rose Bridge: A bridge decorated with roses that crosses the Shinara River in Estramnadon, the Fhrey capital. The meeting place of the Gray Cloaks.

Rostwell: The mammoth dining hall in Caric where all members of the ruling party take their meals.

Roundhouse: A typical Rhune dwelling consisting of a single circular room with a cone-shaped roof, usually covered in thatch.

Ryeteen: The Fhrey term for a simplistic system of markings carried over great distances by birds for limited communication. *Ryeteen* is also used for the keeping of itemized lists.

Sebek (Fhrey, Instarya): The best warrior of the Galantians. He uses two cleve blades named Thunder and Lightning.

Second Chair: The honorific position held by the spouse of the chieftain.

Shahdi: The non-Instarya military group charged with maintaining order in Greater Erivan.

Sharhasa: An aptitude test given to Fhrey who wish to become Miralyith. Those who pass are granted access to the Estramnadon Academy and learn the ways of the Art.

Shegon (Fhrey, Asendwayr): A hunter stationed at Alon Rhist to provide the warrior tribe with fresh meat. He was killed by Raithe after Shegon killed Herkimer (Raithe's father).

Shield: Also known as shield to the chieftain or chieftain's shield. The chieftain's personal bodyguard, and generally the finest warrior of a given clan.

Siegel (Rhune, Dunn): The chieftain of Clan Dunn.

Sikar (Fhrey, Instarya): An officer and patrol leader in the Instarya tribe stationed at Alon Rhist. A friend of Nyphron before the Galantian's desertion.

Strom: One of the three Gula-Rhune clans. The other two are Dunn and Erling.

Stump, The (Rhune, Rhen): The Shield to Konniger, The Stump was promised Moya's hand in marriage—much to Moya's dismay. He was killed by Konniger when he reconsidered his part in the overthrow of Reglan's reign.

Summerule: One of two Rhune holidays (the other is Wintertide). Summerule centers on a huge picnic and a number of athletic competitions.

Suri (Rhune, Rhen): The illegitimate child of Reglan, who had an affair with Maeve (Dahl Rhen's Keeper of Ways). She was left to die in the forest, but was saved and raised by a mystic named Tura. She may be the only Rhune known to possess the ability to use the Art. She's always accompanied by a white wolf named Minna, as the two are best friends.

Talwara: The official name of the Fhrey's palace, where the fane resides and rules.

Tegan (Rhune, Warric): The chieftain of Clan Warric.

Tekchin (Fhrey, Instarya): One of Nyphron's band of outlaw Galantians, Tekchin is a rough, outspoken warrior whose preferred weapon is a thin, narrow-bladed sword.

Ten Clans: The entirety of the Rhune nation, comprising seven Rhulyn clans and three Gula clans.

Tesh (Rhune, Dureya): The orphan boy who, along with Raithe, is all that remains of the Dureyan clan.

Tet: A curse word derived from *Tetlin Witch.*

Tetlin Witch: The universally hated immortal being thought to be the source of all disease, pestilence, and evil in the world.

Tirre: The southernmost Rhune dahl. Ruled by Lipit, it sits at the edge of the Blue Sea, across a narrow strait from the Dherg city of Caric.

Tirreans: Residents of Tirre.

Torc: A rigid circular necklace that is open in the front. In Rhune society, it is a mark of leadership. The Dherg often bestow a torc as a reward for a great accomplishment.

Traitor, The: The moniker Mawyndulë bestowed on Arion for her part in First Minister Gryndal's death while aiding the Rhunes of Dahl Rhen.

Tressa (Rhune, Rhen): The wife of Konniger, ex-chieftain of Dahl Rhen.

Trilos (Fhrey, unknown tribal affiliation): A mysterious person obsessed with the Door in the Garden.

Tura (Rhune, no clan affiliation): An ancient mystic who lived in the Hawthorn Glen near Dahl Rhen; mentor to Suri. She predicted the coming of the Great Famine.

Uberlin: The god of evil worshipped by the Ghazel. The source of all wickedness in Elan, believed to be the father of the Tetlin Witch.

Udgar: The chieftain of Clan Erling of the Gula.

Uli Vermar (the reign of a fane): An event that occurs three thousand years after the crowning of a fane or upon his death, when other Fhrey can challenge to rule. This is done by petitioning the Aquila and being presented with the Horn of Gylindora.

Umalyn: The Fhrey tribe of priests and priestesses who concern themselves with spiritual matters and the worship of Ferrol.

Urum River: A north–south Avrlyn river west of the Bern, and the place where Raithe would like to make a new start.

Valentryne Layartren: A room within the great tower of Avempartha that allows multiple Artists to join forces and work as one. It's particularly useful for locating people.

Vasek (Fhrey, Asendwayr): The Master of Secrets.

Vellum: Fine parchment perfected by the Dherg for drawing maps, made from the skins of young animals.

Vernes: The Rhune port city that grew up directly below Dahl Tirre.

Vertumus (Fhrey, Instarya): The personal assistant to Petragar.

Vidar (Fhrey, Miralyith): The senior councilor of the Aquila representing the Miralyith tribe and new tutor to Prince Mawyndulë.

Volhoric (Fhrey, Umalyn): The senior councilor of the Aquila representing the Umalyn tribe. He also holds the position of Conservator of the Aquila.

Vorath (Fhrey, Instarya): A member of Nyphron's Galantians. He has taken to the Rhune custom of wearing a beard. His weapons of choice are flails, maces, and morning stars.

Warric: One of the seven Rhulyn-Rhune clans, ruled by Chieftain Tegan.

West Puddle: The more affluent area of the Rhen settlement in Tirre.

Wogan: The name by which the spirit of nature is known in and around the Crescent Forest.

Yarhold: The home city of the Grenmorians.

Ylfe: The Fhrey pronunciation of the derogatory Dherg term *elf.*

Zephyron (Fhrey, Instarya): The father of Nyphron, killed by Lothian during the challenge for fane upon Fenelyus's death. Lothian killed Zephyron in an unusually gruesome fashion to make a point about Miralyith superiority and the folly of challenging their rule.

Acknowledgments

From time to time, I'm asked whether I would consider collaborating with someone to create a shared book. My immediate response is: "I don't play well with others, so collaboration would be difficult." That is indeed true: I'm a pretty solitary old curmudgeon and very particular about my writing. But when it comes time to write my acknowledgments, it becomes immediately clear to me that I *do* collaborate, and it is because of the talents and hard work of *many* people that you have this product before you.

Simply stated, I have a lot of people who make me look better than I am, and I would be feckless not to point out their amazing contributions. If you have read my other acknowledgments, you'll see some familiar names. That's because when I find someone who is as exceptional as these people, why would I go looking for anyone else?

I hope you saw the dedication at the front of the book. It went out to Tim Gerard Reynolds, for whom I couldn't have more respect. I've seen

Tim's career blossom over the years, and I'm so happy about that. My only hope is that with his continued success, he'll still have time to narrate my books. I couldn't imagine any voice other than his telling my tales.

Audiobooks are such an important format for me, and there are several people at Recorded Books I would like to thank. Andy Paris saw the wisdom of pairing Tim with my stories, and I think all my listeners are as grateful as me for that. Brian Sweeny and Troy Juliar are the ones who picked up my works for audio production in the first place. They have continued their faith in my writing with generous offers for the Legends of the First Empire series, and I love their enthusiasm for producing more of my work in the future. I'd also like to thank John Nebel, our recording engineer, who has an eagle's eye and fine-tuned ear. I'm impressed that John is also writing musicals, something that takes incredible talent, and Robin and I wish him great success with that.

Speaking of incredible talent, once again the exceptional artwork of Marc Simonetti graces the cover of this book. For those who don't know, Marc has provided the amazing artwork for not only *Age of Swords* but also the French editions of *The Crown Conspiracy, Avempartha,* and *Nyphron Rising.* He's also created covers for the English-language editions of *Hollow World, The Death of Dulgath,* and *Age of Myth.* The last two titles have won him back-to-back Stabby Awards for best fantasy artwork, given out by the wonderful people at the /r/Fantasy sub on reddit—a distinction that is well deserved. Thank you, Marc, and I'm already excited to see the final versions of *Age of War.* The initial concepts blew me away.

If you request a copy of *The Making of Age of Swords* (the bonus material I talked about in my author's note), then you'll see a bit about how much my copy editors have contributed to this book. I've said it before, but it's worth repeating: You, ladies, have saved me from looking like an utter fool. Both Laura Jorstad and Linda Branam have been with me now through multiple books, and my sincerest hope is that they'll continue with me for many more. I owe you both a debt of gratitude for your talent and incredible attention to detail.

As some may know, I'm what's referred to as a hybrid author—someone who releases books both through a traditional publisher and as an indie.

When self-publishing, I have only myself to worry about with regard to whether a book will be successful or not. If one were to fail, I'm the only one who would feel the pain. When I traditionally publish, I feel a sense of responsibility for those who have stood up and said, "This book deserves to be *out there*." I'm especially cognizant that they put their reputations on the line by putting faith in me. It's an obligation I take quite seriously, and I hope I've lived up to their trust. So I want to start out by thanking Laurie McLean from Fuse Literary Agency (who initially sold the first three books of this series), Joshua Bilmes from JABberwocky Literary Agency (my current agent, who is selling the books overseas and has generously helped me and Del Rey work out a release plan that allows new Riyria tales to hit the streets while accelerating the releases of the Legends of the First Empire books), and most especially Tricia Narwani, my editor at Del Rey. She is talented, trustworthy, and a fabulous advocate for me and my work.

Both Tricia and Joshua read and provided excellent feedback for *Age of Swords*, but they were not the only ones who contributed to the final product. I want to also thank the best beta reader team an author could hope to have. These people work without compensation, under a tight deadline, and always provide great insight. While not all the beta readers wanted to be acknowledged publicly, my appreciation goes out to every one of them. My deepest thanks to Robert S. Aldrich, Michael Jay Brunt, Kyle Campbell, Jeffrey Carr, Greg Clinton, Paul Dunlap, Louise Faering, Daniel E. Foley, Cathy Fox, Christopher Haught, Sarah and Nathaniel Kidd, Amy Lesniak-Briggs, Joseph C. Martin III, Richard Martin, T. Anders Mikkelsen, Elizabeth Ocskay, Beth Rosser, and Melanie Sanderson.

No one but myself will ever know the full extent of the contributions made by my wife, Robin. Her passion, her dedication, and the incredibly long hours she has put into this (and all my books) have had more of an impact than the combined efforts of all the people I've written about above. Given the massive contributions of those people, that's saying a great deal. I'm certain that her hours on each book far exceed my own. Again, you can learn more about what she does in *The Making of Age of Swords*. For those who don't pick up their free copy, here are just some of Robin's responsibilities: alpha reader, structural editor, line editor, beta test administrator, project manager, business manager, marketing guru, and liaison to my agents, editors, publicists, and various sales and marketing people. The copyediting, which she managed, on this book was especially challenging due to some scheduling issues. In a perfect world, we would have Linda and Laura do their work serially. In other words, Linda would make her changes first, then Laura would add her revisions to Linda's. To meet the schedule, they had to do their work in parallel, which meant Robin had to collate their changes and deal with my additions from the final read. This was a monumental and time-consuming task and significantly improved the quality of the book.

Before I go, I would once again thank you, my readers, for your enthusiastic support of my work. In a time rampant with piracy and a mindset of "all art should be free," it's encouraging to see people willing to pay for books. Your money provides salaries for the people I mentioned above, and gives me the luxury of living a life I love. I've always said that I write the books I want to read, which is very true. But I also feel a responsibility to you (just as I do to my publishers). I'll always strive to provide you with the best book I can produce, and forever be grateful for your support.

ABOUT THE AUTHOR

MICHAEL J. SULLIVAN is the bestselling author of the Riyria Revelations and Riyria Chronicles series. Like most authors, his road to publication has been both a lifelong dream and a difficult road to travel. Michael was just eight years old when he discovered a manual typewriter in the basement of a friend's house during a game of hide-and-seek. He inserted a blank piece of paper and channeled the only writer he knew at the time . . . Charles M. Schulz's Snoopy. Yes, he actually typed the iconic line: *It was a dark and stormy night.*

That spark ignited a flame, and the desire to fill blank pages became an obsession. As an adult, Michael spent more than ten years developing his craft by studying authors such as Stephen King, Ernest Hemingway, and John Steinbeck. During that time, he wrote thirteen novels but found no traction in publishing. So he did the only sane thing he could think of (since insanity is repeating the same act but expecting a different result), he quit writing altogether and vowed never to write creatively again.

Michael stayed away from writing for over a decade and returned to the keyboard in his forties . . . but with one condition: He wouldn't seek publication. Instead, he wrote a series of books that had been forming in his head during his hiatus. Michael's first reading love had been fantasy, and his hope was to foster an appreciation for the genre in his then thirteen-year-old daughter, who struggled with the written word due to severe dyslexia.

After reading the third book of this series, his wife, Robin, insisted that the novels needed to *get out there*. When Michael refused to jump back onto the query-go-round, she took over the publication tasks and has run the business side of his writing career ever since, and things have been going quite well. Michael has sold nearly one million copies, made the #2 spot on the *Washington Post*'s Hardcover Bestseller List, been nominated for five Goodreads' Choice Awards, and his books have appeared on more than 200 best-of or most-anticipated lists including those compiled by Amazon, Barnes and Noble, *Library Journal,* and Audible.com. He's current working on his next Riyria Chronicle novel, *The Disappearance of Winter's Daughter.*

michael.sullivan.dc@gmail.com
riyria.com
Facebook.com/author.michael.sullivan
Twitter: @author_sullivan

ABOUT THE TYPE

This book was set in Fournier, a typeface named for Pierre-Simon Fournier (1712–68), the youngest son of a French printing family. He started out engraving woodblocks and large capitals, then moved on to fonts of type. In 1736, he began his own foundry and made several important contributions in the field of type design; he is said to have cut 147 alphabets of his own creation. Fournier is probably best remembered as the designer of St. Augustine Ordinaire, a face that served as the model for the Monotype Corporation's Fournier, which was released in 1925.